JOHN LAWTON

FRIENDS
AND
TRAITORS

AN INSPECTOR TROY NOVEL

Atlantic Monthly Press
New York

FIRST EDITION

Published simultaneously in Canada
Printed in the United States of America

First Grove Atlantic hardcover edition: October 2017

Library of Congress Cataloging-in-Publication data available for this title.

ISBN 978-0-8021-2706-8
eISBN 978-0-8021-8921-9

Atlantic Monthly Press
an imprint of Grove Atlantic
154 West 14th Street
New York, NY 10011

Distributed by Publishers Group West

groveatlantic.com

17 18 19 20   10 9 8 7 6 5 4 3 2 1

for

Sara Coward

1948–2017

. . . The only toy he cares for is a box of matches; and up the houses and barns and hayricks go, in crackling flames. That was Burgess's distinguishing mark: the flashing smile of the fire-raiser, full of secret pleasure in mischief and destruction. Even his most loyal friends had no illusion about his favourite toys. Some were affectionate and benevolent people who wanted to help and protect him against this innate viciousness; and some were people who were mischievous and destructive but would not risk their own safety, and found a vicarious gratification in his recklessness.

—Rebecca West, *The New Meaning of Treason*, 1965

A true hero of our time . . . hip before hipsters, Rolling before the Stones, acid-head before LSD. There was not so much a conspiracy gathered round him as just decay and dissolution. It was the end of a class, of a way of life; something that would be written about . . . with wonder and perhaps hilarity, but still tinged with sadness, as all endings are.

—Malcolm Muggeridge, *The Infernal Grove*, 1973

All humanity's misery derives from not being able to sit alone in a quiet room.

—Pascal, *Pensées*, 1670

I

Burgess

§

England: 1958

Someone was following Frederick Troy.

§1

Mimram House, Hertfordshire: July 1935.

He felt foolish. As though he'd rummaged in the dressing-up box and tried on something better suited to his brother.

The damn thing simply didn't fit.

A voice from the doorway. Laconic and softly mocking.

"You look like a twat, bro."

"Sasha, if you can't be helpful, just fuck off will you?"

Just as his mother passed by his door.

"Pourquoi avez-vous appris l'anglais juste pour utiliser tous les gros mots de cette langue?" Why is it that you two learnt English just to use all the worst words it has to offer?

"Il nous reste une demi-heure avant le dîner. Nos invités vont bientôt arriver. S'il vous plaît, les enfants, s'il vous plaît." We have half an hour before dinner. Our guests will be arriving soon. Please, children, please.

With that she was gone. Sasha stayed.

"As I was saying . . ."

"I know I look like a twat. It doesn't fucking fit. I'll be Constable Scarecrow, the laughing stock of Hendon."

"Or worse . . . the mascot."

Troy was legally too short to be a copper. His father had capitulated to his wish to join the Metropolitan Police Force after much argument, but with good grace, and had pulled strings, of which he had plenty, to get his younger son accepted at Hendon College as a cadet. It had pained him, and pained him doubly. Troy was well aware of that. Eighteen months ago Troy had turned down an Open Exhibition, a lesser form of scholarship, to Christ Church College, Oxford, to work on one of his father's newspapers as a cub reporter. Like Charles Dickens, he had begun as a court reporter, sitting on the hard benches of magistrates' courts day after day and recording the fragmentary lives of shoplifters, drunks, and flashers. Then he had graduated to the Old Bailey, to the rank of crime reporter, and after a year of such reporting, his vocation, if such it be, had become apparent to him. He wanted to be a copper. Above all he wanted to be a detective. The uniform was simply a hurdle en route. What he didn't know was how many hurdles he'd have to jump to get out of uniform.

This one bagged around his ankles, sagged at the arse, and would have accommodated another slim-ish person at the chest without bursting its silver buttons.

"It'll never fucking fit."

"Y'know, Freddie . . . it's nothing a good tailor couldn't work wonders with. When do you actually start?"

"Monday of week after next."

"Fine. Whip round to your man in Savile Row and get it tailored."

"I doubt very much whether Foulkes and Fransham bother with uniforms."

"Then find another. God knows *somebody* must tailor uniforms. Think of all those RAF pilots, think of all those Guards officers. Do they go around saggy-baggy? Do they, fuck. Anyway, get it off now and get your black tie and togs on. Ma is right, there'll be a posse of the old man's oddities knocking back the gin any minute."

"Then close the door."

Sasha closed the door.

"I meant from the other side."

She slumped in a chair and Troy realised that she had been knocking back the gin already, that she had, in fact, been holding a large gin and

It in her hand all the time, concealed by the door frame, and that she
might well be more than a bit pissed.

"Don't be silly. We've never given toss about nudity."

Indeed, they hadn't, but . . .

"We're not in the nursery any longer."

She sipped, gulped her gin, but didn't move.

She had a point, Troy knew, they had undressed in front of each
other and his other sister, Masha, since childhood. They had only
one rule . . . never comment on what you see. And he wondered why
self-consciousness should become paramount at this moment, and he
knew the answer. The uniform. It changed everything.

He stripped down to nothing, Sasha looking at him, then not looking
at him, and all the time looking unconcerned, until he reached break
point . . . the fastening of the black tie itself.

"Still can't do it on your own, eh?"

She stood behind him, taller even when she was barefoot, but now
she almost towered over him in heels, her hands at his throat, peering
around him to see them both in the mirror, deftly knotting the bow
tie, whispering about a rabbit down a hole.

"Oddities?"

"Eh?"

"You mentioned the old man's oddities . . . his choice of dinner
guests. Who's coming?"

"Hmm . . . well. There's Rosamond Lehmann."

"I know that name."

"Novelist. Pretty good one actually. Three or four to her name. She's
John's sister . . . you know John. Rod was at Cambridge with him. One
of the Trinity bright boys."

"Will John be coming?"

"Yep. And then there's Moura Budberg."

"Again? Weird."

"Dad seems to enjoy her company."

"Ma doesn't. Moura name-drops all the bloody time."

"I think the Baroness Budberg brings a little bit of Russia back to
the old man, and, needless to say, Ma doesn't need or want any little
bits of old Russia. And Moura makes for a good guessing game. Is she
a Soviet spy or isn't she?"

"I can't see any point in the Soviet Union having spies who tell you they're spies over the fucking soup course."

"And then there's Harold Macmillan . . ."

"And weirder."

"Macmillan's a rebel . . . you know how the old man loves trouble-makers. Mac's a charmer. A hopeless charmer, a backbencher with about as much chance of cabinet office as our cat."

Sasha stepped back.

"You're done."

So he was. Troy looked in the mirror and could see *himself* again, something he had not been able to do dressed as a police cadet-cum-clown.

"If you'd asked me when you were thirteen and spotty if you'd ever be handsome only good manners would have restrained me from saying no, but I will say this, our Fred: for a little 'un you're really rather cute."

Troy said nothing.

Sasha reverted to the subject.

"And then there's that new bloke he's got writing book reviews for one magazine or another . . . Burgess, Guy Burgess."

§2

Troy looked around and felt lost. Eighteen guests strung out either side of the table. His father at one end, his mother at the other. His elder brother, Rod, sat at his mother's right hand. Macmillan sat at his father's right, a rather obvious clue that Alex had an agenda of things he meant to say and meant Macmillan to hear.

Troy was slightly closer to his father, off-centre, next to his sister Masha, twin of the now completely sozzled Sasha. He wondered if he'd been placed there to keep an eye on Masha or she on him. She'd not appeared for cocktails, but had emerged from her dressing room looking like Greta Garbo or Anna Karenina . . . black dress, pale skin, and plenty of cleavage. He wondered who she might be tarting at but could spot no likely candidate.

Centre table was Burgess, on the far side of Masha. She leaned Troy's way, her lips all but touching his ear.

"Who's the new bloke?" she whispered.

"Guy Burgess."

"Hack, novelist, pol?"

"Hack. I gather the old man's taken him on. Rod tells me they overlapped at Cambridge."

"Funny. Never heard Rod mention him."

"Me neither."

"Have you seen his fingernails? Looks as though he scrapes dung off a cow's backside for a living."

"Say it a bit louder and he'll hear you."

"Don't care. I wouldn't let those fingers up me."

"For Christ's sake, Masha."

"Only saying!"

"Only saying what?"

It was Burgess, pricking the illusory bubble that Masha had sought to blow around the two of them.

"That you and Rod were at Cambridge together."

"Oh, yes. Not exactly together. I think Rod came down at the end of my first year. And we never quite mixed in the same circles."

"Rod tells me you were in Russia a while ago?" Troy said, hoping for and getting the desired effect.

No other word would have exploded into the room, slicing through all other dinner chit-chat, quite like "Russia." Facing him were his uncle Nikolai and Baroness Budberg. Within earshot, his father, and, just out of it, his mother. All of them Russian exiles.

Before Burgess could answer Nikolai leapt in.

"When?" he asked simply.

"Last summer. Went Intourist with a Cambridge chum. The quid quotidian—a pound a day to see Moscow. Cheaper than Blackpool or Skegness."

"Ah," said Nikolai. "The fellow travellers' package."

Burgess seemed not to hear the contempt in Nikolai's voice.

"No, actually, I was a fully paid-up member of the Communist Party at the time."

He looked around, well aware that he had taken centre stage, and, as far as Troy could tell, was loving it. Troy could not deny the charm, even as Burgess was uttering such show-stopping lines—bricks cascading down like demolition. If it weren't for the fingernails, and the remnants of the soup course down his shirt-front, Troy might even concede that Burgess had style.

"Such folly," Nikolai gently stabbed.

"Quite," said Burgess. "I resigned last year."

"Ah . . . the visit opened your eyes?"

"Forgive me, Professor Troitsky, if I say that my eyes weren't closed. Let us say that I returned with a different perspective. I did not suffer an overnight conversion to become an anti-Soviet."

"Nor I. But I have been an anti-Soviet since before the USSR existed."

Moura Budberg said something so quietly to Nikolai that Troy did not catch it. All he knew was it was in Russian and sharp of tone.

His father stepped in.

"Nikolai, don't be so hard. Guy has been to Russia, and only a year ago at that. When were any of us last there? I am sure he has things to tell us."

Burgess paused for a few seconds as his audience rearranged their thoughts. A quiet moment broken only by the sound of Macmillan clanking his fish knife. Troy was not at all certain Macmillan had been listening, but then the big, sad eyes looked up as though wondering at the gap in the conversation.

"I came back not so much critical of Russia, that is of the Russian system, as critical of myself, of my own generation. Of all us fellow travellers, if you like. We hitched our wagon to the wrong star. The red star. We fell too readily into the folly, as you put it so aptly, of being starry-eyed utopianists in search of a workers' paradise, and convinced ourselves that the Soviet Union was that paradise. What my visit to Russia taught me was that it may well be a workers' paradise. There is much to admire. But it is a paradise only for Russian workers and only in the context of Russian history. It isn't a model for the West."

"Ah," said Nikolai. "You have seen the future and it *doesn't* work."

Even Troy's mother, a woman who could be fiercely humourless when she tried, laughed at this. It was a twentieth-century classic.

Lincoln Steffens, the American journalist, had summed up the Soviet Union in a single quotable line after his visit in 1919. But that had been the trend . . . the exiles could not return, yet Western intellectuals seemed to descend upon the new country in droves, the publicity value of their visits being immeasurable.

Bernard Shaw, an enthusiast, had visited in 1931 and had vigorously defended the Soviet Union, the Five-Year Plans and the "Workers' Republic" in the pages of the *Manchester Guardian*. His odd choice of travelling companion had been the Tory MP Nancy Astor, a less-than-enthusiast who had boasted to Alex Troy that she had told Josef Stalin that Churchill was a spent force in English politics.

"You're wrong," Alex had replied.

H. G. Wells, lover of the Baroness Budberg, seemed to be in and out of Russia at the drop of a hat . . . but who among living English writers had been quite so troubled by so many dystopias? G. K. Chesterton's sister-in-law had written about her "Russian Venture," and the Labour politician Ethel Snowden had published a book with a title like *Across Bolshevik Russia on a Dog Sled* on her return. Troy hadn't read either. He'd been brought up on the old Russia not the new one. A Russia of fading memories, peeling like the pea-green paint on a decaying dacha. His father had fled in 1905, an escape shrouded in mystery and carpeted with diamonds. His uncle and grandfather had stuck it out until 1910, protected from the Tsar's secret police by the patronage of the most famous writer in the world, Count Leo Tolstoy. With Tolstoy's death the protection stopped, and Nikolai had brought the old man to England to live out his days without learning a word of English, and to die at ninety—author of a dozen pamphlets on civil disobedience and numberless letters to *The Times*—without ever seeing Russia again. Troy doubted any of the old ones at table would ever see Russia again. He felt that Burgess had the advantage of him, of them all. Troy was fluent in Russian, but had never been to Russia. Burgess had. Whilst Troy had all but tuned out to muse awhile, he could see that Rod, whose dislike of Burgess was all too apparent, was listening to him intently. He was serving them Russia on a plate, between the fish and the meat, gently oscillating between reservation and endorsement, warning against expecting miracles whilst expecting them himself.

Troy stopped daydreaming just as Burgess was saying something about encountering a woman on a Moscow tram with a pig under each arm.

"It's almost impossible to imagine how close contemporary Russia, in the midst of the most directed and planned society on earth, in its urban capital, is to the nineteenth century and to peasantry."

Nikolai was smiling now. He had no difficulty whatsoever in such a feat of imagination. Macmillan was smiling too.

"I met a chap with an Aberdeen Angus on top of a 38 bus in Blooms-bury once," he said.

Troy thought his father and brother might die laughing. Burgess too—well, at least he could laugh at himself. No small virtue.

§3

Troy's mother always liked him to play the piano after dinner. She liked to show him off. Troy's father always liked him to play the piano after dinner. He liked the Great American Songbook, however indifferent the interpretation.

Troy was partial to Fred Astaire and Ginger Rogers and had only recently seen them dance their way through *The Gay Divorcee*, which had taught him some new Cole Porter songs. His repertoire already included "Love for Sale," "You Do Something to Me," and half a dozen others, and after rambling through them he settled on a new one, "Night and Day."

Much to Troy's surprise, Burgess pulled up a chair next to the piano stool. Stuck his minute coffee can and his outrageous, bloated brandy balloon, in which he had what looked to be at least a triple shot, on the top of the piano.

"Do you play, Guy?"

"I tinkle. I don't really think I'm much of a pianist. But you are."

"I don't practice enough. Now, before my dad slides over and requests 'Puttin' on the Ritz' or something just as raucous, do you have any requests?"

"Not really. I suppose I like the odd music hall song . . . never quite got to grips with all this American stuff . . . the odd hymn too, you know, sort of thing we used to sing in school assembly . . . And of course one can never get enough Haydn or Mozart."

"Quite," said Troy. "But if I belt out *Eine kleine Nachtmusik*, the *nacht* will soon be over."

And a demon whispered in his ear.

"Glorious things of thee are spoken . . ."

And Burgess joined in with the second line:

"Zion, city of our God!"

He had a poor voice, Troy's was not much better, but as long as the same demon whispered they sang it through to the end.

> *Fading is the worldling's pleasure,*
> *All his boasted pomp and show;*
> *Solid joys and lasting treasure,*
> *None but Zion's children know.*

And then they both burst out laughing.

His mother appeared at his side.

"Quoi, t'es devenu complètement fou? L'hymne national allemand?" Have you gone completely mad? The German national anthem?

"Maman, it's also an English hymn. Music by Haydn, words by some long-forgotten English poet. Rod and I used to sing it at that very expensive school you sent us to. Apparently they sang it at Eton too, eh Guy?"

"S'il te plait, Freddie, joue quelque chose anglais." Please, Freddie, play something English!

Then she was gone.

"Music hall, you said?" Troy asked.

"Fine by me . . . if you think it will placate your mother."

Troy struck up "My old man said follow the van . . ."

Burgess joined in and they played a version for four hands and two voices:

> *My old man said: "Follow the van,*
> *And don't dilly-dally on the way."*
> *Off went the van wiv me 'ome packed in it.*

I walked be'ind wiv me old cock linnet.
But I dillied and dallied,
Dallied and dillied;
Lost me way and don't know where to roam.
And you can't trust a "Special"
Like the old-time copper
When you can't find your way home . . .

Across the room his mother glowered at him, and his father raised his glass and grinned.

§4

It occurred to Troy that Burgess was the kind of bloke who'd never leave a party until physically thrown out.

Lady Troy was long abed, his father was postmidnight pottering in his study as was his wont, his sisters were in the kitchen giggling their way through the Calvados, he'd no idea where Rod was, and every other guest but Burgess had left at the witching hour. It occurred to Troy that Burgess was probably pissed, but he hardly seemed incapable.

They sat on the west-facing verandah in the last vestiges of summer warmth. Troy often listened to the foxes and the owls this way, but now he was listening to a man, who whilst certainly not without charm, struck him as an endless blabbermouth.

"Your brother tells me you're a copper."

"Cadet. Well, almost. I don't start for a week or so."

"Odd choice, if I may say so."

"You may. You were a cadet yourself, I hear."

"Oh, that was different."

Burgess reached down for the brandy decanter and finding it empty set it back down, the silver tag clinking gently on the Waterford crystal. Troy did not offer to fill it up again.

"That was Dartmouth," Burgess went on.

"I know," Troy said. "There are rumours."

"Oh fuck. Is there anyone in England who hasn't heard? Completely untrue of course. I was not expelled for theft, although I think I'll probably spend the rest of my life denying it."

"What was it?"

"Oh, I dunno. General dissatisfaction, I suppose. Realising before it was too late that a life in uniform wasn't for me. I was good at it. Passed everything with flying colours. I shone . . . that might be the word . . . I always have . . . that's what I do, I pass exams with bugger all effort. I've never really failed at anything."

There was a long, sigh-soaked pause that Troy would rather not shatter.

"Which . . . which is why I find this current feeling so odd. I feel I have not got off the ground since Cambridge. And that tastes remarkably like failure."

"When did you leave Cambridge?"

"Oh, just now. In the spring. I've chased a couple of jobs. Eton wouldn't touch me with a barge pole, and Tory central office passed on a glorious opportunity to hire me. Your father kindly took me on as a reviewer. A couple of other proprietors have been equally generous, and I've enough to live on quite comfortably. And I'm not a fussy man. I'm . . . I'm easily pleased. All I need to be content is wine, books, and the *News of the World*."

Burgess's own joke set him giggling, a high-pitched whine.

"Don't ever let my old man hear you say you like the *News of the World*," Troy said.

Burgess drew breath and continued as though Troy had not spoken.

"But . . . but I always thought my life would have taken off by now. And it hasn't."

"Dreams of flying?"

"We all have them. You too."

"Maybe. I turned down Oxford a couple of years ago."

"Bloody hell. How old are you?"

"Twenty next month."

"Hmm . . . you look fifteen."

"Usually I'm told I look twelve. Glad to make it into the teens."

"And you turned down Oxford?"

"Open Exhibition, Christ Church."

"I bet your old man was furious."

"No. He heard me out, then asked what I might be doing next, as he was rich enough to keep me but did not think it good for my soul to be kept without working. I asked for a job on one of his papers and he sent me to the *Post* as the lowest of the low—court reporter."

"Like Dickens?"

"Giant footsteps to follow in. And that sparked my interest, my taste for crime."

"You want to be a beat bobby?"

"Well, you can't trust a special like the old-time copper."

Burgess giggled.

"No," said Troy. "Of course I don't want to be a beat bobby. I want to be a detective at Scotland Yard. I don't mind being in uniform, but I'd be a damn sight happier if I had one that fitted. I tried it on just before you got here. I look like a weasel lost in a sack of spuds."

"I used to get my Dartmouth cadet togs tailored at Gieves in Old Bond Street. They make uniforms for all our armed forces. Tell you what . . . if you're doing nothing Monday morning, meet me there and I'll introduce you to the old boys who stopped me looking like a weasel in a sack."

§5

Mayfair, London

They met at Gieves, 21 Old Bond Street, in the heart of what could be termed "a Gentleman's London," a little to the left of Savile Row and Cork Street, a little to the north of the Burlington Arcade, a district with more than its share of gold cufflinks, those stretchy things like dog collars that shorten your sleeves, and old school ties . . . windows full of stripes . . . Repton, Marlborough, Sherborne, Harrow, Eton. Burgess,

Troy observed, wore his old school tie. Troy didn't. He could happily do without a morning reminder in the mirror of what a hellhole school had been.

Gieves flaunted no old school ties. They had settled for a window display that was simplicity itself—the dress uniform of a rear admiral, circa 1835, mounted upon a stuffed mannequin, complete with cocked hat, as in "knocked into."

Burgess had not been vague in describing the tailors as "old boys." Mr. Tom looked seventy-five, and Mr. Albert old enough to be his father.

They measured Troy all over.

Burgess watched with an appraising eye, though precisely what he might be appraising, Troy was not quite sure. And when it was over, they took his blue-black serge uniform and said softly that it would be ready on Thursday.

"We don't have many police officers among our clients, sir, but we are pleased to say that the chief constables of both Hertfordshire and Kent are amongst them."

Out in the street Burgess said, "I think they just anointed you."

"God, I hope not."

"You're not in any hurry, are you?"

"No. Are you?"

"The life of a freelance hack is much like that of the unemployed. There's never a hurry about anything. Let's adjourn to the Burlington Arms for a snifter."

"Of course," said Troy, uneasily uncertain of what about him might make a man of twenty-five or so interested in a "boy" of nineteen.

They stayed in the Burlington on what Troy began to perceive as the Burgess pattern, until chucked out at closing time.

It was odd to be surrounded by midday boozers. Men, scarcely a woman in sight, who had nothing better to do than drink. Men of undetectable means, men in Savile Row suits, men in raggedy sleeves and elbow patches who'd look more at home on a Hertfordshire cabbage patch—all with the time and means to booze away the day in a fog of cigarette smoke and a hubbub of unrestrained gossip. He knew he didn't look like one of them, he knew he didn't look eighteen . . . but then no one was looking in the first place.

Burgess asked a thousand questions.

"Still living at home?"

"Almost. It's obligatory to live in at Hendon. But when my training's done, I'll be posted somewhere in the Met district, to one division or another, so my mother has picked out a small house just off St. Martin's Lane for me. It's central. There's almost nowhere in London I couldn't get to pretty sharpish."

"Any preferences when you are posted?"

"I've asked for J Division. It covers most of the East End. Stepney, Whitechapel, Limehouse, and so on."

"Ah . . . the mean streets."

"If you like."

"Good luck with that. It sounds like you might have a taste for Chinese opium dens and the odd bit of rough trade."

"What's 'rough trade'?"

Burgess giggled, the same high-pitched snort Troy had heard at Mimram . . . all but choking on his pint of mild.

"My God, Freddie. Are you really such an innocent?"

§6

Church Row, NW3

It was near four in the afternoon when Troy got back to his father's town house in Hampstead. He still felt tiddly and hoped it didn't show. He'd no fondness for beer but had been told that a chap doesn't let a chap drink alone, so he'd drunk what Burgess drank, and to his detriment.

Rod and his father were in the old man's study. Men there were who held their studies to be hallowed ground. Alex was not among them. His room was open to all and sundry, a hub of activity from which he could retreat regardless of what was taking place right under his nose—and while being far from a model of neatness, he always seemed to know where everything was. The walls lined with books of every language the old man spoke, every surface littered with souvenirs of his past lives . . . the gun with which he claimed to have shot his way out of Russia . . . the typewriter on which he had recorded Lawrence's entry into Damascus, the signed copy of Freud's *The Interpretation of Dreams* inscribed "Dream on" . . . and the art . . . a life-size bronze copy of Donatello's *David* . . . an original, if small, Van Gogh . . . a South Seas nude by Gauguin . . . half a dozen pale Turner watercolours—so pale, so watery you might look in vain for the colour. As a boy Troy had poked around in every corner, he felt he had got to know his father as much by reading the objects in his life as by listening to him. His father was standing behind his desk now . . . with that look on his face he had when he regretted giving up smoking.

Rod was fuming.

"You've been with that bugger, Burgess!"

"Eh?"

"Sasha saw the two of you together. Swanning up Cork Street. Arm in arm."

"We were most certainly not arm in arm, and I haven't a clue what you mean by swanning."

"Freddie, are you completely bloody naïve? You're courting the company of one of the most notorious buggers in London!"

"Ah. Sorry. When you called him a bugger just now I thought you were just being coarse, I didn't take it literally."

Alex intervened.

"Boys. Stop. This is hardly the point."

Rod turned on him, puffed up in self-righteousness like a squawking pigeon.

"I rather think it is. Freddie, if 'bugger' is too ambiguous for you, how about arse bandit?"

"Something new every day if not every hour. I've only just learnt 'rough trade.'"

The booze swam north and bumped into Troy's head. He sat down on the nearest chair and burped softly into a clenched fist.

"But, yes. I think I understand you," he all but whispered. "I had begun to wonder."

"To wonder? He's as queer as a coot."

Alex spoke up again, more forcibly.

"I say again, this is not the point, and if you do not permit me to get to the point we'll still be here at midnight. Now, do as your brother has done. Sit down and hear me out."

With bad graces and a sour face, Rod took the armchair next to Troy.

"Freddie, I cannot tell you how to choose your friends. Everything Rod has told you is true . . ."

"Everything? It amounts to one prejudicial opinion that might be a fact."

"Hear me out, my boy. Burgess is a homosexual. I knew that when I hired him. It doesn't matter. He is also a Soviet agent and that does matter."

Rod and Troy looked at each other. Silent and wide-eyed.

"And I did not know that when I hired him."

"How can you be sure?" Rod asked. "I know he was in the Communist Party when we were at Cambridge. He makes no bones about it, even admitted it at dinner the other night. Dozens of blokes were. It hardly amounts to more than being in the Boy Scouts. A phase some of us have to go through."

"I would agree with that. But Nikolai does not. Nikolai says the inherent contradictions in Burgess's arguments smack of a man told to disassociate himself."

Troy said, "Methinks the lady doth protest too much."

"Exactly. Burgess is burrowing like a badger."

"Mole," said Troy. "Like a mole."

"As you wish. He's stopped fighting England because he's been told to join it. He's reinventing himself with every word he utters."

"All this from one conversation?" said Rod.

"No. Nikolai has his sources. I do not ask what they are. Links to the old country I'd rather not know about."

"So what are you going to do? Sack him?"

"No. He's rather good at what he does. I see no reason to sack him."

"Then why are we sitting here? Why did you tell me to get Freddie in here as soon as he got home?"

Troy said, "Surely just to give you the opportunity to tell me not to consort with queers? Or what was it you called him? A bum bandit?"

"Fuck off."

"Boys, please. That is but a fraction of the truth. The bigger picture is this. As long as we know what Burgess is, we can and must be careful. We are vulnerable. We have been since the day we landed in this country twenty-five years ago. Every Russian, however well-received, is an object of suspicion. They buy my newspapers, they read my books, they pile on the honours . . . I can lunch at the Garrick, prop up the bar at the RAC club, I can consort with Churchill, with Macmillan, with Eden . . . but if I, if any of us, consort with a Russian spy we can never forget that he is a Russian spy and that we as a family are at risk from both sides."

Eventually Rod broke a silence that Troy never would.

"You believe Nikolai?"

"Of course."

"Then one question remains. Who do we tell?"

"Rod, we have no idea what is going to happen in the next five years. The map of the world might rearrange itself. Or Hitler might rearrange it personally. We do not know what side Russia will take . . . what deals Stalin might make . . ."

"I say again. Who do we tell?"

"Tell? We tell no one."

§7

In the absence of a verandah Troy took to the back garden. Not so much the London pocket handkerchief as the London tablecloth. Hollyhocks instead of willows. A lone hooting owl, a visitor from the nearby churchyard, where he no doubt feasted on London's abundant rats, instead of the competitive barking of Hertfordshire foxes. A warm August dusk. He'd sat here countless times. It might even be part of his first memory, and it was certainly part of a thousand subsequent childhood memories. A sickly child, wrapped up like a railway parcel awaiting collection by the porter, blanketed and cushioned while his grandfather read Russian folk tales aloud to him.

He had no memories that were not English. His brother and sisters had been born on the long five-year trek around Europe while his father made up his mind where they might settle. Rod even professed to have memories of their days in Paris, although Troy was not wholly certain he believed him.

Rod flopped down next to him now. Mellowed by food and drink.

"Where's Dad?" Troy asked.

"Gone back to messing about at his desk."

A pause. A silence. Another one Troy would not fill.

"Look. About what happened earlier. I'm sorry."

Troy hated Rod's apologies. The man could make decency oppressive.

"I was overreacting . . ."

"Rod. Do shut up. You're drowning out the owl."

"I was only trying to protect you."

"What? From the queers?"

"Yes. You don't know how you appear to people. Women want to mother you . . ."

"Well . . . you got the tall gene. I can't help being short."

Rod all but ignored this.

"And you can't help looking cute."

"Cute? You think I'm cute?"

"Of course I don't. Don't be an ass. I'm well aware that you are a malevolent little prick with a capacity to go . . . what's the word . . . rogue?"

"I'd prefer feral. Or do you want me to fetch you the *Oxford Dictionary of Fraternal Abuse*?"

"Whatever . . . women want to mother you . . . men . . . well, a certain kind of man . . . wants to fuck you."

A pause. A silence Troy had every intention of filling as soon as he'd strung Rod out for a minute or two.

"I'd prefer the other way around."

Rod appeared to be thinking about this. Then he smiled, and the smile became a grin, the grin became a giggle.

Troy knew he could wring yet more contrition out of his brother, but could see no point in so doing. If Rod had relaxed enough to laugh then it was a hatchet successfully buried. Until the next time.

"Speaking of protection," Troy said. "There was really nothing I didn't know, couldn't have guessed at, in what the old man said about our vulnerability, as he put it . . . it almost didn't need saying, and but for this new development, he might well not have put it into words. But it does give rise to wonder."

"Not quite with you here, Freddie."

"Are you the one who's pissed now?"

Rod equivocated with his left hand, like a rudder.

"*Così così*. I can still spigga da Inglish."

"What does he think he did when he whipped us all into exile? What is he manifesting when he talks of it. Guilt?"

"Well . . . I've known him twenty-five years . . . you a tad less . . . but I determined long ago that the characteristic the two of you share almost completely is you don't feel guilt. It can be scary sometimes. You exude a total confidence that whatever course of action you have embarked on is unarguably the right course of action. No regrets, no guilt, no looking back."

"He looks back all the time. His entire narrative is one great big act of retrospection."

"But devoid of guilt. It is the narrative that matters to him. It's not looking back in the sense that the English would normally understand it. The telling of the story is no indication that he is reappraising himself or any of his actions."

"Well . . . he got that from his dad. All he ever did was tell stories."

"I missed most of them. School, university, so on . . ."

"I think I copped the lot. I was his captive audience . . . and after that I was Dad's captive audience. The lot of the last-born. The lot of the sickly child. To be forcibly entertained and educated at home by a man who knew everything and never shut up. But . . . we are off the point. How does he see us? I see an us, you see an us, but surely not the same us. What is the Troy family to him? What is this risk he now seems to have become so acutely aware of?"

"He's not just become aware of it. It's the ongoing condition of exile."

"Then what do you make of all the risks he's taken in the past?"

"Such as? Sorry, silly question. I mean pick one. Fukkit. There've been dozens."

"How about . . . 1924?"

"I wasn't exactly politically savvy in 1924."

"Nor me. I was eight, but I knew what he was doing. I sat next to him while he typed his editorial. He even had me correct his spelling."

"Oh. That. The fucking Zinoviev letter."

"That would be my idea of risk. Putting his name to an editorial denouncing it as a fake after the *Mail*—or was it the *Express*? I probably never knew. As I said, I was only eight—after whichever right-wing rag published the letter."

"He wasn't the only one to call it a fake, and it was a fake. Either anti-Soviet Russian exiles or our own dear secret services faked it. If we live long enough we may even find out which."

"All the same, he stuck his neck out."

"I think Dad would call that a calculated, perhaps even a contained risk. He said what half the country thought, plenty of people backed him, and he said it from behind the shield of money and a title. I don't know which the English respect more."

"And that's another thing . . . the title, which has suddenly become 'piling on the honours'. All a bit baffling."

"A baronetcy *is* an honour."

"OK. One honour. Hardly a pile."

"A slight exaggeration. Understandable given how close he sailed to the wind in getting it."

"When was it? During the war?"

"1919. Lloyd George whacking out the awards. And the truth about that and countless other knighthoods and peerages nearly came out a couple of years ago."

"Truth?"

"He bought the baronetcy off LG through a middleman named Maundy Gregory. Chap set up a pretty lucrative business as LG's middleman, and quite literally brokered deals for titles. The old man paid £5,000. Most of which ended up in the coffers of the Liberal Party. I think he got a bargain. Ten years later the price would have more than doubled."

Troy felt he should be shocked by this, but the only shock he felt was at not knowing sooner.

"1919?"

"Yep. You'd have been about three, going on four."

"And in what way was this 'sailing close to the wind'? It sounds as though half the toffs in England paid for it."

"A couple of years ago Maundy Gregory approached the wrong bloke. Some naval officer, personal friend of Mountbatten. He shopped him. Solicitor-General had no choice but to prosecute and the new toffs of old England went into panic. Our dad was a new toff, but he doesn't bother much with panic. He told me it was a storm in a teacup and that an English principle was 'you consume your own smoke.'"

"I'll have to look that up in *Brewer's*."

"Be my guest, but the old man was right. Maundy Gregory cut a deal. Consumed his smoke. Pleaded guilty and in exchange he got eight weeks in the Scrubs and named no names. If he had . . . well, we'd have been exposed, vulnerable as the old man chooses to emphasise. There would have been risk."

"Embarrassment might be a better word."

"He's sticking with risk, because he is risk-averse. It was why he wanted the damn title in the first place."

"It made us more English?"

"On the button, Fred. We could not shuffle off our origins but we could obscure them, we could waft a smoke screen around them. It was a shrewd move. He could have bought a barony or a viscountcy, but that would have seated him on the red leather benches, the fake lord, betrayed at every move by his accent. A baronetcy was perfect. No territory, no obligations, no ermine. No less the Russian in his own eyes, a bit more English to the English. Sir Alex Troy—pillar of the community. Not so much a press baron as a press baronet. Free to write his own editorials and denounce whomsoever whensoever. I can think of only one down side."

"Which is."

"In ten or twenty years I'll inherit the fucking thing."

Troy mused awhile.

"A point of order if I may, eldest son and heir."

"Certainly, last-born son of no significance."

"If we are becoming more English as the years pass, the student princes of the class system . . . at what point do the English consume their own smoke screens?"

This set Rod laughing like an idiot, fit to drown out the hoots of even the loudest owl.

Troy brought him back to earth in two terse syllables.

"Burgess."

"Oh fuck. Burgess? Is this still about bloody Burgess? I think this is where I came in."

"Do you seriously think he's a risk? Is he not too much the clown to be a liability to anyone but himself?"

"He's not a clown. He's a gobshite. He was one of the 'apostles' at Cambridge. A self-electing coven of gobshites. He's a filthy, arrogant gobshite. And I refer to his personal habits not his sexual preference."

"Yes. Masha did have something to say about his fingernails."

"I can imagine. A remark as filthy as Burgess's nails."

"Yep."

"Then I don't want to know. And the short answer to your original question is yes. Burgess is a risk. If the old man says he's a risk, he's a risk."

"Suppose," Troy went on, "that Burgess were a German spy rather than a Russian spy. Would he be less of a risk?"

"It says something about the state of England that he probably would be. It may be acceptable to admire Hitler, much as all those railway timetable idiots have admired Mussolini. You can't admire Stalin. If you do, you're at worst a Commie, at best a fellow traveller. And it might go without saying that as Russian exiles we cannot fellow-travel. It is not an option permitted to us."

"Is it not better to fellow-travel hopefully than to arrive?"

Rod suppressed a smile.

Troy pursued the argument.

"It remains, however, that for the moment, and it may be a very long moment, Burgess is an aspiring hack of some talent, a patchy pianist blessed with the curiosity of a kitten but cursed with the manners of a slob, who went to the right school and the right university. Just like you."

"Not just like me. Not just like you. He's English. The English will never trust us. They'll like us. They'll never trust us. Right now, they trust Burgess. Burgess is one of their own."

"But . . . it's why the old man sent us to that bloody school. Not to be educated, but to become 'one of their own,' to become old Harrovians. Ever after."

Rod was wearing his old Harrovian tie just about half-mast, much as Burgess always seemed to be wearing his old Etonian tie. He flipped the sharp end, looked momentarily at the pattern—the light from the room behind him just enough to pick out the silver stripes.

"Why do you wear that damn tie?"

"I suppose I like it. I've got plenty of others, but four days out of five I seem to pick this one. I'm not making any statement."

"Really?"

"I can't argue this one with you, Freddie. Of course it was another attempt to make us more English, which, in your case, clearly didn't work. I cannot deny I quite liked my time at Harrow."

"And I hated it."

"As you are ever wont to tell me. But . . . but . . . it doesn't mean I bought the package. I have the kit . . ."

Rod waved the end of his tie.

" . . . I forsook the caboodle."

"And you now would have me forsake Burgess."

"Forsake? You've not known him two minutes!"

"True. But four days out of five I quite like him."

"After all I've said?"

"Yep. Arse bandit, arrogant gobshite, queer as a coot . . . have I missed anything out?"

"You omitted 'Russian agent.'"

"Oh, so I did."

"Be as cheeky, as sarcastic as you like, Freddie . . . but don't let this man be your undoing."

Rod stared hard at him. Troy said nothing. Noted that Rod had swapped the plural "our" that had dominated their conversation, for the singular "your." It was no longer about the Troy family, it was about Troy.

"Do you have any plans to see him again?"

Troy said nothing. Rod waited. Troy wondered if he might just bugger off, but he kept up the stare . . . looking nowhere near as pissed as he had fifteen minutes ago.

"No," said Troy at last. "I haven't."

And he recalled how he and Burgess had parted outside the Burlington.

Burgess had said, "Let's make it soon, eh?"

And Troy had replied, "Soon it shall be."

It wasn't. Looking back, years later, Troy tried to remember when "soon" had arisen, when he had next met Burgess. It had not been soon. It had been years. It had been 1939 or 1940. The world had been rearranged. There might even have been a war on.

§8

Mayfair: Thursday, September 26, 1940

There was a war on. It had lasted a year already and, until the fall of France in May, had seemed remote and unreal.

Shortly before the outbreak of war, Troy had been plucked from his East End station, promoted to sergeant, and installed at Scotland Yard on the Murder Squad under Stanley Onions—a man of whom it might be said: "a legend in his own lifetime."

"Нарядный. Impressive," his father had said. "How long were you in uniform?"

"Three years. Hendon to Stepney and out."

And it was impressive. So much so that most of Troy's new colleagues at the Yard regarded him with suspicion. A bit of a tosser. And if education and a toff accent were not enough, he was also a "boy wonder."

He'd slung his uniform in the back of the wardrobe, neither caring nor bothering to imagine that he might need it again.

Onions's attitude to both "living legend" and "boy wonder" was the same curt two syllables: "Bollocks."

"I chose you. Stand on that."

Troy had solved a few murders that might have baffled ordinary coppers. He had garnered praise, and more suspicion. But tonight's body baffled only the ordinary copper who'd called it in. Troy wished there'd been someone else available to take the case. He had far bigger fish to fry than this body on the pavement opposite Selfridges in Oxford Street. Just another black-out fatality. Unlucky enough to be dressed in black and hit by a car in the first dimness of dusk. Calling Troy out had been a waste of time.

Then the raid started.

Of late the Luftwaffe had switched from bombing RAF airfields to bombing cities, London and the East End in particular. Occasionally one or two bombers had strayed past Tower Hill, all but immune to anti-aircraft fire, to hit the City, Westminster, and Mayfair. Now, a month into the Blitz, all London was their target. This had produced not the mass panic predicted by the dystopian novelists of *things to come*—lurid tales in which whole cities were levelled like cornfields in a downpour—so much as mass caution. Anywhere that might provide bombproof shelter, from church crypts in the East End to the basements of the grander hotels up West. The deep-level tube stations on the Northern, Bakerloo, and Piccadilly lines might have been the logical choice, but London Transport still insisted on closing them after the last train—a state of affairs surely surviving on borrowed time? The Dorchester hotel was new, opened in 1931, and built of modern concrete; the Ritz, a generation older, had opened in 1906, its seemingly timeless façade wrapped around a steel skeleton . . . both had quickly come to be regarded as safe in an air raid, and it may be that they were, but the same reputation had spread without regard to age or structure to other hotels . . . the Savoy . . . Claridge's . . .

Troy was crossing Mayfair when the sirens struck up their wail. The Luftwaffe would be swarming in, following the Thames like an AA road map. While night raids might be thought to be the worst, death raining out of darkness, the bombers could come at any time, day or night. You might die at noon as readily as midnight. Only the RAF stopped them bombing around the clock.

He cut through into Shepherd Market—a warren of alleys with a notorious reputation, just south of Curzon Street—heading for Piccadilly, and then home to Goodwin's Court via Leicester Square and Cecil Court. The sky might flourish a bomber's moon, but very little light penetrated to ground level in streets as narrow as Shepherd Market. Yet, prostitutes had cheated Darwin and evolution in a single leap and developed cats' eyes. Twice, despite walking slowly and carefully, he bumped into a soft body, apologised, expecting a curt "mind yerself" to hear "Fancy a good time, dearie?" instead.

Troy did not fancy a good time.

Some confrontation was taking place in the doorway of a boarded-up barber's shop near what he took to be the junction with White Horse Street. A torch was waving—Troy didn't give a damn for the ARP and their self-righteous pronouncements—and voices were raised. Coming closer he could see the outline of the man with his back to him, a shape quite like no other—a London bobby, pointy hat, truncheon and all—and the torch was being shone in the faces of two men. The younger man was in tears, the older looked bored as though this sort of thing happened all the time and "could it all just be sped up a bit?" Troy didn't know the young man, but the streets off Piccadilly were littered with pretty, young draft-dodgers, peddling their backsides, as commonplace as the tarts—Troy cared no more for the Vice Squad than he did for the ARP—but he knew the older man: Guy Burgess.

"May I be of some assistance?"

The copper turned, shone his torch on Troy.

"You'd assist me best by minding your own business."

Troy held his warrant card in the beam of the torch.

The copper glared at him. He wasn't about to offer any deference to rank.

"What's the problem?"

"What does it look like? Queers."

"Doing it in the street?"

"What?"

"Frightening the horses?"

"What bloody horses?"

"Let me put it another way: Did you see a lewd act, did you hear either one of these men proposition the other?"

The copper said nothing.

"Quite," said Troy.

The younger man chose his moment to run for it, and the copper made no attempt to chase him. Burgess, far too casually to cause anything but offence, took out his cigarette case, offered his fags around, and finding no takers lit up.

The copper pocketed his torch, adjusted his chinstrap, muttered, "You should have better things to do" at Troy, and plodded off, cheated of his prey.

Burgess exhaled a cloud of smoke. Waited until the copper was out of earshot.

"It's been a while, Freddie," he said.

"Did you proposition that boy, Guy?"

"Of course I bloody did. He was up for it. We'd even agreed a price. He was cheaper than the boys in Hyde Park. Far cheaper than the painted dolls at the 'Dilly. However, I'm not so stupid as to let a beat bobby hear me."

"But you'd have let the boy suck you off in a shop doorway?"

"My, how a few years on the mean streets coarsens the tongue. Look, I feel I owe you a drink. Shall we go on somewhere and let Göring do his worst while we do our best?"

"I was just on my way home," Troy said.

"In an air raid? We're a hop and a step from the Ritz. Let's nip into the basement bar for shelter and snifter."

Troy had no idea why he was not simply brushing Burgess off, but he wasn't.

"OK," he said.

"Splendid," said Burgess. "Simply splendid."

They set off in the direction of Piccadilly. It wasn't splendid, but curiosity, which killed many a cat, was the primary modus operandi of any detective worth his salary. The warrant card no more than a licence to be nosy.

"I see you made the papers," Troy said.

"Oh, you mean the driving under the influence? The beak at Marlborough Street was very understanding, I pled the importance of the job—and of course the minute you mention war work, secrets and hush-hush in the same sentence . . ."

Troy could scarcely believe this.

"You're in Intelligence?"

"I was. I was in a section that instructed chaps on sabotage and survival in occupied countries."

"Hmm," said Troy. "Do you know much about that kind of thing?"

"Of course not, but nobody in MI6 . . . or was it 5—I forget which is which most of the time—anyway no one in MI what-have-you thought to ask. I gather I'm considered knowledgeable about propaganda because I produced programmes for the BBC, but all that means is that our secret masters regard the BBC as being entirely propaganda. Even the shipping news is propaganda to them—they're probably wondering about the German Bight even as we speak. They trust us and suspect us simultaneously. Mostly I gave lectures to the Home Guard about politics and unions and . . . stuff . . ."

Troy was uncertain how long he might be able to keep a straight face. Suddenly the "phony" in Phony War was all too resonant.

"Did the Home Guard need your stuff?"

"Not for a single moment. But . . . but all that came to an end in the summer. One department got rolled into another and I got rolled out."

"So, no job."

"Worse, no fucking Get-Out-Of-Jail-Free card. Thank God I was nicked while I still had the job. The next time it will be a bit harder to talk my way out of it."

"You could try staying sober."

"Freddie, for crying out loud, there's a war on. Nobody's sober!"

"Strapped for cash?"

"It'll be a cold day in hell before I go skint—there's money in the family, although I imagine anyone looks poor standing next to a Troy—on the other hand, who couldn't use a few more readies? However, the real problem with having no gainful employment is getting called up. It's get a job, chase a commission, or let myself get stuck with an ill-fitting uniform and square-bashing till a Nazi bullet puts me out of my misery."

"I could ask my father."

"What? Back to book reviewing? It was fun for a while, but it feels like another lifetime and another Guy Burgess, so thanks but no thanks. I've a few irons in the fire and my Micawbers are riding high at the moment."

"Something will turn up?"

"It had bloody well better."

§9

The downstairs grill-room at the Ritz had become another world in the first year of war. Not that Troy would spot the difference. He had occasionally visited upstairs at Le Rivoli, but never downstairs to the bar-grill that had become La Popôte . . . a demotic—"the canteen"—rendered exotic in translation.

It was a descent into a circle of hell.

The walls had been lined with sandbags and wooden struts, so that it looked like a Great War trench writ large. Graffiti were scrawled everywhere, mostly obscene—"Jimmy J. sucks cock," "Dennis takes it up the . . ."—and some, no doubt written in desperation or optimism, were just telephone numbers.

There were murals depicting both the last war—a panorama from the Western Front—and this one—the Siegfried Line, crude cartoons of Hitler and Mussolini—and there was a bar, a stage, a band, and a dance floor—and it was packed.

"How," said Burgess, "can you tell there's a war on?"

Troy had no idea what Burgess was driving at and said so.

"Alrighty. Let me put it another way. Take a look around. What is different in here, what is happening that might not have been happening in '37 or '38?"

Troy looked. It seemed at first sight to be the same old hectic toffdom. His own class at leisure with the added ingredient, fear. Another crowded, noisy London bar—and from his point of view utterly unappealing.

"Why not '39?"

"No. Last year there was trepidation. I hesitate to call it panic—it wasn't, but the place would have been as empty as a cobbler's curse. Think back to before the war."

"I couldn't say. I've never been here before."

"You're kidding?"

"No. I'm not."

"Never been in the Ritz bar? You'll be telling me next you're still a virgin."

Troy hoped he wasn't blushing. He wasn't a virgin. He was, he knew, by the standards of a man like Burgess, inexperienced. He had lost his virginity in circumstances he would never disclose to anyone. Except that he had. Sasha had wormed it out of him, and his sisters had all but toasted his loss in champagne.

"You sound just like my sisters, Guy."

"I'm flattered. But . . . you really should get out more. However, you are out and we are in, as it were. What's different is the sense of urgency. Everyone you see is a bit drunker than they would have been in '38, a bit more desperate, a damn sight easier—at least in the sexual sense of easy—and a lot happier. Feeling everything more keenly for '39's seeming brush with nothingness that turned out to be a brush with nothing much. It might well have been the same in the last war, of which I have scarcely more memory than you have yourself, but I doubt that somehow."

The more he looked, the more Troy saw Burgess's point, the more he looked, the more it struck him as parodic. Less a reality than a contrivance. A diminution of fear by embracing the fact of war whilst pretending it was all a joke. A celebration too loud, a jollity too forced, a hedonism too readily extolled. A scene from a silent Hollywood epic depicting the fall of the Roman Empire. The British Empire had been waiting years for this. All through the Great Depression, the farce that had been "National Government," appeasement, the shabby years. Just what the doctor ordered, but delivered by the Führer—an excuse not to give a damn.

He thought he might be the only sober person in the room. And keeping a safe, yet friendly distance from Burgess, quite possibly the only body not to be wrapped around another.

"There'll be fortunes made in this war," Burgess was saying. "By arms manufacturers, but above all by hoteliers and publicans. I put my spare change into Rolls-Royce. Aero engines and such, and if I had a bob or two more to spare I'd stick it in a pub or in BSA. Did you ever wonder how many people riding their motorbikes even realise it stands for Birmingham Small Arms? But, I digress—"

Small arms draped themselves around Troy. Fingertips rustled his hair, and a voice husky with fags and booze said, "My my, Guy, you old rogue . . . you have landed yourself a pretty boy."

She stepped to one side. A beautiful blonde in her late twenties in a backless, near arseless dress, blew him a kiss.

"You don't know each other?" Burgess said. "The Hon. Venetia Maye-Brown—Frederick Troy."

Troy did know Venetia and wished he didn't. She'd been one of his sisters' dissolute friends a few years back. It was obvious she didn't remember him or hadn't until Burgess made the introduction. Anything in trousers, he thought, probably didn't include short trousers.

"Not the one who caused the scandal about five years ago?"

"Not to my knowledge," Troy replied.

"Oh . . . silly me . . . not the same family . . . there was a Troy . . . you know, *those* Troys . . . Sasha's younger brother . . . forget the name . . . but he joined the police. Imagine. A copper! A London beat bobby! Everyone was talking about it. Imagine, having a copper for a little brother . . . you'd have to hide the reefer every time he came round. Speaking of which, Guy, you don't happen to have—"

Burgess cut her short.

"Venetia, George Brook-Benton's waving at you from the bar."

She turned.

"Oh God. I should never have let him buy me champagne. He'll expect a fuck now. Still, let it not be said Venetia Frances Adelaide Maye-Brown does not pay her debts. See you later, boys."

"If you were looking for proof . . . well, she's no different from what she was before the war," Troy said. "She had my pal Charlie when he was sixteen."

"She's a bit more blatant, you might agree. She'll give George his way in the Ladies. But Venetia is a class act. Won't do it in the Gents. Before the war she might well have insisted he book a room. And for all we know one or two other hopefuls might get lucky in the loo before the Ritz calls time."

"Are women becoming men?"

"Dunno. And don't much care. The voracious vamps and the todger dodgers don't bother me. As long as men . . ."

Burgess paused, a mischievous twinkle in his eyes.

". . . Stay men."

"What about all those women who dress as men?"

"Ever met one?"

"I might have. But not tonight."

"Very coy. No Freddie, that one doesn't wash for a simple, perhaps crude reason. Any man who mistakes a tweed-and-trousers hussie for a chap has no sense of smell."

Troy looked around La Popôte again. Felt distinctly out of place. As though garbed in a police uniform invisible to all but him. Burgess was right. There were so many senses of the word in which he was still a virgin, on the outside of the party looking in.

"Speaking of which."

"Speaking of what?"

"Men. Of men . . . you're in the minority here . . . La Popôte isn't the only nickname—"

"I know. The Pink Sink."

"Ah . . . so much for your much-vaunted innocence."

"Guy . . . it's the most notorious queer bar in London. And if you're suggesting we wade farther in and meet a few 'chums,' the ones oblivious to Venetia's charms . . . well, I can't. I'm a serving copper."

"But you're not Vice. And you just saw off that prurient flatfoot in Shepherd Market."

"That was . . . different. I hold no brief for Vice, and no brief for buggers either, but if a copper is to do his duty and abide by the law it is better that the blind eye he turns stays blind. Whatever you do in the Pink is of no importance to me . . . but don't ask me to look any more closely than I have already."

"Ah, blind. Blind as a bat, blind as a . . . What is the old adage? In the kingdom of the blind, the one-eyed trouser snake is king?"

"Goodnight, Guy."

"We'll keep in touch?"

"Of course we will."

§10

Troy walked home alone. Piccadilly was far from deserted. People doing just what he was doing himself. Blundering on in darkness, eyes turned to the roaring, sparkling heavens, the pops, the starbursts, the snaking fiery trails, all but oblivious of danger, hypnotised by the illusion of their own immunity. At the Circus, more than fifty people sat by the hoardings, staring down Regent Street at the glow of Southwark burning.

On a level he did not care for, he found he shared the wantonness of La Popôte. He had no wish for sex with strangers or to be the spare prick at an orgy, but he could not deny that something in the way of restraint had been cast off like a winter overcoat with the onset of bombing. Even less did he care for Burgess being the one to awaken this knowledge in him.

§11

Friday, October 4, 1940

Troy had been in the wars. One war in particular had caught up with him. This one. His immunity had run out.

He had spent weeks investigating the murder of several rabbis in the East End. The case had climaxed on an autumnal Wednesday in the middle of an air raid. He had spent two nights entombed in the remains of Heaven's Gate synagogue, with a seductive killer who now lay in the London Hospital with a bad case of concussion. They'd been dug out on Friday morning.

The hospital had discharged him. He'd gone straight back to his investigation. To the house of his chief suspect in Belgravia. There, he'd had the rotten luck to encounter his boss, Stanley Onions.

"You're on sick leave, go home," Onions had said. "I'll be round in the morning."

And Troy had had no choice. Kicked off the case, he caught a cab home, dipped rather than soaked himself in the meagre warmth of a shallow bath, and tried to sleep away the day as he had been advised. His head hurt. Why would his head not hurt? His back ached. Why should his back not ache? But at least he was at home. Just as well. He couldn't face Zette Borg right now. He could not face Zette, dead or alive. He wanted her to wake up and thanked God she hadn't just yet. He didn't mind that she had seduced him. He minded that he had got used to it. He minded that he had found her irresistible. The wicked woman a fortune teller had foreseen in his tea leaves. He didn't mind that she was wicked, that her wickedness had turned deadly, only that he hadn't seen it coming, for all the warnings in the tea leaves and for all the warnings she had given him herself—and his professional pride was bruised.

Kolankiewicz cared not a fig for wounded pride, only for his wounded head.

"I hear you took a knock, my boy. I need to give you the once-over."

He stood on Troy's doorstep in Goodwin's Court. Utter darkness but for the sky overhead, criss-crossed by searchlights and tracers and the popping of ack-ack shells. Off to the east and west bombs whumpffed and bullets rattled. London was copping it, somewhere towards Mayfair, somewhere towards Clerkenwell, but St. Martin's Lane was not.

"Why do you come out in the middle of a raid?"

"You let me in, and I won't be in the middle of it."

Troy closed the door behind him.

"Blackout curtains stop no bombs," he said. "We're still in it."

"Of course not. It just feels that way. When I draw the blackouts at home, I feel safer. I feel wrapped up against the world. Much the same as wearing your favourite overcoat, or going to bed early on a wintery night with a hot water bottle. Who knows, I may never take them down. When this war is over I may still black out."

"You'll be the only man in England who does."

Troy had little time for doctors, and any injury he usually referred to Ladislaw Kolankiewicz, senior pathologist at Hendon—a man more accustomed to dealing with the dead, but guaranteed to keep secrets, of which Troy had plenty.

Kolankiewicz examined his head, listened to his heart, said, "OK, smartyarse, so you're immortal. Now . . . you got anything you want to tell me?"

Troy said nothing. Too many secrets. Ones he could never share with anyone.

Kolankiewicz would not wait for the all-clear—that could be after dawn—and bustled out as rapidly as he had bustled in.

Troy flicked out the light, opened the door to let him leave, and Kolankiewicz all but stepped on a man standing just outside the door. As Kolankiewicz muttered his apology, the man slipped in. Only with the door shut and the light back on did Troy have a clue who it was.

Burgess.

"I heard," he said simply.

"I find that hard to believe."

"You called your sister, who called your other sister, who called Venetia Maye-Brown, who just told me . . . in the Ritz."

"So, she finally figured out who I am?"

"Yes. And I fear she is after you, you'd better guard your virginity more closely."

Troy thought of the ravages of Zette Borg. How she had roared through his veins. He had known all along that he would regret his relationship with her. Now she lay unconscious, he wanted nothing more than that she would wake up. Beyond that he could not see. He had invested too much in her—as he thought of it, he had built castles in the air on a relationship that began in the gutter. He could boast idly to Burgess about an affair of the heart that was so much an affair of the flesh. She hadn't been his first. It just felt that way. But he owed himself no boast and he owed Burgess nothing.

A boom from hell cracked across the sky and set the windows rattling.

"If we're going to sit this one out, Guy, I think we're going to need a drink."

"I'm a Scotch man, if you have . . ."

"I know. I heard."

"Really? I'd no idea I was the object of so much gossip."

"Yes, you have."

Troy produced a couple of single malts. An Arran and a twelve-year-old Lagavulin. He also found a bottle of Johnnie Walker that he kept for Onions, who preferred blended whisky. He'd no idea for whose pleasure he had acquired the single malts, but it now appeared that both bottles had been expecting Burgess all along.

"There are people who think you have Scotch for breakfast."

"Harrumph. Bloody cheek. I breakfast at the Ritz. Almost every day. I'm a scrambled-egg-and-bacon man. There for anyone to see. I dread the day eggs become scarce. Can't go to work without a neggie. On a sloppy day you can read the history of breakfasts past on me ole school tie. And I daydream of breakfasts yet to come."

"Then you start on the Scotch."

"Never before ten thirty. Good God, Freddie. One has to have some standards."

"Don't make me laugh, Guy, my head hurts too much."

He lay back. A glass of Armagnac in his hand. Closed his eyes. Let Burgess prattle. That was the dreadful thing about an air raid—you couldn't just kick a bloke out when you'd had enough of him.

The lights went off. So familiar. Less than twelve hours after he'd been dug out and here he was again plunged into blackness thick as onion soup.

But now there was another danger. Alone in the dark with Burgess. If he makes a move, thought Troy, do I have the strength to deter him?

For several minutes all he could hear was the rasp of Burgess breathing. Then another piece of doom cracked overhead.

"Don't you," Burgess said, "find all this . . . a bit erotic?"

From somewhere Troy would summon enough energy to kick him in the balls if he had to.

"All what?"

"All this . . . Hitler's own *son et lumière*."

Troy did and was loth to admit it. Entombed in the synagogue, death a closer prospect than it had ever been, he and Zette had fucked like rabbits. He could tell himself it helped to pass the time, and what a colossal lie that would be. They had fucked to fuck. They had fucked to die and hoped to live.

"I suppose it is."

"Not just me, then?"

"No. You, me, Venetia, and half London I should think."

"I mean. Just imagine how much shagging is going on at this very moment."

"I'd rather not."

"London's always been easy. But never as easy as it is now. There is just so much cock out there just . . . waiting for the chance to strut its stuff. And before you queer me on that . . . there's an absolute ocean of quim too. Wet as a washday Monday."

"Guy . . . the last time we met . . . you had propositioned that boy."

"Of course."

"Do you do that often?"

"No. Perhaps two or three times a week."

"And how often do they say yes."

"About two or three times a week."

"And how often do you have to deal with a constable?"

"It's happened once or twice. The blackout's been a gift. They can't see what's going on under . . . don't take this literally . . . their noses . . . on second thought, do take that literally, as I got blown by a beat bobby last March . . . but this one was a bit of a bastard. Normally, they'll flick on their torches . . . got to be against regs hasn't it? . . . I mean where are the bloody ARP when all you want is a quiet blow job in the dark . . . 'Ere put that light out! Ere suck that cock!' . . . they just check you both look over twenty-one and tell you to get lost. It's a rare kind of bastard who really wants to nick you. They'd sooner thump you. It's the war. Better things to do. Won't last, of course."

"Do you ever worry that one day you will get nicked?"

"I did get nicked a couple of years ago. Gents bog at Paddington. I'd done the circuit—"

"The what?"

"The circuit. There's a gents bog at practically every station on the Circle Line, so you pay your two farthings and you go round, one way or the other, doesn't matter which, and try the gents at each stop until you find someone else doing the same thing. I was going clockwise. Started out at Sloane Square. Rotten luck. Nothing at Gloucester Road, High Street Ken, or Bayswater, but I thought I'd scored at Paddington. Turned out I hadn't and the plod was lurking.

But, I am nothing if not eloquent. After he heard me, the beak threw the case out in court. That means I have not a stain on my character—to say nothing of the clap, a dose of syph, and several cases of crabs, still I am spotless in the eyes of the law. But . . . on a lower level, beneath thought and most certainly beneath speech, every homo wonders about getting nicked. However . . . I have two things going for me, three if I count you turning up out of the blackout and blue . . . I've always felt I was a lucky sort of chap, I get out of scrapes as easily as I get into them, and you'd be amazed at how intimidating RP and the King's English can be. Of course that copper the other night was having none of it. He'd have nicked the Duke of Windsor."

It seemed to Troy that in a little less than a month the Blitz had divided Londoners into two types—shelterers and watchers. Both had sub-types. Frightened and not-frightened was not the line. It was closer to . . . the *introvert* shelterer, who stuck a mattress up against the window and hid under the kitchen table or, if better prepared, found one of the rare public shelters . . . or the *extrovert* shelterer, who looked upon being up all night as merely an extension of his habitual practices and regarded an air raid as an excuse for a party. Class and money had a lot to do with it. The watchers who worked . . . worked. They stayed on the surface, drove ambulances, put out fires, and lived or died along with those in their care. Troy saw himself as the other type of watcher. His job gave him a legitimate reason to be out, but he was no part of safety or rescue and so looked skyward more than those who were. And alongside him were the watcher-starers who were out in the blaze for no better reason than that they were fascinated by it. It was odd—falling just short of morbid. Only the job saved Troy from being such a starer. Burgess, Troy concluded, was an up-all-night subterranean reveller who'd really quite like to be a starer.

"Have you ever just gone out in a raid and looked up?"

"No. Spend most of my time looking down. Once the siren goes you can hear the fly buttons pop in every basement bar in London."

"So you've never really seen Hitler's *son et lumière*?"

"You don't think you're labouring the point a bit? It was a throwaway remark."

"No it wasn't. You want erotic. Follow me. I'll show you erotic."

Troy found a torch and led the way to the top floor.

Burgess followed. As they passed the bedrooms he said, "Am I reading this situation wrongly, Troy?"

"In all probability."

He handed the torch to Burgess and slid the bolts on the roof hatch.

"We're going to get a view from the gods. Put the torch out now."

Troy climbed out onto the tiles, held out a hand and yanked Burgess after him.

"I might be a bit fat for this sort of caper."

"You may well be. But look up and stop thinking about yourself for a moment."

Troy wedged his back against the chimney stack. Burgess sat just below him, one foot wedged in the trapdoor. He had carried the bottle of Lagavulin up with him. Nothing, it seemed, and certainly not the Luftwaffe, would part him from his grip on it.

It seemed to Troy that the night sky was short on sky's own colour—blue. Reds it had aplenty, from the bright, post-office-van scarlet of the flames that leapt heavenward from burning buildings to the colouring-book-and-wax-crayon carmine of tracers and the paintbox burnt orange of ack-ack shells popping uselessly among the beaten-metal pewter hue of the barrage balloons. Incendiaries burnt white to silver, and the searchlights sliced up the night with long fingers of pure, clear light. Rarely had he seen a plane hit, either ours or theirs, but when it happened every colour in the rainbow might burst forth.

He stared.

Let Burgess stare.

Cocooned in noise and light.

Burgess swigged Scotch, burped and sighed.

"You're right. There is a most appalling beauty to it all. I am put in mind of Yeats . . . a terrible beauty."

"I'm not. I don't think this is what he meant."

Three massive explosions shook the air around them . . . crump, crump, crump off to the east—buffeted by a giant hand.

Burgess sighed.

"Speaking of terrible beauty . . ."

Burgess burped.

" . . . What will you do about the lovely Venetia?"

"Avoid her. Shouldn't be too hard. I've managed to avoid her the last five years. Besides I have rather a lot on my plate at the moment."

"A woman?"

"More than one woman, I'm afraid."

"Ah . . . you have grown up, after all. Then I won't mention your virginity again."

"Good. I'd be grateful for that."

A pause, in which man was silent and metal was loud.

Troy saw a glint of hot steel flash in the sky to the south of them, like sparklers in the giant's hand, then a shower of ack-ack shrapnel hit the roof of the Coliseum theatre. He had no idea what happened in a theatre during an air raid—must the show go on? Did the show go on? What, after all, could be darker than a London theatre—designed to keep light out, they surely also kept it in?

A lull. The illusion of silence after so much noise. He could even hear the pop as Burgess took the Scotch bottle from his lips.

"Bloody hell. That was close."

More swigging of Scotch. Then the pleasing non sequitur that alcohol found in his befuddled brain:

"What's playing there at the mo'?"

"I believe it's a revival of *Chu Chin Chow*."

"Really? Pity it wasn't a direct hit, then."

"My brother rather liked it."

"And where is he now?"

Troy pointed upwards.

"Really. You mean . . ."

"Not quite. He's with a Hurricane squadron, Hampshire or Dorset way."

"Shouldn't that be secret?"

"No idea."

"Any other secrets he shares?"

"He says we're winning."

The flash once more, the sweep of the giant's hand, and fragments of shrapnel dashed a deafening clatter along the roof to stop only inches from Burgess's left leg.

He dropped the Scotch bottle, sent it rolling towards the gutter, and his impulses sent him lurching after it, an arm outstretched to the bottle. Troy grabbed hold of the back of his coat and heaved, hoping he wasn't so heavy that he'd pull both of them over the edge. Burgess slithered to a halt with his head in the gutter, Troy's hands knotted in the hem of his overcoat, the bottle smashed in the yard below them.

For a few moments neither of them moved, Troy hoping that Burgess regained some control and shared the burden of his bulk, his live weight, before they both fell as dead weight.

"Bloody hell. I mean . . . bloody hell."

"Guy. For God's sake, just shut up and push."

Then Troy felt the pull on his arms relax as Burgess used the flat of his hands to push himself slowly back up the roof towards him.

"Did I say something about a *near* miss? Me and my big mouth."

He stretched out on the tiles. His left leg twitching involuntarily, his chest heaving, his breath sounding like an approaching hurricane.

"Thank you. I think you might have saved my life."

"As long as I don't come to regret it."

"Freddie, there are people even now who wouldn't thank you."

For some reason this induced a fit of giggles.

Troy could not think it odd, giggling in the face of death, because he could not think what normal might be. Was it normal to be stuck on a London rooftop in an air raid with a drunken and notorious homosexual, debating the erotic nature of war?

"Tell you what, Freddie. Let's give thanks. I think we should pray."

More self-perpetuating giggles of profanity.

"I don't know any prayers, and I doubt you do either."

"Or . . . how about a hymn? What was the one you played me out at your dad's house . . . da da daaah!"

"It was Haydn's 'Glorious Things of Thee Are Spoken' . . . and if you recall my mother stopped us because it has the same tune as the German national anthem. I cannot think how you or I would explain to the nosy buggers in the ARP what we might be doing sitting on the roof serenading the Luftwaffe with 'Deutschland Über Alles.'"

But Burgess was away with the fairies, humming softly to himself.

"Da da daaah da daaah da dada . . . I will glory in thy name . . . something something worldling's pleasure . . . what's a worldling? What on earth is a bloody worldling?"

"You are," said Troy, and he began to tune Burgess out. A magenta and orange burst in the sky over Waterloo and he couldn't hear him anymore.

§12

The all-clear sounded around four o'clock in the morning. It woke Troy. He wondered if he'd be able to go back to sleep. Ten minutes later he heard the front door close and knew Burgess had abandoned a night on the sofa for a few hours in his own bed.

Troy did not stir again until past ten.

He opened the front door to find a fine layer of ash covering everything. He blew it off the top of the milk bottle, and closed the door.

On the small table in front of the sofa was a piece of paper that hadn't been there last night.

It was a pen-and-ink sketch. A man, recognisably Troy, although far too Adonis-like in the body, was having intercourse with a woman, recognisably Venetia, although the body far too buxom, bent into the dog position, in front of the statue of Eros at Piccadilly Circus. A policeman's helmet lay discarded in the foreground. One of Troy's hands rested on the curve of Venetia's hip, the other held a truncheon upright, as if saluting, priapic, as if symbolising the hidden penis. And in the bottom right-hand corner . . . "Morituri te salutant." Those about to die salute you. Petronius, Suetonius? Troy couldn't remember. On the back Burgess had scribbled a note:

I think we agree. War was made for fucking. And, the complications of your life set aside for the moment, if I were you, if I could ever imagine the attraction of a woman, I think I'd fuck Venetia Maye-Brown under floodlights in the middle of a hundred-bomber raid. That'd show 'em.
Yrs Ever,
Guy.

Show who? Troy wondered for a fraction of a second. But the answer all but preceded the question. Show *them*. Not the Germans. Not the ARP . . . *them*, the ubiquitous *them* that were not us. The real and imagined oppressors of Guy Burgess in the world Burgess had made for himself. What was troubling, but he'd hardly lose sleep over it, was that Burgess lumped Troy and himself together in this defiant, unarticulated us.

There was a knock at the door. Troy quickly stuffed Burgess's sketch in his pocket. Opened the door to find Superintendent Onions on the step. He'd said he'd call. It had completely slipped Troy's battered and Burgess-burdened mind.

"Tell me," Troy said.

"Stick the kettle on," Onions said.

Half an hour later Troy was no nearer a solution to the case that had led him from one dead rabbi to another to being walled up in the synagogue with Zette, but he had clearly, if silently, been told to file his report and drop it.

In an abrupt change of subject, on his feet ready to leave, Onions said, "London's gone sex mad. The Commissioner's getting reports from beat bobbies of people shagging in Hyde Park in broad daylight. Would you believe it?"

Troy would.

He'd done it himself.

Onions left the door open, light from the Indian summer sunshine reflecting off the far wall and into the otherwise gloomy sitting room.

Troy pulled out the sketch. It struck him as unbelievable cheek. It struck him as absurdly funny. Then a shadow took the light. A figure in the doorway again. What had Stan forgotten? But it wasn't Stan. It was his mother. Quickly he screwed up the sketch and lobbed it deftly across the room into the wastepaper basket. If his mother ever saw it his life wouldn't be worth living.

§13

London: October 1948

Almost falling off the roof proved to be the high and low point in Troy's relationship with Burgess. Throughout the war he found himself invited to endless parties at Burgess's flat. Once in a blue moon he would run out of excuses and accept. He found himself a fish out of water and usually left early.

One day in 1948 he was crossing Piccadilly Circus to find that the statue of Eros was being replaced on its plinth. It had been removed to safety on the outbreak of war. The revellers who'd swamped the 'Dilly on VE night had gathered around a boarded-up, empty plinth, plastered with advertisements urging thrift and the purchase of war bonds. But the war had been over three years. Like so much else in England normality was painfully slow in returning. The war ended, and then it hung around for ages, kicking its heels, reluctant to go home in case anything else happened. Rationing stretched out to infinity. The peace seemed like an inert interlude. The erotic charge spent. Surely something else would happen one day . . . some day . . . any day?

A crane swung the statue up off a flatbed truck and three men in boiler suits and cloth caps guided Eros into place. One clunk, a couple of twists, and it was home. Wings spread, heel up, head down, the arrow shot. Love struck. The small crowd that had gathered applauded. Troy remembered the vulgar drawing Burgess had done of him all those years ago. Burgess had included Eros—the sketch would have made less sense without it. Love in an air raid, presided over by the skinny youth with the bow and arrow. He hadn't, to the best of his knowledge, seen Venetia Maye-Brown since 1940. He couldn't remember when he had last seen Burgess. Last year? The year before? Burgess had gone back to the BBC, and from there to the Foreign Office . . . but what he did for the Foreign Office, and whether he was still at the Foreign Office . . . and why the Foreign Office would want a man as indiscreet as Burgess . . . all went unanswered.

But, to think of the man was to conjure him up.

That night, he took the cellist Méret Voytek, a woman renowned for her performance of Bach, a survivor of Auschwitz, and someone he strongly suspected of being both a murderer and a Russian spy, for an evening of British bebop at Club 11, only yards from Eros. He had not expected to find Burgess there. He did not mind finding Burgess there, but if everything he and Rod had long assumed about him was true, then it was odd to bump into him at precisely this moment, and Troy wondered if it was just a coincidence. Had she told him, had he told her? Were they total strangers? Or was he piggy in the middle?

As he introduced them there was not a flicker of recognition on Voytek's face. Guy was harder to read. He greeted everyone as though he had known them all his life. He slid into instant, if illusory, relationships as readily as putting on old slippers.

He seemed to be under the influence of a mixture of Scotch and dope. An overly large drink in one hand, and a waving joint in the other. Troy had no difficulty not minding any of this. He'd seen Burgess light up a reefer in public countless times, and he'd scraped him off the pavement outside the pubs and clubs of Soho a dozen times. The only thing to mind was when Burgess held out the reefer to Voytek, which she accepted with a cheeky grin, and pigged Troy in the middle once more. It was as though they'd both be happier if he did mind. The self-regarding defiance of naughty children.

Bebop, as played by Ronnie Scott, could drown out an air raid. Conversation with Burgess got as far as "What are you up to these days?" and not as far as an answer. When they parted in the street, Troy having declined all suggestion that they might "go on somewhere," he realised the nature of his apprehension. He did not want a relationship to develop between these two. It was a complication too far. He was uncertain where investigating Voytek might lead. She might be innocent of everything, and even if she weren't, he had little inclination to arrest her—he simply wanted to know. And to that process of knowledge Burgess, with his kitten's curiosity, could only be an obstacle. Voytek-Burgess was a consummation not to be wished.

About a month later Troy knew everything, and knowing there was not a damn thing he could do about any of it, he stuck Voytek on a cross-channel ferry to Calais on the assumption that she would lose herself before she was exposed. That she had exposed herself in an anonymous tip-off to the *Daily Express* was a secret they'd share for the rest of their lives.

It was easy enough to keep. A few days later, his right-hand man, Jack Wildeve, stuck the *Express* in front of him. There was a headline:

RUSSIAN SPY FLEES ACROSS CHANNEL

And a photograph of Méret Voytek.
Followed by . . .

SCOTLAND YARD SEEK MYSTERY MAN

And a scrappy sketch of someone Troy took to be himself.
As Jack had said, "His own mother wouldn't recognise him."
Indeed, she didn't.
Alas, someone else would.

§14

December 20, 1948

Troy had been at school with Neville Pym. He had seen nothing of him since leaving school, until he had reappeared in Troy's life in 1944 as Squadron Leader N. A. G. Pym, liaison officer between MI5 and the Yard.

He was more obviously queer than either Guy Burgess or Tom Driberg, and Troy had concluded that the only reason he had not been victimised or ostracised was a certain wilful incredulity on the part of his masters in military intelligence. How else had Burgess got away with it all these years? Burgess had ascribed it to luck. Pym's luck ran out.

The London copper felt no need of willed incredulity. Troy thought Burgess's assessment of "they'd sooner thump you than nick you" to be pretty well accurate, but there was always just one bastard waiting in the wings, or in Pym's case in the gents in the Holloway Road.

It was Driberg who asked Troy to intervene, and Troy was sad that his intervention yielded no hope for Pym. As the copper had put it:

"You should have better things to do with your time than running errands for queers. He's going down, Mr. Troy, and that's all there is to it."

Troy had broken the news to Pym himself, rather than leave it to Driberg. It was what he felt he owed to an acquaintance who had never really been a friend, and whom he'd never much liked.

On the nineteenth of December, in his rooms at Albany, on Piccadilly, Pym had shot himself through the roof of his mouth, a bullet straight to the brain, his brains spattered across the wall, and left a suicide note which pointed Troy to Jimmy Wayne, a suspect he had lost track of four years ago. Of a kind, it was gratitude. It sharpened Troy's sense of failure and his resolve. He'd been given a lead on a case that had gone cold as the grave.

At the moment he's running the airlift in Berlin.

Troy had called Rod, a junior minister at the Air Ministry, and scrounged a flight to Berlin. Then he waited. He waited at home and when he got fed up waiting at home, he waited in the pub.

It was only a few days before Christmas. Soon he would be able to have a quiet drink in a pub without being overwhelmed by dozens of office workers hell-bent on having a noisy drink.

Troy sat alone in the back room at the Salisbury in St. Martin's Lane— the velvet box, as someone had appropriately dubbed it—reading that day's *News Chronicle* . . . record snowfalls in New York, the US military government of Japan about to hang war criminals, a tortured, ambivalent editorial on the state of Israel, West Berlin still under siege, the RAF shuttling planes in every minute . . . and taking a large gin and drinking it as slowly as he wished. There was hum and hubbub arising in the main bar, but nothing he could not ignore.

He could not, however, ignore the man looming over him. The best he could hope for was to fake a little bonhomie.

"Guy, fancy seeing you here."

Burgess had a rather tatty briefcase with him, tied up with bits of string. He slid off a couple of loops, took out a folded newspaper, and let the briefcase slide to the floor.

He unfolded the paper, the *Express* from a couple of weeks ago, and spread out the headlines, with Voytek's mug shot and the unfathomable your-mother-wouldn't-know-you artist's sketch.

"I may be wrong," Burgess said. "But isn't this the young woman you were with at Club 11 the other night?"

The other night? It was more than six weeks ago.

Troy stood up.

"Guy. Your tiny hand is empty. Let me get you a glass."

He went into the main bar, and bought time and a triple Scotch.

This was no coincidence.

This was no question.

The bugger knew.

The issue was—surely?—was this nosy old Guy, or had he clicked into spook mode and was investigating Troy as surely as Troy had investigated Voytek? Was he here for Voytek, or possibly, just possibly Pym? But . . . how could he know about Pym? The man had been dead less than twenty-four hours. But queer had its own grapevine—the "Homintern," as some wag had put it. Was this a spook thing or a queer thing? Was he asking stupid questions because he felt like asking stupid questions or because whoever ran him, paid him—whatever—had told him to? Was he arseing about or checking him out?

"Striking young woman. Shame about the white hair. Old before her time would be the phrase."

"She's under thirty, Guy. Auschwitz can do that to you."

"Then it is the same woman?"

"Of course it is. You knew that before you sat down. I'd go a little further than striking, wouldn't you? Unforgettable would be the word."

"Quite. But if she's on the run, she surely wants to be forgotten?"

"I did suggest hair dye."

"So she is on the run?"

"I don't know. I've no idea where she is."

Burgess mused a moment over Troy's denial. Took a hefty swig at his triple Teacher's. If he downed it quickly enough, Troy would simply line up another. For once he wanted Burgess pissed.

Burgess tapped on the sketch on the front page of the *Express*.

"You took a risk, you know."

Troy said nothing.

"I mean. If I spotted it for you. Bloody hell! Who else did?"

Troy said nothing.

Burgess knocked back his Scotch in one searing gulp and cheekily held out his glass for a refill, as though he'd heard Troy's thoughts.

"Tell you what, Guy. I think I've a bottle of Cragganmore under the sink. A rather nice Speyside, or so I'm told by them as likes it. Why don't we nip across the road to Goodwin's Court?"

"Lead me to it!"

Burgess leapt up so quickly his foot collided with his briefcase, knocking it to the middle of the room, spilling its contents out across the tiles.

Troy bent down and picked up a couple of documents, intending simply to help Burgess repack. Each one was stamped "Top Secret" in red ink. He handed them back without a word.

Burgess stuck them back in along with his copy of the *Daily Express*.

"What's to become of me, eh? Clumsy as a clown after just one drink."

§15

Burgess plonked his briefcase on the coffee table, sloughed off his coat and jacket, and began to prattle.

"Odd thing, bumping into you twice so soon. I don't seem to run into you in any of my clubs. Although I suppose you're not a clubbable sort of person. Of course your father was. And I'm pretty sure I first met him in one club or another. I forget which. The Reform, Brooks's, the Garrick? Come to think of it, it probably was the Garrick. He was a member, wasn't he? An awfully good choice now I come to think about it. After all, it's the actors' club. Unlikely to be full of fellow hacks. And I suppose what anyone wants from their club is a haven. Perhaps even an escape. Did he ever put you up for membership? But I suppose policemen aren't really clubbable, are they?"

Troy hit him in the sternum. More of a tap than a blow. Just enough to send Burgess backwards into the sofa.

"How quickly you catch on."

"Bloody hell," said Burgess. "I mean, bloody hell."

"Stop pretending, Guy."

"Stop pretending what?"

Troy picked up the briefcase. Yanked on one of the many pieces of string holding it together and scattered a dozen sheafs of paper across the table. White, buff, and red covers. Every one of them stamped "Secret" or "Top Secret."

"In case you've forgotten, Guy. A red cover means 'Do Not Remove From Office.' You didn't knock your briefcase over accidentally. I know you can be a clumsy fucker, but after one drink? Guy, whisky is to you as mother's milk is to a baby. It's the stuff of life. There's nothing you can do sober that you can't do pissed. You knocked it over just to be certain you had my attention. You were doing what you've done as long as I've known you. You were flirting with me. But for once the object of your interest is not my perfectly formed arse."

Burgess stared at the pile of secrets for a few moments. Made no effort to gather them up. The magician whose props have been exposed. The bottle, the glass, the rabbit, and the pigeon all tumbling from the top hat at once and all mystery dissolved.

Then, smiling faintly:

"Did you mention something about a bottle of Cragganmore?"

"Stay there. Do not move. If you run, I will only come after you."

Troy returned with a half-full bottle, two glasses, and the small jug of water. He'd no intention of joining Burgess in a drink, but as long as he poured for both of them Burgess was unlikely to notice if Troy left his untouched. Left long enough, he'd probably drink it himself.

They sat opposite one another in a temporary if spacious silence. Troy knew Burgess would probably say nothing until he'd necked his first drink, all the same the speed with which he downed it was startling. Troy topped him up at once.

"You didn't," he said, "just bump into me tonight. You sought me out. You'd probably called here first and tried the next logical place. You didn't just happen to have the *Daily Express* on you. You've been carrying it around for days."

Burgess said, "I do drink in the Salisbury every so often, you know."

"I'm sure you do. But not tonight. You were looking for me. Don't even bother to deny it. It doesn't matter. What matters is were you looking for me that night at the Club 11?"

Troy topped him up again.

"Guy?"

Troy didn't think he'd ever had occasion to describe Burgess as sheepish—until now. It was at least thirty seconds and a full glass of Scotch before Burgess would look him in the eye.

"No," he said softly. "I wasn't. It really was pure chance running into you there. I suppose I was slumming. Odd notion, really. You probably think my whole life is slumming. I just wanted to hear what this bebop thing was all about. Miss Voytek, or rather what Miss Voytek plays, is much more what I'm about than any kind of jazz. Of course I recognised her. I'd just no idea you knew her."

"But then you saw the *Express*?"

"Then I saw the *Express*. And I knew at once that you were the one who spirited her out of the country. And as the rest of the papers picked it up, suddenly the connections were clear . . . she was Viktor Rosen's protégé . . . Viktor Rosen was an old friend of your brother's . . ."

"That's not the way it was. Viktor was her mentor . . . Viktor was her lover . . . Viktor taught me piano . . . but I never met her until this year. Now, I'm sure you've a dozen questions. And I'm not going to answer any of them. We will both be happier if you just concentrate on answering mine. What's your interest in Méret Voytek?"

"Nosiness, plain old-fashioned nosiness. That and . . ."

"And what?"

"I'm not sure how much to tell you. I'm not sure how much you know."

"I know what you've told half London for the last fifteen years. Is it not your practice to get pissed and tell whoever you are with that you're a spy?"

"I wouldn't say it was. I may have let slip, once or twice, here and there . . ."

"For God's sake, Guy."

"I mean, did you know . . ."

"Well, if I didn't, you've gone out of your way to tell me tonight, haven't you? You threw down your calling card. I think you thought for one witless moment that we were two of a kind and I might do the same."

Burgess looked a little word-bludgeoned, but stuck to his guns.

"I mean, how long?"

"It was pointed out to me the first time we met."

"I see. Your brother was there that night, wasn't he?"

"Yes, he was. But like a lot of people he chalked it all up to the times we were living in. Not so much pro-Stalin, as decidedly anti-Hitler. The one thing we neither believed was you joining the Anglo-German Fellowship. You might as well have glued a red star to your forehead."

"And now?"

"You had your youthful indiscretion, your case of the Communist measles. The least offensive way of putting it is that he sees you as a buffoon promoted beyond your talents. Plus, your private life is hardly likely to gain approval from a man who's never looked at another woman since the day he met his wife, let alone at another man. And come to think of it, the problem with your private life is that it's rather public. He warns me about you from time to time. I just tell him to fuck off."

"He's always polite to me if we pass in the corridors at the Commons."

"Politeness in the hands of a man who exudes decency the way my brother does is a deadly weapon. But we stray from the point. You and Miss Voytek."

"Curiosity. Real curiosity. The only people I know in this . . . business . . . oh God, it's not a business is it? . . . and it's not a game either . . . are . . . people I don't or can't have much to do with, but are people I've known for almost twenty years . . . friends who are . . . strangers—and a few grim-faced Russian agents whom I meet in caffs in the East End. It's quicker and more mercenary than a paid blow job in the gents. Quicker still and utterly faceless are the dead letter boxes in Limehouse or on Hampstead Heath. It's all a bit isolated. Comrade really isn't the word, there's no bloody comradeship at all. I found the idea that she might be doing the same thing . . . the stupid possibility that you might be . . . hmm . . . reassuring. And I wished I'd met her sooner. I wish I'd known who or what she was when I met her."

Troy pondered this. It was close to pathetic and he'd never thought of Burgess as pathetic.

Burgess filled the silence.

"I get lonely."

Troy topped up his glass, pushed it across the table to him.

"You may well be the most gregarious man I know, Guy."

The Scotch necked in an instant, the glass held out for more.

"I say again. I get lonely."

"And I say again, what do you know?"

"About Miss Voytek? Only what I read in the papers."

"And you came here seeking more?"

"I don't know why I came here. I was sober at the time. That so rarely happens. I make all my best decisions pissed. Nobody sent me if that's what you're asking."

Troy leaned in a little closer, lowered his voice.

"Guy, we each have our secrets. A bucketful apiece. But whereas your bucket is small, enamelled, and cream with a yellow stripe, perfect for making sandcastles, mine is a five-gallon galvanised slop bucket into which you seem hell-bent on stepping. I can keep your secret—nobody seems willing to believe it anyway—but you must keep mine. You never met Méret Voytek, you never talked to me about her . . . she is never mentioned in any report you make to the Russians . . . and if you ever get to Moscow, you keep your mouth shut even when they get out the lead pipe and the rubber hoses."

Burgess seemed to perk up at the word Moscow, a glimmer of pointless self-respect surfacing in the pool of booze and self-pity.

"Moscow? Why in God's name would I ever go to Moscow? You forget. I've been there. Bloody awful place. I just couldn't do it. I could never live in Russia. My soul would wither on the vine."

"And as ever, Guy, you have the advantage of me. I've never been there."

"Don't . . . don't don't . . . I have seen the future and it's boring. Boring boring boring. Moscow . . . Moscow makes you want to wear red underpants and learn to tap dance. Moscow makes you want to teach the dog to Charleston . . . Moscow . . . is a Primitive Methodist Sunday school on a winter's afternoon in Yorkshire . . ."

"Poetic as that sounds, can you stick to the point? Méret Voytek."

"Who? . . . never heard of her."

"So glad we agree."

"We appear to be out of Scotch, Fred."

Burgess had downed about half a pint all on his own. No matter. The man's ability to function through the haze of booze was little short of legendary. Troy doubted he'd forget what he'd just said. And he doubted he'd ever renege on it. A curious thing to think of a spy and liar, but Burgess had always struck Troy as being a man of his word—but then there were so many words.

"I believe I have a drop of Bell's somewhere."

§16

It was past midnight when Burgess staggered to the door.

"What say we meet over Christmas?"

"'Fraid not, Guy. I'm leaving for Berlin as soon as I can get a flight. The air corridor is rather crowded at the moment as you may imagine."

"Berlin? What's in Berlin?"

Troy was never going to answer that.

Burgess stood in the doorway looking up at a clear, cold winter sky.

"No raid tonight. Makes a change."

"The war's been over three years, Guy."

He twitched. Shook his head as though trying to dislodge an insect from his hair.

"Eh? What? Bloody hell, so it has. Must be more pissed than I thought. Who'd ever have thought we'd end up missing the war? Hot war . . . cold war . . . that's a joke . . . this isn't a cold war . . . it's a luke-warm egg custard of a war."

Burgess trundled off down the yard towards St. Martin's Lane, to the corner where Ruby the Prostitute had stood until a matter of weeks ago—unsteady on his feet, happy as a newt.

If there really had been a raid on, Troy would have left him on the sofa under an eiderdown rather than booting him out on a cold December night. But there wasn't. There might never be again, and Troy saw no reason to take him in.

As Burgess turned the corner Troy wondered if, this time, he might actually have seen the last of him.

§ 17

Tuesday, July 18, 1950

Troy sat at his desk. The *Manchester Guardian* spread out in front of him.
From our Moscow Correspondent:

Méret Voytek, the Austrian cellist who vanished
from her London home nearly two years ago, was
seen in public yesterday for the first time
since her disappearance and her exposure in
this and other papers as an agent of the Soviet
government.

At a ceremony in the Kremlin, Miss Voytek was
awarded two medals by Deputy Prime Minister
Bulganin: Hero of the Soviet Union [Герой
Советского Союза] and People's Artist of the USSR
[Народный артист СССР].

The USSR has never admitted that Voytek was
an agent. And while the Artist's award might
be considered self-evident, the award of Hero
of the Soviet Union might also be considered
an admission that her services to the USSR went
somewhat beyond playing the cello.

Her Majesty's government had no one available
for comment.

Troy wondered how strong his pact with a drunken Burgess really
was. Of course, sooner or later she had been bound to surface, and
when she did she'd strain Burgess's sense of secrecy as his overwhelming
sense of curiosity took over. He had occasionally wondered if Burgess
had understood the pact. He had been loth to spell it out. He thought
it simple enough. If Moscow learnt that Troy, a Scotland Yard CID
inspector, had helped Voytek escape, then sooner or later they would

conclude that she had denounced herself—the balance of doubt would never be in her favour—and her life wouldn't be worth two kopecks.

Troy's deputy, Jack Wildeve, stuck his head around the door.

"Chap on the phone for you. Jack or Jim somebody. Northern accent. Didn't give a surname."

"Then why should I talk to him?"

"Well . . . he did give a surname, just not his own. Burgess."

Oh fuck. So soon?

"Put him through."

"Freddie . . . Jack Hewit here."

Burgess's live-in. Troy could not abide him. He'd always struck Troy as a cross between Uriah Heep and Count Dracula.

"Are you free on Friday evening? A bit of a do for Guy."

Another one? They came around as regularly as a 38 bus.

"A farewell do, as a matter of fact."

"Really?"

"Yes. Guy's been posted to Washington. Second Secretary at our embassy. He'll be off in a matter of days. Anyway. Seven thirty Friday. All the old crowd will be there and he'd love to see you."

Old crowd? Was he part of an old crowd? God forbid.

And what lunatic in the Foreign Office thought Washington was a fit posting for Burgess?

§18

Friday, July 21, 1950

Troy had no idea how to dress for an orgy, so he made no attempt. He wore his black suit, one of many, and went straight from Scotland Yard to Bond Street, leaving as late as he could in the hope of missing something.

A warm night, the windows open, and the sound of Burgess's farewell was audible almost as far as Piccadilly. Someone had brought Nat Gonella records. Trumpet raucous.

Two young men were leaning in the doorway, smoking, as Troy walked up Old Bond Street. Camp-looking, lean street-trades. Troy could swear they were wearing eye shadow, and perhaps mascara too.

"Who's a pretty boy?" In a Cockney accent.

He was used to that. A certain kind of man and the occasional woman, who talked to him as though teaching a parrot to speak.

"I am," he said, and pushed past them.

Burgess's bedroom was just by the front door. Troy added his raincoat to the pile on the bed and stepped into the sitting room, hoping against hope that Burgess had invited a few ordinary people too.

He had, and at first sight there was not a lot of difference between this party and those his father had thrown before the war.

The ever-present Baroness Budberg—getting stout now and looking more like a real babushka with every pound gained. Burgess's old boss at the Foreign Office—Hector McNeil MP. A bloke he knew by sight but didn't think he'd ever spoken to—Anthony Blunt, a cousin once removed (or possibly more, Troy never understood the term) of the Queen, and the appointed "surveyor of her pictures," whatever that was. Guy Liddell of MI5, with whom he'd had professional dealings and hoped to have no more. The writer James Pope-Hennessy—Troy had met him several times. He had shared a flat with Burgess just after the war. And . . . he was a man on a mission—the English country house, and as Troy owned one, Pope-Hennessy had invited himself to Mimram. They'd got on rather well, and having no real wish to talk to Liddell or Baroness Budberg, Troy helped himself to a drink and cut a path across the room to greet him.

"Fancy meeting you here."

"James, I think I might be in the minority in not being fancy."

Pope-Hennessy looked around.

"I wouldn't worry about that, Guy is catholic in his taste. Friends across the sexual spectrum, although I think one or two of them must be aghast at the rough trade Guy's roped in tonight. Personally . . . I rather fancy the sailors."

Troy followed his gaze to two uniformed naval subalterns deep in conversation with a handsome young man who looked much like the two Troy had encountered on the doorstep.

"Do you think he just invites them in off the street?"

"I know damn well he does."

"Risky?"

"You don't think of the risk. You think of the man, and inevitably you think of the pleasure. The sheer delight in a young body. Speaking of delight. I have one for you. An old body. Blunt wants to meet you. You'll like him. Smart as they come. There's nothing Anthony doesn't know. He could get culture a good name."

Pope-Hennessy was right. Troy took to Blunt. Blunt asked a dozen questions about things he'd no idea anyone outside his family knew— about the paintings and statues Alexei Troy had collected on his travels.

"Is it true he knew Gauguin?"

"Doubt it," Troy replied. "My father didn't leave Russia until a couple of years after Gauguin's death. His collecting begins with his exile."

"Picasso?"

"Doesn't everyone know Picasso?"

Blunt smiled at this.

"Yes. My father knew Picasso. About the African time . . . '08 . . . '09 . . . he told me once he'd called on him at his studio and the painting he described Picasso working on was *Les Demoiselles d'Avignon*."

"Or something very like."

"Well said. He couldn't swear to that, and indeed, he bought a 'something very like.'"

There seemed to Troy to be only one good-mannered satiation to Blunt's good-mannered curiosity. He threw out an invitation to visit Mimram and see for himself. He'd take it up or he wouldn't.

After Blunt, the wagging finger of Baroness Budberg beckoned. Troy prayed for an intervention, and after a couple of minutes it came in the shape of the elusive host.

"You've been neglecting your guests, Guy."

Burgess grinned wickedly.

"S'awright. They haven't been neglecting me."

And the grin broadened.

"So soon in the evening, Guy? The night is yet young."

"And the roughs are even younger. Take a look at the chap taking off his shirt right now. Pecs like scallop shells. A bum like a peach."

Troy turned. It was one of the two boys he'd encountered earlier, stripping off—much to the amusement of the two Royal Navy officers.

The shirt whirled around his head and flew across the room.

"Guy, you don't suppose—"

"Oh yes."

And in seconds the boy was naked, shoulders back, belly out like a dancer in a Moroccan club—but that which shook was not his belly.

The muttered "I say" and "Good Lord" drowned out by the whistles and cheers.

The first cock out had divided the room.

People would make their excuses and leave now or stay on to see what happened next. Troy was unsure which camp he was in.

As the young rough shimmied around the room, Burgess's old boss, Hector McNeil, Minister of State at the Foreign Office, came up to him, forcing a smile and bidding him goodnight.

"Guy. I have known you for years, and you are dear to me, and whether you like it or not I have shielded you from your enemies just as long. I feel I have earned the right to offer a word of warning."

"Fire away, old man."

"For God's sake, Guy, remember three things when you get out to the States. Don't be too aggressively left-wing. Don't get involved in race relations, and, above all, make sure that there aren't any homosexual incidents which might cause trouble."

For just long enough Burgess seemed to be giving it the consideration McNeil clearly thought it deserved. Then . . .

"I think I understand you, Hector. I'll be OK as long as I don't fuck Paul Robeson."

Anyone within earshot burst out laughing at this. It was Burgess at his worst and best. But worse was waiting.

"Hang on a mo' you bunch of cynics. It's not that funny. There is a serious point to be made here."

The look on Burgess's face told Troy the opposite was far more likely.

"I give you . . . before your very eyes . . . you lucky people . . . the words of the Vice-Marshal of our Diplomatic Corps . . ."

Cries of "what?" and "who?" went up across the room. "Diplomatic what?"

Burgess pulled a scrap of paper from his back pocket.

" . . . the one, the only Sir Magnus Lowther, author of Guidelines for the Diplomat Embarking on Overseas Service. HMSO. Revised edition, 1947. Section 3, paragraph 1 . . . 'When in Washington . . . But . . .'"

Burgess switched from his variety-theatre routine, his Tommy Trinder/Max Miller persona, to a parody of the accent of three-quarters of the men in the room. Posh enough to crack a wine glass.

"'But . . . if protocol should present few problems, there are more general standards of behaviour which Mr. and Mrs. John Bull will ignore at their peril.'"

A cry of "when was this written? 1850?"

Burgess had to pause a moment to be heard over the laughter he so relished.

"'To be shy is a defect.'"

The room exploded. For what seemed to Troy like several minutes, Burgess could not go on. This was better than any music-hall routine and all the funnier for being real.

"'To look bored is an error.'"

Now it was Burgess consumed in his own mirth, shouting above the hubbub.

"Bored. Bloody hell. Me? Bored? Do I ever look bored? . . . and I save the best for last . . . 'But to appear superior is the eighth deadly sin!'"

It might have been a Roman emperor cuing the next round of the gladiatorial circus, the next bout of coupling in the orgy. It was a world away from the man who'd owned up to feeling lonely. How lightly the star of the footlights rested upon the sad and lost individual to be found at the bottom of the Scotch bottle.

McNeil had had enough. He hadn't joined in the laughter. Rod had told Troy that McNeil had privately expressed relief when Burgess had transferred to the Far Eastern section of the FO. How relieved must he now be to have him out of the country altogether? Troy doubted McNeil would stay a moment longer, and resolved to leave when he did in the interests of discretion. His mind was made up. If this really did turn into an orgy he wanted no part of it.

A few minutes later he sought out Burgess and made his farewells.

"I was just thinking," he said. "We've been at peace with the USA since 1814 or thereabouts."

"You think I can fuck it up all on my own?"

"Surprise me, Guy."

Walking home, Troy found relief mixing with alarm. The Burgess cocktail—stirred not shaken, since Guy managed to stir up everything he touched. Relief, that he might be free of the social quagmire that Burgess pulled him into every so often, a world that was over-sexed, loud, careless rather than carefree, and constantly striving to outrage. Alarm that World War III might be just around the corner and that Burgess might be the blue touch paper.

He parted from McNeil at the next corner. They said goodnight, and Troy could not for the life of him recall that they had exchanged any more words all evening. They had both been out on a limb, and neither wanted to mention it. They had both put up with Burgess for years out of a mixture of affection and apprehension, and neither wanted to mention that either.

Troy wondered if this time he really had seen the last of Burgess.

§19

It was scarcely even dark. A month after the equinox, to the day. One of those seemingly endless summer evenings that made him want to be out at Mimram, on the verandah, looking westward, all the windows open, a bottle of Pouilly-Fumé, Tommy Beecham turned up loud . . . "Summer Night on the River" . . . "A Song of Summer" . . . not stuck in London.

He sat an hour watching the light vanish, undecided. It was Friday night. He could just drive out. Nothing to stop him. Or he could stay and get up at dawn. Drive north on empty roads. His car keys were not in the drawer of the hall stand. He picked up the Macintosh he'd worn in that day's brief morning shower, the one he'd just walked home in. The keys were in the left-hand pocket, but his black policeman's notebook wasn't.

He thought back to where the coat had been hung. On a peg in his office? If it had fallen out he'd surely have noticed. On the bed in Burgess's bedroom? Oh bugger. He could easily have missed it there. The last thing he wanted was his notebook falling into the hands of one of Burgess's disreputable friends.

He went in search of it. Across Soho, to Mayfair and Bond Street once more.

The party was winding down. Only stragglers left. Men like Burgess who only left when they were thrown out. Not that Burgess would ever throw anyone out. A dozen men, not a woman in sight, were hunched around the ashtrays, cavemen around a campfire, talking loudly, no one listening to anyone, flicking fag ash everywhere, spilling whisky, nodding off, throwing up.

Burgess was not among them.

"Where's Guy?" elicited no response.

Troy asked again.

"Fucked if I know. Bedroom mos' likely."

That was what Troy had feared.

He tapped lightly on Burgess's bedroom door. Then he tapped a little louder. Then he eased the door open.

A bedside reading lamp cast its arc halfway across the room. Burgess was stretched out on his back, snoring intermittently, stark naked, half-priapic, the cock just beginning to wilt.

On the floor was the discarded uniform of a Royal Navy commander. Three rings and a loop on the cuffs, a peaked cap with a dash of scrambled-egg braid. Burgess had got lucky, sex with a sailor. Troy's idea of lucky would be to find his notebook and get out without Burgess waking up.

It was on the floor, half-hidden by a chest of drawers. As he picked it up the pile of bedding next to Burgess moved. The sheets and blankets slipped to the floor in a cotton avalanche. A man he'd never seen before sat bolt upright, as naked as Burgess, and saluted Troy.

"Captain on the bridge!"

He stayed rigid, as though cast in plaster. It occurred to Troy that pissed as he was, naked as he was, the man was at attention, as erect as his cock, waiting for Troy to return his salute.

Troy saluted.

"At ease, commander."

"Aye, aye, sir."

And with that he fell back on the mattress, cock waving like a hoisted pennant.

§20

Enough was enough. Troy went home, threw a bag in the back of his tatty old Bullnose Morris and drove out to Mimram. Now, he was fairly confident that Burgess was the bad penny in his life. He'd never "see the last of him," the man would always turn up somewhere—and by and large Troy would not mind, but right now he'd rather have a Beecham than a Burgess.

He wound down the window, blew Old Bond Street, queer London, and Burgess out into the summer night.

§21

London: May 25, 1951

Ted Wilmott was an old-school copper. Or perhaps he was just old. He had been pushing forty when Troy had joined J Division at the Leman Street nick that served Whitechapel and Stepney. He was well-liked, and as he lived in the community handled the occasional—perhaps frequent—arrest of people he knew with aplomb. Aplomb is not the same as discretion and was frequently accompanied with what Ted called "a punch up the bracket." He was not Troy's mentor, that had been George Bonham, a gentle giant of a man, lacking Ted's rumbustious sense of humour, never known to sing on duty, and a man who handled street fights by lifting a combatant in each arm and banging them together like conkers. Troy had not seen Ted—or heard Ted, as he unfailingly *did* sing on duty, especially "Men of Harlech" and "A Bicycle Made for Two"—for several years.

On May 24, 1951, just after noon, Ted was on point duty at the junction of Sidney Street and the Mile End Road, opposite the Blind Beggar, when a Bedford truck loaded with first early potatoes from Jersey ran over him. By one thirty he was on a slab in the morgue of the London Hospital, two hundred yards down the road.

Bonham had called Troy.

"Run over by a lorryload o' spuds. Would you believe it? A bloke as larger than life as Ted."

Troy could not help but wonder if Ted had been singing at the time, and what he might have been singing.

"Perhaps it was the way he might have chosen to go."

"Eh?"

"Well, he was awfully fond of a bag of chips."

"Y'know, young Fred, the longer you spend at the Yard, the less I understand you. Talk about iron in the wossermacallit. Funeral looks to be next Tuesday. Gladys Wilmott'll have her hanky out and be in tears till the first bottle of stout gets popped. Try and find something pleasant to say to her. Oh, and dust off your uniform."

"Eh?"

"We don't bury coppers in our civvies. At least not in Stepney we don't."

This presented a dilemma. The obligation to attend was inescapable. But Troy could not remember when he had last worn uniform.

At home, in Goodwin's Court, he found it, at the back of the wardrobe in the spare bedroom. Surprisingly, it fit. But the moths had been at it, and it still bore sergeant's stripes on the sleeves. He was short an inspector's pip or two or three on the shoulder.

Bugger.

He'd have to get it fixed.

He needed a tailor rather urgently.

In particular, he needed Gieves and Co. of Bond Street, who'd tailored his cadet's uniform all those years ago, and who had made this one bespoke for him just before the outbreak of war.

The next day, the twenty-fifth, he left Scotland Yard around half past two and headed for Bond Street.

§22

Mr. Tom and Mr. Albert had long since retired. Mr. Harold served Troy. He too looked to be about seventy-five, as though the firm had an unlimited supply of men of just the right age.

"You don't think, Inspector Troy, that perhaps a new uniform might be in order. The moth damage is considerable and when we remove your sergeant's stripes, there will more than likely be a visible scar."

"You may well be right. However, I need the uniform by Tuesday morning. A funeral, you see."

Troy hated the thought of spending money on a uniform he might never wear again. Troy hated the thought of wearing a uniform ever again.

"One moment, Inspector. I'll have a word in the workroom and see if we can expedite."

Troy drifted round to the other side of the large glass display case that divided the counter. A stoutish bloke was trying to open the locks on a second-hand suitcase, a case bedecked with exotic labels that might make its owner the envy of all who saw it—Cunard, P&O . . . Cairo, Jerusalem, Damascus, Istanbul, Trieste, Venice, Belgrade, Cracow, Moscow—an account of a pre-war, probably pre–Great War grand tour in stick-on labels, the paper triangles and circles of record.

Two loud clicks as the locks and the lid flew open.

The man turned to see who was standing next to him.

Burgess.

"Guy?"

"Troy!"

"Back so soon? Washington didn't work out?"

Burgess looked sad for a moment and shook it off with a flick of his often errant forelock.

"No. Did not work out in spades, as a matter of fact. My fault, in all probability. What on earth made me think I could live in a nation of prudes? I mean they can't even bring themselves to say arse . . . they call your backside an 'ass.'"

"You didn't . . ."

"Of course I did, but not in public. Not in the street. Didn't want to frighten the Cadillacs. No, I got done for speeding, the epitome of innocence, but enough for the zipped-up buggers at our embassy to send me packing. Can't say I mind all that much. Got back a couple of weeks ago. Bit of a break. Look for a new job. Overseas back pay. Not exactly broke. *Daily Telegraph* interested in taking me on. The world might just be my oyster, after all."

This sounded false. Every word of it.

Gieves's man approached with a white Macintosh. Held it open while Burgess slipped his arms into the sleeves.

"Whaddya say, Fred?"

"White doesn't suit you."

"Except when used in the same sentence as sepulchre."

"Oh no. I'd never accuse you of that."

"You're too kind, sir, too kind."

"And now you sound like Sydney Greenstreet."

"Do I? . . . oh bugger. It would be so good, so rare to sound like me."

This Troy understood. The false self was a concept he grasped and was quite certain Burgess did too. Oh, the relief in being who you are.

Gieves's man reappeared.

"Will sir be purchasing the suitcase?"

"Yes, yes, and I think I'll take the mac too."

He sloughed it off. Gieves's man took it away to be wrapped.

"Planning a trip, Guy?"

"Yeeees. S'matter of fact. Chap I met on the *Queen Mary* coming over. An American. I thought I might show him a few bits of Blighty. Y'know, the North . . . Scotland . . . all those bits one never thinks about if at all possible."

"Do you know Scotland?"

"No. I was thinking of Glen This, Strath That. You know, Scotland . . . as in . . . Scotland . . . as in whisky."

"So you're clueless?"

"Pretty much."

"And you're not really going to Scotland at all, are you?"

"Nope. But try not to think any the less of me. It would help enormously to know that someone believed in me."

"If that really bothered you, you could just tell me now. Whatever it is."

"No, I couldn't. And if I did, I'd be doing you no favours."

He reached into the open suitcase, just before the neatly wrapped macintosh was dropped into it.

"Hullo, what's this? Can't read a word of it."

He handed a large, time-faded sheet of paper to Troy.

Отель Метрополь
Театральный проездъ
Москва

12. августа 1908 г.

за внимание

Господина Родерика Спода

₽295

При первой возможности

Съ сердечным уважением Менеджера
ПРОСРОЧЕНО

"It's a bill from the Hotel Metropol in Moscow. An unpaid one. See . . . that large red stamp reads 'overdue.' Overdue since August 1908."

"You owe them two hundred ninety-five rubles. The manager sends his compliments, but he'd like you to settle the bill 'at your earliest convenience.' All rather understated and English, wouldn't you say?"

Burgess began to giggle. And the giggle ripped to laughter. For the best part of a minute his mirth seemed uncontrollable.

"Well, fuck me. Story of my life. A trail of unpaid bills and in debt to Moscow before I've set a foot outside of London. At my earliest bloody convenience? God, life piles on the little ironies, doesn't it?"

Out on the pavement, Burgess's mood seemed to change, the man to sag, as though drained by his own laughter. Troy was about to ask what he was thinking when Burgess said, "Do you ever get out to that Georgian pile your old man had in Hertfordshire? Or did you sell it when he died?"

"No, we never sold it, and probably never will. I get to Mimram most weekends. My mother still lives there. Hearty if not hale."

"Childhood. Childhood enshrined?"

"If you like."

"That book. Came out in the war. Can't remember the title. Something like *You Can't Go Home Again*?"

"I think it was called that. Never read it, I'm afraid."

"I remember a line from it . . . quite haunting . . . 'You can't go back home to your family, back home to your childhood, back home to romantic love, back home to a young man's dreams of . . . something something . . . back home to exile.'"

Troy said, "I don't think I understand that. Home, yes. Exile, yes. But back home to exile?"

"Me neither. Till yesterday. I went back to Ascot, to the house my people had until about ten years ago. Never been back before, never much wanted to. But I did. God knows why. Nothing had changed. I think it might have been better if things had. Changes that would rightly rob me of nostalgia and void the maudlin mood in which you find me. But nothing had changed, except my mother doesn't own it anymore—and so it was home and so it was exile."

"I still don't get it," Troy said.

"Oh, I'll send you a postcard," Burgess replied, a faint smile returning to his face.

They parted on the pavement, quite close to Burgess's flat. Burgess, ever the one to be "going on somewhere," did not ask him in, did not suggest a local pub. That in itself struck Troy as odd. But everything about Guy was odd—his abiding characteristic was to be odd. The cryptic hints, or the lack of hints, about where he might be going and with whom weren't worth a moment's thought. There was almost always a lover involved and Troy had long ago learnt that some were secret and some were not. And try as he might he could make nothing of "try not to think any the less of me" and "back home to exile." So he didn't.

II

Burgess & Maclean

Burgess and Maclean must have felt, as they worked out their long stint of treason, that they were proving themselves much better adapted to their time than any saint or hero could have been.

—Rebecca West, *The New Meaning of Treason*, 1965

§23

London: Twenty Minutes Later

Burgess dumped the suitcase in his flat and walked over to the Courtauld Institute in Portman Square on the far side of Oxford Street. Blunt was in his office, facing south-west, summer sun streaming in. He was viewing slides—just holding them up to the beam of light between thumb and forefinger, the image screened across his face in vivid blues and reds.

"Titian," he said simply as Burgess entered.

"Well, we all like a bit of Titian now and again," said Burgess, hardening the second T.

Blunt looked grumpy and set the slide back in its tray.

"I do hope you haven't come with a problem, Guy? You did buy the tickets, didn't you?"

"Of course I bloody did. I did everything you told me. Rented the sodding car. Even bought a suitcase. Just came over to . . . to say . . . goodbye."

"Goodbye?"

"Can't a chap say goodbye to his oldest friend?"

"You're only going away for the weekend."

Blunt paused, pushed the box of slides away, and stood up, head and shoulders taller than Burgess, in faux headmaster mode—an attitude he could switch on faster than Burgess could crack a joke.

"Or are you? Guy, listen to me."

Burgess felt like the reprobate of the Lower Fifth . . . the "Fat Owl of the Remove."

"Do not even think of going the whole way with Maclean. Whatever state he's in—and believe me I know him a damn sight better than you do. When you get to Saint-Malo put him on the train to Paris, finish the cruise, and come back. No one will be suspicious. It's a floating knocking shop. Permanent Secretaries and their mistresses . . . junior ministers and their shorthand typists. Anyone who sees you will assume you had an assignation—of some sort."

"Really? I shall look forward to sniffing out the whiff of illicit sex."

"Guy, do take this seriously."

"I am, honestly. And you're right, I don't really know him. Truth to tell I've seen bugger all of him since Cambridge. He came to the occasional party at my last flat, but he never really fitted in and . . ."

Blunt put a hand on each of Burgess's shoulders.

"Guy! Put him on the train and then come home."

Burgess almost winced at the word home, but forced a smile and said, "Yes. Of course."

Blunt removed his hands.

Then Burgess held out his hand.

"Goodbye, Anthony."

Blunt shook it, lightly, cold-fingered, like a leaf that had floated down from an autumn canopy.

"I think you mean au revoir."

§24

The RAC Club: An Hour Later

Ever since he'd thought up the scheme, Blunt had told him not to blab about it. In fact, he'd said, "Put them off the scent, Guy. I don't think they're watching you, but they're most certainly watching Maclean. Leave a false trail."

This would be the fun part. Rather like a party game for the under-twelves.

Burgess hailed a cab in Oxford Street and was dropped off at his club—one of his clubs—the Royal Automobile Club in Pall Mall. It was coming up to five o'clock—five o'clock on a summer Friday . . . half the skivers in half the ministries in Whitehall would be knocking off early and slipping into the club for a snifter or two before the homeward commute back to the rolling pin. He'd have plenty of witnesses.

He tackled Willie, surname unknown, who'd served him drinks, steered him into cabs when pissed, and on occasion reminded him to button up his flies, since before the war.

"Maps, Willie."

"Maps, sir?"

"Yes. North of England . . . Scotland . . . or are they the same thing?"

"As a native Dundonian, sir, I can assure you they are quite different places."

"But roughly in the same direction?"

"Quite, sir. Scotland is second star to the right and straight on 'til morning."

"Can't miss it, eh?"

"Yes, sir. Hasn't moved in years."

Willie took maps from a rack by the main desk, and gently spread them out in front of Burgess.

"Bartholomew's, Ordnance Survey, MacTavish's Highlands and Islands, and of course our own RAC edition."

"Jolly good. I'll be in the Long Bar. Large Scotch and soda when you've a mo', Willie."

None of the small tables were large enough, so he laid his first map on the floor and knelt down, unfolded it to the size of a tablecloth, stiff and starched. He thought of watching his mother's cook cut out a dress pattern on her day off—shears pinking, fat arse in the air. He must look much the same. He glanced up. Sure enough, eyes were staring and eyebrows rising over the tops of glasses.

He knew sod all about Britain north of Cambridge. Willie appeared with his Scotch and politely pointed out that he had the Highlands map upside down.

"A motoring holiday, sir?"

"Oh yes. Been meaning to take one for ages. Then I met this nice young American on the *Queen Mary*, coming over, and we hit upon the same idea—Scotland and points north. He seemed very keen on seeing a place called Inversomething. Do you know it?"

"Possibly. But going to Scotland in search of Inversomething is rather like going to Wales and asking for Abersomething. It's close to ubiquitous."

"Really? Where would you recommend?"

"Skye, sir. Quite beautiful in May. The wild thyme is about to flower. Stay till June and the island will be an eiderdown of mauve."

"How do I get there?"

"Motor to Mallaig and take the ferry."

"Mallaig?"

Willie put his finger on Mallaig.

"Ah, I get it. The Skye boat. Speed bonny boat like a . . . something something."

"Bird on the wing, sir."

§25

Burgess packed for the weekend. A cruise on the *Falaise*. Overnight from Southampton, a couple of stopovers at French resorts, and back on Monday morning. Dinner jacket. Tweed suit, three hundred quid in white fivers—far more than was necessary, but he'd have to change some of that into francs—new razor, old badger-hair brush . . . and his *Complete Jane Austen*. Two things an Englishman should never go abroad without—Jane Austen and a badger-hair shaving brush. Even so, there was still spare room in the suitcase. Perhaps a bit of George Eliot, but *Middlemarch* weighed as much as two bricks, and pocket-sized and light as it was, *Silas Marner* had never been his favourite. He picked up the bill Troy had read out to him. It was certainly from a hotel—even he could make out that word—but he wouldn't put it past Troy to have made up the rest as a leg-pull. He stuffed it in his jacket pocket.

§26

Tatsfield, Surrey: Later the Same Evening

In his time, Burgess had driven a Rolls-Royce—lurid in gold—and a Lincoln—ludicrous in the way all American cars were ludicrous, too much of this, too much of that. Both of which made getting into an Austin A40 feel like trying to shove a pork sausage into a matchbox. But it was what the doctor—in this case, the professor—had ordered . . . nondescript. So many of them on the English roads as to be utterly unremarkable.

Burgess could imagine why Maclean wished to live in the "mundanes," not suburb, not country, and above all not city. Once he'd established to his own lack of satisfaction that he wasn't queer, quim was bound to get him. Marriage to Melinda. Two kids. A large, ugly house in Tatsfield, Surrey. It all went with the ostensible Foreign Office job in Whitehall and a daily commute into Charing Cross.

Maclean was certain beyond any doubt that a couple of plods from Special Branch followed him all around London, but equally certain that they stopped following once he'd boarded his train each evening, whether from caution or sheer laziness neither he nor Burgess knew.

"I'll pick you up. Before eight," Burgess had said.

"Needs must I suppose, but could we make it around nine?"

"OK, but that's cutting it rather fine."

"There is a complication. It's my birthday. Melinda will have cooked something special."

"Can't be helped. Dinner in Surrey? Breakfast in Wormwood Scrubs?"

"I know. I don't need to be persuaded, but Melinda will have something to say."

What she said, between clenched teeth, was, "I blame you, you bastard." As soon as he was across the threshold.

"Roger Styles," Burgess replied heartily. "Old pal of Donald's from way back when."

He leaned in. Whispered.

"Play the game. The house is probably bugged. Pretend we've never met. Do not use my name."

Melinda scowled. But her words smiled.

"Oh, yes, Roger. Donald often talks about you. Let me give him a shout. He's just upstairs, saying goodnight to the children."

"Couldn't miss his birthday, could I? We'll just nip out to the local for a pint or two."

Her eyes burned him alive.

"He'd love that. But, Roger, don't make it too late."

§27

Maclean slung a small bag onto the back seat. No more than you'd take to the tennis club of an afternoon.

"Is that all?" Burgess said. "I've got a whole suitcase."

Maclean ignored this, gave him one of his cold-fish looks, the pouty bottom lip poutier than ever.

"What's all this Roger Styles nonsense?"

"Oh. Just thinking on my toes. After all, it's going to be a mysterious affair, isn't it?"

"If we miss this boat it's going to be a deadly affair."

§28

Burgess awoke to the boat gently rocking. They were in harbour. Saint-Malo, on the coast of Brittany.

From the top bunk a strangled voice, shot through with self-pity, moaned, "I feel sick."

"Donald, we've docked. The boat isn't even moving. And it's past nine . . . if we don't shake a leg we'll miss the boat train."

"I have to eat something. I have to—or my gut will just churn on empty."

"Alright. We'll grab breakfast and I do mean grab."

But Maclean dawdled over bacon, eggs, and fried bread, asking for more bread and a second pot of tea.

Burgess gazed around. Few had disembarked. The mess—or whatever they called it—was still pretty full. He looked at older men, beaming with the lineaments of gratified desire at women half their age, and concluded Blunt had been right—a floating knocking shop in which two single men might as well be invisible and everyone else blind.

Burgess hoped they were deaf as well.

"Y'know," Maclean was saying, "I can't tell you the strain of the last few weeks. I'm so glad we're out of England. If Five had nabbed me I wouldn't have held out for five minutes, I'd have blabbed the lot. Really, I would."

"Do shut up."

They stepped ashore into a fine drizzle. Maclean's only foresight was that he'd brought a hat, and Burgess hadn't.

"Fuck. We've missed it. The bloody train's gone."

"It crawls," Maclean said. "From here to Rennes. Only picks up speed between Le Mans and Chartres. If we can find a cab in the square there's a good chance we can get to Rennes before the train does."

They did, and in the back of the cab Maclean, looking over his shoulder, said, "This might even be better. Nobody's seen us board a train, we just walked off into town like a couple of tourists."

"Aren't you being just a little paranoid?"

"Guy, you haven't a clue what it's been like. It wasn't you the buggers were following around London. They were so close last week that when the cab I was in braked a bit sharpish the idiots ran into the back of us."

"Is there a car behind us?"

"No, the road's empty."

"Then relax."

But once he'd said it, Burgess knew he was no more relaxed himself. He'd left his suitcase on the *Falaise*. He could do without the tweed suit. It was just part of the Scottish illusion he'd fostered to the old duffers at the RAC. He'd packed it unconsciously, deceiving himself as well. What practical purpose could a tweed suit possibly have in France when it was nearly June? Pointless. And the three hundred nicker? Stuffed into a bulging wallet. He wasn't leaving readies for some light-fingered steward to find. But—but his *Complete Jane Austen* was in the case too. If he got shut of Maclean at Rennes, he'd have nothing to read on the way back.

Rennes? Maclean? He should never have got into the damn cab. Once they got to Rennes, the man was whining.

"I can't do this alone."

Torn between "You'll have to" and the fresh memory of "I'd have blabbed the lot," Burgess bought two tickets to Paris and told himself that he'd get home via the Gare du Nord and Calais and think of something, some excuse, for the cruise proprietors, retrieve his case—tweed or no tweed—get back to Bond Street, and . . . and what? Resign before the FO fired him? Look for a job? Deny all knowledge of Maclean? It was not as if their names were linked like Naunton Wayne and Basil Radford. Cambridge was more than fifteen years ago. Yes. Deny, deny, deny. Perhaps a job on a newspaper? Reviewing this and that for the *Telegraph*. Of course he'd be no more use to the Russians. The Russians? The Russians? And then a gentle tide of relief began to wash over him, as though instead of leaning back into the hard cushions of a second class SNCF compartment, he had slipped into a warm bath. No use to anyone at all—bliss.

§29

It was less than three miles from the Gare Montparnasse to the Gare d'Austerlitz. Ten minutes in a taxi, but Maclean was hungry again.

"I must have lunch. Perhaps I have an ulcer? Why shouldn't I have a fucking ulcer? Don't I deserve an ulcer? I think I've earned an ulcer."

Burgess really didn't mind. Montparnasse was littered with good restaurants, and if his memory of Moscow served him well, he would not be the one to deny Maclean his last decent meal. He even encouraged him to ask for a pudding and coffee.

"You've never been to Russia before, have you?"

"Of course I bloody haven't."

"Then have two of everything, and read the menu as though it were a novel. Think of each dish as a character. An unforgettable character, like Natasha in *War and Peace*. Or Becky Sharp. Or, better still, Julien Sorel. A model for us all. You'll need a storehouse of menu memories to get by in Moscow. Lay in some mental foie gras, a whopping great dish of beef bourguignon, a couple of soufflés, lay down a few cases of decent claret . . . a bottle or two of Armagnac . . . all in some dusty corner of the mind."

Maclean tucked into soupe à l'oignon, jarret de porc, and tarte au chocolat avec crème anglaise . . . with a bottle of Burgundy . . . and three cups of coffee. Burgess ordered just the soup, pushed it away half-finished, and smoked half a dozen cigarettes with no hint of impatience. As far as he was concerned, they could sit there forever. Lunch in Paris. There was nowhere he wanted to be. Who knew . . . sit there long enough and his appetite might return? And if the sun broke through they might hop from one pavement café to another—the moveable feast.

$30

While Maclean bought his ticket for Berne, Burgess sat on a bench. Rain pelted down on the glass roof, trains roared and belched, whistles blew—and in between it all he could hear silence, like punctuation . . . the commas and colons of minute nothingness.

He stared up at the roof.

He wondered if he should ever have told Troy about his visit to Ascot. Stupid, really. He didn't know why he'd gone there. Still less why he'd told Troy. What might Troy with his Freudian tendencies read into it? And then he thought of his last meeting with Blunt. He should have told him about the guitar case full of love letters—love

letters like sticks of dynamite, enough to blow London society apart.
And then he wondered why he was wondering. And suddenly he knew.
Part of him wanted to go with Maclean. A small, hidden part of him,
another dusty corner of the mind, one he didn't understand. That
which killed the kitten.

He lowered his eyes. A small, good-looking woman had seated herself next to him. Beautiful conker-coloured eyes and tits Jane Russell
might envy.

She handed him a railway ticket.

"He won't make it alone," she said simply.

He looked at it.

Berne, 2ème classe

Typical Russian stinginess.

"And you are?"

"Let's just say 'Peter' sent me."

"Peter," the code name of his KGB control in London, Yuri Modin.

Burgess took the ticket in both hands and slowly began to tear it
down the middle. When he'd put a surprisingly noisy one-inch tear in
the ticket he looked her in the eye.

"OK. OK. Stop! I'm Larissa Fyodorovna Toskevich. I'm a KGB
major . . . and they call me . . . Tosca."

It required a lot of thought. He gave it none—so many emotions in
play.

"Berne," Burgess said. "Berne and not an inch farther."

"Deal," she said.

Maclean was approaching. The look of a drowned dog. A streak of
crapulous misery in wet gaberdine. They stood up. Burgess slipped the
ticket in his pocket.

"If I'd known how far I was going I'd have had a proper lunch," he
said.

She smiled and walked away without so much as a glance at Maclean.

Burgess wondered how long the journey was to Berne—eight hours?
Ten? Twelve? Twelve hours alone with a man about as much fun as a
dead codfish. Stuck on trains as a boy, he and his brother would play
"I Spy," but it hardly seemed less than ironic now—and they'd be fed
up with it before they reached the Paris suburbs.

"How long have we got?"

Maclean shot back his cuff and looked at his wristwatch, still on English time.

"About fifteen minutes."

"Good. I'm just nipping off to see if I can buy a toothbrush."

§31

Maclean seemed about to deliquesce—twitching rather than trembling, and ghostly pale. It was like having a little brother in tow, a Burgess minor, only allowed out if he wore a scarf and kept his chest warm, a child who couldn't quite play the game . . . couldn't catch the ball or kick it. He let Burgess do everything from buying snacks on the train to flagging the taxi in Berne, to talking to the Russian officials at the Soviet Embassy.

Burgess was startled. They were expected. He thought they'd improvised the route, yet here was a smiling Soviet attaché who knew who they were and asked them to kindly wait a few minutes. Then it dawned on him, the woman who'd turned up in Paris . . . Major Tosca or something like that . . . she'd given him the ticket. The Russians had known all along they were heading for Berne.

Maclean sat nursing his solipsism. Burgess stood and smoked. Ten minutes later the attaché returned and handed him two British passports.

"Two?" Burgess said. "I'm not going on to Moscow. Look at him. One long streak of jaundice. He's all yours."

The man said nothing, just pointed to the two heavies by the door— two six-foot slabs of Slavic muscle and brutality who looked as though smiling hadn't been invented east of Berlin, and who hadn't been there five minutes ago.

Burgess opened the passport.

Mr. D. W. Craig—an old photograph of Maclean, occupation: "teacher," next of kin: Mary, wife, in Edinburgh.

Mr. T. P. Dalton—himself, a slightly more recent photograph, occupation: "journalist," next of kin: Gladys, mother, in Harpenden.

Maclean appeared at his shoulder. He snapped the passport shut and handed it to him.

"Be grateful for small mercies, Donald. At least they made you Scottish."

He turned to the attaché, still smiling as though welcoming them to a five-star hotel not a one-star state.

"And how far will these fakes get us?"

"All the way, Mr. Dalton. They're fakes, but they are good fakes. You will take the train on to Zurich. At Zurich, you will catch a plane to Stockholm. Here are your tickets. The plane makes one stop before Sweden—Prague. Get off at Prague. You will be met."

"And that's . . . it?"

Maclean snatched the tickets away.

"And the rest is history. For Christ's sake, stop arguing, Guy. I am exhausted, one hundred per cent knackered. Let's go. Just go. Moscow or Mongolia. I don't fucking care."

On the train to Zurich, Maclean, head back, eyes closed, said, "It could be worse."

"Could it?" Burgess replied.

"It cuts both ways, y'know. I can think of people I'd far rather have eloped with than you."

"Thank you, Donald. I shall always remember you for the small kindnesses. The little things that mean so much."

§32

At Prague they walked unmolested from the international transit area to the domestic side. There stood a lone individual, clearly looking out for them. No heavies, no Slavic muscle, just one man in his late thirties in a well-cut single-breasted blue suit looking more like the Liberal candidate in a rural English bye-election than a KGB officer. All he lacked was a rosette.

"Mr. Dalton, Mr. Craig, I am Yevgeni Ivanovich Dragomirov." He held out a manicured right hand. "A pleasure to meet you both."

Maclean shook the hand, but said nothing.

Burgess shook and asked, "We weren't at school together by any chance? You look awfully like a fag I used to have at Eton."

Dragomirov laughed softly.

"No, Mr. Dalton. We have no fags in the Soviet Union."

Maclean said suddenly, as though waking from a trance, "We're not actually in the Soviet Union though, are we?"

Dragomirov seemed to read his mind.

"No. But you're safe now. Believe me, you are safe."

"And me?" Burgess said.

"You too are safe. Whether you go back or join us on the flight to Moscow."

"Do I have a choice?"

Dragomirov gestured with a sweep of his hand to the almost empty concourse.

"Of course. There are no hidden guards. I'm not even armed. You have done . . . as you might say . . . sterling work, Mr. Dalton, but it's over and we are grateful and if you wish to leave no one will stop you."

Maclean coughed once into his fist.

"I'm grateful too, Guy. I know I've been a bit of a wet blanket . . . but y'know . . . couldn't be helped."

Burgess looked from the one to the other. The dishevelled ragbag that was Maclean, the Burton's showroom dummy that was Dragomirov.

"I've come this far. I might as well see a bit of Russia. A couple of weeks away won't do any harm. All I have waiting for me in England is the sodding dole queue. It can just wait a bit longer. What's a fortnight in June . . . it's a holiday, isn't it?"

Looking back, years later, he was shocked at the ease with which he'd made the decision.

§33

Moscow: Later the Same Day

A hotel balcony somewhere near the Kremlin
A pleasing sunset

"Is this vodka any good? I've never really had much of a taste for the stuff."

"Seems OK, but there's vodka and vodka, isn't there? I mean . . . some chaps prefer a blended whisky and know not the joys of Laphroaig or Glenthingy."

"Morangie. It's Glenmorangie not Glenthingy."

"Scottish pedant."

"If you say so, you Sassenach prick."

(pause)

"Two weeks, you said?"

"Did I?"

"In Prague. You said two weeks. A bit of a break. A holiday."

"So I did. Might make it a month. June's the silly season. Everyone I know will either be at Broadstairs or Bognor."

"You know people who take holidays in Bognor?"

"Course I don't. It's a metawotsit, isn't it. I mean . . . you can never get hold of a chap in summer for one reason or another and if I'm to land a job when I get back . . . *Telegraph*, *Economist*, even *Punch* . . . I'll need to call in a few favours."

"People owe you favours?"

"Come to think of it. Probably not. I might have recourse to a bit of blackmail."

"Do you mean the queer thing?"

"I suppose I do. After all, I know half the arse bandits in London."

(pause)

"You'd do that? Blackmail some bloke you've done the nasty with?"

"Probably not."

"So it was just another metaphor?"

"I suppose it was. I've got to do something. More vodka?"

"Don't mind if I do."

(pause)

"And you?"

"What about me?"

"What will you do?"

"Oh, Russia will find me something, and whatever it is, I'm going to have to look very co-operative if I'm to get Melinda and the kids out of England."

"But you're safe now."

"Oh yes. Safe but suspect. The game is still afoot."

(pause)

"Speaking of which. Look down there."

"At what?"

"All those people. Milling around like ants. Right now that's MI5 and Special Branch, blindly milling around. Insects with no sense of direction. Looking for you everywhere. Dover, Calais . . ."

"Broadstairs."

"Bognor."

The mention of Bognor, even on his own lips, set Burgess giggling like a schoolboy. Infectious. Maclean caught it, grinned, sniggered and laughed out loud—spattering vodka out over the balcony. The two of them—laughing like idiots until some inner comedian cued them simultaneously and they yelled into the warm night air of Moscow, "Bugger Bognor!"

III

Voytek

§34

Moscow: 1952

The day they delivered a grand piano, she reluctantly realised that she was safe. Safe and unsuspected. It was the final, the telling gesture on behalf of people she would have to learn not to regard as her captors. It meant more than medals.

About eighteen months ago, Major Tosca had asked if there was anything she needed.

"Such as?"

"Anything. Anything in our power."

She had asked for a piano. With her own piano she could expand her repertoire. It had always been her second instrument, but apart from a battered Victorian upright in her London flat—more suitable for a pub than a concert hall—she'd never owned one. Owning one didn't matter. Having one in her own apartment did. She could rehearse in total privacy. She had hoped for a Blüthner or a Bösendorfer (both possible) or a Steinway (unlikely), but as they winched a Becker baby grand up the side of the building she felt no disappointment. A Russian piano in Russia. A pre-revolution instrument, hand-made in St. Petersburg, finished in a light, almost red chestnut, that had survived forty years of turmoil without a scratch. Once it was tuned, she'd christened it with a Rachmaninoff prelude, the short, lively C Major, dating from 1910—the same year as her piano.

It had not always been this way.

In 1948, there'd been questions. No more than half a dozen, but the same questions over and over. The same account of her leaving London for Paris, and then Austria, and her "defection" at the Soviet Embassy in Vienna. Then the questions.

They'd produced the front page of the *Daily Express*, the one with the police sketch artist's impression of the "Mystery Man" who was said to have accompanied her to the cross-channel ferry.

"Who is this man?" Colonel Ronin had asked.

It was Troy, but it looked nothing like Troy.

"Who is this man?"

"Nobody."

"*A* nobody? Or nobody you know?"

"Nobody at all. I made the journey to Dover alone. This is some fantasy of the English press."

"You don't know him?"

"He doesn't exist."

"He didn't help you to escape?"

"I didn't know I was escaping. I was on my way to concerts in Paris and Vienna. Only when I got to Vienna did I learn that I had been betrayed. I had a return ticket to England in my purse. Once I knew, I had little choice but to take refuge in the embassy."

Throughout the interrogation—and there had been no threats, verbal or physical—she wondered how much they really knew. That she had denounced herself? That Troy had put her on the ferry to Calais? That he'd mailed her letter of denunciation to the English press? That they'd timed it for her arrival in Vienna? That she'd dumped the gun with which Troy had killed four Czech agents into the English Channel?

Her lifeline had gone silent. Major Tosca, for so long her guardian angel, had been present at each interview, but had said nothing—left everything to Ronin.

At the end of the third day, Ronin had left and Tosca spoke.

"It's over."

"They believe me?"

"They were always going to believe you. The network in London was falling apart. Skolnik's murder, Rosen's suicide . . . if you hadn't left they'd probably have had to pull you out anyway. Besides . . . the information you got out of London was priceless. You're a hero. But I think you know that."

She said nothing. She'd been the conduit from Los Alamos, to Harwell, to London, to Moscow. She'd given Russia the bomb. A hero.

"What now?"

"Oh . . . the usual retirement package . . . a better than average apartment, a dacha, a pension, a couple of medals . . . if you're lucky Marshal Stalin will pin them on you in person."

She searched for any hint of irony or sarcasm in Tosca's voice. "Retirement?"

"You're blown. We can't use you. But I think you know that too. Go back to the cello. Moscow has more concert halls than it has urinals. Moscow will love you."

"I don't have a cello."

"So? I'll get you a cello. After all, I've done that before."

Indeed, she had. Somehow, shortly after the war ended, Tosca had found her Matteo Groffiller cello, the one she had been forced to abandon in Auschwitz, and had shipped it to her in Paris.

"But not my cello. That's in London."

She kicked herself at once. Three days of questions and precise, evasive answers . . . and now she had given a hostage to fortune. Why did she not say Vienna? If she was leaving to perform in concerts in Paris and Vienna, why had she not taken her cello with her?

"No," Tosca replied. "Not *your* cello. Just a cello."

Tosca knew. Voytek knew that she knew. Each could see it in the other's eyes.

"Trust me. I'll get you a cello."

And eighteen months later they delivered her piano too. Not *her* piano. Just a piano. Far better than her piano.

§35

Peredelkino: 1955 or Thereabouts

The years in Kuybyshev had felt like infinity. An infinity modelled on a drunken Saturday night in Glasgow circa 1880. It felt like punishment. Cultural deprivation. Hell among the proles. Kuybyshev was somewhere east of Moscow, about halfway to Chelyabinsk, his housekeeper had told him, but as he wasn't allowed to own an atlas and he'd never heard of Chelyabinsk, he settled for thinking of it as that point where Russia ceased to be Europe and became a bit Asian. The housekeeper also told him that Kuybyshev was its Soviet name, and that when she was a girl it had been called Samarra, a name he thought he knew from the tales in *The Arabian Nights*—and then he remembered, the Somerset Maugham story, "The Appointment in Samarra," a tale told by Death in which the moral appeared to be "you can't cheat death."

"Oh God," Burgess thought time and again, "let me not die in this shithole."

He knew that there were people back home who might very well think him pig enough to thrive in a shithole, but he didn't. Oddly, Maclean did. Unremarkable, blatant drunkenness in the street, the Russian modus vivendi, gave him an outlet for what Burgess had mistakenly perceived as melancholy and he now recognised as rage. They grew apart. Never close, they drifted. Drifted to the point where Burgess would have been glad of the company, on the principle of a malign presence being better than none at all, but Maclean didn't much want to know him. Tant pis. He wouldn't miss the violence, those bitter, booze-fuelled orgies of vandalism when not an ornament or a window was safe from him. The Russians found this funny. Burgess didn't. A happy drunk for much of his adult life, he could not understand miserable drunks. Being drunk and miserable was a waste of God's good alcohol.

After what felt like infinity—in reality, no more than a few years—they were allowed back to Moscow. Suspicion if not abandoned then at least suspended. Suspended along with the irregular but tiresome interrogations. Interrogations in which, "I believe I answered that question in 1952, 1953, and again in 1954" would have been unacceptable and possibly fatal.

His first interrogator had been the woman he'd met at the Gare d'Austerlitz. Major Tosca. Silent at her side, a Colonel Ronin, who spoke only to say hello and goodbye. Perhaps they had not been hard enough. After their fifth visit they were replaced by Blodnik and Bolokov, who played hard man and soft man like a couple of bumbling Scotland Yard flatfoots. Blodnik would ask the same old questions Tosca had asked, with none of her charm, as though biting them off a tree trunk with his jaws only to spit them out . . . Bolokov would whip out a packet of fags and slide one across the table. Disgusting as they were, camel-shit and sawdust, Burgess accepted. It wasn't torture. It was boredom. All it required was patience. Occasionally he had wondered how Maclean was coping with it all, but Maclean dismissed them as "Mutt and Jeff" and changed the subject.

Moscow . . . "aah, Moscow," as Olga, Masha, and Irina dreamed and sighed. A brand-new Moscow apartment . . . and his own dacha in Peredelkino. About forty miles south-west of the city, he could go there every evening if he chose, and often didn't, but weekends in summer . . . that was when the dacha came into its own. Once the private estate of the Dolgorukovs, who had married the Romanovs, run the court and whatever, and most of whom seemed to have perished in the revolution, it had, at Maxim Gorky's suggestion, sometime in the thirties, become a writers' and artists' colony. A wooden Toytown of talent. Initially he had wondered where he fitted in . . . Babel had lived there, Pasternak still did—he'd never read a word of either—slaving away at his translations of Shakespeare. But then the one word that mattered surfaced—privilege, privilege made manifest in walls and roofs and a small garden he conspicuously neglected. He was still watched, still listened in on, but his new housekeeper—name so unpronounceable he dubbed her Doris—assured him that not every room was bugged, just most of them.

"Well . . . which one isn't?"

"The bedroom."

Ah . . . he could let fly a morning fart in freedom and peace.

Peace was compromised. Maclean had a dacha not a hundred yards off. It was possible to avoid him, much as he was being avoided, but neither mode felt natural or comfortable. They were separate and inseparable. Still, the village had its own bar and social life was tolerable, except when Maclean gave in to the magmatic rage that seethed within him and trashed the bar. Best not go in for a day or two, lest he be held accountable as well.

This was one of those mornings after. Doris had told him. Maclean had broken chairs and picked fights with two blokes twice his size. Better to take a stroll in the opposite direction. Away from the bar, away from any chance encounter with a hungover Scotsman.

A dozen dachas on, a furniture van was unloading—an upright Bösendorfer piano, very much like the one Frederick Troy had had in his small house off St. Martin's Lane, was being manhandled up the path to the front door by four very grumpy *furnitchniks*.

Burgess had what he called "kitchen" Russian, the vocabulary of his London clubs rendered into rough Russian that Doris could understand . . . mostly nouns . . . words like gin and sausage and tea and mustard . . . but he knew enough to recognise the force of their complaining.

« Дерьмо, дерьмо, дерьмо! » Shit, shit, shit!

So . . . a musician moving in among the writers and the prominenti. Interesting.

He hung about for a few minutes as the men manoeuvered the piano inside, hoping that the pianist himself might appear, hoping for a bit of a chat. But he didn't.

Undeterred, Burgess walked back that way after lunch the following day.

To his delight, the new chap was at the piano practising. The sound of a Brahms intermezzo wafting through the open door into the summer lane.

Brahms was not exactly Burgess's favourite—a bit late in the century for him, but he was a musical beggar, not a chooser. He stood by the door, peering into the dim interior and seeing nothing. He waited until the pianist stopped and then rapped on the door with his knuckles.

"Please God, in whom I do not believe, let this bloke understand a bit of English."

Out of the gloom a young woman appeared. Thirtyish, thick black hair, pale skin, slender unto skinny, but quite beautiful in her ghostly way.

She shielded her eyes and Burgess concluded she could not make him out, such was the contrast between the interior and the bright sunshine behind him. He turned sideways, she stepped out, looked up at him and said, "I know you."

He didn't know which was the more shocking, the more pleasing. That she knew him or that she really had spoken in English—accented though it was.

"You do?"

"You're Guy Burgess."

"And you have the advantage of me."

"Club 11. Great Windmill Street. 1948."

"You mean in London?"

"Of course. Is there a Great Windmill Street in Moscow? You came and sat with us at our table."

"I did? I mean . . . 'us'?"

"Me . . . Me and Troy."

The penny dropped, clunked down in his befuddled memory.

Voytek. Méret Voytek, the atom spy who'd done a bunk a couple of years ahead of him. The woman Troy had told him to forget.

"Good Lord."

"Quite, as Troy always said. Now, Mr. Burgess . . . *aimez-vous Brahms*? I was just practising the E-flat Major Intermezzo. I shall finish soon. Come in and sit quietly until I do."

§36

Miss Voytek had mastered the samovar. Made a good cup of tea. He never had, and accepted Doris's disgusting brew with grim patience. Any East End caff would tip tea as stewed as Russians seemed to like it. Cuppas like creosote.

"We can talk now," she said.

With one hand he held the glass of delicately scented tea, the right amount of hot water, the *kipyatok*, added to the dark, overbrewed tea concentrate; with the other he pointed at the ceiling and described circles in the air.

"Oh," she said. "The house isn't bugged. They stopped bugging me in 1949. I'm a spent force. No use to them and so no threat."

"My dacha is bugged, so's my Moscow flat. They have a minimum level of decency—they don't put microphones in the bedroom."

"If you're still bugged, then you still matter to them. There's something they still want from you."

"They know everything. I was interrogated every few weeks until earlier this year. Two clowns called Blodnik and Bolokov. I couldn't have made up names like that if I tried."

"Ah . . . I got Tosca and Ronin. They weren't clowns."

She had her back to him momentarily, thumping a cushion into shape. Then she turned, sat, and gestured to him to sit on the other end of the sofa.

"Little woman? Eyes like conkers . . . rather well . . ."

He described the arc of Tosca's bosom with his right hand.

"Ah. You've met?" Voytek said.

"Oh yes."

"She was your London control?"

"Oh no. That was 'Peter.' I didn't meet Major Tosca until I was on the run. She was my first interrogator. Brighter than all the others put together. I rather liked her."

"I see."

"And you didn't like her?"

"I had . . . have . . . very mixed feelings. She rescued me from the Nazis. But then she made me a Soviet spy and put me into London. I have reasons to be grateful and reasons to resent her."

"I still see her from time to time. I often think she misses London as much as I do. We have a drink together and reminisce."

Voytek had paused. The needle pulled suddenly from the groove.

"I'm not sure I'd want to."

"I find I can talk to anyone with approximately the same memories I have. There are times I think I'd relish a chat with a chap from Nottingham or Derby and I've never been to either. Desperate, isn't it?"

"Of course . . . I'm not tied to this house or to Moscow or even to Russia. I can travel. All the Warsaw Pact countries, and the neutrals too . . . Sweden, Switzerland . . . Austria. I suppose I'm not desperate."

"I can't go anywhere. Would you believe I'm still a secret? The British may be ninety-nine per cent certain where I am, but Moscow won't tell them. It reinforces my isolation. I'd love to come clean, to be able to say 'Guy Burgess is alive and well and living in Moscow.'"

"And what would that gain you?"

Burgess could feel tears gathering.

"Letters," he said softly. "My mother would have an address for me. She'd write me letters."

He paused as one lonely tear ran down his cheek.

"And I would write back."

§37

Moscow: Район Хамовники
улица Большая Пироговская 53-55, квартира 68
1956

It pained him to heft his bitch tits—all the same, he did so two or three times a week. Usually in front of a full-length mirror. The true reflection of the most distorting aspect of his nature—vanity.

His London controller, "Peter," on one of his fleeting visits back to Moscow, had been the first to point out that he was putting on weight.

"Well, if the fucking diet here wasn't so fucking stodgy I fucking wouldn't be, would I?"

"Still dreaming of London's restaurants, Guy?"

"I close my eyes and I can still smell Wheeler's fish soup. I can taste the Arbroath smokies in Simpson's. I could reach out and touch the filet mignon at the Ritz."

And then his new suit had arrived from Savile Row, with a polite note from his tailor, "Sir, we note the change from 32 waist to 34. If you would be so good as to advise us of any further changes."

It was tempting to write back and say he now dressed to the left, but what was the point? They'd never get the joke. What, indeed, was the point of anything?

Burgess was not a happy man. Those fleeting moments when happiness seemed possible, tangible, only heightened his frustration. Such as the day his harmonium arrived from England.

Tom Driberg had shipped it for him. Along with most of his books. A sentimental, self-deceiving man—and Burgess was both—might be able to recreate the illusion of the flat in Bond Street. But every so often, or a hundred times a day, he'd find himself looking out of the window at the Novodevichy Cemetery, next to the Orthodox convent, and no illusion of home could sustain itself with such a view. Not that he disliked the cemetery. With hours to kill he often killed them there—he'd drift from Chekhov's tomb, to Gogol's, to Bulgakov's (not that he'd read a word of Bulgakov), to Nadezhda Stalin's, and on . . . and on . . . to Sergei Eisenstein's. He'd sat through *Oktober* and *Battleship Potemkin,* and quite enjoyed both. He'd tried sitting through *Ivan the Terrible* and failed utterly to enjoy it or stick with it to the end.

He'd have felt better if the harmonium had worked, but its lungs were shot, its leather bellows perished.

The arrival of his books, however, had revived his "frenetic bibliomania." He'd felt an acute sense of loss without them. He tried to feel lucky, feeling no more lucky than he felt happy; after all, he'd known people who really had lost their books during the Blitz—blown up and burnt up, nothing left but ash. His pal Duncan (or was it Denis? Couldn't have been much of a pal) sitting over breakfast in the Ritz one day in 1941, tearfully drawing up a list of lost books, then producing, wrapped in a damp, snotty hanky, the charred corner of a book.

"*Oxford English Dictionary,*" he said. "Volume 12: *Supplements.* Page 381. It's all that's left."

Trying for uplifting levity, Burgess had said, "Fond of 382, were you?"

And Duncan (or Denis) had wept buckets into his pre-porridge Scotch and soda.

There was his copy of Somerset Maugham's *Of Human Bondage,* a tale of pointless love for a worthless woman, which had fired and fuelled his adolescence. His copy of Walter Sickert's essays, edited by Osbert Sitwell—newish, only a few years old, but it had become one of his most treasured books.

But . . . but . . . but the one he really missed was: *Partridge's Dictionary of Slang and Unconventional English.*

He'd had the newest, updated edition, dating from 1949. It had a column and a half just on the word "Bum

"Bum-clink"

"Bum-perisher"

"Bum-feagle"

It had been a treasury of delight in the English language, a riot of filth and double entendre, and his favourite bedtime reading. Almost made insomnia worthwhile.

Even more on cock.

"Cock-maggot (in a sink hole)"

"Cock-quean"

"Cock-smitten"

And the classic, the timeless entry:

"Fucked, more times than I've had hot dinners, she's been."

The taxonomic pleasure of typing a line like that. He wondered how Partridge had ever been able to type such a line and keep a straight face.

The possibilities, the endless possibilities for insult. Oh, to have it back again. To be at large in a country where few, if any, spoke English, armed with the thinking, drinking man's bible of abuse. He'd give up his hand-annotated two volumes of the *Selected Marx and Engels* and throw in his copy of Murchison's *The Dawn of Motoring* too just to be able to refresh his reservoir of insults from Partridge. But—he'd left it in Washington. Not happy. Philby had promised to ship it. He never had. Not lucky.

But . . . but . . . but there were now regular letters from his mother.

§38

Moscow: ул. Петровка
Институт Паганини

It was the interval.

Miss Voytek had invited him to a recital at the Paganini Institute, a chamber venue that reminded him more than a bit of the Wigmore Hall—tasteless shades of brown more than compensated for by the acoustics.

He'd enjoyed the first half. Schubert's "Arpeggione" Sonata. Voytek on piano and some young Russian bloke . . . Rostripov? Rostropich? . . . on cello. He wasn't sure what an arpeggione was, but had vague memories of something that looked like a cross between a cello and a guitar. No matter, it had been a treat. The second half was new stuff. Prokofiev. He thought he might sit it out in the bar and then go through the motions of congratulation with Voytek and Rostripthing. All artists were readily flattered. As long as he smiled and enthused, he'd get away with it.

A big man, a fat man, fatter than he was getting, was looming up above.

"Mr. Burgess?"

Burgess just looked at him.

"Jack Dashoffy. US Embassy."

"Come to see if I have horns and a tail?"

"May I?"

Dashoffy gestured at the chair opposite.

"I'd say it's a free country, but you'd just laugh."

Dashoffy grinned, sat, held out a hand Burgess did not shake.

"I suppose you're a cultural attaché?"

"Correct. Culture, Information, and Arts."

Burgess began to crack up.

"Ah . . . I was with the Baked Beans and Chips for a while."

"That so? I did a spell in radio too."

"Cheese, Burgers, and Sausage?"

"Nah—No Bum Cheques. How long can we keep this up?"

"I think we just shot our bolt. Tell me, how are things in Culture, Information, and Arts?"

"Well, we're on the road to forgiveness."

"For whom? The British? For what? Suez?"

"No—I was thinking of you."

"I did nothing, you know. Nothing at all."

"Really? All those unpaid speeding fines from your time in Washington?"

Burgess giggled.

"Uncle Sam sent you here to collect on my speeding tickets?"

"Of course not. In fact, Uncle Sam didn't send me at all. This is just me. On my own."

"You're that curious?"

"I'd love to know."

"I'd love to tell. A weight off my mind. But I won't."

"Aw. C'mon. Spinach In Seattle would never know."

"I prefer to think of them as Shit In Sawdust."

"Just so long as we know who we're talking about."

"We do. But I've no reason to trust you."

"No. You haven't. But maybe we could horse trade."

"We could?"

"Depends entirely on what you want? I could get you things from England. Y'know, things you might be missing."

"I have all my books. I even have my harmonium. My account at my tailor is still active—I get a new suit every so often. New ties in Eton stripes when I can't scrape the congealed egg yolk off the old one any longer. And my mum writes twice a week. The only thing I really want I doubt you'd give me."

"And what would that be?"

Burgess lowered his voice to a stage whisper.

"To go home."

"Aw shit. Just when I thought we were getting somewhere."

"All the same, there are things I miss."

"OK. Such as?"

"I miss the little things. The trivia. The unimportant things. In England I missed the important things—ideas."

And as he said it, he realised he had said it before. Yesterday? Last week? Last month? And that he would be saying it the day he died.

"Ideas might be the other thing I cannot give you."

"No matter. I have an idea. The biggest idea there is."

"Which is?"

"Russia."

"Aw shit. I was afraid you'd say that."

"On the other hand . . ."

"I'm listening."

"A small tin . . . or perhaps two . . . of Patum Peperium . . ."

"What?"

"They call it the Gentleman's Relish. Although they let rogues like me eat it. Can't get it in Mother Russia for love or rubles."

"Let me write that down . . . Pat . . . Pat . . ."

"Patum Peperium. They make it from anchovies. You might try Fortnum's."

"Gotcha. Consider it done. I'll set my old pal Joe Wilderness on to it. He's a regular at Fortnum's. It'll be in the bag from London next week. Then maybe we could talk again."

"Of cabbages and kings?"

"Nah—let's stick to Shit In Sawdust."

§39

"Don't get your hopes up."

At Novodevichy, walking the long aisles between the dead. Three tins of Patum Peperium nestling in the pockets of Burgess's jacket.

"I thought you said you lot were in a mood to forgive?"

"We are. The problem isn't Washington. It's London."

"Bugger."

"Have you made any approaches to them?"

"No. It's only been a matter of weeks since the Russians agreed to let us, I mean me and Maclean, go public. Prior to that no one in London officially knew where I was. We held a farce of a press conference, you probably heard about."

"Of course. It's what enabled me to approach you without, how shall I put it? . . . incident."

"Any approach by me would have been impossible. I was the invisible man."

"Things may change. In time, things may change. Give it a while and ask. You get nothing if you don't ask. I can't ask on your behalf. That really would be an incident."

"Meanwhile, I could die waiting."

"We all might die waiting for something. However . . . I do have some good news. Your friend Tosca got out."

"Out? You mean defected?"

"I'm not sure I do mean that. She'd been in one of those KGB Little Lubyankas they have dotted all over town for weeks and the spook gossip is she escaped in transit to some other prison. Sometime in the last month."

"Escaped where?"

"I don't know. But the only way is west, isn't it?"

$40

Peredelkino: May 1956

Voytek did not know how to take the news. Regret was part of it, relief another part—and the sum a wish that she'd said goodbye.

"I gave her a note for Troy. Must have been a couple of years ago," Burgess was saying. "You know, just on the off chance."

"Off chance of what? Her getting out? Her reaching London? Her surviving?"

"No, the off chance of her bumping into Troy."

"Bump? I didn't even know they'd met."

"Oh yes. Didn't I tell you? She used to talk about him. She did a couple of years undercover in London during the war. Met him then. They were . . . well, you know . . ."

"I don't know anything. You're saying they were lovers? When?"

"In '44, I think. They met a few weeks before Moscow pulled her out."

"You knew her there too? I thought you met her here?"

"Good Lord, no. One Russian spy knowing another? Only if there was a purpose and in this case there was none. No, I met her here. I'm certain I told you—she managed some of my de-brief. I think our masters thought she had a handle on London . . . or something."

"Yes, you did tell me that. How could you not tell me about her and Troy?"

"Dunno. I suppose it's not the kind of relationship that's ever interested me. You know . . . men . . . women . . . women . . . men. Even the gossip's second rate."

"Suddenly I feel as though I'm part of a conspiracy."

"Well . . . we both are, aren't we? It's called Russia."

"I meant one I didn't know about. Not a Soviet conspiracy . . . they're ten a penny . . . a divine one. The gods playing games with us."

She fell silent. Burgess had a high tolerance of silence, but this one had gone on far too long.

"Tell me," he said

"I was musing. Pointlessly."

"On what?"

"Where is Troy? Where is Tosca? Will she ever find him?"

IV

Gus

§41

Vienna: May 1956

Gus Fforde was a rogue. A rogue, a wag, and an old friend. He and
Troy and Charlie Leigh-Hunt had been schoolboys together. Charlie
was the leader, Troy and Dickie Mullins very much the NCOs, and Gus
the inspired, reckless subaltern. It was Fforde who had taught Troy how
to disable a car by shoving a potato up the exhaust, how to blow out the
down-pipe on a lavatory cistern with guncotton so that the next poor sod
to flush the bog got a free shower, and how to catapult stink bombs in
chapel. Of these, Troy had only found the first to be of any lasting value.

Fforde was also First Secretary at Her Britannic Majesty's Embassy
in Vienna, capital of the newly reconstituted Austria. The Austrian
democratic government was only weeks old, the Russian and American troops that had been in the country since 1945 having departed a
matter of months ago.

Troy wondered, as he had so often, what outlet life as a British diplomat provided for the inherent anarchist in Gus. A world that revolved
around gin and tonic, fours at bridge, and constant glad-handing could
hardly satisfy the need to create chaos in a man happier knocking up
home-made bombs.

"A passport, you say?"

"Yes, Gus. For my wife."

"She's not English, then?"

"Of course not."

"Okey doh. And when did you get married?"

"Tomorrow. You can be a witness if you like."

"Freddie, there wouldn't be anything . . . how shall I say? . . . untoward
about this, would there?"

"Untoward, no. Downright dodgy, yes. In need of discreet assistance
from an old friend, yes."

"Quite," said Fforde. "What are old friends for? Now, I'll need a name and some sort of identification."

Troy slid Tosca's passport across the table to him. Her *real* passport. *One* of her real passports. The real *American* one.

Gus read the name out softly to himself.

"Larissa Dimitrovna Tosca. Well, there's a mixed bag of origins for you. Dostoevsky and a dash of Puccini."

"Russian . . . Italian . . . all America's a hybrid of some sort."

"Quite," said Gus. "Born April 5, 1911. New York. You and older women again, eh Freddie?"

Troy said nothing.

Gus did his bit. Witnessed a civil wedding, pronounced Tosca, even with her haggard look and pancake makeup, to be "a stunner," discreetly intervened when the clerk raised the vexatious matter of "residency", popped the champagne and served the Sachertorte in the lobby of the Hotel Sacher, and rushed through a British passport, asking no questions and stepping lightly over embassy staff who remarked that it was all a little irregular.

Gus did not give a damn about the irregular. Little or large.

"However, there is one thing," he said sotto voce, towards the end of the second bottle of champagne. "The ambassador would like to meet you."

"For God's sake, why?"

"You're the brother of a man who'll be Foreign Secretary after the next election. Effectively the ambassador's boss. Isn't that reason enough?"

"What's his name? Do I know him?"

"Sir Francis Camiss-Low. New to the job, but then so are we all."

"Nope. Never met the bloke and now is not the time for a double-barrelled Englishman."

"He's just a diplomat trying to be diplomatic."

"So am I."

"Fine, Freddie. Don't tell me."

Troy shrugged it off and mourned the days when they had all told each other everything.

What were old friends for?

§42

Tosca unfolded the marriage certificate out on the bedspread. Riffled the pages of her new British passport.

"As instant as a cup of Maxwell House," she said.

"Almost," Troy conceded, not knowing where this was headed.

"But is it real?"

"How real do you want it to be?"

"I want my real to be real. I don't want fake real. I want real real."

"We're the real."

"Are we, Troy?"

"I'm here. You're here. The paperwork is all real, but that doesn't matter. You're real, I'm real."

She walked across the room. Stared at herself in the full-length mirror. Folded her arms. Cocked her head to the right. She was looking at a stranger. Troy knew this.

He stood behind her. Short as he was, he was still taller than Tosca. He wrapped his arms around her, cupped her elbows with his hands.

"You've always been you," she said. "I have had so . . . so many . . . identities. So many 'me's. Slough 'em on and off like snakeskin."

"And who do you see now?"

A deep breath. Exhaling a sigh.

"I guess I'm looking at Mrs. Frederick Troy. And like I said . . . is she real?"

Troy slid his hands back and squeezed her right hand. The Russians had taken pliers to her hands.

She winced. Her reflection screwing up in the mirror.

"Sorry. I keep forgetting."

"S'OK. At last, something real. Pain."

V

Troy

My body, now close to fifty years of age, has become an old tree that bears bitter peaches, a snail which has lost its shell, a bagworm separated from its bag; it drifts with the winds and clouds that know no destination.

—Basho, circa 1694

Fading is the worldling's pleasure,
All his boasted pomp and show;
Solid joys and lasting treasure
None but Zion's children know.

—John Newton, 1779
to a tune by Haydn

§43

Someone was following Frederick Troy.

§44

Hampstead, London NW3: Saturday, August 3, 1957

Sir Rodyon Troy, Bart, MA, DSO, DFC, MP, Shadow Home Secretary, a man never entirely sure in which order his plethora of initials should follow, awoke one morning to find he was fifty.

He decided to ignore it, and told every member of his family to ignore it under penalty of him getting a bit grumpy.

§45

Hampstead, London NW3: Sunday, August 3, 1958

Sir Rodyon Troy, Bart, MA, DSO, DFC, MP, Shadow Home Secretary, a man never entirely sure in which order his plethora of initials should follow, awoke one morning to find he was no longer fifty.

"Oh fuck," he said to no one, for the room was empty.

"Oh fuck."

He remembered the opening of Orwell's *Coming Up for Air* . . . "It was the day I got me new false teeth . . ." but then his mind drifted to *The History of Mr. Polly*, whose awareness of the rigidity of middle-age was summed up in the words, "Hole, rotten beastly hole." This struck him as more appropriate—he was in H. G. Wells's old house, in H. G's old bedroom, and in all likelihood in H. G's old bed . . . all bought as a job lot by his father in 1910.

He was not unprepared for this. For weeks now his wife had been saying things like . . . "We ought to get the family together" or "Do you fancy a bit of a do? You promised a bit of a do if we ignored your birthday last year."

The shock of being "over fifty" was not one of intellectual revelation. It was visceral. The knowledge in tendon, bone, and gut that he was "over fifty."

"Oh fuck," he said to no one, his wife having risen some half an hour before.

He knew where she was. A smell of Twinings Blue Mountain medium-roast coffee was wafting up the stairs from the kitchen five floors below. He could see her in the mind's eye. Blonde mop tucked up in a towel. Her blue silk dressing gown, so long it swept the floor. Perhaps it all augured well. Perhaps he'd get breakfast in bed for his fifty-first. Perhaps there'd be hanky-panky and high jinks to follow.

And his mind drifted back to the willowy, captivating blonde he'd met in the late spring of 1931, when he'd gone back to his old college—Trinity, Cambridge—for "a bit of a do," and found himself drawn to this gorgeous twenty-one-year-old, just about to graduate from Newnham in Applied Biology.

"To what do you apply it?" he'd said, thinking himself the soul of wit.

And she had applied it to him. And he to her. Ever after.

§46

If he smoked he'd be blowing smoke rings at the ceiling. But he didn't smoke. When his father's physician had advised the old man to give up cigars—long before the war—the entire household had had to give up any form of smoking. The old man would not have it any other way. Rod was not in the habit of defying his father. He left that to his sisters—who surreptitiously did what they liked, let libido rule reason, and deceived rather than defied—and his little brother, Fred, who openly argued with the old man. But if you don't smoke . . . what do you do after sex? What do you say? Twenty-seven years of monogamy had not left him at all certain of the protocol.

"Thank you," whilst sincere, did not seem appropriate.

"Did the earth move for you?" sounded like he was fishing for a compliment, and was more than likely to elicit a reply from Cid along the lines of, "Not all of it, but parts of Africa and the Middle East might have rumbled."

"You're miles away again," she said to him now.

"Was I?"

"Daydreaming. Family characteristic. The Troy male's modus operandi. Your father, you . . . young Fred. Come back to planet Earth. Tell me what we should do with ourselves. The day has arrived with not a plan in place. We could have given dinner for thirty. We could have had a dirty weekend in Paris for two . . ."

"Well, I certainly wouldn't want a dirty weekend in Paris for thirty!"

"Shut up. Your sisters would love that. Shut up and listen. We will do something. Not today perhaps, but something while the House is in recess. Once Parliament is sitting again, I'll never get you away. So think on, my boy. Apply your mind to this and come up with a plan by teatime today. Or else."

"Or else what?"

"Or else no more Applied Biology."

§47

Frederick Troy was at home in Goodwin's Court, London WC2 some three or four miles from his brother's house in Hampstead. He too was in bed. He too was the grateful recipient of breakfast in bed, followed by hanky-panky and high jinks. He too stared at the ceiling, but less in need of something to say than utterly content with silence.

His mistress, Foxx, had just returned from topping up her mug of tea—that part of the Northern mind that desired to start the day with tea was impenetrable to Troy, but he had long since ceased to wonder at it—and she had tossed the morning mail to him. A single airmail letter floated onto the sheet. A pale blue multi-folded piece of origami, lighter than goose down, that defied being opened in any manner that prevented tearing, unfolded into something the size of a bath towel and was best read by rotating the single page . . . this way, that way . . . until something resembling meaning hove into view.

It was from his wife. Troy had married Tosca a little over two years ago, and a little less than two years ago they had parted. He had not seen her since. Foxx surely knew who'd sent him an airmail letter and question or comment could not be more than seconds away.

"It's postmarked Chicago," she said before he had taken in more than the date.

He twisted the outer face towards him.

"No return address, though," he said.

"Then she doesn't want you to know where she is. Anyone could have posted that for her."

Troy read on. Foxx slurped tea for emphasis.

"What does she say?"

"No."

"No?"

"No. She does not agree to a divorce."

"Oh bum. Does she say why not?"

"More or less. The last year . . ."

"She's been gone nearly two!"

"The last year has been difficult for her. It would be a decision made in haste and stress . . . and besides, what she's not saying is that she knows damn well I can sooner or later divorce her in absentia on grounds of desertion."

"Later?"

"Sooner."

"All meaningless, isn't it?"

"Yes."

"So we stay as we are?"

"Yes."

"And that suits you just fine, doesn't it?"

§48

It felt like a summons. The following Sunday. To tea with his brother. A handwritten note, ending "or else."

"Or else what?" he said, standing on the doorstep of the Hampstead house.

"Just a nudge to get your attention, Freddie," his brother replied.

Foxx stepped between them, ever the peacemaker. Kissed Rod continental-style on both cheeks.

"I agree," she said. "So much simpler than taking all your clothes off."

And breezed past them both, and into the house.

In the library, facing front onto Church Row, Troy found most of his family assembled, balancing crockery and shedding crumbs.

His uncle, Nikolai Rodyonovich—quietly staring at nothing, head full of thinking and remembering.

His sister Sasha—knocking back the Canadian Club at ten to four of a Sunday afternoon.

Her twin, Masha—seemingly content with a cup of tea and a fig biscuit.

His brother-in-law Lawrence—a man who got by on four hours' sleep a night, edited two national newspapers, and never looked exhausted.

His sister-in-law, Cid, and her children: Alex, the second set of twins, Eugènie and Nastasia, and her youngest, Lydia—all about twenty, having appeared in a rush of fecundity just before the war.

Of his other brother-in-law, Hugh, there was no sign, but he was a complete gobshite and Troy didn't much care if he never saw him again. Perhaps Hugh's representative on earth was his younger son, Arkady, a gangly monster of seventeen or so who was blessed in resembling neither parent in shape or nature, enough for Troy to wonder about paternity. Hugh and Sasha's elder son, Maximilian, a man born to the pith helmet and alpenstock, always seemed to be up a mountain or crossing a desert with a team from this or that university in search of this or that lost/undiscovered/buried/sunken/stolen something or other. Troy tried to remember him at birthdays and Christmas and habitually failed, as he did with most of the nephews and nieces.

Masha and Lawrence had put off having a family, which implies more choice than there had been, until after the war. Their kids, two boys, hardly even adolescent as yet, would be at home with an aunt or a nanny or a dog or television set. Otherwise, Troy thought, the full dramatis personae had taken to the stage.

"Who's died?"

"Freddie, please," Cid reprimanded. "This is a joyous occasion."

"Joyous?"

"Happy, you cynical bastard!" said his brother.

"Now," Cid went on. "Thank you all for the birthday cards and presents you sent Rod last Sunday . . ."

Oh fuck, thought Troy.

". . . but this Sunday Rod and I have a present for all of you."

Foxx whispered in his ear, "You forgot his birthday?"

"S'OK. He's fifty-one. It's not a big deal. Not even a round number."

"We want," Cid was saying, "to mark Rod's fiftieth . . ."

Foxx elbowed him sharply, muttered, "Idiot."

". . . with a holiday. Now, I appreciate the invitation is a year late, but would you all please accept an invitation from Rod and myself to accompany us in October on the last Grand Tour of Europe."

Silence, followed by murmurs of curiosity, and a muttered "I don't get it" from Foxx.

"Sorry if that sounds vague, I mean . . . we'd like to recreate the journeys of Rod's parents across Europe in the years before the Great War, stopping off where they stopped off. Alex kept copious diaries and, apart from the odd hotel or restaurant that's folded in the intervening years, I'm sure we can trace their steps. Obviously we can't include anywhere that's now behind the Iron Curtain. So, the route would be . . ."

Cid consulted a white card, nestling in her hand.

". . . in the order we can travel now rather than the order in which Alex and Maria actually travelled . . . Paris, Siena, Florence, Venice, Vienna, and Amsterdam. We would like to take this at a leisurely pace, over a fortnight or more . . . so would you all please free up your calendars, rope in missing husbands and children, and be our guests."

More silence. The first to break it was Sasha, rising to her feet to say, "Fucking hell, I need more booze."

If looks could kill, Rod would have nuked her.

Then Nikolai spoke.

"Forgive me, my boy. I would love to, but I fear my old bones will not permit me."

"That's alright, Nikolai. I quite understand."

Then Lawrence.

"I'm terribly sorry, I can't get away in October. We launch the new colour supplement in November. There aren't enough days in the month as it is."

"Really?" said Rod, cold enough to crack tooth enamel.

"Er . . . er . . . I go up to Oxford in October, Uncle Rod," said Arkady. "Rotten timing."

"Well, Arkady," Sasha said. "You're not just letting Rod down, you're letting me down. 'Cos I want to go . . ."

"Thank you," said Rod. "At last, a modicum of enthusiasm."

". . . But I'll be fucked if I'll go with your father. If that bastard's on board you can count me out!"

Troy thought Rod might weep.

Instead "Jesus wept" and he went downstairs.

Cid, possessed of more sangfroid than any Troy, simply said, "More tea anyone?"

And the look in her eyes told them they were not off the hook just yet and that her legendary powers of endurance and persuasion had only just begun to kick in. This was a woman capable of organising Christmas dinner for forty, and of addressing the South Herts Labour Party Women's Group without notes, and of drawing the tombola winners without fear or favour. A Grand Tour of Europe was kid's stuff to Lucinda Troy.

§49

"Go after him."

"Eh?"

"Go after him. Fifty? Fifty-one? It doesn't fucking matter. Just tell him we accept gratefully," said Foxx.

Troy found Rod at the kitchen table. The black cloud around him all but visible.

"I have the list."

"What fucking list? Hell's tits, you'd think I'd invited them to three nights in Wormwood Scrubs not the best hotels on the Continent."

"Foxx and I will happily take the tour. I have leave due. And you've given me plenty of notice. Masha will leave the kids with Lawrence and accompany Sasha. With you, Cid, and your children that makes ten of us. Enough for every meal to be a party and probably about as many as you could manage, if you think about it."

"So . . . no in-laws?"

"No. I'll miss Lawrence. He can keep the conversation rolling better than anyone else I know, just the right measure of fact and gossip—but would you really want Hugh along? Did you really invite him? He calls Sasha a drunken bitch ten times a day, and I doubt they can get from Monday to Friday without her threatening to kill him."

They both knew the levels of anger, if not violence, of which Hugh was capable. To Troy's knowledge, he had not hit Sasha since the day she had hit back and broken his nose with the back of a hair brush. And he claimed to have beaten one of her lovers, no doubt intending the classic cuckold's cliché "to within an inch of your life"—but the man had died. Troy had never wholly believed Hugh's assertion—a boastful wanker at the best and worst of times—but had never been able to dismiss it either. It had been swept under the carpet. Family before all else. If Sasha had left Hugh, things might have been different, but she hadn't and Troy did not know why she hadn't. He could only surmise that she thought she could make him more miserable by staying, more miserable by having more affairs. Without a shadow of a doubt, she was having an affair right now—she'd never say who, but she'd make damn sure her husband knew about it. She had him on a hook, and she would twist and she would twist and she would twist.

"Well," said Rod. "He has it coming, hasn't he?"

"Yes. I'd just prefer she hire a hit man rather than shooting him herself."

Rod got up and opened a cupboard next to the fireplace.

"My mad sister isn't the only one who needs a drink. Scotch OK?"

"Not for me."

Rod sat back down, with the bottle, a tumbler, and a jug of water. Knocked back half a glass of over-diluted Scotch.

"Speaking of which. Do you think she's mad?"

"They've both of them had that potential for years. But I think Masha might be pulling back from the edge. I see she's on tea and biscuits upstairs."

"A courtesy to the missus. Not getting plastered before six o'clock."

"And if Sasha were going to tip over that edge I think she would probably have done it that Christmas when Hugh dropped his killer bombshell. Right now she seems determined to live long enough to get even."

Rod rested his forehead on the deal table.

"I'm the one who's mad. Why the fuck did I let Cid talk me into this holiday? Dragging those mad tarts around Europe. I need my head examined. I'm doing this why exactly?"

He lifted his head to look at Troy.

"Because she asked."

"I'm doing it because I'm 'over fifty.' Ask me how I feel about being over fifty."

"How does it feel?"

"Too old to be doing this."

"It'll be fine," said Troy, more in hope than anticipation.

$50

Paris

To begin in Paris was to begin at the end. Paris had been his parents' last jumping-off point. From here they could only land in England. England and stability and permanence after five years of traipsing—his father's word, the old man loved collecting anglicisms . . . as a boy Troy could not be lost or bewildered, he was always "a dog at a fair"—traipsing around Europe in the last days of the ancien régime (how many ancien régimes could one continent have?) in the Edwardian haze. Along the way they had picked up a son (Vienna) and twin daughters (Paris).

Paris held more than enough to occupy the next generation. They shopped, they climbed the Eiffel Tower, they shopped, they drifted aimlessly around the Left Bank, they shopped, they paid lip service to the Louvre, and they shopped . . . while the previous generation made a pilgrimage. To Père Lachaise Cemetery . . . in search of Oscar Wilde.

All the way up the cobbled lane from the metro station, past seemingly countless tombs standing like abandoned sentry boxes, Rod complained about his feet.

"Suffer for your art," Troy said.

"What art?"

"This."

They had arrived at a vast monument in the Egyptian style, carved by Epstein, a god of some sort, floating or perhaps gliding . . . cock and balls flying free.

Rod looked baffled.

"Can you see any relevance to this?" he asked.

"Quite a lot, actually," Troy replied. "He did write *Salome.*"

"Is that the best you can come up with?"

"And—"

"I thought Salome was Jewish not Egyptian. You know, Herods and things, not Pharaohs and things."

"And . . . as I was saying . . . it may well reflect his rather odd way of spending his nights."

"Good bloody grief."

"OK. I give up. It has heaps of classical allusion, it has a knob, it has bollocks. What more would Oscar ask?"

"Don't make me regret this any more than I already do, Freddie."

"There's nothing to regret."

"I know you've got lots of friends who are . . . er . . ."

"Queer. The word you cannot utter is queer."

"Alright . . . queer it is. No more euphemisms."

"Queer is a euphemism."

"If you say so. You have friends who are queer."

"And some of my *best* friends are Jews."

"Now you're just taking the piss—stop it. All I meant was—"

"I know what you meant."

"I meant I just don't get it."

"What's to get?"

"The thing. The whole thing. The queer thing."

"Does it matter?"

"Yes, it does. For one thing, there's a Commons vote on Homosexual Law Reform not long after we get back."

"Well then, you know how to vote, don't you."

"I do?"

"Vote for Oscar. It's fifty years too late, but vote for every queer who's ever been sent down for hanky-panky in a public lavatory."

Slowly descending the hill, after several silent minutes, Rod said, "If I could only understand why it has to be in public lavatories."

Troy said nothing.

"Disgusting places at the best of times."

Troy said nothing.

"Y'know . . . I've got my doubts about my PPS, Iain Stuart-Bell. Before the war we'd have just thought him a bit effeminate . . . now I have to ask myself if he might be one of those."

Troy had met Iain many times. He didn't have doubts. He was sure.

"Why don't you try asking him," he said.

"Because," Rod replied, "I'd rather not know."

§51

Siena

The weather had favoured them so far. Sunny autumn days, warmer days than many an English summer, and they had drifted up and down cobbled streets, without faction or acrimony.

Rod had been pleasantly surprised to find his children still not averse to culture after several days of exposure. They had listened patiently while he explained the frescoes in the Sala dei Nove at the Palazzo Pubblico, the allegories of good and bad government, meat and drink to a politician—which he described as "refreshingly secular, not a Madonna and bambino in sight" without any of his children sniggering.

And they had wandered around the Duomo in awe of the Tuscan blue-starred ceiling, baffled by the marble floor panels, until Rod had told the story of the Sybil—how Tarquinius Superbus did one of the worst deals in the history of the second-hand book trade, letting the Sybil burn six of the nine before he finally stumped up the money.

"So she's a pagan myth, right, Dad?" Nattie asked. "In a Christian church?"

He floundered a little at this.

"I suppose she is."

Troy came to his rescue.

"She's a myth, the books were real."

"They were?"

"Mentioned by Tacitus in his *Annals*. How Augustus scoured the empire to reconstruct the text. Finally lost forever in the fifth century."

But, at last, as they all knew she would, Sasha spoke up—just as they were leaving, stepping into the Piazza del Duomo as the afternoon sun faded and beat her in a contest to bring a chill to the air.

She pointed at the statues of Romulus and Remus that framed the space, as they did so many of Siena's public piazze.

"OK, smarty-pants. Explain this. All these kids and all these bloody wolves. I've never seen so many babes sucking on wolf tit in my life. I ask you . . . one or two statues? . . . wouldn't be in bad taste perhaps . . . but a suckling wolf on every street corner? I don't know about you, but I am frescoed out and I am titted out!"

"Oh God," Rod sighed. "She's off again."

"I've bumbled around enough for one day," Sasha was saying. "You can have too much of a good thing. Certainly too much fresco and too much tit. I'm going to put me feet up. One of you pick a decent restaurant and let me know when dinner's up."

The gender divide divided. In less than a minute the three men, Rod, Alex, and Troy, found themselves alone.

"Was it something I said?" said Rod.

"It's nothing," said Troy. "*Di niente*. Let's find a bar on the Campo and watch a blue sunset. There are things I need to tell you, and Alex is a journalist . . ."

"Yep," said Alex simply.

". . . So nosiness is second nature to him."

At the top of the Campo's fan-shaped slope Rod seemed to be searching for something, looking at tables, then turning around to check the view over the Torre del Mangia.

"What's up?"

"The old man brought me here when I was thirteen. Blowed if I can remember where we sat."

"I can."

"You weren't here."

"No. But I came with him in '39. And we sat there, one rib of the fan and two bars over."

Troy pointed to an empty table. Rod stood in front of it.

"Y'know, I think you're right. OK, let's get a waiter and a bottle of Brunello over, and hope we don't get one of those blokes who insists you have to eat beef with it, because I'm going to drink it neat."

So they did.

As Rod poured himself seconds, as Troy stared at the cobalt sky above the palazzo, the moment arrived.

"You're not up to anything, are you? Either of you?"

"Not with you there, Freddie. Explain."

"Alex, you're not investigating anything . . . shall we say . . . dodgy in your cub reporter's outfit?"

"No. I'm lucky if I get to cover a jumble sale in Primrose Hill."

"Rod?"

"Such as?"

"Have you been assigned a bodyguard?"

"Now you're just being silly. Bodyguard? No member of the opposition gets a bodyguard. If Macmillan called an election they'd assign a Special Branch bloke to Gaitskell, but only to Gaitskell. Who cares if the rest of the shadow cabinet gets shot before the votes are counted? Why are you asking daft questions?"

"Because we're being followed."

"What?"

"I spotted him in Paris. Wasn't wholly certain, but as we sat on the stone bench at the Porta Romana yesterday, he passed by on the far side. An old trick. Get ahead of the person you're following. When we passed the *Ospedale Psichiatrico*, on the way back into town, he was just inside the gate. He gave us about thirty paces and then resumed tailing."

"I don't fucking believe this!"

"Then try harder."

"If we're being followed, then where is this bloke now? The Campo's deserted. We're the only customers at this bar and I doubt there's more than a dozen drinking at all the other bars put together."

"I don't know. I last saw him near the Duomo just before we went in. He won't be far away. There's a dozen alleys leading off in every direction. He could be watching us from any one of them, and we wouldn't be able to see him."

Alex intervened, "Dad, there's nothing preposterous in what Freddie's saying."

"On the contrary, it's cloak-and-dagger bollocks."

"But," Alex went on, "he won't be following me. So which of you two is it?"

"I don't know that either," said Troy. "But I'll find out."

"How?" said Rod.

"I'll take a walk after dinner. If he follows me, then it's me. If he doesn't, it's you."

Rod's exasperation showed in the vigour with which he beckoned the waiter and ordered a second bottle, and the scarcely audible repetition of "I don't fucking believe this."

Alex said, "In 1939? Wasn't there a war on?"

Troy admired the boy's tact, switching back to the ever-present subject, his grandfather and namesake, Alex Troy.

"It hadn't got far. Poland was a battlefield. France was still safe, and Italy still neutral. We were, I found out on this very spot, on our way to Rome to meet Mussolini. I think your grandfather saw himself as the fixer who might persuade him to stay out of the war. Probably futile, but we never got there."

With another glass in his hand, Rod began to mellow.

"That was our dad. The fixer. The man for all seasons. The Sybil."

"Eh? The Sybil?"

"He sat where I'm sitting now and prophesied. 1921. The first war had been over less than three years. A Europe desperate for peace, and he sat here and told me, a spotty thirteen-year-old, to think of it as a cricket match."

"Eh?" said Alex again.

"Peace as a cricket match played in an English village over a long summer weekend. Sooner or later rain would stop play."

"And you think I'm a cynic," Troy said.

§52

Rod seemed to Troy to have put the problem, if indeed that was how he saw it, behind him at dinner and let himself relax. Troy had long thought his brother a happy man in so far as happiness was his default condition, that to which he reverted when the pressure was off. Happiness was not Troy's condition, nor was it his nature.

They sat, all ten of them, at a vast round table in the Osteria Domenico Scarlatti on Banchi di Sopra, a room papered with sheet music, and with alcoves housing half a dozen different busts of the great man. Troy thought it would be little short of the magical touch if someone actually came in and played the harpsichord propped open in the corner, but no one did—and he resisted the promptings of his sister-in-law to play himself with "Can you imagine how heavy-handed I would sound after forty years playing the piano? My hands would feel like sledgehammers."

Instead, as they chattered all around him, he unwound the thread of Scarlatti's delicate, addictive B-Minor Sonata (K. 27) in the mind's ear, as he had heard it played by Dame Myra Hess in 1940 or 1941, and as Cid saw his fingers form a chord upon the tablecloth, one hand closed over his and she squeezed.

They had worked their way through several bottles of very expensive wine over antipasti, primi, and secondi—the palimpsestic layers of the Italian menu—drinking in the direction of dolci, when Troy said:

"I think I must get some air. So if you'll all excuse me, I'll see you back at the hotel."

No one seemed to mind—boozed into bonhomie.

He was standing in the street, buttoning his overcoat against the night, when he realised he was not alone.

"What do you want?"

And Sasha said, "Same as you. A bit of air."

"I'm going for a walk. Quite a long one."

"Then I'll join you. One can have quite enough of family."

"Has it ever occurred to you that you might be the family of which one can have quite enough?"

"I'll pretend I didn't hear that."

Troy felt there was little left in his arsenal except "fuck off," but as he looked at her—black jacket, the expensive hide of something dead and furry, black slacks and flat heels—it occurred to him that she was dressed to keep up with whatever pace he set and that to have her along might diminish the possibility of the tail thinking he'd been rumbled.

He leaned in close.

"I'm being followed. Don't fuck it up."

She whispered back, "Don't fuck what up?"

"I mean to tackle him."

"Bloody hell! I can't wait. Lead me to it."

"Just do as you're told."

Troy headed north and west, uphill, away from Il Campo, in the direction of the Basilica di San Domenico. Sasha slipped an arm through his. He did not discourage her—the touch of intimacy added to the air of innocence he wanted to create.

"Where is this chap?"

"Dunno for sure. Somewhere behind us. It would be almost impossible for him to be dodging ahead of us or walking a parallel street. The streets are too narrow and this part of the city's like a maze."

Halfway up Costa Sant'Antonio they took a sharp left into an alley less than six feet wide and emerged onto the Via Camporegio, with the basilica looming up ahead of them.

She whispered, "Not another bloody church?"

"Churched out, are we?"

"Yep. And I think you might have lost him."

"No, I haven't. Stick with me."

And they began the long descent down the Camporegio steps into one of Siena's urban valleys.

"Put a spurt on."

All he'd meant was "walk a bit faster," but Sasha began to hop from one giant step to the next, like a little girl playing hopscotch, left foot to right, right foot to left. She reached the bottom well ahead of Troy, and Troy for his part hoped they were both well ahead of their tail.

At the bottom of the steps stood an ancient, ornate, fortress-like building that housed the three fountains that had supplied Siena with water for a thousand years.

Troy pulled Sasha under the first arch. The light vanished completely. He put one hand across her lips.

"Now. Keep your voice down."

"Where are we? I can't see a damn thing."

"We're in the Fontebranda. Your eyes will get used to the darkness in a few seconds, but he'll be as good as blind if he looks in."

A minute passed. A figure appeared as a black outline in the curve of the arch. It seemed to Troy that the man was looking straight at him, utterly unable to see him.

Troy's first punch doubled him over. The second knocked him cold.

He wasn't a big man. Taller than Troy but skinny as a rake. Troy dragged him to the lip of the fountain, rested his head against the low wall.

Sasha seemed ecstatic. All but hopping from foot to foot again.

"Do we torture him now? I'm still good at Chinese burns, y'know."

"I hit him too hard. I only meant to knock him down, not out. Scoop up a handful of water. Torture or no torture, I need to talk to him."

Sasha splashed water onto the man's face. His eyes opened, he shook his head gently and groaned.

"Right, you bastard," she said. "Start talking!"

"Sasha, please."

The man groaned again.

Troy squatted next to him.

"Why are you following me?"

"Wurr . . . wurr . . . wurrrr."

Sasha took his wrist in both hands and delivered the Chinese burn with which she had tormented Troy when they were children. Troy let her. It might be productive.

The man screamed.

"Answer, matey—or I start on your bollocks!"

"Sasha! For God's sake."

"I'm . . . not . . . following you."

"I spotted you in Paris. If you're not following me, then you're following my brother, Rod."

"No."

A pained shake of the head to emphasise the syllable.

He had Troy baffled now. It didn't sound like a lie or the simplicity of denial.

"Then who? You're following someone."

He raised his burning wrist and pointed.

"Her," he said.

"What?" said Troy and Sasha simultaneously.

"Not following you. Following her."

Troy rocked back on his heels. This made no sense at all.

Sasha said, "Me? You're following me? You cheeky bugger!"

"P . . . p . . . paid."

"Paid? By whom?" Troy said.

"By her husband."

Sasha caught the man with a deftly aimed right hook and knocked him cold again. Then she straddled him and began to pound his chest with both fists.

"Bastard! Bastard! You complete and utter fucking bastard!"

Troy pulled her away, her legs pedalling in the air on some invisible tricycle.

"Calm down. Calm down and go back to the hotel."

"No!"

"Sasha, for fuck's sake, leave this to me."

Her legs drooped. Troy felt her body sag.

"I'm going to kill Hugh. This is the last fucking straw. I'm going to kill him. What did he expect to find? That I'm shagging every gigolo from Paris to Siena? I'm going to fucking kill him!"

"Just go and leave this to me. Please, Sasha."

He released his grip. She pulled her coat around her a little tighter, and just when Troy thought she might go quietly, she landed a kick to the balls at the unconscious gumshoe.

"Bastard! Don't be long, Freddie. I want to know everything."

When she'd gone, Troy scooped up another handful of water and revived the man.

"Bloody hell. My head hurts. Oh bloody hell. My bollocks hurt. Has the madwoman gone?"

"Yes," Troy replied. "But if you don't start talking I'll get her back."

"I don't envy you a childhood with that harpy."

"Get to the point."

"I'm ex-Met, like yourself, Mr. Troy. Bob Thornton. I was a beat bobby at Paddington Green nick until '55. Been private ever since."

"I'm surprised you make a living. You're not very good at it."

"This is all a bit new. Most divorce jobs take you no farther than Brighton. It's a bad day if I have to go as far as Eastbourne."

"So Hugh is paying you to gather evidence for divorce?"

"No. He never mentioned divorce . . . he just wants to know about all the . . . what he calls 'fancy men.'"

"To what end?"

"I don't know, Mr. Troy. Just to have something on his wife."

Troy held out a hand and pulled Thornton to his feet.

"I think the job's over, don't you?"

"Too right it is. I'm not going near that madwoman again."

"Can't say I blame you. Go home, go back to England and tell Hugh exactly what happened. Leave nothing out. Be sure to pick up your fee. And offer him a piece of advice from me."

"OK."

"That when he next meets my sister, his wife, he should wear his cricket box because his bollocks will be her first target."

"I've a dim recollection of her saying she'd kill him. Or did I imagine that?"

"She might well, but she'll start with his bollocks. Sorry I hit you so hard, by the bye."

"S'awright, Mr. Troy. No hard feelings."

§53

"Paranoia," said Rod.

Troy had found him waiting up in the hotel lobby, sitting surrounded by newspapers in half a dozen languages in a jungle of overstuffed armchairs and sofas, a whisky and soda to hand.

"Yours or mine?"

"Well, it's not likely to be mine, is it? I'm not the one with the dodgy profession."

"Hmm," said Troy. "Are you sure you have the right frame of mind to become Home Secretary? I work for Scotland Yard. If you lot get lucky at the next election, I'll end up working for you. Dodgy profession, my arse."

"How can I put this without adding further insult? You are a dodgy individual in an otherwise respectable profession."

"You failed. I'm insulted."

"Freddie . . . I had no reason to think that chap was following me until you put the thought into my head. You're the one who . . . dammit . . . dammit, Freddie, you sail close to the wind and you know it. It was more than likely that that chap was following you. He might have been CIA or the other lot, or who knows what. Any of the acronyms you seem to upset on a regular basis."

"Instead, he was following our errant sister, in search of high jinks."

"Which surprised both of us."

"Quite. But he'll stop now. Sasha scared the living daylights out of him."

"Suppose Hugh just hires somebody else?"

"Then we ignore him. Whatever Sasha gets up to is her business, and now she knows that Hugh wants to know, I wouldn't put it past her to deliver the goods."

"Oh hell. She'll be fucking taxi drivers and tour guides."

"Altar boys and traffic cops."

"The archbishop of Florence . . . the Doge of Venice . . . in the street, frightening the horses."

"But at least we won't feel paranoid anymore."

§54

Florence

Troy watched Sasha's rage drop to a simmer. She did not raise the cause of her anger in conversation, as though storing it up for future reference and deployment. Had he given her the benefit of the doubt, he might have concluded that she was trying to make the holiday work for Rod's sake, but he felt no urge to be her beneficiary. She was plotting something. He just didn't know what.

It was their second night in Florence before he saw the glimmer of a smile. A bar in Oltrarno, with a view of the river, after a morning inside Brunelleschi's Duomo, and an afternoon in the Bargello, where she had gazed rapt at Bartolomeo Ammannati's *Leda and the Swan*.

"Unbelievable. No . . . I mean the opposite. Believable. You really can believe the swan . . . well . . . you know . . ."

Silently Troy agreed, whilst finding it predictable she would fall for the most erotic sculpture in the city. It was something about the beak-to-lips kiss, something about the way his wing was held in the crook of her thigh and calf.

"I mean to say," she had said, "all those dozy buggers standing around in the piazza with their box cameras, snapping away at David's willy, about as erotic as yesterday's cold rice pudding, and here's this, tucked away inside . . . a hidden whatchermacallit . . . thingy . . . gem! . . . and I'd never heard of it!"

Sasha stood, wrapped up in a shawl, on the bar's open terrace, looking across the river towards the Uffizi.

She turned as Troy approached, and then he saw the smile. So unexpected. He realised the temptation was to read too much into it. Forgive and forget were not concepts the woman understood.

"What's making you smile?"

She put an arm through his, pulled him close, whispered into his ear—not that anyone would have heard if she'd spoken out loud.

"My imagination."

"And what are you imagining?"

"Fucking a swan."

§55

Venice

Venice passed without incident or acrimony. Rod even read chunks of his father's diary out loud to everyone at breakfast with scarcely a groan or an unexcused absence. They listened to a description of the city as it had been in 1907—of Alexei and Maria Troy, fugitives footloose on a Continent not yet capable of imagining what might be to come, the empires and kingdoms not yet lost—the children not yet born. Troy began to think they might be able to pass for a family, after all.

§56

Someone was following Frederick Troy.

§57

Vienna

By treaty in 1955, Austria's post-war occupation had ended. The country's neutrality was both guaranteed and enforced. It would not join the Warsaw Pact, nor would it be part of NATO. The last twenty-odd thousand Russian, French, American, and British troops departed—the zones of the country abolished and the sectors of Vienna restored to their civil status as *Bezirke*. All things considered, Vienna fared better than Berlin by 1958. Nobody was arguing over it any more, almost overnight it had ceased to be the most spied-in and spied-upon city in Europe, and if it didn't immediately settle back to a life of swaying waltzes and strong coffee . . . well, you can't have everything.

Berlin was still two cities, divided by a fairly neat if meandering line between the Russian sector in the east and all the other sectors in the west. Vienna's dividing line had never been quite so clean. In fact, it was more of a mess. The French had a tidy cluster of districts, so did the Americans, but the Russians and the British jigsawed. And the whole of the city centre was subject to four-power administration, resulting in four-men-in-a-jeep, jack-in-the-box patrols consisting of one soldier from each army, a motley formula that might have led to a United Nations in miniature (and on wheels) but more often than not merely led to arguments about lunch and beer. And lest you forgot whose turf you were on, there had been regular white pavement-demarcation stencils.

Troy found himself looking at one, scuffed and fading on the cobblestones that marked the line between the Landstraße Bezirk (3), which had been British, and the Wieden Bezirk (4), which had been Russian, on the Schwarzenbergplatz:

СОВЕТСКИЙ СЕКТОР

He wondered if there'd ever be a day when the Second World War wasn't a visible remnant in half the cities in Europe, scars upon the body politic. This one could have been scrubbed away. Its survival was deliberate. An act of conservation, not an error of omission.

He scraped at it with the sole of his left shoe.

"You're destroying a bit of history," said Gus Fforde.

"Really? I wonder how many poor Russian conscripts wasted days of their own history going around painting this on every street corner?"

"Marginally better than whitewashing piles of coal, I should think. And God knows plenty of our Tommies did that."

"Touché, Gus," Troy replied. "However, you will appreciate that where Britain and Russia once met might blur the definition of 'our' in my case."

Gus had met Troy outside the Hotel Sacher on his way to work, as First Secretary at the British Embassy on Rennweg, only a few yards from where they were standing. Gus and Troy had been at school together. Their mutual loyalty was boundless. In 1956, Gus had arranged Troy's marriage in Vienna to Larissa Tosca, knowing full well that she had been a Soviet agent. He had pulled every string at his fingertips, told a dozen lies, and given her the security of a British passport. And loyal still, he had asked no questions when the marriage had exploded later the same year and Tosca had vanished yet again.

Troy had skipped breakfast to walk with Gus. His first morning without family in the best part of a fortnight. "Family and friends" was a phrase used so often to define emotional territory as to be little short of cliché—one that baffled Troy. They weren't the same thing at all. Troy thought they needed a stencil to make that clear:

You Are Now Leaving Family—This Is A Friend
Вы покидаете семью—это друг

"I hope Rod's enjoying this," Gus said, just as they reached the embassy.

"Oh yes. He was nostalgic by proxy all the way here. Reading the old man's diaries, retracing the journey. It's different from now on. He's nostalgic for himself. He's reliving the Vienna he knew before they kicked him out after the Anschluss in '38. And he's imagining the Vienna he never knew. He was born here, after all."

"Jolly good."

"Why do I find that ominous?"

"God—am I so bad at dissembling? Not ominous, no. It's just that I might be putting a bit of a damper on the fun."

"How?"

"Someone back in London told the ambassador Rod's here. I know this is a holiday, but the ambassador is not the sort of bloke not to take a politician's visit seriously—in this case, too seriously. Wanted to know why I hadn't told him. Pooh-poohed me saying it was a private visit and is pretty insistent on . . . dunno what to call it . . . not black tie . . ."

"Just as well. None of us travelled with evening dress."

"And not a reception as such . . ."

"A bit of a do?"

"Exactly."

"I think Rod will be delighted."

"Really? And you?"

"I'll tolerate it. Just see that you water my sister's wine if you don't want a diplomatic incident."

"Ah . . . Sasha. *Plus ça change.* I'll never forget her thrusting her hand down my trousers when I was fourteen and tweaking my John Thomas."

"Gus. I do wish you hadn't told me that."

"Shall we say tomorrow night, seven thirty for eight, here?"

"I'll tell him."

§58

The following afternoon the Troys were walking through the Innere Stadt, like a caravan, it seemed to Troy—all they lacked were camels and music and sunlight and shifting sands. They had walked from the Danube Canal, the length of Rotenturmstraße in the direction of St. Stephen's Cathedral.

Someone was still following Frederick Troy, although in the absence of further paranoia he was now telling himself that someone was following Sasha Darbishire.

"We've picked up another tail," he said to Rod.

Rod's head jerked as though on a string.

"No, don't turn around. We'll get out to middle of the square and I'll nobble him."

"I'm getting fed up with this."

"Leave it to me."

He slowed his pace, let the family pull ahead as they passed the southern corner of cathedral, and as they reached the chapel on the far side, Troy turned and walked quickly back across the square to face his pursuer.

It was a little bloke, quite unlike the last. Short and tubby. A black winter overcoat and a rather tatty homburg, and shoes soled in leather that rang on the cobblestones. Not a hint of gum about the shoe.

They stood face-to-face, almost nose-to-nose.

Troy could almost swear the man was blushing.

"Look. I'll tell you what I told the other chap. Fuck off back to London and tell my brother-in-law to grow up."

"*Sie sind Herr Troy?*"

"What?"

"*Herr Frederick Troy, aus London?*"

"You know bloody well who I am."

But the man didn't seem to understand a word he'd said.

"*Ja,*" with exasperation. "*Ich bin Frederick Troy.*"

"*Ich habe einen Brief für Sie.*"

He stuck an envelope in Troy's hand, turned on his heel, and walked away without looking back.

Troy watched in disbelief, felt as though he'd just been served with a summons, felt tempted for a moment to go after him and grab hold, to thump him as hard as he'd thumped the last dim-witted gumshoe, but the moment passed and he tore open the envelope.

No letter, no note, just a ticket for the Großer Saal at the Konzerthaus— Stalls seat D18, that same night.

KONZERTHAUS
GROSSER SAAL
LOTHRINGERSTRASSE 20, WIEN

Wolfgang Amadeus Mozart
❖

KLAVIERKONZERT 20 IN D-MOLL
SINFONIE CONCERTANTE IN ES-DUR
& SYMPHONIE 41 IN C, 'JUPITER'
DIE MOSCAUER KAMMERORCHESTER
DIR. ANATOLI CHERTKOV
SOL. LAVRENTI KUTUZOV
❖

D18

And he'd no idea what this was about.

§59

Predictably, Rod was furious.

"What do you mean you're not coming? It's your pal arranged this dinner."

"He's your pal too. You've known Gus even longer than I have. And you know the ambassador, Sir Francis Whatsisname. I've never even met the man."

"It's bad form, Freddie."

"It's fucking awful form, but it's what I have to do."

"What's so important you have to skip dinner at the embassy?"

"Something *more* important, obviously."

"Oh my God . . . it's not spook stuff, is it?"

Troy had no idea what it was, but "spook stuff" was a useful concept. It was a forbidden country and if Troy told Rod it was "spook stuff," he wouldn't go there.

"Might be," he said.

"You know, that's the sort of answer you gave to questions when you were ten!"

$60

From his centre aisle seat Troy would have a first-rate view of the pianist. His benefactor might well have given him the best seat in the house. Four rows back—usually considered the best for sound—but close enough for him to see Kutuzov's hands move across the keys. As the lights dimmed, as Chertkov took to the stage, as the first round of applause went up, the seat next to Troy remained empty. He wondered if it had been reserved for a purpose, if he was meant to meet whoever had been given the ticket.

As the applause tailed off, Chertkov, tall and stunningly handsome, one of the young Turks of Russian music in the relaxed post-Stalin era, was still facing the audience. He wasn't taking bows. He was, against tradition, about to speak.

Troy's German was poor, but Chertkov's was simple.

"I am sorry to say that Lavrenti Kutuzov is indisposed."

Kutuzov was not one of the young Turks. He was seventy-five if he was a day. Was this a tactful way of saying he was dead? A huge sigh rippled out across the audience, most of whom had probably paid the earth to see one of the most famous pianists on the planet.

"However, we are lucky, we are privileged to have one of Vienna's own step into Lavrenti Rodyonovich's shoes. I might say at no notice, and we are, sadly, completely unrehearsed together, but be assured you will not be disappointed. Ladies and gentlemen—Méret Voytek."

The applause returned with a bang, and suddenly it all made sense to Troy—it all fell into place . . . everything except the empty seat.

He'd not set eyes on Voytek since the day he'd stuck her on the ferry to Calais ten years ago. At twenty-four she'd looked older than her years, her hair prematurely, brazenly white after a year in the hands of the Nazis. Now, she had more flesh on her bones, she had dyed her hair back to its youthful black, no longer wearing white as her badge of suffering.

It wasn't a happy face that looked out at her waiting, appreciative audience, but the habitual frown he had known had softened into a more neutral expression, as though the soul inside might be one prepared to give life a chance.

Her dress was pleasingly immodest. Skintight, up to her throat at the front, practically down to the crack of her arse at the back, the unbroken paleness of her skin in stark contrast to the concert black of the fabric—the only hint of colour was a single narrow strip following the seam from the right shoulder to the hemline, just above her knee, a line of crimson piping no wider than that on the cap of a London clippie, that spoke a defiance that might be visible from the moon.

She took her seat. Chertkov faced the orchestra, turned once to look at Voytek, nodded and raised his baton. The rhythm of the string section, almost syncopated, Troy thought, struck up with a deep murmur, a bass rumble of anxiety, apprehension and fear . . . a sudden drop into nothingness and nowhere—a dark, dark opening to any concerto.

Unless the conductor was a galloper trying to break the mood, a good two and a half minutes usually passed before the pianist was cued, by which time it could feel to the listener as though one had passed *une saison en enfer*. Most pianists sat with their spine straight, their hands in their laps, and let the sombre mood of the music dictate. At the first notes, Voytek had reached out a hand to the top of the piano and leaned her head on her arm. Within thirty seconds she had buried her face in her hands. After a minute she took them away and spoke to Chertkov. Neither Troy nor anyone else in the audience could hear what she said, but, with his baton in his right hand still conducting, Chertkov had turned to her, extended his left, and said:

«Ты можешь это сделать» You can do it.

Troy could guess at her reply.

Chertkov said, «Да, ты можешь. Ты играла это и в прошлом сезоне.» Yes, you can. You played it only last season.

Her hands returned to her face. There were now only seconds left to her cue.

«Méret, ты же хорошо знаешь эту пьесу.» Méret, you know this piece so well.

Her left hand still clutched her chin, her right reached out to the keyboard and played the first delicate notes of Mozart's melody. The left hand touched down and, for the next half hour, she put not a finger wrong, and whilst there might well have been people in the audience still wondering what the opening fuss had been about, they rose as one to applaud her.

Troy kept his seat for the interval. Just after the bell sounded the man he'd encountered in the Stephansplatz came out from the wings and handed him another envelope.

"We can't go on meeting like this," Troy said.

But the man merely smiled and said, *Entschuldigung.*"

Inside was another concert ticket for tomorrow night, Mozart's Twenty-seventh, and a handwritten note:

"Stay in your seat when the lights go up. MV."

He grew impatient during the Sinfonia Concertante. More so during the symphony. The "Jupiter" was so well known as to be sing-along-a-Mozart and right now, for once in his life, he cared more about the mystery than the music.

The hall had emptied of all but cleaners by the time Voytek appeared, dressed in mufti—slacks and a duffel coat, clutching her music case.

She hugged him silently for a moment.

"If I say you don't know how glad I am to see you, it's only because you haven't spent the last ten years in Russia."

"That was marvellous," he said.

"Victory from the jaws of defeat, eh?"

"What happened?"

"Oh, Kutuzov had a stroke less than forty-eight hours ago. Anatoli called me yesterday, pulled a few strings, got me the necessary papers, and I was on a plane by lunchtime today. No time to rehearse, so I studied the score on the plane. Unfortunately the wrong score."

She patted the music case with her free hand.

"What were you expecting?"

"The Twenty-first."

"And you were expecting me?"

A smile, concealing more than it revealed.

He didn't press the point.

"I asked Anatoli to have one of the stage hands find you. So pleased he did."

Troy gestured at the row of seats.

"Found me, but not the other chap, eh?"

The same flickering smile.

"Oh, just a friend I thought you might like to meet. A no-show, as it happens. Deeply unreliable person. Still, I've invited him to tomorrow night's concert as well, so perhaps . . ."

The sentence trailed off in air.

"I'm flying out tomorrow. Amsterdam next stop."

"Stay, Troy. Please. It's important."

"I . . . er . . ."

"Whatever it is, get out of it. For me, Troy. Do this for me."

Troy didn't believe a word of this.

§61

Predictably, Rod was furious. He hid it well in front of his wife and children, but he spoke through gritted teeth.

"You've been trying to fuck this up all along, haven't you?"

"That's unfair. Consider that I'll owe you one. Next time I'll go anywhere you like, and I'll pay—but I have to stay on here for a day."

"Just for a day?"

"Maybe two."

"Well, if you can't make your mind up there's no point in me offering to reschedule, is there? So I'm off to Amsterdam, Freddie—and fuck you."

"Rod. This can't be helped."

"No, but it could be ameliorated. You might at least tell me why you have to stay on. But you're not going to do that, are you?"

Troy said nothing.

"Fine. You keep your trap shut. Say nothing. Drop me in it. Leave me alone with the mad sister from hell!"

"You're far from alone. You have all your immediate family with you. And you have Masha."

"She's no bloody use! What's that phrase you use for them? One dreadful woman with two bodies, isn't it? Masha's just a time bomb that hasn't gone off yet."

§62

Again, seat D17 was empty. Voytek's unreliable friend was still unreliable. Troy didn't care. The mystery was not the empty seat, it was the woman herself. She'd sent a stage hand to find him and deliver yesterday's ticket—how had she even known he was in Vienna?

None of that mattered a damn while she played. She'd send him back to London with a mission to lock himself away and listen to Mozart's Twenty-seventh with fresh ears.

In the interval, the same stage hand appeared, smiled faintly at Troy, as though embarrassed by the routine, handed Troy another envelope.

"*Wird unser Freund auch mitkommen?*" Troy asked. Will our friend be joining us?

Again all Troy received by way of reply was "*Entschuldigung.*"

It paid to know nothing.

Inside the envelope was another of her notes.

"Come to me after the Brahms. Dressing room #3. MV."

Brahms? He'd not even asked for a programme. Brahms? What Brahms?

But when the first notes, the descending and ascending thirds of what Troy thought might be the most haunting allegro in music, struck up, he knew it was the Fourth Symphony, and that the mystery of Voytek could be set to simmer while the mystery of Brahms burned.

§63

Backstage in a theatre always reminded Troy of being "backstage" in a police station. All pretence vanished. The art of illusion ceased at the frontier. No more red, no more gold, no more velvet. Nobody was wasting so much as a threepenny bit on paint or fabric. The walls were always two tones of faecal misery in high gloss, divided by a black line.

He picked his way through pockets of men in tailcoats, all smoking and laughing, as though in need of comic relief after the passacaglia angst of Brahms's last movement.

There was laughter coming from dressing room #3 as well.

He tapped at the door.

Voytek yanked it open, a glass of red wine in her hand, hugged him, kissed him.

"So glad you came. Mmm." And kissed him again.

A fat bloke in what looked like a fake beard was sitting by the illuminated dressing table, framed by twenty unshaded light bulbs, knocking back the wine.

"You remember Sir Roderick Spode, don't you, Troy?"

The unreliable friend at last.

"No," said Troy. "I'm afraid I don't."

But there was something terribly familiar about both the name and the man—the thing was . . . they just didn't go together.

The fat bloke stood up.

Pulled off the fake beard.

"Fooled ya!"

Burgess.

Guy bloody Burgess!

"Well, say something, Freddie. Or I might get the idea you're not pleased to see me."

"I'm not. It really is a gun in my pocket."

Burgess corpsed. A fit of the Guy-giggles that sprayed red wine everywhere.

For a fraction of a second Troy felt annoyance with Voytek, but he knew all along she was setting him up for something, so what did it matter now he knew?

She ducked behind the folding screen for a quick change from stage black to mufti. It seemed to Troy that she'd put off the moment till he was there—never leave a Burgess alone, they'll just break something.

Burgess was offering Troy a drink. He took it, sat down.

"It's been a while," Burgess said. "When did we last—"

"You know damn well when. You know exactly how long it's been. To the minute, I'd imagine. So stop faking."

"I've missed you."

Plaintive and wry at the same time.

Troy said nothing.

"This is where you say you've missed me. According to the social code."

"I haven't and you don't give a fuck about the social code."

This just brought on another fit of the giggles.

Voytek emerged in her duffel coat and slacks.

"I shall leave you boys to it. I have ordered sandwiches, and another bottle. The room is yours until midnight. Then they boot you out."

The look she gave Troy told him nothing.

And then she was gone.

"You came from Moscow with her?" Troy asked.

"Yes. Last minute sort of thing . . . wanted company . . . once she'd . . . as it were . . . stepped up to the podium."

"Too many hesitations, Guy. You're lying to me. Let's start again. Méret didn't ask you to come with her, at the last minute or any other, so why are you here?"

"To see you."

"No lie?"

"No lie whatsoever."

"I'm listening."

There was a badly timed tap at the door. The same stage hand who'd carried messages for Voytek came in and set down a tray for them. An open bottle of red wine. A plate of beef sandwiches.

Burgess swallowed a sandwich almost whole.

It gave Troy a minute to weigh him up. He looked grey, his neck sagged, his fingers and teeth were coppered with nicotine. His suit was filthy, but then it always had been. He'd aged fifteen years in half that time. Troy tried to remember how old he was. Perhaps three or four years older than he was himself, which still put him under fifty.

As his hand reached out for another sandwich, Troy said, "I'm still listening."

Burgess paused. A visible if momentary hesitation in his eyes.

The plate changed direction in mid-air.

Troy took the proffered morsel.

"I want to come home."

"Yes," Troy said softly. "I'd guessed as much."

"I miss it all. I miss London. I miss the clubs. I miss the pubs. I miss the Dog & Duck. I miss the Salisbury. I miss the Reform. I miss the RAC. I miss the Gargoyle. I miss that bloke in the pub in Holborn who could fart the national anthem. I miss Tommy Trinder. I miss Max Miller. I miss Billy Cotton. I miss Mantovani. I miss my mother. Oh God, I miss my mother. I miss my flannelette stripy pyjamas. I miss the weather. I miss fog. I miss drizzle. Who would ever think anyone in their right mind could miss drizzle? I miss Penguin books. I miss the pelicans in St. James's Park. I miss the blow jobs in St. James's Park. I miss the *News of the World*. I miss the *Daily Mirror*. I miss sniffing the fresh inkiness of the late edition London evening papers. I miss the *The Beano*. I miss Desperate Dan. I miss Wilfred Pickles and Mabel. I miss *Much-Binding-in-the-Marsh*. I miss Kenneth Horne. I miss Stinker Murdoch. I miss Arthur Askey. I miss *Mrs. Dale's Diary*. I still worry about Jim. I miss Pathé News. I miss Bob Danvers-Walker. I miss the Proms. I miss Malcolm Sargent. I miss Pomp and Circumstance. I miss the Gang Show. I haven't had a "ging gang goolie goolie wotcha" in years. I miss nipping down east for jellied eels and a bit of rough. I miss the circle jerks in that gents in the Holloway Road. I miss the randy guardsmen. I miss the sexy sailors. I miss chopped liver at Bloom's. I miss egg and chips in Endell Street.

I miss the soufflés at Boulestin's. I miss breakfast at the Ritz. I miss lunch at the Caprice. I miss tea at the Café Royal. I miss cocktails at the Criterion. I miss crawling round all the bars on the Circle Line. I miss getting tipsy at King's Cross. I miss getting legless at Sloane Square. I miss pissing off the platform at Liverpool Street. I miss the number 19 bus. I miss Eccles cakes. I miss Mars Bars. I miss Walnut Whips. I miss sherbert fountains. I miss licorice allsorts. I miss Bertie Bassett. I miss the enamel golliwog you get if you save enough marmalade labels. I miss the little blue bag of salt at the bottom of a bag of crisps. I miss Ovaltine. I miss HP Sauce. I miss chips with mushy peas. I miss the tickle in the nose when you first slosh the vinegar on the peas. I miss steak and kidney pud. I miss spotted dick. I miss apple charlotte. I miss custard with everything. I miss toffee apples and brandy snaps. I miss pork scratchings with a pint of mild. I miss roast beef and brussels sprouts—"

"You've missed out tripe and onions."

"Noooo!—I get all the tripe and onions I can eat. Russia is the world capital of boiled offal."

"Guy, I don't wish to sound heartless, but what do you expect me to do about it?"

"Ask, Freddie. Just ask. Just ask them back in Britain. In the absence of an honest broker, be the honest copper. Just . . . ask them."

"Them?"

"You know everybody."

"I don't think I do, Guy."

"But you could ask your brother."

"Let's leave Rod out of this, shall we?"

"Then . . . there's that pal of yours at the embassy."

"My, but you have done your homework. You're referring to Gus Fforde, I take it? What took you so long? Why do we have to get through brussels sprouts and drizzle before you bring up Gus's name?"

"You will ask him?"

"I could. I could walk around to the embassy and report this meeting. But you could do that for yourself."

"No . . . no . . . I couldn't. Honestly, I couldn't. This needs to be done . . . properly."

"Is that what the Russians have told you? Is that their condition?"

Burgess shrugged.

"Leaving was a cock-up. Who'd want my return to be as cack-handed?"

The logic was obvious. Troy didn't need to ask. Burgess would stay on neutral ground until some kind of political or legal safety net was in place. He could imagine the conditions—immunity from prosecution in return for a full confession, which would, in the end, be anything but full.

"Guy, if I do this, there's one thing you need to assure me of or we're both wasting our time."

"What's that?"

"That Russia really will let you leave."

The hands flapped in the air, as though inviting contradiction that would never be made manifest.

"Well . . . they've let me get this far. I even have a British passport in the name of Spode. Fake, of course, but a good one."

"You realise, Five will want to de-brief you?"

"Of course."

"And the KGB are happy about that?"

"As I said . . . they've let me get this far . . . and whilst I don't know who or where, they can hardly be far away even as we speak, can they? There's nothing happening they don't know about."

That was too true to be anything but painful. Paranoia was its own reward. Without a doubt, someone would be following Burgess, and if they were following Burgess they were now following Troy.

It required little thought, but Troy thought it as well if he gave the appearance of thought.

"OK. I'll do what I can."

"Splendid."

"Yes, I am."

That brought a smile to his face. Burgess's mood lightened. Troy thought he might get the giggles again. Instead, appetite restored, he swigged red wine and wolfed sandwiches and asked a thousand insignificant questions.

"Do you see anything of the old crowd? Y'know . . . Guy Liddell . . . Goronwy Rees . . . I don't suppose you've seen anything of my brother, Nigel . . ."

And the list went on and on.
Troy was patient.
Midnight could not be far off.

§64

In the morning Troy called on Gus at the British Embassy.

"I need a secure line to MI5 in London."

"May I ask why?"

"Vienna has a visitor."

"Stop being coy."

"Guy Burgess is holed up at the Imperial not half a mile from here."

"Oh fucking hell!"

Gus reached for the phone.

"Give me a moment, Freddie. Hello . . . yes . . . put me through to Leconfield House on the scrambler."

He put one hand over the mouthpiece.

"Do you want anyone in particular?"

"You'll get a duty officer, but the man I want is Jordan Younghusband."

"Hello? Yes . . . Fforde, Vienna Station here. I have Chief Superintendent Troy for Jordan Younghusband. Yes, yes. I quite understand. Yes, it is rather urgent. Thank you."

He put the phone down.

"Jordan's in the building. Somewhere. He'll call us. Might take a while. I'll ring down for coffee. You can tell me all about it while we wait."

Over the next half hour Troy was as frank with Gus as his sense of caution allowed. He did not mention Méret Voytek. He wouldn't mention Méret Voytek unless he really had to.

"It's a mess," said Gus simply.

"Why's that?"

"Burgess is trouble wherever he goes. If I had a choice about his what d'ye call it? . . . de-defection . . . I'd rather he'd shown up in Berlin or Timbuctoo . . . anywhere but Vienna."

"Do you know Jordan?"

"Yep."

"Then we'll agree, he's quite capable of handling Guy."

The phone rang.

Gus listened for a minute and passed the handset to Troy.

"Jordan?"

"Yep."

"Freddie, what's up, old son?"

Troy told him. Jordan heard him out without questions.

Then he said, "I'll need to run this Upstairs. But I'll be on a plane out as soon as I can. Just hang on to our friend and I'll take over."

"Jordan. I'm leaving today. I want nothing to do with this. It's spook nonsense. Worse, it's Burgess nonsense."

"Freddie. When Upstairs hears this there won't just be ripples, there'll be a tidal wave. Please, just stay there . . . till I can get there. Overnight at the most. Honestly. I'll call you back as soon as it's clear what happens next."

He rang off.

"I really don't want to do this, Gus."

"All rather depends on one's sense of obligation, doesn't it?"

"What, Queen and Country?"

"I was thinking rather more of your obligations to Jordan."

"And I was trying not to."

"Tell you what. Let's give it another half hour, another pot of java, and see if he gets back to us before lunch. We can forget the elephant in the room and just catch up. So much seems to have happened since we last met."

A pleasanter half hour passed. They rehashed the sins of Sasha, the farce of Troy thinking foreign agents had followed him halfway across Europe only to find them waiting in Vienna, and Troy told Gus enough about Shirley Foxx to bring a twinkle to his eye.

"This could be the real thing, eh, Freddie?"

"Perhaps," said Troy.

The phone rang.

Gus held it out to Troy.

"Jordan?"

And in a stage whisper, pulling a face, Gus replied, "Onions!"

Oh shit.

"Can you hear me?"

"Of course I can."

"Good. Stay put!"

"What?"

"I said, stay put. Sit on that bugger, Burgess, till the bloke from Five gets there."

"No . . . no . . . Stan, it's got fuck all to do with you, me, or Scotland Yard. I'm coming home this afternoon."

"You're a serving Met copper. You'll take orders. And the order is 'Stay put!' I will not have this coming back to be laid at our door. Those twats in the Branch lost Burgess in '51. I will not have it said that Scotland Yard let Guy Burgess escape . . . twice!"

The line went dead.

Troy said, "Ouch!"

"Quite."

"Who would have thought Stanley Onions had a nark inside Leconfield House?"

"I think this calls for an early lunch, don't you?"

§65

They walked back into the Innere Stadt, to the Café Frauenhuber in Himmelpfortgasse, home in its time to Mozart, Beethoven, and Schubert.

"Can you imagine a London street named Heaven's Gate, Freddie? Seems so un-English."

"I'm sure it does. But there used to be a synagogue of that name in the East End. Bombed out in the Blitz. I was there when it happened."

"Ah . . . yes. You told me about that. Don't think you ever named the place before. Well, it's not that I'm trying to bring back bad memories for you. But they know me here. If anyone calls for me at the embassy, the embassy will phone here and the waiter will give me the nod."

The nod came around twelve thirty.

Gus unfolded a note at the table.

"Jordan says he'll be on a noon plane out of London tomorrow. He'll call us in the morning if there's any hold-up. Otherwise, meet him at the airport around three fifteen."

"And then I can go home?"

"He doesn't say."

"Perhaps I could get on the plane as he gets off?"

"Nice try, Freddie, but I think we can assume he wants you to introduce him to Burgess."

"Why? He can hardly fail to recognise him."

"Think, Freddie. Although it might pain you, try for a moment to think like a spook. You have been first contact. That matters. Matters hugely."

"The duckling emerging from the egg?"

"Precisely. The perfect metaphor. You are Guy Burgess's Mother Duck."

"Guy Burgess?

　　　—Mother Duck?

　　　　　—Oh fuck!"

§66

Troy took Burgess to a traditional Viennese restaurant—the Café Landtmann.

They sat in a red booth, a burgundy island in a sea of silver mirrors.

Burgess stuck his nose in the menu.

Troy ordered wine.

"You've eaten here before?" Burgess asked.

"A couple of times, yes."

"What would you recommend?"

"Bangers. Classic Austrian food."

"Nothing wrong with a good banger."

"Ask for the sausage plate. They'll bring you a variety. Try them with black bread and goulash gravy. Think I'll plump for the trout."

The wine arrived first. By the time they had bangers and trout in front of them, Burgess had all but finished the first bottle and Troy asked for a second.

He'd always taken Burgess for a bit of a trencherman—his shape alone bespoke a man who liked his grub—but it seemed to Troy that he cut up his food, rather in the American style, nibbled at it, and for the most part just pushed it around his plate. The wine, on the other hand, was necked effortlessly. His lips went slobbery and his eyes had that maudlin look of barely contained misery.

"I do miss England, y'know."

"Yes. You told me last night. At length."

"But it occurs to me . . . I have expectations that may be too high. I mean, it's been seven years . . . how much has the old place changed?"

"I can't answer that. I'm in it . . . so I don't really notice it. And of course England may have expectations of you."

"Doubt that."

"No, really. Can't you see your memoirs in the Sunday papers in six parts . . . *Guy Burgess—My Life and Hard Times*?"

"Take the piss all you want, Freddie. I shall say fuck all. When I get back to England, England will see a new Guy Burgess."

"Sober?"

"Silent."

"Anonymous?"

"Invisible."

"Discretion?"

"Soul of."

"No more cottaging? No more gents bogs at Paddington Station?"

"Absolutely not. I'll stick to Marylebone. But . . . seriously."

The pause dragged out. The ever-mobile fork stopped stirring at his rapidly cooling bangers'n'mash. His left hand gripped the stem of his wine glass and for several moments all he did was stare at the tablecloth.

When he looked up the sadness in his eyes was brimming over.

"Seriously. I wonder if I'll get what I really want."

"I take it being back in England isn't the be-all and end-all. Simple though that would be. So, what do you want?"

"I want . . . I want . . . I want . . ."

He paused so meaningfully Troy took it as his cue and prompted. "Yes?"

". . . To be allowed . . . to be allowed . . . to fade away."

At last they'd got there.

Troy knew what Burgess meant, yet the devil had his advocate.

"Anonymous . . . silent . . . discreet . . . all the things you are in Russia. You don't need to come home for that. If you want to be yesterday's man, yesterday's spy, well Russia's the place, isn't it? In England, Guy, in England you'll always be a headline."

"No . . . noo . . . nooo . . . stoppit! You don't know the pain I'm in. Yes, of course, I'm yesterday's spy to them. Neither use nor bloody ornament. But anonymous? God, no. They watch everything I do. I can't take a piss they do not know about."

"So you want to fade away?"

"To fade away, to be allowed to fade away would be bliss. To be a nobody would be very heaven."

Troy ordered a third bottle, pushed his own plate away, and suggested the waiter bring the dessert of the day.

"Do you remember when we sat on the roof of my house during the Blitz?"

"'Course I do. I may be pissed but there's nothing wrong with my memory."

Troy felt there might be much wrong with Burgess's memory but let it pass.

"You thought we should pray, and as we neither of us knew any prayers you sang a hymn."

"Da da da daah . . . that one. I think you said it was Haydn. Forgotten the words. But I can hum it. Da da daaah da daaah da dada . . ."

"Fading is the worldling's pleasure."

"Right. I asked you what a worldling was and you told me I was. So . . . it's my right to fade away, isn't it? I'm not one of the whatchermacallit?"

"Zion's children. Those who know solid joy."

"Solid joy? The kind you can touch? Absofuckinglootly not. Joy eludes me. I am a worldling fading. I know not joy."

"Does it really matter where you fade away as long as you fade away?"

"I see. You think coming home's a mistake?"

"It might be. England expects."

"Expects what."

"I don't know. But it will expect."

"And if I don't come home?"

"Stay in Russia. Learn to fit in. Learn the language. Let the country you adopted adopt you."

Burgess paused again as more wine and two portions of lemon tart arrived. Stared down into his tart accusingly, as though it had sinned against him.

Softly, "I hate Russia. I fucking hate it."

He looked up.

Troy concluded the tart was blameless. He was probably the one to blame.

"It all smacks of 'made your bed, so lie in it.' A cliché I have done so much to earn I should get a royalty every time it's used. But—it's easy for you to say, Freddie. You're one of *them*, aren't you? You speak the lingo. You'd fit in. You'd get all the anonymity that I can't. You could go into a gents and know you're not being watched. They'd think you were one them . . . not one of *those*."

"Easy"? Troy did not like "easy." Time to kick back with a few home truths.

"What's my first language, Guy?"

Burgess looked baffled. Gave the question more drunken thought than it required.

"I s'ppose I should say Russian, but it's got to be a trick question, hasn't it? Otherwise you wouldn't bloody ask. Oh, I dunno. Welsh? Esperanto? Swafuckinghili?"

"My first language is probably French, because it was my mother's first language. My father was a great advocate of the English language. He said to me, 'Forget that Russian has twenty words for snow, English has twenty words for penis. How could you not love a language so rich in obscenity?' And mostly he spoke to his children in English. Russian . . . Russian was the ambient language of the household, it was on like a light bulb or a radiator. My grandfather spoke it, wrote it, and never learnt a word of English other than 'fuck off' and 'kiss my arse,' which my father taught him in much the same way you'd teach a parrot to swear. My Russian's as good as my English but it comes a poor third on that scale, on a scale of identity."

It was too long a speech. The look on Burgess's face told Troy he didn't get it.

"Guy, it's this simple. I don't think I'd fit into Khrushchev's Russia any better than you would. It would be an effort for me. It will be an effort for you. Perhaps one you might make. I would say I have only one advantage."

"Which is?"

"A personal invitation from Comrade Khrushchev."

"You know him?"

"I've met him. I was bodyguard-cum-interpreter-cum-spy on his English tour in '56. Just about the time you and Maclean were surfacing to tell your pack of lies to the western press."

"Had to tell them something."

"No, you didn't."

"We did, we did. If I was to, as you say, surface, then a statement needed to be made, and I needed to surface because I wanted communication with England, which meant the English knowing where I was. I wanted to be able to write to my mother with a return address in the top right-hand corner . . . I wanted my stuff . . . I wanted my books . . . I wanted my harmonium . . . I wanted . . ."

The booze was wearing Burgess down rather rapidly. Troy wasn't sure how long he'd stay awake, and was damn sure he'd need someone to put him to bed.

"What was wrong with telling them the truth?"

"Every bloody thing. Betrayal. Too many people still to betray. Names not to be named. Who's the third man? All that kind of crap. The press never seem to relent. Who's the third man? Who's the third man? Do they honestly expect me to name names?"

"No. Not you. Somebody, not you."

"Who's the third man? Who's the third man? Bloody hell . . . who was the first man?"

"I rather think you were."

"Why? Because me name begins with B? Do we take our spies in alphabetical order, like calling the bloody register in a prep school?

Arkengarthdale? Present, sir. Arseworthy? Present, sir. Burgess? Defected, sir. Six of the best when the boy gets back! Ah well, you can always rely on the alphabet, never lets you down."

"And Maclean would be number two?"

"Would he really? Maclean's a shit? A turd? A number two! Well, whaddya know? Go on, then, ask me who was number three."

"Fine," said Troy. Let's play the game. "Who's on thoid?"

"Thoid?"

"Abbott and Costello."

"Fuck me, are they spies too? No, the third man was Philby."

"Surprise, surprise."

"Lowest form of wit, y'know . . . sarcasm."

"Was there a fourth man?"

"I thought you said some other bugger would be the one to name names?"

"Humour me."

"No, you humour me. You . . . you sc . . . sc . . . scratch my back and I'll scratch yours."

"You don't think asking me to get you home is a big enough scratch? Guy, it will leave scars. And I've quite enough of those already."

Burgess swigged more wine. Looked huffy in a drunken sort of way. Then the glass went down with a clunk, and he snapped out a single word: "Blunt."

He paused, breathed in deeply, as though gathering energy and girding loin.

"If ya must know. Blunt. Blunt, bloody Blunt."

His voice dropped to a growl of a whisper.

"D'ye know Anthony is second cousin to the Queen!"

A moment's reflection set in.

"Or was it the old Queen? Queen Mary? Whatever. Talk about fuckin' treason. It's a bit like selling your virgin sister to the gyppos."

"And the fifth . . ."

Troy knew he'd answer this. It was too obvious to both of them for Burgess to want to duck it. Whether he could tease him past a fifth, to the unknown sixth, Troy did not know. He could but try.

"Charlie. My ole pal . . . your ole pal, your ole school chum . . . Charlie Leigh-Hunt. Good ole Charlie. I do miss him. The best boozing companion a man could have . . . unless totty hove into view of course, then he was off up some tart's skirt like a rat up a wotsit."

Burgess was woozy now, his eyes swam like goldfish in a dirty bowl.

"I hesitate," Troy said without hesitation, "to ask if there's a sixth man."

"Sixth man? Siiiiixth maaaaan?"

He put as many syllables into the phrase as Edith Evans had put into "haaaanndbaaag?"

"Sixth man? Nosey parker . . . nosey parker . . . b . . . b. . . b . . . bub . . . bub . . ."

And with that he fell face down into his lemon tart.

Rain stopped play.

§67

London: The Palace of Westminster

There were perks to being on the front bench, even in opposition. One perk of Rod Troy being Shadow Home Secretary was an office he didn't have to share with anyone. Not a fellow MP, not a Parliamentary Private Secretary. Rod had a Parliamentary Private Secretary, housed somewhere down the corridor and off to the left a bit. Occasionally he got lost trying to find him.

It was always better if the PPS found him.

When Rod got into his office around nine fifteen, Iain Stuart-Bell, who had been his PPS since 1956, was waiting for him.

An affable young man, only just thirty, who'd been one of the youngest MPs elected in '55—handsome, tall, always slightly nervous, and with an engaging, disarming Dundee accent. One day, and not that far off, when the war no longer mattered and "what did you do in the war?" would be a question no longer asked, men like Iain would run Britain. It was their turn. All he had to do was hang on to his seat.

"I'm afraid I have to resign."

"Eh? What?"

"Resign. I'm really very sorry about this."

"You mean quit being my PPS?"

"No, I mean quit Parliament."

"In God's name, why?"

"To save you and the party from the scandal."

"Iain, you're talking in riddles. What fucking scandal?"

"No . . . it's not a fucking scandal . . . it's a cocksucking scandal."

Rod dropped his briefcase onto the floor with a thump. Slumped into his chair, not looking Stuart-Bell in the eye. On a deeply sub-conscious level, somewhere in the Freudian catacombs of the mind, he'd always dreaded this moment. He'd known on that same level that Stuart-Bell was queer, he'd never been certain how queer. And there was no way he'd ever have taken his brother's advice—"Just ask."

Until now.

"Tell me," he said, still not looking at Stuart-Bell.

"It was about ten o'clock last night. It had been a long sitting, and by half past nine it was really rather obvious that there'd be no vote at the end of it, so I sloped off. Down Birdcage Walk and into the park. A route I take quite often, because . . ."

He ground to a halt.

"Because?"

"Because . . . one can be pretty certain of meeting the odd off-duty guardsman."

"Odd in the same way you're odd?"

"Yes."

"Who blew who?"

Even to his own ears Rod thought he sounded like an owl saying this.

"I blew him."

"I see."

"It's what I . . . like."

"So you've done this before?"

"Lots."

"Red jacket and busby?"

"Good grief, no, that would be asking to get caught. No, they're always in khaki. This boy was a private in the Coldstreams."

"And how did you get caught?"

"Two bobbies with bike lamps. They'd probably been watching him for a while. I was just unlucky."

"Did money change hands?"

"No . . . would that matter?"

"It would add soliciting to indecency so . . . yes. Are you up in front of the beak?"

"Today at eleven."

"Then I think you'd better apply for the Chiltern Hundreds before you go. I'll tell Gaitskell. He'll hit the roof."

"He turns a blind eye to so many things."

"He turns a blind eye to Tom Driberg's antics, if that's what you mean. Driberg's led a charmed life. You haven't."

"He really has blown guardsmen in busbies and red tunics—and he's got away with it."

"Oh Iain, I do wish you hadn't told me that."

§68

The Prime Minister had more than one PPS, and the one who now stuck his head around the door was Toby or Tony somebody, and was utterly confident as he spoke that Rod was alone, enjoying his perk.

"Sir Rodyon?"

Rod wished they wouldn't call him that. But how do you unteach good manners?

"Ah . . . Tony?"

"Tim, actually, but no matter. The PM asks if you'd care to take tea with him at four."

"Today?"

"Yes. Today."

"Where? Sorry, I mean delighted, of course. But where exactly?"

"At Number 10. In the PM's apartment. The copper on the door will let you in. Top floor. Just walk up."

And with that he was gone.

Rod had been to 10 Downing Street many times. After the war, newly elected, Labour in power, he had been one of the "new Labour bright boys," and an occasional visitor. Someone to be shown off. By the end of the forties, holding a sub-cabinet appointment at the Air Ministry, he had become a frequent visitor. In opposition, having known Winston Churchill all his life, having witnessed the spats between Churchill and his father, Alex, he was sometimes the token socialist invited as leavening at international get-togethers. But, he'd never been to the PM's private apartment, and he'd not been to No. 10 since Macmillan became Prime Minister almost two years ago.

An invitation to tea at No. 10 was one thing. Tea in the apartment quite another. Most of Downing Street being offices, what few realised was that the second most powerful man in the Western World lived in an apartment not much bigger than a council flat in Debden or Haringey. If Macmillan asked him upstairs, it could only mean one thing. Privacy.

"Mind how you go, sir," said the copper who'd let him in. "The bannister's a bit wonky. If you ask me the whole place is falling apart."

Rod climbed past the portraits of the great (Palmerston, Melbourne, Gladstone, Disraeli) and the disgraced (Chamberlain, Eden) to find Macmillan at the top of the stairs, tea pot in hand. He was in mufti, a raggy cardigan and old slippers.

"Ah, bang on time. I've just this minute put the kettle on."

"Prime Minister, surely you have someone to do that for you?"

"Apparently not. Take a seat. I'm sure I have a packet of ginger nuts around here somewhere."

Rod sat down, little short of shocked. It was a big enough kitchen, but . . . what was the word? . . . tatty, it was tatty. It looked much as it must have done in the twenties. A scrubbed pine table, cracked linoleum, a single shaded light bulb dangling from the low ceiling. Every Ideal Home Exhibition, the annual pride of the *Daily Mail*, that effervescent display of the latest, shiniest gadgetry of household convenience, had passed this room by. It struck Rod as ironic that most of those gadgets were described as "Labour Saving," and were conspicuous in their absence.

"No ginger nuts," Macmillan was muttering. "We'll have to make do with Arrowroots."

He lifted the whistling kettle off the gas ring and sloshed water into the teapot, which he crowned with a hand-knitted cosy, patriotic in red, white, and blue. Surely Lady Dorothy did not knit?

Macmillan read his mind.

"Present from a loyal voter in Stockton many years ago. Getting a bit worn now. Just like this house. If you ask me the whole place is falling apart."

He glanced around as though seeking confirmation in the faded paintwork and scuffed skirting board, then he reached out an arm to the dresser and handed Rod a single sheet of paper.

"Got this last night."

Rod read it. "Top Secret." His heart sank. Oh fuck.

"I see why we're meeting up here."

"Quite. You got back from Vienna when exactly?"

"Just last night. The trip ended in Amsterdam, pretty much on time."

"And your brother stayed on in Vienna?"

"Yes. He didn't say why. I asked and he wouldn't tell me. I had been puzzled . . . until now."

"It's a bit of a pickle," said Macmillan with classic Macmillian understatement. "But young Fred seems to have done the right thing, so far. Contacted the embassy, got through to some chap at MI5."

"So far?"

"Rod, this isn't just a courtesy call. There's something I need from you. Reassurance."

"You're asking me to vouch for Freddie?"

"That would be one way of putting it. You know as well as I do he has . . . shall we say . . . a reputation for recklessness. The chap from the Branch who dogs my every footstep tells me that Freddie and that subordinate of his are known as the Tearaway Toffs at Scotland Yard."

"I can't deny any of that. And I'm not sure I can vouch for him, particularly as I don't know what it is you want me to vouchsafe."

Macmillan poured tea, split a packet of Arrowroots onto a saucer.

"Feel free to dunk. I always do."

Rod waited. No idea of where this conversation was headed.

"It's like this," Macmillan continued. "I met Burgess just the once. At your father's dining table. Can't deny the wit, but his manners were deplorable, and his personal habits disgusting. You could raise a crop of spuds in the dirt under his fingernails."

Rod was wincing inwardly. Burgess pretty well disgusted him too, and with some success he'd managed to avoid him between dinner and defection, but this seemed like a moment to make agreement seem tacit rather than articulate. Mac was surely heading for a point? Some point? Any point?

"I don't want Burgess back. There'll be no de-brief, no attempt to bring him in from the cold. He burned his bridges in '51. He can just bugger off back to Moscow. I don't want Burgess back—at any price."

At last.

"And Freddie? He's just the unfortunate middleman?"

"Indeed, he is. But Burgess chose Frederick Troy because he knows him."

"They were never the best of friends. Let's not shoot the messenger."

"All the same . . . I don't want your brother adopting Burgess as a cause. As I recall, your brother is very like your father. A man with many causes, you will agree."

"My father edited newspapers, Prime Minister. The many causes went with the job. My brother is a copper, that's his job, that's his cause. And he is fiercely loyal to it."

"Good. Good. Then let's say no more about it. Your brother comes home. Burgess goes back to his igloo in Moscow, and we shall forget he ever asked to return. Now . . . about young Stuart-Bell and the Cold-stream guardsman. At least it wasn't a Grenadier. A small mercy there."

Rod's inner voice uttered a painful, "Oh God."

His outer voice said, "Ah, you heard?"

"Will he go quietly?"

"He *has* gone, Prime Minister."

"Good. Pity, all the same. Always liked him. Fellow Scot, after all. I'm sure you and Hugh had high hopes of him. But . . . awful timing."

"In what way?"

"The debate on homosexual law reform next week. Free vote. I dunno which way it'll go, but one of our own up in front of the beak for . . . for whatever . . . and please don't tell me . . . it muddies the waters, don't it? We should all be thinking about the issue in the abstract, a matter of principle and law, not individuals. Instead, you'll be thinking about poor Stuart-Bell and I shall have difficulty not thinking about that bugger Burgess."

Macmillan had neatly linked the two issues together, as though they were two pieces of the same jigsaw puzzle. Rod did not see the puzzle. He saw coincidence and nothing more, and it would be a while before he attached any further significance to his conversation with the Prime Minister. But then, the old man could be amazingly elliptical, subtle to the point of obscurity, to the point where half the nation had willingly misunderstood his "never had it so good" speech.

However, there was nothing elliptical about "I don't want Burgess back—at any price."

§69

Vienna

The next morning Troy and Gus sat at the embassy, both unsure whether they were expecting a call or not.

But Jordan called at nine thirty.

"Troy, I'm afraid I won't be coming."

"I'm not handling the bugger alone!"

"Just hear me out. We're sending someone. You won't be on your own. It just won't be me."

"Then who?"

"Dunno yet. I was never the best choice. Not my area of expertise. It will mean a delay, though."

"How long?"

"You'll have to babysit him at least another day."

Troy said nothing.

"Troy? Troy? Are you still there?"

"Jordan. I'm not happy about this."

"Me neither. I was all packed for couple of days away. Just keep tabs on him, and get what you can out of him."

"I am not—no, I *will* not interrogate him!"

"Sorry. Bit of a lapse on my part. Far too cheeky. Just a throwaway remark. Ignore me. Troy, just whip the old fraud out to dinner and relax. I'll call Gus when my replacement's on his way."

"Thank you, I'll be sending Five the bill. Jordan, there is one more thing. Please tell Foxx what's happening. All she knows is I had to stay on here. I don't want her kept in the dark any longer."

"You didn't tell her?"

"What was to tell? That I'd received an anonymous invitation? Enough to alarm her, and no reassurance I could give."

"If you're sure she can be discreet, I'll tell her everything. Let our fat friend take the blame."

"Don't worry, she's already sitting on secrets."

"And Rod?"

"Rod doesn't need to know."

They hung up.

Gus sat at his desk, listening on an extension, the last to put down the telephone.

"Did you get all that?"

"Oh yes, Freddie."

"And?"

"He's been pulled."

"In what way is that different from being replaced?"

"Just a feeling. Jordan's a senior field agent. My idea of just the right bloke to de-brief Burgess. The 'not my area of expertise' was a bit disingenuous to my ears. Still, could be wrong. You never know."

"And now I'm stuck with Burgess for another day and another night."

"Love to help out. I'd be intrigued to meet him, but it would be terribly bad form to have official embassy contact with him."

"You're missing very little. He's the shell of the man I used to know."

"In fact . . . it would be a bit of a sticky wicket if he'd come to us direct. Right now you're invaluable to both sides."

"Yep. That's me. Piggy in the middle."

"Cheer up . . . you might get a medal for services to Queen and Country."

"Or six months in the Scrubs. No Gus, whatever I do now it won't be appreciated. And I can't face a third night with him. I'll go round to the Imperial now and tell him it won't be happening tonight, but that's all."

§70

"At least have a drink."

"Guy—it isn't even noon."

"It's noon in Moscow."

Irrefutable logic.

"Just the one."

One became two, became three. Troy kept swapping his full glasses for Burgess's empties and by half past two Burgess's head lolled back against the cushions, exhaling his Scotch-and-garlic patented halitosis, and Troy snuck off silently. If the staff at the Imperial couldn't handle a comatose drunk in their lobby in the middle of the afternoon they were in the wrong business. All they had to do was ease off his shoes and, when he awoke, remind him of his room number.

§71

The person he most wanted to see now was the person he felt oddest about seeing. He felt, with no apparent logic, that he and Voytek had compromised one another.

He killed an afternoon walking around in drizzle, hopped from café to café, and in the evening bought a ticket for the Konzerthaus. He sat at the back of the stalls, far enough away never to be spotted, and listened to Voytek play Mozart's "Jeunehomme" concerto, the Ninth in E flat—one that he'd never much bothered with before.

The second half was Beethoven's Second Symphony. One few orchestras would ever tackle. Troy found he could live without it and left at the interval.

He turned in at the Sacher, ridiculously early. Found himself buzzing from too much strong Viennese coffee. Found he'd no interest in any of the novels in his travelling bag. Lay back. Locked his fingers behind his head and watched the rippling reflections of street lamps in rain play across the ceiling as curling ribbons of light.

§72

Troy wondered who to curse for the brevity of the note in his hand. Gus for taking it down so curtly, or Jordan for being so elliptical in the first place.

All it said was: "5 p.m. Schwechat. Blaine."

He'd caught a cab for the ten-mile drive out from the city centre and sat in one of the airport's makeshift buildings, little better than a British post-war prefab, wishing he'd brought a warmer coat and thicker gloves.

He could hardly miss Blaine. One runway, few landings, and when the BEA flight from Heathrow touched down, only seven passengers.

He could hardly miss Blaine. He was huge. A least six feet four. Everything about him was big—from ears like the doors on a Rover 90, a nose Jimmy Durante might be envious of, and soft hands the size of frying pans that gripped Troy's like a closing clam.

"Bill Blaine," he said, in the same received pronunciation as Troy. "Old firm."

"Troy," said Troy. "Even older firm."

"Ha, ha. Jolly good!"

And the big blue eyes lit up behind their thick spectacles in a way that made Troy think he might well be able to like Bill Blaine if only he could be bothered, but he couldn't. All he wanted of Blaine was to dump Guy Burgess on him and have done.

In the cab Blaine attempted a little small talk.

"I'm surprised we haven't met before."

"Well, my job doesn't much overlap with yours," Troy lied.

"No. I meant personally . . . rather . . . socially. Your sister's a pal of my sister-in-law. They go back years. To schooldays, I think."

Troy didn't ask which sister. One could have quite enough of sisters, and of late he had come to feel about sisters the way Bertie Wooster felt about aunts. He changed the subject.

"Will you be escorting Burgess back to England?"

"If all goes according to plan, yes. I have that authority."

"Do you also have a passport for him?"

"No. I mean . . . Good Lord . . . no one thought of that."

"I think you should know he's travelling on a ringer."

"Eh? A ringer?"

"A fake. A Russian fake of a British passport. He hardly speaks a word of Russian, after all, so they couldn't give him one of theirs. I haven't actually seen it, but he assures me it's a good one, and certainly the Austrians haven't spotted it as phony."

"In his own name?"

"Now, that would ring a few alarm bells. No, he calls himself Sir Roderick Spode."

"Hmm. I suppose you have to admire his nerve, and his wit. He seems fond of those initials. He ducked out of England in '51 calling himself Roger Styles. Of course, it's possible he won't need a passport. I just stick him in the diplomatic bag."

"Is that safe?"

"Oh, it's only a metaphorical bag. Wouldn't want the old bugger to suffocate now, would we?"

§73

The embassy had provided Blaine with a guest room. By the time he had dropped his suitcase, gone into a closed-door chat with Gus—Troy cooling his heels in the lobby, only too delighted not to be included—it was seven thirty.

Blaine emerged from Gus's office, with just his briefcase, looking a trifle flustered.

"It's going to be a stinker of a night," Gus said. "Rain and more rain. There'll be a cab at the door in five minutes. If the evening proves to be a long one, I'll see you both in the morning."

"What?" said Troy. "You bloody well won't. I'm off as soon as the dog sees the rabbit."

"Freddie, please. See that Bill gets to the Imperial in one piece, and be so kind as to escort him back. He doesn't know Vienna, do you Bill?"

"'Fraid I don't. Not my beat, as it were."

"That's OK. Every cab driver in Vienna knows Vienna."

Gus took him by the arm, steered him into a huddle.

"Freddie. Just do this. Need I remind you? Egg, duckling, Mother Duck."

"Make that Mother Goose and we've got a fucking panto! Which is pretty much what this feels like."

"Just do it!"

It was a short hop to the Imperial.

Troy said, "Surely you've met Burgess?"

"Oh yes. Bumped into him a few times during my years with Five. He always seemed to be turning up. Proverbial bad penny. But even before that, we overlapped at Cambridge. Can't say I knew him, but his set were very high profile, always being seen, always wanting to be seen."

"Then you probably overlapped with my brother too."

"Yes. But I didn't know him either. We never really overlapped in what we did. He was very much Cambridge Union and debating."

"And you weren't?"

"No, I rowed."

I might have guessed, thought Troy.

"A blue in 1930. We beat Oxford by two lengths. Nineteen minutes nine seconds. Pretty good time. Second fastest since the end of the war, but in '34 we took more than a minute off that. Of course, I'd come down by then . . ."

Troy tuned out.

§74

Burgess was his usual dishevelled self as he opened the door. If he remembered Blaine from their Cambridge days nothing in his face showed it. But, why would a man like Guy Burgess ever notice a Cambridge "blue"? A nice, muscular arse notwithstanding, "blue" was just a four-letter word to Burgess and so was "bore."

"Mr. Blaine," Troy said. "I'll be on the floor below. Room 707. Just knock on the door when you're ready to leave."

As Blaine stepped into the room, Burgess looked blankly at Troy. He'd nothing to say. Just as well, there was nothing Troy wanted to hear.

§75

Voytek seemed surprised to see him.

"How did you know I'd be here?"

"I'm a detective. On Wednesdays you only play a matinee. Besides, I asked at the desk on my way in."

"Are . . . what do I call it . . . are 'things' happening?"

"Things are happening even as we speak. MI5 are upstairs de-briefing Guy."

"Ah. I've been through that. It's wheels within wheels, circles in circles. You learn fifty different ways to say the same thing. But tell me, are we just killing time?"

"We are and we aren't. I'd say I've a couple of hours, but I wanted to talk to you anyway."

"Then let us walk."

"It's still wet . . . drizzling as I came in."

"I don't care."

§76

They stepped out into the brightly lit Kärntner Ring, one of the wide boulevards created when some emperor or another had decided Vienna could at last do without its city walls.

A tram rattled by at slow speed and deafening volume, and when something close to silence resumed, she said, "I missed you yesterday. I wanted you to come to the concert."

"I was there."

"You mean you hid?"

"I suppose I did."

"From me?"

"From the questions I feel I must ask you."

"And now you're not hiding?"

She drew her coat tighter about her, dug her hands deep into her pockets, and tapped her forehead gently against his chest like a bird bobbing on its wooden perch.

"Then ask me. I've had ten years of distance from you. I don't want the added distance of your suspicion."

"Kutuzov didn't have a stroke, did he?"

She drew back, eyes to his eyes, not avoiding his gaze.

"Yes, he did, but that was in September. And that's the only lie I told you. Why do you ask that?"

"Because all this took planning."

"Ah. I suppose it did."

They walked on, her head down now, eyes looking at the puddles as she stepped around them.

"Burgess has been asking to leave for two years now. He is like Oliver Twist in the queue for gruel. The Russians decided they'd let him earlier this year. I think they just got fed up with him. He's a pest, but I think they know he'll never name anyone the British don't already know about, and what he's learnt in Moscow you could jot down on the back of a post-age stamp. But then, it was Burgess himself who hesitated. He's no idea what the British have on him. He wanted to go home to Mayfair, not to Pentonville. The Russians could have just flown him into Berlin and let him walk across, but Burgess insisted he needed someone he trusted . . . a broker or a conduit . . . or he'd just end up in prison. So the Russians waited. Then, at the end of August, they got news of Rod's Grand Tour."

"What? How?"

"Was it meant to be a secret? Perhaps the cleaning lady at Westminster goes through your brother's wastepaper bin, perhaps the doorman at the Garrick goes through his pockets . . . it could be any one of a dozen sources . . . but the simple truth is it was in the diary page of the *Morning Post*."

Suddenly Troy felt stupid, and stupid by proxy, at that. The grin on her face as she spoke told him he was being stupid.

"They asked him if he would trust Rod . . . trust him to be the safe conduit he said he needed. Burgess said he needed someone he could trust more than Rod, and that was you. So they cooked up the idea of a visit to Vienna. Then in September Kutuzov had his stroke, and Anatoli approached me to play here in his stead at exactly the same time you and Rod would be here. I told Burgess . . . I suppose that was a mistake . . . and the next thing I knew he'd told the Russians he needed someone he could trust more than you . . . and that was me."

"And I told the stupid bugger never to mention your name and mine in the same sentence."

"It doesn't matter, they haven't put two and two together and they never will. They'll never know I denounced myself. They'll never know it was you got me out of the country. You are safe. I am safe. I'm a defector, a decorated spy. A Hero of the Soviet Union. I've got the medals to prove it."

"Why the pretence that this was all a last-minute thing? Why not tell the Konzerthaus? Why pretend Kutuzov would be the soloist, when both you and Chertkov knew he wouldn't be?"

"Would you have accepted the ticket if it had had my name on it?"

"Of course I would have."

"I could not be sure. You will understand. Ten years in another life. In a life you may try harder than most to imagine, but nevertheless you cannot. Ten years. You might not have wanted to see me again. The last time we met I was fleeing . . . a murderer . . . I had killed for the first and last time in my life."

"I'd killed too. Four of them in a matter of minutes. They weren't the first or the last. We were . . . equals."

She shook her head as though trying to shake off the idea like an insect caught in her hair. Then she looked at him, a glint of tears in her eyes.

"And that's something I've never tried to imagine. Never wanted for one second to imagine. Yet it comes unbidden. Summoned by silence. But it, all of it, was enough to give me doubt. Doubt I should never have had about you, Troy. I'm sorry. But . . . but . . . the secrecy was not my decision, it never was going to be my decision. And even if it had been, I can only assume the KGB wanted to create the illusion of spontaneity."

"That's absurd. Who in MI5 would ever believe Guy could get as far as Vienna without their sanction?"

She shrugged this off.

"You know Russians. They couldn't be seen simply to hand Guy back. I don't know, perhaps too much loss of face. As I said, they could just have flown him to Berlin and pushed him across the border. So, a simple, childish plot—me, you, Vienna, Mozart, a fake passport, the pretence they aren't watching his every move. In the end, what Guy needed was what they wanted. Guy prosecuted is a risk. Guy accepted, in whatever ignominy, is not. They wanted the conduit, the safe option, as much as he did."

"And now they've got it. A pointless de-brief of a de-defecting agent by an MI5 officer, who'll get nothing out of Guy that the Russians don't want him to say. All watched over . . . or listened in to . . . by a loving KGB. I thought it was a pantomime, but it's a farce."

"Yes. It's a farce . . . and I never even got to rehearse my part in it."

Troy looked back towards the hotel.

"I wonder what's being said in that room right now."

"I don't. I don't give a damn. I just want this to end. I've grown fond of Guy, but now I want him out of my life."

"And I feel much the same. Poor Guy. He's just a game of pass the parcel, isn't he?"

It was raining harder now. Voytek turned up her collar, shivered.

"Let's go back. If all we have to do is wait, let's wait in my room. I'm tired."

"I'm not surprised. You've played a Mozart concerto and tried to second guess the KGB. All in one day."

§77

Voytek had kicked off her shoes and lay on the bed. Troy sat in an armchair. He thought she might be sleeping. He flicked off the reading lamp and stared at nothing.

"Troy? Lie with me."

He hesitated, had not moved a muscle when the inevitable knock at the door sounded. He put the light on.

"That's Blaine. I have to take him back to the embassy."

"How long?"

"Less than an hour."

"Then come back to me."

§78

Outside the Imperial, the rain had eased, the street glistened.

"Any chance we could walk?" Blaine asked.

"Oh, it's close enough."

"Good. I feel . . . what's the word . . . closeted. I could do with fresh air."

"Closeted with Burgess is closeted indeed."

"Exactly. The room was full of him before I even got there. I take it you knew Burgess before his defection?"

"Yes," Troy replied. "I did. I was one of millions."

They left the Ring in the direction of Karlsplatz. Troy hoped Blaine would have no more questions. Let him play the Englishman and just talk about the weather.

But once he'd established that one fact, no doubt prompted by something Burgess had said, Blaine seemed to retreat into himself. He was a mutterer, a man who talked to himself—the kind of oddity Troy had recalled being abused at school with the nickname "chunter." It went with the unnatural bulk of the man, less athletic than awkward in middle age, and with the solid glass barrier between self and other that spectacles could provide to those who sought it. Rowing had probably been his salvation, a team sport that wasn't a team sport, no ball to pass or fumble. You took your place in a thin blue line and you beat your strokes in time.

Troy decided to take a shortcut via the Red Army War Memorial. The Russians had bunged up their memorials at the speed of light, commemorating their dead even as they were dying—so fast, in fact, that they had built the Berlin memorial before the final division of the city had been completed, and it stood to this day in the British sector, close to the Brandenburg Gate, guarded by Soviet troops demonstrating the goose-step to Berliner and visitor alike every couple of hours. In Vienna, they got the geography right. The memorial was in the former Russian sector—just. It was a few yards from the stencilled white line, and only a couple of hundred yards from the British Embassy—in what had until very recently been known as Stalinplatz. The new Austria had given guarantees for the safety of the monument, and the curving colonnade of pillars that framed it, but none as to the permanence of Stalin's name. However, the forty-foot high monument to the liberators of Europe still bore his signature, there for all to see in the glare of floodlights that burned all night.

As they reached the vast Victorian fountain—the Hochstrahlbrunnen—in front of the monument, Blaine looked up at the statue.

"Good Lord. It's monstrous!"

"Are war memorials known for their good taste?" Troy replied. "If you'd been here a couple of years ago there'd have been a T-34 tank parked in front of it as a reminder."

"Rubbing salt in the wounds, eh?"

"Something like—"

The first bullet sent chips of stone flying from the paving flags between them. Troy ducked under the broad lip of the fountain. The second bullet hit Blaine in his right thigh and his legs shot from under him. He rolled towards Troy with too little momentum to get clear, but enough for the third bullet to ping uselessly off the stone behind him.

He was scrabbling inside his coat.

"Troy!"

His hand emerged clutching a gun. He sent it skidding across the flags towards Troy a split second before a fourth bullet struck him in the chest. Then he moved no more.

Troy rolled out of cover, grabbed the gun, and rolled back too hard. His head hit the side of the fountain and the world turned billiard-table green, then Florentine blue, and finally Bible black.

He had no idea how long he'd been out. Asked to be objective he'd have said seconds, but that seemed impossible. There were boots everywhere, boots walking, boots standing—and right in front of him shiny black shoes and the hem of a trench coat, just at eye level.

"Put the gun down, Herr Troy."

Eh? What gun?

Troy realised he was holding a gun in his right hand. He'd no memory of this.

He looked up at the owner of shoes and trench coat. A man of his own age. Rimless glasses, good haircut. Every inch the flic. And he wasn't coming any closer till Troy surrendered the gun.

Troy flipped the gun. Held it out to the flic butt first. Then a helping hand pulled him to his feet. He was unsteady. He looked around. There were uniformed Viennese coppers everywhere, one or two sporting sub-machine guns. Blaine lay where he'd fallen, in an oceanic slick of his own blood.

Then a green surge passed before his eyes and he was out again.

§79

He came to in the back of a police car in front of the Marokkanergasse Police Station. There was vomit down his coat and trousers.

Inside, they sat him down, took his coat and jacket.

A police surgeon examined the lump on the back of his head and said he would be fine.

"No need hospital. *Verstehen Sie?*"

Troy nodded.

"*Wasser*," he said simply, wanting to rinse the taste of vomit away.

Instead, two uniforms escorted him backstage, and he found himself locked in a cell. It was the same faecal colour scheme, but it was warm. He put his head down and slept. At least they hadn't taken his tie and shoe laces.

Nor had they taken his watch, and when the flic reappeared he looked at it. They'd taken an hour and a half to get around to this.

Behind the flic was a uniform, clutching a tray. On it were a glass of water, a sandwich, Troy's passport, warrant card, and the gun. He set it down and left. The flic pulled up a chair.

"You want to tell me about it?"

"What haven't you figured out?"

"In your own words—please."

"We were on our way . . . Mr. Blaine and myself . . . from the Hotel Imperial to the British embassy. Mr. Blaine is a guest there. As we reached the fountain there were shots. Four, I think, if there were more I was out cold and didn't hear them. I'd say they came from the direction of the war memorial, perhaps a man behind one of the columns, but I could be wrong . . . it sounded to me like a rifle . . . a rifle with a decent telescopic sight, and the gunman could have been in a building on the Rennweg. Blaine was hit twice. The second shot probably killed him."

"Or," the flic said. "Perhaps this did."

He held up Blaine's automatic pistol.

"No. That hasn't been fired."

The flic held the gun up to his nose, close enough to smell.

"Perhaps, perhaps not, but until we get a ballistics report you may appreciate . . . you were found with a gun in your hand."

Troy thought back to the moment when he handed over the gun.

"Have you fingerprinted Blaine?"

"Of course."

"Then you should fingerprint me. My fingerprints will overlap Blaine's, not his mine."

"And what would that prove?"

§80

Troy declined to say more without a representative from the embassy. But it was eight in the morning before Gus appeared.

"Where the fuck have you been?"

"Freddie. They called me less than twenty minutes ago. I think, to use police jargon, they were trying to sweat you."

"Pointless. They have both my passport and my warrant card. They know I'm a copper so they know I can't be sweated."

"What have you told them?"

"About Blaine? Nothing. I can hardly just tell them Blaine was MI5, can I?"

"No. I suppose not. The ambassador wouldn't think much of that."

"Get on to London and find out what their cover story for Blaine is going to be. We'll have to tell them something sooner rather than later. And if Jordan says he has to run 'Upstairs' with this one, tell him to make it quick."

Gus sighed.

"It's a mess."

"I'm the one in jail, Gus."

"And I'm the one trying to get you out. But . . . but . . ."

"For God's sake, Gus!"

"But you were caught holding a smoking gun."

"A delightful cliché, and so rarely does anyone get to use it, but it's not true. It wasn't smoking. And the gun was Blaine's. I think I must have picked it up after he drew it. I don't honestly remember. His prints will be on it as well as mine."

Gus sighed again.

"I wonder. Are we being set up?"

"Maybe. If so, it's a bloody clumsy attempt. No, Gus. Speaking professionally, I think they're just incompetent. Their idea of procedure is a joke. I'm all they've got. I was at the scene of the crime. I'm a suspect. If I were them, I wouldn't be turning me loose without answers to questions. But they're not asking. They just leave me here to cool my heels. They're pinning it all on ballistics—and if they think I shot Blaine with his own gun, well, ballistics will produce two rifle bullets that won't match Blaine's pistol. And, lest there be any doubt, if I'd just shot him, what was I doing with the gun in my right hand when they found me?"

"Eh?"

"I'm left-handed, Gus. You know that. I might have picked up the gun with my right, but if I wanted to shoot him it would be with my left. I couldn't hit a barn door right-handed."

"Oh, of course. The old left-handed solution. Pure Perry Mason. Hamilton Burger gets it wrong yet again. No, I meant are we being set up by . . . by our friends in the east, by . . . ?"

"Just say it, Gus."

"OK. By Burgess. Has it all been a set-up from start to finish? From the moment Burgess approached you . . . a set-up. Did Burgess exploit a friendship with you to lure poor old Blaine out here and facilitate a KGB hit?"

"Well . . . we'll all be asking ourselves that, won't we? I imagine it'll be the first thing they think of when Jordan runs 'Upstairs.'"

"Y'know . . . I hate being made to feel like an idiot."

"And I hate being in a fucking cell. Get me out. Pull every diplomatic string you have."

§81

It was dark before Gus returned. Troy had been fed, allowed to wash, but his trousers reeked of dried vomit and he'd sell his soul for a tooth-brush and half an inch of Gibbs SR.

"I'm afraid it's going to be another night, Freddie."

"Like hell it is. Gus, get me out of here."

"They won't release you on my recognisance. They're waiting for the ballistics report. I can send for a lawyer, if you like, but London would take a dim view of that. They ask that you don't make a statement. Any statement. You haven't, have you?"

"Of course not."

"All London asks that you don't make waves. They want this dropped, not debated. The ballistics thing ought to kill it stone dead. Then you're out."

"Who do the police think Blaine was?"

Gus looked sheepish, embarrassed by the answer rather than the question. Two words spoken softly.

"Cultural attaché."

"Cultural attaché? That old lie."

"If Blaine hadn't had a diplomatic passport on him we'd have passed him off as a tourist."

"An armed tourist? An armed cultural attaché? A ballet-and-opera man with a shoulder holster and a Browning automatic? I said they were incompetent, not stupid."

"I know. It's completely implausible, but it's what's been agreed. No one's going to own up to this one. It suits Five and it suits Sir Francis."

"Who?"

"Sir Francis Camiss-Low. The ambassador. The bloke you so curtly refused to meet when you were here last."

"Ah, I forgot his name. Mea culpa. My diplomatic blunder. But . . . I ask—what am I supposed to have been doing out with a gun-toting cultural attaché at ten o'clock of a Wednesday night in the middle of a rain-sodden Vienna? Shooting divas? Popping off at ballerinas? Assassinating the fucking hurdy-gurdy man?"

"No one's asking that. No one but you."

"And that doesn't strike you as odd?"

"I suppose it does."

"You suppose? Gus, go back to the embassy, bypass the fucking ambassador, and call Onions. If his narks at MI5 haven't told him what's going on, you tell him."

§82

On Friday morning before it was light, a uniform opened the door to Troy's cell and handed him all his possessions, his wallet, his warrant card, his passport, his overcoat, and led him to the front desk.

Gus was waiting.

The flic who arrested him was waiting.

"You are free to go," he said in English, and handed him a typed page.

Troy said nothing.

Read enough to learn that the bullets that killed Blaine had been 9mm, and the handgun 7.65mm. Well, he knew that all along.

He screwed up the page into a ball and thrust it back.

"A formidable policeman, your Mr. Onions," the flic said with a hint of a sneer.

"And you're not," Troy replied.

Out in the street, Gus said:

"I know it's early, even earlier in London, but Stan is at the Yard. You'd better call him. I gather he read the riot act to that flic. Your brother's name got used like a cudgel. Brother of a man tipped to be Prime Minister and blah blah blah. Not the approach Five or the ambassador wanted, but . . ."

"But I'm out, and your chickenshit tactics would have had me sitting in a cell till doomsday."

"For the ambassador to step in would mean a diplomatic incident. No one wants a diplomatic incident, Freddie."

"For Christ's sake, Gus. It's been a diplomatic incident from the minute Burgess showed up in Vienna."

"Then perhaps I mean 'crisis' rather than incident."

"Gus—bollocks! What the hell has happened to you? When we were at school you were team leader, top tearaway, the first over the wall . . . mad, bad, and dangerous to know."

Gus stopped, paused, faced Troy.

"If this is your rude way of saying I've lost my nerve, then I take all the offence you intend, Freddie. But I haven't. You're an outsider. I'm half insider. You haven't a clue how much the names of Burgess and Maclean still sting the British Establishment, the insiders. The cock-up of a lifetime, the 3-D Technicolor cock-up of the twentieth century. You could have come to me asking for asylum for Hitler, Stalin, and Genghis Khan and caused fewer ripples. You could have told me Martin Bormann and Dr. Mengele were waiting tables in a Viennese coffee bar and scarcely raised an establishment eyebrow. After all, neither of them went to Eton. But Burgess? Guy bloody Burgess? The man who let the whole side down? The man who didn't play with a straight bat? Personally, I don't give a toss, as you well know, but I answer to an ambassador who does. If you were to ask me if I think Sir Francis is a pusillanimous prick, a man who makes me wonder why I ever bothered to enter the diplomatic service, a man ideologically and patriotically opposed to the Soviets but, more importantly, scared shitless of the queers, I would privately agree with you. But for your sake I have outmanoeuvred this pusillanimous prick, incurred his future pusillanimous wrath, and God knows what else. And your reproach is unwarranted."

"OK."

"I'll take that as 'sorry.'"

"Please do."

They walked through the breaking dawn to the embassy, less than a quarter of a mile away. Drizzle again, one of the things Burgess said he missed about England, and which seemed to be ubiquitous in Vienna.

Gus got through to Scotland Yard on the scrambler.

Handed the telephone to Troy.

"Get out now," Onions said.

"There's been a murder."

"I know there's been a murder."

"Murder is my business."

"Do as you're told."

"It's not a week since you told me to stay. A man's dead. There are questions to be asked here."

"I just moved heaven and fucking earth to get you out of jail. Do as you are fucking well told and leave now!"

Troy held the telephone away from his ear. It did little to diminish the volume of Onion's rage.

"OUT! NOW! GET ON THE NEXT BLOODY PLANE! YOU'RE NOT INVESTIGATING THIS ONE. DO YOU UNDERSTAND ME?"

The phone was slammed down. Troy was left with an electrical buzz.

"Not one for subtlety, is he?" Gus said.

"No. All the same, I'm not getting on the next plane."

"Freddie, the man just got you out of jail."

"I only need a few hours. Get me on a flight after lunch. Stan won't know what time I get back to London."

"Freddie. You can't make up for the shortcomings of the Vienna police all on your own."

"I've no intention of trying. Onions is right about that. Not my case. I was merely pointing out the irony of him ordering me to guard a spy, but ignore a murder. But he doesn't do irony either. There are other questions besides 'who shot Bill Blaine?' And there are other ends, ones I'd rather not leave loose."

"I won't ask."

"Then let me ask. Gus, why did you become a diplomat?"

Gus mused, twirled a pencil in his hand, tapped on the desk with the rubber end.

"I suppose I could reply by asking why you became a copper. Unlikely choices both if you think of us at fifteen or so. But it's a conversation for another time in another country. Now, you'd better get off. Your ends are getting looser by the hour."

§83

Troy went back to the Sacher, showered, changed, scrubbed his teeth viciously. Felt the quasi-erotic pleasure of a freshly laundered shirt on bare skin.

He was at the Imperial by nine o'clock.

"Herr Spode checked out on Thursday morning, sir. Would you be Herr Troy?"

"Yes."

"Then this is for you."

The desk clerk handed Troy a hotel-embossed envelope. Inside was a scrap of lined paper folded over several times:

Oh shit. What a mess. Looks like it's back to the life sentence and the Moscow rock pile. How I long for Pudding Island.
Thanks for trying.
TTFN.

Yrs ever,
Spode.

P.S. Nip into Simpson's and eat a bowl of porridge for me, would you. Salt, no sugar.

Troy stuffed the note in his pocket.

Perhaps he'd be allowed to go home now?

Perhaps this time he really had seen the last of Burgess?

§84

He found Voytek in the small rehearsal room at the back of the Konzerthaus. Almost half the room was taken up by the huge Bösendorfer concert grand—ninety-seven keys, the best part of ten feet long. She always looked small, dwarfed by her piano.

She was working out, playing, for the exercise of her fingers, the Schubert E-flat Impromptu—a piece so fast it made Troy's brain ache and it was a good day when he could play it through without making a mistake. To finish it lifted the heart, to finish it without error was bliss.

He heard her out. She knew he was there and would no more stop halfway through the four-minute keyboard blitz than he would have done himself.

After four minutes and forty-six seconds, she lifted her fingers from the keys, rested her hands on her thighs, breathed deeply, and looked at Troy.

"You didn't come back. I missed you. I thought you'd gone back to England."

"I've been in jail."

"That must make a change for you."

He ascribed the sarcasm to the fact that however long he might be banged up, it was nothing to her experience. A night in the damp and deep Rossauer Lande prison and nine months in indescribable Auschwitz.

"The man the English sent to interview Guy is dead, and Guy is gone."

"So . . . no trip back home?"

"Did you ever think there would be?"

She stood up, came to within inches of him as he stood in the curve of the piano, took his left hand in both of hers and squeezed.

"Troy, please do not see a conspiracy where there is none. If the Russians used you, then they also used me. Burgess asking to go home was real. I don't know what's happened—"

"Gunned down in the street. An MI5 officer gunned down in the street. That's what happened."

She leaned her head against his chest.

"Oh God. I am so sorry. But believe me. I knew nothing of this. And I doubt Burgess did too. Troy, he really wanted to go home. He really believed the Russians would let him."

Troy put his arms around her.

"And you?"

"Where's my home? Fucked if I know. I have to go back to Moscow. What choice do I have? You may say the English have nothing on

Burgess. They have too much on me. It's a simple choice. A lifetime in the Soviet Union or a lifetime in prison. But for you, I'd never have had even that choice."

He lifted her head gently. Tears bursting in the corners of her eyes. "And now?"

"Oh. That's easy. I don't need to think about now. Lavrenti Kutuzov's stroke paralysed his left arm, and while we both know there are pieces for left hand, I've never heard of a concerto for right hand. No. I must stay in Vienna, almost till Christmas. Till the twenty-third. Fulfil all Kutuzov's obligations. I don't mind. He undertook to play most of the Mozart concertos. Nineteen out of the twenty-seven. It'll be a challenge to play them almost back to back. I've never done that.

"Then 'home'—that ironic term—home to Moscow, and back to Vienna for just two days, and back to the cello for the New Year's Eve concert with the Philharmonic and Willi Boskovsky at the Musikverein. Strauss, Strauss, and more Strauss. The sugary icing on the sugary cake."

"All the same, that's quite an honour."

"Yes. It is. Unimaginable when I was growing up in this city. Unimaginable while Vienna was occupied too. I suppose neutrality has its uses. Tell me, Troy. Does anyone play my cello?"

Voytek had pawned her two-hundred-fifty-year-old Matteo Goffriller cello for a few pounds just before her defection in 1948. Troy had redeemed it and lodged it in his brother's study in Hampstead. If he ever went broke, selling the cello could be his life's pension.

"Yes. My niece Nattie, Rod's daughter, plays it. She's twenty now. Not bad at all. Not you, but not bad. We duet occasionally. A little Brahms, perhaps a little more Schubert."

"Duets you never got to play with me."

"No. I missed that. But, I can ship the cello, if you'd like. Guy had his books and his harmonium shipped, after all."

"No. I'd far rather your niece kept playing it. I'd far rather be able to think of you playing a duet when I'm stuck in fucking Moscow. A pleasant thought, and I can get so short of pleasant thoughts."

They kissed.

Far longer than friendship.

A duet without instruments.

VI

Wilderness

§85

MI6 HQ, 54 Broadway Buildings, London SW

The British Counter-Espionage Service, MI5, and the Secret Intelligence Service, MI6, answered to different branches of government—MI5 to the Home Office, via which it had access to the Police Force in the rough shape of Special Branch, and MI6 to the Foreign Office. If that were not enough to make them suspicious of one another, add that MI6 had its own counter-intelligence section, and add further that Dick White, who had been head of MI6 ("C") for the last couple of years, had previously been head of MI5, and had been a deputy head at the time of the "Missing Diplomats" crisis of 1951, and a pattern for mutual mistrust was established.

MI5 had cocked it up at the time, and Dick White knew it. Letting Burgess and Maclean escape had been so stupid, so easily avoided. MI5 had not so much egg on their face as a whole omelette. They might go on apologising to the Americans for ever. White might blame himself as well as blaming those above him—he had, after all, been one of the many who dismissed whisky-sodden, garlic-munching "Guy the Spy" as too improbable for words—but in 1958 he felt no inclination to let MI5 handle the death of William Blaine, despite the fact he was their own agent, not Six's. But, it would be as well if MI5 never knew that.

White sent for his most trusted advisor, Lt. Colonel Alexander Burne-Jones—whose rank had not changed in twenty years, whilst his powers and responsibilities had grown exponentially . . . but as Burne-Jones often said, there's no such thing as a pay grade or a rank once you don the cloak and pick up the dagger.

Burne-Jones hated visiting C in his den—his fourth-floor office, from which he rarely descended to meet "the troops." It reminded him of a doctor's waiting room. All that was missing were a stack of outdated magazines depicting a fiction of the English countryside . . . riding to hounds . . . county shows . . . pseudo-debutantes. He always kept the curtains drawn, never lit the fire, never offered you a sherry, and had never found so much as five minutes to take you down the rogues' gallery, the photographs of his predecessors . . . all those moustaches . . . all those intimidatingly misshapen English teeth in fading monochrome.

C was reading. Glanced up as Burne-Jones came in. Waved him into one of the oversized leather armchairs that faced his desk. Burne-Jones found himself looking at a bank of telephones. Perhaps a qualification for getting the top job was knowing which phone to pick up? He had three and would invariably answer the wrong one. C had four. Three black, and the green scrambler, next to the overflowing ashtray and the open packet of Senior Service cigarettes. If C got through this meeting without lighting up Burne-Jones would be amazed.

White stopped reading. Closed the folder and spun it around to let Burne-Jones see the cover. The Vienna embassy's report on William Blaine.

He simply tapped on it with his finger.

"Alec, you've read this, I suppose?"

"Of course. Came in on the teleprinter about an hour ago."

"Do you think Five have any leads?"

"No. They have nothing. There was only one witness, one survivor, if you like, and that was Chief Superintendent Troy."

"What was he doing in Vienna?"

"Family holiday, I gather."

"Is that believable?"

"His brother's fiftieth, so . . . probably."

"Do you know him?"

"No, but the brother in question is Rod Troy."

"The Shadow Home Secretary?"

"The same."

"Bugger."

"There's worse. His brother-in-law is Lawrence Stafford at the *Post*— a man known to tell us where to stuff D-notices when he's a mind to. There's a rumour that one Home Office underling trying to make him accept a notice questioned his patriotism, only to have Stafford offer to return his George Cross to the Queen. But, on this occasion he appears to be complying."

"Not averse to looking after his own, then."

"Quite. This will need careful handling or there'll be ripples. I hear Five want to put a watch on him, but young Troy has dealt with the Branch countless times so he's capable of running circles round a couple of dumb coppers in beetle-crushers and bowlers. He was temporarily assigned to the Branch to cover Khrushchev's visit in '56, he has good Russian, after all, and it's hard to tell who hated who more. But that's the other thing—he's run afoul of them far too often. Put politely, they have their suspicions. Put realistically, they've had it in for him ever since Khrushchev's visit."

White had been asked to take control of MI6 immediately after Khrushchev's visit—his predecessor, Sir John Sinclair, more or less fired by the Prime Minister himself—and the espionage fiasco that had surrounded it. His career had been diverted, rewritten around that incident, and he was not about to allow it to be used as any kind of yardstick. He had taken charge at the low point of SIS's history and the only way was up.

"Doesn't make him a wrong 'un."

"No, but on the other hand, it would appear he and Burgess were old friends, and in '51, when Five pulled in everyone who'd ever known Burgess, they overlooked Troy. Peter Wright's Burgess-crony hunt has become an obsession. It would be easier to list the people he hasn't interviewed. That he missed Troy is little short of amazing. Troy is just the sort of man Wright despises. Although it's probably fair to say Wright despises anyone who doesn't buy his suits off-the-peg."

White seemed almost to flinch at this. Yet another cock-up come to light. Another damn thing he'd got wrong.

"Man's an idiot," he sighed, reaching for his cigarettes.

A contrived pause as he struck a Swan Vestas and lit up.

"And," exhaling a cloud of cheap tobacco fumes, "we're off the point."

"Of course. Sorry," Burne-Jones said. "It might have been chance that the entire Troy family was in Vienna, but it was no mere chance that Burgess approached Troy. He must have planned it. If Five have any sense they'll put Jim Westcott on to interrogate Troy, keep Wright well out of it, and ignore anything the Branch say. If Troy is a wrong 'un Westcott stands a better chance than anyone of finding out . . . and if he's not they'll be able to clear him without his family making a fuss."

White did not look happy.

"I'm not happy," he said. "Burgess was one of us for however long it was—?"

"It was just a few months in 1940. Section D, till it was wound up. He went back to the BBC after that."

"Which is all the excuse I need. Put one of our own on to Troy. Someone Troy won't run circles round. Someone you can trust absolutely. What's that son-in-law of yours up to at the moment?"

"I've just assigned him a spell abroad."

"Oh—of course, I was forgetting—Beirut. When does he go out there?"

"In two weeks. He's on embarkation leave right now."

"Cancel it. Put off his departure by ten days and assign him to young Troy. I can think of no one less likely to be intimidated by the English Establishment than Joe. The Troys may own newspapers, have a man in the Commons, another in the Lords, DSOs, DFCs and GCs . . . gongs and ribbons galore. It won't mean shit to Flight Sergeant Holderness. This calls for an oik, not someone on the old school-tie network. Let's get it right this time. One Guy Burgess cock-up in my career is quite enough."

Oik?

Burne-Jones blinked at this. He knew plenty of people who might and often had used that term to describe Joe, along with "spiv," "wide boy," and "chancer"—he just hadn't expected to hear it on White's lips. Perhaps there was an irony he was missing? After all, White was putting his trust in Joe. But . . . orders were orders. All the same, he couldn't help wondering what his daughter would say. She could and would be resentful in the extreme at the loss of Joe Wilderness's embarkation leave.

But it worked out well. All Judy said was:

"Dadyoucompleteanduttertotalfuckinbastardgobshiteofafatherhow canyoufuckindothistoyourowndaughter!?!"

Burne-Jones did not pause to parse.

§86

Foxx and the Fat Man met Troy at Heathrow. A leisurely ride home in his own car. Enough to conceal the fizz of anger bubbling below the surface.

Foxx hugged him. Tears in her eyes.

"The messes you get into."

The Fat Man said, "Wotcher cock," stuck Troy's suitcase in the boot, and drove while Troy and Foxx took the back seat.

She rapidly curled into a foetal sleep, her head in his lap, and the soothing sound of the Fat Man's front-seat narrative, cast softly across his shoulder, was almost like music—how the vegetable garden was winter bare, but for . . .

"That foreign stuff you're so fond of. That 'orrible, smelly, poor excuse for a nunnion."

And Troy realised he was talking about the garlic.

"An' a few winter carrots. Mind, the rabbits are robbin' us blind. Now, I know where I can pick up a Bren gun for twenty nicker, an' if you was to 'old the torch—"

"Absolutely not."

"Suit yerself, old cock."

"How is the pig doing?"

"I'll swear she understands everything I say to 'er. She misses you, though."

Troy doubted that, and as the Fat Man embarked on what would very likely be another long chapter in his tales of life-with-pig, he tuned out, let meaning sink beneath the music . . . a fat man's sonata in B flat for pig and veg.

He dropped them at the end of Goodwin's Court with a "See yer at the weekend."

With the door closed, Foxx draped herself around him once more.

"I've been so worried."

"I have to make a phone call," he said, sounding callous even to his own ears.

"Now? Can't it wait?"

"'Fraid not."

He called Jordan at home.

"Am I the first person you called, Freddie?"

"Of course."

"Good. I'll be right over."

§87

Foxx stayed up long enough to greet Jordan. Put on a brave enough face to bring a twinkle to his wicked blue eyes.

When she'd gone upstairs, Jordan said, "Why you haven't married that woman is beyond me."

Troy said, "Let's not waste any time. If I could answer that question I would, but I can't and won't. Perhaps being married already might have something to do with it?"

"I forget."

"And I can't. So . . ."

"So?"

"So, where were you?"

Jordan shrugged off his coat and sank into the sofa, not bothering to conceal the weariness showing on his face.

"I got pulled. Right at the last minute. I was actually heading for the door when I got the call. I was told someone else was taking over. And that was it. Bill Blaine's name wasn't mentioned till later."

"You didn't ask why?"

"Freddie, that may be the way the Yard works, but when Five ask you to do something you don't ask questions. If you do, you will rapidly get a reputation as a troublemaker. Now, we're both well aware that that has long been your reputation, but I'd hate it to be mine. Sending Bill made sense in its way. The Cambridge lot were his subject. He'd known half of them when he was up at Cambridge himself. I talked to him about his time at Cambridge on odd occasions. He was usually little short of vitriolic. Self-deluding, fair-weather Marxists—or if he was feeling particularly bilious, a bunch of poofs who were in it for the rough trade."

"Well, that certainly describes Guy."

"How long did Bill get with him?"

"No more than a couple of hours. He was shot as we were walking back to the embassy."

"Five were very keen that Bill talk to him. Did he comment?"

"No."

"Did he leave any notes?"

"Probably not. He'd not have talked to Guy with a pencil in his hand, surely? If it had been me, I would have left the note-taking until I got back to my hotel—but Blaine didn't get the chance."

"So Five have nothing?"

"Not a sausage."

"Except . . . they have you."

"Jordan, I don't think I'm following you here."

"It looks like a set-up."

"I suppose it does. Guy pretends he wants to come home, Five send out Blaine for the de-brief. The KGB bump him off, and Bob's your uncle. One British agent less."

"Quite."

"But for the fact that I was expecting you—not Bill Blaine. Nobody was expecting Bill Blaine."

"I honestly don't know what to make of that. Nevertheless, from Five's point of view you are the last person to see Blaine alive, and apart from him, the last person to talk to Burgess. That alone makes you interesting to Five. The fact that Burgess seems to have asked for you in the first place makes you little short of fascinating."

"Why do I suddenly think 'fascinating' is a sinister description?"

"Because they want to talk to you. I think that was predictable. What's not predictable is that they have brought Jim Westcott out of retirement to question you."

Westcott was MI5's master of interrogation—the spycatcher. The man they'd set to tackle the atom spies, Klaus Fuchs and Karel Szabo.

"Good God. Are they really barking so loudly up the wrong tree?"

"Yes. They'll approach you tomorrow. Try to act surprised. In the meantime, don't expect to see any mention of this in the papers. It's had a D-notice slapped on it."

"For Christ's sake, why?"

"It's a no-win situation. Vienna has only just stabilised, and I hate to say this, but hanging on to the pretence of its neutrality matters more than the life of one secret agent. If we hit one of theirs we get into a tit-for-tat battle. If we complain at diplomatic level we expose the illusion. The government is far more concerned to keep doors open than go back to what we had up till '55. We need a neutral ground where we can do business with the Russians. Somewhere a damn sight less hostile than Berlin. Of course we could snatch Burgess—"

"No, you couldn't. He's back in Moscow."

"But that would be to rack up the tension . . . and besides, I doubt very much whether anyone really wants him back after this."

"So, the KGB get away with murder?"

"More or less. The investigation will be left to the Vienna police, who, needless to say, will not solve the death of one innocent English cultural attaché . . . victim of a mindless killing . . . and blah de blah."

"It could have been you."

"Yep. Someone just walked over my grave."

"Are you familiar with that English turn of phrase which has always had me slightly baffled. I can think of no equivalence in Russian. 'Consume one's own smoke'?"

"Very English, very public school, and very accurate. That's exactly what we're being told to do. Let one of our own be murdered and just stick out the stiff upper lip."

All this required thought and booze.

Troy looked under the sink for the bottle of green-tinted Polish vodka he kept for Kolankiewicz's visits.

Jordan knocked his shot back in one and held out his glass for another.

"Just the ticket, eh?"

Troy said, "How much do your people know?"

"About what?"

"Let's start with my wife."

"Nothing to my knowledge. Jim may well ask you, after all, her absence is a little odd. But you married an American. I'd stick to that line if I were you."

"And the Czechs?"

Jordan sniffed at his vodka, leaned back, and breathed out at length. This was tricky for both of them. In 1948, four Czech assassins had come for Troy. They were the four principal reasons he had stuck Méret Voytek on a cross-channel ferry. Troy had killed them all and called on Jordan to clean up the mess. Ever since, they had had an implicit understanding never to mention the incident again. Jordan had disposed of the bodies. Troy had no idea how, and until now had never thought he would need to ask.

"No, they don't know about that either. I'm often amazed at how many secrets one can keep in an organisation dedicated to prising them open. As far as Five is concerned, I took out the Czechs. I even went to the trouble of splashing a bit of blood around in that crummy hotel they'd been staying at in Fulham."

"And the cleaners?"

"They were my men. Loyalty still counted for something in those days. One is dead now, the other two have retired. There's nothing to worry about there."

"I'd love to have nothing to worry about, but I'm not sure I share your confidence."

"As I said. Try to act surprised."

Troy paused.

"Jordan—why kill Blaine? It doesn't make sense. The Russians must have approved of Burgess going to Vienna or he would not have been there. Hence, they knew the possibilities, and may even have engineered the one that came to pass. But why shoot the messenger?"

"Perhaps because they could?"

"They could have taken Blaine out on the streets of London. A discreet hit as he crossed some London park at dusk. A bullet to the head and pop! They didn't need to lure him or you to Vienna with Burgess as bait."

"I don't know, but it does seem as though Burgess asking to come home was just a ploy."

"I talked to Guy. Far, far longer than Blaine did. It wasn't a ploy. He wasn't faking. He wanted to come home and he believed Moscow would let him."

"And how believable is that? Does Moscow show mercy?"

"Dunno. Perhaps he picked up too many young comrades in too many public lavatories. Perhaps they feared he'd corrupt an entire generation and destroy the Soviet Union more effectively than an atom bomb. Gives a whole new meaning to 'Fat Man' and 'Little Boy,' doesn't it? Or it may be Guy just bored them, and they'd sooner he bored us back here."

Jordan sniggered at the truth of this. Knocked back his second shot.

"As I said, Freddie. Just try to act surprised."

§88

Troy's first morning back in his office would be telling. Stan was unpredictable at the best of times. Troy wasn't sure which way he'd jump—or how much he knew.

He had half listened to Eddie . . .

"Mr. Wildeve's in High Wycombe. A poisoning. The Hoxton Boys go on trial at the Bailey on Wednesday. He'll be back for that. Mostly it's just a mountain of paperwork."

"A small mountain?"

"No, an alp. Mont soddin' Blanc. You've been gone three weeks."

. . . but all of him listened out for Stan.

Just after ten, he appeared in Troy's office.

Closed the door behind him.

"We're in a pickle."

"We are?"

"Branch want to see you."

"In which case, your immediate use of the plural personal pronoun has me somewhat baffled."

"Eh?"

"I'm in a pickle, apparently. Not you."

"When one of my officers is under investigation by . . ."

"OK. I get it. Who, when, and where?"

"Jim Westcott."

Troy faked the raising of one eyebrow.

"I'm flattered, the last Branch man to try and turn me over was Charlie Walsh in 1940. Suddenly I'm playing in the First Division."

"For God's sake, Freddie, take this seriously. This could be where your chickens come home to roost."

Troy stared at Stan. Above the chalk-stripe suit, the rumpled collar, and the decidedly non-school tie was the face of an implacable man.

"Chickens?"

"The whole fuckin' hen house."

"Meaning?"

"I've told you repeatedly—"

"To have nothing to do with the Branch. Yet in 1944, you told me to investigate the murder of a Branch detective sergeant against the express wishes of the Branch itself. Two years ago, you assigned me to a Special Branch squad guarding Khrushchev. Need I say more?"

"I should knock your block off for cheek like that, but if you think about what you just said, it makes perfect sense of 'we.' We're both in this."

Troy kicked himself. He should have known better than to antagonise Stan.

"Sorry, Stan. When and where do you want me to meet Westcott?"

"He's on his way down now. Set up a meeting with him and clear off."

"Clear off."

"Take leave until this is over."

"I've just had three weeks leave."

"I'll not have the Branch questioning one of my serving officers. They want you on leave and so do I."

"Agreeing to that . . . putting me on leave is telling them I'm guilty of something."

"No—it's not. It's telling them we play by the rules. It's a neutral condition. If an officer is under suspicion, it's right that he has no cases until he's cleared."

"No cases? I've just got back to three weeks of fucking paperwork!"

"Leave it. It's why you hired Eddie Clark, isn't it?"

Troy looked out of the window. Anything not to have to look at Stan. What he said next needed the most careful phrasing he could manage. He turned back.

"It is also something else. Something that might not be obvious."

"Fine. I've not had me breakfast yet. Give me an egg to suck."

"Stan, please. It's a tactic on the part of MI5. Suppose I were whatever it is they might suspect me to be . . . a secret agent . . . a spy . . . to suspend me is to tip me off . . . and that might give me cause to contact my handlers. They want me to break protocol . . . they want me to run . . . just like Donald Maclean."

"Then you've nothing to be afraid of, have you? First off, you're not a bloody spy, and second, if they keep tabs on you the way they did on Maclean you'll be in Moscow by Thursday lunchtime!"

The faintest flicker of a smile on the grim Lancashire face. Troy wished he'd opened their conversation with that small vote of confidence, but he hadn't.

§89

Westcott was coming down the corridor as Troy stood in the doorway of Eddie's office. He'd not set eyes on him for about three years. On a day-to-day level, Troy happily followed Stan's advice and had as little to do with the Branch as possible. At "plod" level, he despised them. Mindless thugs in black boots and macintoshes. An insult to the name of copper. But not Jim Westcott. Westcott was pure mind, with a fearsome reputation. A fearsome reputation and an unprepossessing appearance. He seemed to Troy to follow the Stanley Onions school of fashion, which was no fashion at all. He didn't *wear* a suit, it simply hung on him as it would on a scarecrow.

But he was smiling, and he was offering Troy a hand to shake.

"Mr. Troy. I think we should talk, don't you?"

At least he hadn't used any euphemism along the lines of "a bit of a chat."

"I'm sure you do, Mr. Westcott. Equally, I'm sure you'll understand when I say, 'not in this building.'"

"I think I do, Mr. Troy, I think I do."

"Then what say we meet on neutral territory?"

"You have somewhere in mind?"

"I do. Meet me at the corner of Garrick Street and St. Martin's Lane, just below Seven Dials . . . at—"

Troy looked at his watch.

"Shall we say four o'clock?"

"Four will be fine."

Yes, thought Troy, "unprepossessing" was the word.

He called Rod, from his office.

A simple request.

"And I suppose I'm not supposed to ask why?" said Rod.

"No," said Troy. "You're not."

§90

Westcott was at the corner on time. Troy watched him walk up St. Martin's Lane from the Trafalgar Square end. Smaller than he had first seemed. Very grey, and just a little shabby, his moustache permanently stained with nicotine. Troy would put him at sixty or so, but was pretty certain he was younger. His generation had not worn well. A childhood in the over-romanticised Edwardian Age, an adolescence spent wondering if the Great War would last long enough to kill him, and then thrust out into the twenties, into the General Strike and the Depression—the Age of Disappointment—and the thirties, what Auden had called "that dirty, double-dealing decade"—one not designed to leave a man with any memories of heroism, camaraderie, or death. A dullness, a flatness, a slow-grinding hardship without redemption.

Troy felt that parity of rank—Westcott was also a Chief Superintendent, albeit in and out of retirement as MI5 had recourse to his talents—would prevent Westcott from any pulling rank, and that he would probably be inclined to treat Troy as an equal whilst doing his job with all his much-vaunted tenacity. He would not keep Troy waiting, there'd be no cheap tricks designed to upstage or wrong-foot Troy. He'd play fair.

Troy wouldn't.

"You live around here, don't you, Mr. Troy?"

"Yep. But my house would hardly be neutral territory. We'll just walk along to the Garrick. It's just over there."

"You're a member?"

Westcott could hardly keep the incredulity out of his voice.

"No. Coppers are not clubbable, you will agree. My father was, and just before the war he offered to put my brother and myself up for membership. Rod accepted, went on the waiting list and got in quite quickly. A few places freed up by wartime casualties, I would imagine. We're his guests. He'll show us to a quiet corner and then bugger off."

"Am I dressed alright?"

"Yes. They're not complete and utter snobs except where women are concerned. They even keep spare jackets and ties at the door so they never have to turn anyone away. That said, I don't recommend turning up in shorts and sandals."

Rod was just inside, hovering by the porters' desk.

Troy could sense the nervousness in him. He doubted Westcott could. Rod pulled out the vox humana on his politician's keyboard, pressed the flesh, resorted to flattery.

"Mr. Westcott. Not often I get to meet a living legend."

Westcott ducked into the mask of modesty that was probably one of his most useful tools as an interrogator.

"Nor I, Sir Rod. I was too old for the last war, and too young for the first, but I have read almost every book about the Battle of Britain and I think you're more likely to be the legend."

"Too kind," Rod replied with just a flicker of embarrassment. "Let me show you around."

"Of course," Westcott seemed to ramble on as they climbed the overly grand, over-elaborate staircase, "I was a serving copper during the war, but off duty I was on duty, as it were—Home Guard in Queen's Park."

Troy had hated the Home Guard, the ARP, the part-timers and all those officious old men drummed into service. Not so much chocolate soldiers as hot-milk-and-Horlicks soldiers.

"We all did our bit," said Rod, in a mode Troy thought of as his political auto-pilot. "Except Freddie, of course. Couldn't drag him away from Murder."

The baffled look on Westcott's face broadened into a brown-toothed smile as something in his brain heard the capital M on Murder.

Troy said nothing.

Rod had set the tone nicely for phase one, but the sooner he buggered off the better. Phase two—Troy wanted Westcott to be overwhelmed by their surroundings, he wanted Westcott awed and intimidated. A little Sir Rod, a dash of RAF hero, a pinch of Shadow Home Secretary had helped—but their uses were limited. Let the Garrick do its work, let it wrong-foot an old copper in a Burton's off-the-peg suit, on less than a grand a year, whose breath smelt of fags, whose clothes whiffed of stale sweat, whose ill-fitting shoes pinched his bunions, let him feel the cultural clout of Establishment England . . . feel the slings and arrows of Troy's dirty-tricks campaign. Besides, there was nothing in what he or Westcott had to say that he would care to have said in front of Rod. Rod would no doubt be full of questions the next time they met, if he could wait that long, but Troy was adept at fending Rod off. Now—he needed to get Westcott alone.

A quick tour, not quick enough for Troy, but no doubt furthering the slow process of intimidating Westcott, and Rod took them back down-stairs and showed them to a cranny known to members as "Under the Stairs"—a curtained-off area of the main, ground floor lobby, beneath the main staircase—leather armchairs, and it being December, a coal fire. It was often full after lunch, but at four thirty on a winter's afternoon, empty.

"I've ordered tea. The man'll be along in a minute or two. All on my slate. I'll leave you to it."

Westcott pulled out his Player's Navy Cut, the packet with the sailor on the front, a man bearing a striking resemblance to the late Tsar. He lit up, and when tea arrived flicked ash into the saucer, even though the Garrick provided ashtrays galore—the habit of a lifetime, thought Troy. And he began to see that impressed as he was by his surroundings, Jim Westcott was not going to let class intimidate him.

"Do you remember the first time you met Burgess?"

"Of course. Dinner, at my father's house in Hertfordshire. Round about 1935, I think. The Prime Minster was there."

"Mr. Baldwin?"

"No, the present Prime Minister, Mr. Macmillan."

Westcott dragged on his cigarette without a flicker. Name dropped, name sunk, thought Troy.

"And the last time?"

"Vienna, obviously. Or we wouldn't be sitting here talking about him."

"No. I meant the last time before . . . as it were . . . the old days, before his defection."

"That would have been May 25, 1951. Around three in the afternoon. A Friday, I believe."

"How can you be so precise?"

"It was the day he skipped the country. I have a different tailor for suits and a different tailor for uniforms. Mine needed stitching. Guy was there."

"At Gieves?"

"Yes."

"Why didn't you report this at the time?"

"At what time? It was weeks before the government admitted he and Maclean had done a bunk. When the story broke in the papers I was up to my neck in a couple of very gruesome murders in Cardiff, and had no time to follow the story. It would be the end of that summer, perhaps autumn, before I pieced it together and realised I'd seen him on his last day. Then there was an election in October—I usually take a bit of leave to help my brother. By the time that was over, we had a new government and Burgess and Maclean were old news."

"You didn't consult your notes?"

"I don't take notes when visiting my tailor, and neither do you."

"Did you talk?"

"Briefly. Guy seemed to be planning a holiday. Scotland, the North. The only odd thing about it was he hated being out of London. Hated the suburbs, hated the Home Counties. If he ever went north of the Trent in his life I'd be amazed. The idea of him in Scotland was unimaginable. As far as Guy was concerned, the world ended at the Circle Line and Camden Town was a foreign country."

"So you knew he was lying to you?"

"No. I knew he was just rattling on. It was . . . Guy nonsense. I don't remember what I thought. Perhaps a smokescreen to disguise a queer liaison—but he'd never bothered with any pretence in the past. He just did what he did all too blatantly. We chatted, we parted."

"You realise, you might have been the last person to see Burgess?"

"No. That was probably one of your blokes. It seems pretty clear you were following Maclean and managed to lose him. Perhaps you lost Burgess too? Or were you not following him?"

Westcott lit up a new fag from the stub of the old. Troy thought the stench appalling, but said nothing. This was a London gentleman's club—it was tobacco-coloured.

"Did you like him?"

"Hard to say. He had . . . has a grotesque charm. I don't dislike him. I don't share his tastes, except for music."

"Do you know why he approached you?"

"Opportunism. Coincidence."

"We're policemen, Mr. Troy. We think coincidence is a dirty word."

Troy said nothing.

"But . . . as you say . . . also opportunism. You were there. He was there. And you shared a taste in music?"

"Méret Voytek?"

"I was coming to her, yes."

"Ten and more years ago, Miss Voytek and I had the same piano tutor, Viktor Rosen. I investigated Viktor's death in 1948."

"Was she a suspect?"

"No, no one was a suspect. It was suicide. I established that almost at once."

"And when she defected?"

Time to lie.

"When she defected I was as surprised as anyone else."

"You'd no idea?"

"I didn't need an idea. I investigate murder and this was suicide. My involvement lapsed once that was clear. The question ought to be, did your people have any idea?"

"So—you were surprised to hear from her in Vienna?"

"Yes, pleasantly so."

"And when Burgess appeared?"

"It didn't take a genius to work out that they might have met in Moscow, two exiles in need of company, a common love of music. And from Burgess's point of view, a common language. Miss Voytek has toured repeatedly behind the Iron Curtain for years—she is one of the most acclaimed cellists on earth, and a pretty good pianist as well. And as Austria's neutrality is guaranteed by all concerned, she is hardly likely to be snatched by our people or the Americans off the streets of Vienna. I gather she has played there quite a few times since 1955. That the Russians let her is no surprise. The real surprise was that they let Burgess get that far. To the point where he could de-defect."

"Unless, of course, they had other reasons for letting him out of his box?"

Westcott didn't use metaphor. His vocabulary was largely literal. This use of imagery, however slight, was telling. Burgess in his box.

Westcott looked at his watch.

"I think we might call it a day—for now. Thank you, Mr. Troy."

Westcott had asked no questions about the shooting of Bill Blaine— but he wouldn't, would he? He had a copy of the police report from Vienna. Troy had nothing to add to that, and Troy knew full well he wasn't suspected of pulling the trigger, he was simply suspected. The incident was not the object of Westcott's enquiry . . . Troy was. Troy and Burgess . . . as though ever to have known the man was a culpable act. Troy thought of all the irritable, irritating warnings Rod had grumbled at him about Burgess over the years, yet he could not bring himself to regret his friendship with Burgess. He wouldn't even try.

As they left the Garrick, parting with a handshake like two shy friends who'd never got onto Christian-name terms, Westcott set off back in the direction of St. Martin's Lane, and Troy set off in the opposite direction to the corner of New Row.

He felt behind him the quickening shadow, the silent boot, the invisible, flapping gaberdine mac of Special Branch.

§91

Someone was following Frederick Troy.

§92

Someone was following Frederick Troy.

Of course Jim Westcott would have him followed. It would be madness not to have him followed.

Troy led his followers—two of them, clumsy, obvious, flat-footed buggers, he thought—across Covent Garden's rotting vegetable remnants, slippery as ice, an excellent place to lose them if he so chose, onto Long Acre, across Seven Dials and Great Newport Street, into the Charing Cross Road. It wasn't quite a full circle from the Garrick, but close enough for him to be sure they really were following him, and close enough for them to work out that he knew they were following him—but he didn't think they'd do that. They stuck to orders to the letter, they did not think for themselves. Robby the Robot would give more thought to the job in hand than they would.

Not knowing how long he'd be at a loose end, or how long he'd have to keep this up, he dropped into Dobell's Jazz Record shop at 77 Charing Cross Road, just south of Cambridge Circus. He was an occasional rather than a regular, but was known to spend large amounts of money when he did visit, and so was on first-name terms with the proprietor. His indifference to the occasional aura of pot trailed by other customers like clouds of glory helped him to fit in. Douglas Dobell thought of Troy as a customer first and a policeman, if at all, second.

"It's been a while, Freddie. How're things in Murder?"

"Bloody as ever, but I'm on leave for a few days . . . so what's new on vinyl?"

"It's been a good year. I'd say one of the best. Stereo is really taking off."

"It's a gimmick, Doug. It'll never catch on."

"It's more an illusion than a gimmick, and take it from me, it's here to stay."

"I shall be listening on my old electric gramophone, come what may, so . . ."

"They call them record players now, Freddie. Electric? I'm amazed you don't still have one with a wind-up handle."

"Do you want to make a sale or not?"

"Are you buying for you or the missus?"

"Both, I suppose."

"There's a new Billie Holiday. Great title. *Lady in Satin*. Miss Foxx'll love it. Stan Getz has teamed up with Oscar Peterson. A great jam session."

"I've always thought 'jam session' musician-speak for arsing about."

"No, trust me. It's great. A wonderful ten-minute medley in the middle based around "Bewitched, Bothered and Bewildered." Then there's Duke Ellington's *Indigos*, Ella's recorded *The Irving Berlin Songbook*, and Miles has a film score out . . . Asc . . . Asc . . ."

"*Ascenseur pour l'échafaud*. I've seen the film. Jeanne Moreau and I forget who else. Stick one on in a booth, would you?"

"Which one?"

"Any. I won't be listening."

Troy reached up and twisted the light bulb, and the booth dropped into semi-darkness. Troy could just make out the two coppers on the other side of the road. The Charing Cross Road was so well lit, it would have paid them to retreat into a shop doorway, any one of the dozens of second-hand bookshops that lined the street.

Doug changed records, played him a track off each LP he'd mentioned. It was well past five now and Troy wondered at what point the Branch would call it a day. The taller of the two coppers had been glancing at his watch every couple of minutes, and on the dot of five thirty they both set off down the road in the direction of the tube station. Predictable as clockwork.

Troy emerged from the booth.

"Which is it to be?" Dobell asked.

"I'll take the lot. And while I'm in spending mood, is there anything new from Coltrane?"

Dobell reached under the counter and held up *Soultrane*. "Fine. I'll take that too. Cheque OK?"

§93

He walked home, untroubled and unobserved via Brewer Street. If one shop could constitute a Little Italy, then London's Little Italy was Lina Stores, which had opened in the last year of the war, not long after Italy, with commendable good sense, had changed sides and hundreds, if not thousands, of POWs and internees had been released, and one could once again get a decent Italian meal in the middle of the city.

A couple of hours later, armed with fresh spaghetti, a chunk of Parmesan, tinned tomatoes (it was November, after all), a bulb of foreign "nunnion" and twelve ounces of mince, he had rustled up spag bol for two, and he and Foxx were sprawled on the sofa with the last glasses to be tipped from a bottle of Chianti.

He'd put on the Miles Davis.

Foxx did not care for it.

"It's a bit harsh. Austere even."

"Yep. Let me find something a bit more relaxing."

He put on the Stan Getz LP.

"Oh, don't you just love saxophones?" she said.

Troy said nothing.

Waited until Stan and Oscar had reached "Bewitched." Until he could hear the unuttered "wild again" in the mind's ear.

"Over the next few days . . . let me know if you notice anything odd."

Foxx was curled into a ball, her favourite position, head on his lap. She twisted onto her back so she could see his face.

"Eh?"

"Just anything out of the ordinary."

"Such as?"

"I'm suspended. Subject to a Special Branch investigation. I'm being tailed. They may stick to me, but they might also follow you, and they may try and turn over the house when we're out. Illegal, but they may try all the same. Just tell me if you notice anything out of place. Objects not where you left them, that sort of thing."

"Oh bloody hell! It's that bugger, Burgess, isn't it?"

"Yes."

"Oh God. I wish you'd come home with me and not met up with him."

"What's done is done. Besides. He was a friend. Traitor or not, I would not have refused to see him."

"And now you're a suspect? . . . they think you're a traitor too?"

"They're clutching at straws. Looking for someone to blame."

"Are we in trouble?"

Troy's second first-person-plural pronoun of the day. He might never feel lonely again.

"No. If I can't see this one off I'm a poor excuse for a copper. We may run into extra time, I may kick the odd penalty, but believe me, I will score."

"I hate it when you use sporting metaphors."

"Why?"

"Because you haven't a clue what you're talking about. You wouldn't know a silly mid-off from a centre-half."

"I'll win all the same."

"You'd better," she said, and squirmed back into position.

§94

More time passed with no further word from Westcott than Troy would have anticipated. Westcott was stringing him out, and in turn Troy was stringing out Westcott's men. Plod and Plod followed him around London, and he took particular delight in long lunches in Soho that kept them standing around in the cold, no doubt bursting to pee. One day he managed to stretch lunch at L'Escargot out to three hours, and the next day managed to read half of Camus's *L'Étranger* leaning against a bookcase in Foyles while it rained buckets outside.

It was the next Friday afternoon before Westcott called him at home.

"I thought we might meet for another session after work today."

Ah, so he'd now done enough homework to feel he could tackle Troy more forcefully? This would be a tougher session. There'd be no gaps in his knowledge, he'd have Troy's curriculum vitae off by heart—but, equally, he'd have learnt nothing from the followers.

"I'm not at work, Mr. Westcott. As well you know. I appear to be on leave and at four o'clock today I shall be setting off to spend some of it in the country."

"Hertfordshire?"

"Yes. Mimram, to be exact."

"Of course," said Westcott, who probably knew what newspapers Troy read, where he got his hair cut, and so most certainly knew where his country house was.

It might be impossible to put Westcott off, but distinctly possible to control both time and place . . . to open with the white pawn.

"Look, why don't you come down for lunch tomorrow?"

Troy counted to five while Westcott hesitated. He wasn't going to say no, he'd just rather not say yes. Troy thought an outright refusal would be out of character.

"That . . . er . . . that sounds fine, Mr. Troy."

"Jolly good. King's Cross to Welwyn, change to the Branch Line and get off at Tewin Water. The trains aren't frequent, but I believe there's a 9:45 that connects rather well and will get you to Tewin Water around 11:30. I'll have you met at the station. We can talk before lunch, and after lunch, if the weather holds up, we can take a walk around."

§95

Troy called his brother and told him not to show up until Saturday evening.

"It's not really all that convenient, you know. I have constituency surgery in Welwyn tomorrow morning from ten until noon."

"Then find a pub and prop up the bar for a couple of hours. Don't show up here before three at the earliest."

"Freddie, what are you up to?"

"You would not thank me for telling you."

"Fine. Be like that."

He'd tell Rod sooner or later, preferably when the storm had evaporated from the teacup, preferably when there was some advantage in telling him. Now was not the moment.

§96

He let the Fat Man collect Westcott, let him prep a thoroughly London, utterly urban copper with pig tales. Westcott was impossible to intimidate—the Garrick had proved that—but it might just be possible to divert him, confuse him, disorient him in much the way the Larkin family did with the tax inspector in *The Darling Buds of May*. Troy had had many a moment when he had wished the Fat Man would just shut up. This was not one of them.

Westcott stepped from the car, trying to smile, poorly concealing his boredom and his bewilderment.

"I've just heard all about raising pigs in the middle of Chelsea, during the Blitz."

"I know," said Troy. "Just when you think you've heard every Blitz tale, along comes one you'd never expect."

"I was in the Home Guard. I thought I'd seen everything."

The Fat Man winked at Troy from behind Westcott's back.

"I'll go and nudge cook along, young Fred. I'll give you and yer pal a shout just before she dishes up the jubbly."

Westcott looked around. The long, winding drive lined with leafless trees, the lawn gently rolling to the river, still wet with dew, and the house itself, rendered ramshackle with the accretions of many owners and many generations.

Then he turned to Troy.

"I feel I have to ask, Mr. Troy, but we are alone?"

"My brother, you mean? No, he won't be joining us. It would be quite wrong for two police officers to talk as we must talk in front of a man to whom both of us might be answerable after the next election. And, who knows, the Prime Minister might call one any day now. After all, we've never had it so good, have we?"

"And . . ."

"Miss Foxx is out shopping. The only other people are the driver who just picked you up—he'll take lunch with us but then vanish into his potting shed—and the cook. She goes home before two, so yes, we'll be alone."

He showed Westcott into his study. It had been his father's study before it was his, and in almost fifteen years Troy had left next to no mark on it. It was still a room belonging to another century, another man, but most certainly not another country.

He'd lit a fire, and they sat on either side of it, much as they'd done at the Garrick.

"You seem to attract trouble, Mr. Troy?"

"I know."

"In fact, people seem to die around you."

Yes, this was going to be a much tougher session.

"I'm not even sure where to begin," Westcott said.

Of course he was sure. He hadn't even bothered to take out a notebook. Just his packet of full-strength fags. He'd got Troy's track record off by heart. Asking to be coaxed was just a ploy.

Troy pushed an ashtray along the hearth to him.

"Try chronology."

"In 1940, you were part of a team responsible for the internment of aliens, led by Chief Inspector Steerforth. His report doesn't show you at your best."

"Steerforth was an unconscionable bastard. He assaulted me twice in the course of that operation. I made no complaint, but I was glad when it was all over and I could get back to the Murder Squad. I was only on Steerforth's team because I speak a couple of foreign languages, neither of which I got to use, and because I'd been a beat bobby in Stepney, which is where most of the aliens were at that time."

"Steerforth disappeared without trace shortly afterwards."

Indeed, Steerforth had disappeared, but not without trace—Troy knew exactly where he was. Under the remains of an East End synagogue. One day they might find what was left of him, but as several magnesium incendiaries, capable of igniting steel, had followed Steerforth into the pit, Troy doubted they'd find so much as a tooth.

"As I recall, he disappeared during the Blitz. So many people did."

"And you worked with Walter Stilton on the same operation. In '41, Stilton was murdered."

"Walter was shot by a German agent, whose cover was that of an American officer attached to their embassy. I investigated Walter's death, but the case was solved by another American officer, a Captain Cormack. All of which was in my report."

"In '44, Detective Sergeant Miller of Special Branch was shot in Manchester Square."

"I investigated that too. If people die around me, as you put it, don't you think it might seem that way because my job is to investigate suspicious death? And if you intend to bring up every case I've ever investigated we'll be here till midnight."

"I'm focussing on the deaths of fellow officers. And you were told *not* to investigate Miller's death."

"Only by your people. Onions had other ideas. I can quote him word for word. 'Nobody shoots coppers on the streets of London and tells me to look the other way.' I followed orders. Took awhile, but I arrested the killer in 1948."

"And caused some diplomatic ripples."

"John Baumgarner had no diplomatic immunity, and since I could never be certain he'd pulled the trigger in person, I charged him with the murder of one Sydney Edelman, tailor of Stepney Green—a crime to which Jack Wildeve, who is now a chief inspector under me, was a witness—not the murder of Sergeant Miller. If you feel so inclined, that case is still open."

"In '56, you were part of the team monitoring Khrushchev's visit. A team led by Inspector Cobb. Cobb also disappeared. This time without the cover of an air raid."

"I gather that was some time after Khrushchev went home. I was on other cases by then. Cases, I regret to say, that are also still open two years later. Cobb's disappearance never was my case. It would only be my case even now if a body turned up, and if your people asked me in."

Of course, Troy had killed Cobb. He had no idea where the body was and as long as it never turned up, he didn't care. Cobb had been another "unconscionable bastard"—so many of them were.

"To single out my involvement with dead coppers, particularly coppers killed in wartime, may be a way of cataloguing my sins, but it is to lose focus on what I do. I catch killers, Mr. Westcott, and while one or two have slipped through my fingers, my track record is better than most."

"I can't dispute that, Mr. Troy, nor would I want to, but as the issue at hand is, as you might put it, 'yet another dead copper,' in the shape of Mr. Blaine, you'd expect me to review your cases in that particular light, would you not?"

"I most certainly would expect, but I can hear that dirty word 'coincidence' muttering in the wings—"

The Fat Man appeared in the doorway. "Grub's up."

"And now I expect you to eat lunch."

§97

After bangers and mash and beer, Troy invited Westcott to put on his overcoat and take a walk. He led him through the vegetable garden, where brussels sprouts leaned like Pisa, and the bright green tips of garlic thrust up through the loam like frogs' tongues, and down to the bank of the river. A change of venue and a change of tack.

"I suppose I might have begun with this question a while ago, but I didn't. Politics, Mr. Troy."

"My politics?"

"Yes. Never pays to presume too much about a man's politics. Pays to ask."

"Of course. If we all went by the old school tie, we'd get so much of it wrong. Just as we did with Burgess."

"And?"

"I don't have any politics."

"Then what do you believe?"

"I believe in the pursuit, arrest, and fair trial of the criminal. I believe in the blindfolded lady atop the Old Bailey. I believe in justice. I'd be in the wrong job if I didn't."

"Quite so. But you vote?"

"I do."

"And how do you vote?"

"I vote British, Mr. Westcott. The Soviet Union puts up no candidates in rural England."

Westcott could not stop himself from smiling at this.

"But," Troy went on. "Since you've asked what no gentleman should of another . . . I vote for my brother."

"So you vote Labour?"

"No, Mr. Westcott, I vote 'Family.'"

Troy had cued Westcott. Inadvertently he had offered the perfect sequitur.

"Ah . . . I would like to ask about your family, if you don't mind."

"I've nothing to hide, Mr. Westcott, indeed much of my background is common knowledge. A famous father, a famous brother—I am the most anonymous member of the family."

"You're too modest. You might well be the best-known copper in the land, after Mr. Fabian of course."

"And Dixon of Dock Green."

"Real coppers, Mr. Troy, real coppers. And you're not the most anonymous member of the family—there's your uncle."

"Nikolai? Well . . . he's always held a very ambivalent position with your people. They accept him without trusting him. He has worked for our secret services without ever being one of them. Yet every shade of government since Baldwin has relied on him to interpret scientific data coming out of the Soviet Union."

"Do you really need to wonder why? Until 1951, he had a soap box at Speakers' Corner in Hyde Park. He was a rabble-rouser."

"And you sent Plod to watch him, didn't you? Well, if you'd sent someone with half a brain, and if they'd listened to what Nikolai had to say, you'd know damn well he wasn't preaching Communism, that he has no more love for the Soviet Union than he had for the Romanovs, and that he is a follower first and foremost of Count Tolstoy, author of *War and Peace*, a well-known pacifist, and secondly of Prince Kropotkin, a proponent of co-operative movements, author of *Fields, Factories and Workshops* . . . both of whom were spied on by the Russian secret police in their day—and both of whom are rather bad for rabble-rousing as few amongst the rabble have ever heard of them. My uncle is undeterred by futility. No, Mr. Westcott, Nikolai Troitsky is no one you need suspect of anything, no one who has ever been seriously suspected of anything, and, in the words of an idiot schoolmaster who once taught me, the policy of our secret services seems to be 'don't let your right hand know what your left hand is doing.'"

"We had him vetted at the time of the aliens scare."

"You had me vetted too. We both passed. You even interned my brother. How stupid can it get?"

"A lot stupider than that, I'm afraid."

"Then let me save you time and stupidity. Since this all appears to be about my family, let me assure you of my family's loyalty. My uncle has opposed every Russian government since the time of Nicholas II—Kerensky, Lenin, Stalin, that bloke no one remembers, and now Khrushchev. He has been loyal to his adopted country for nearly fifty years. My brother is so loyal to England he risked his life God knows how many times during the war and emerged a highly decorated RAF hero . . . by your own admission, a Battle of Britain legend . . . he may well be Prime Minister one day. My father, my mother, and my uncle were all born in Russia. A fact which the small minds of MI5 can never cope with. My father was born a Russian but died a loyal Englishman, quoting Yeats in his last words. I was born in this house. I am his only English-born child. My mother called me her 'little Englander'—and I've never been to Russia.

"Years ago, my father told me and my brother that however English we were, we would always be regarded as Russian, a suspect condition in itself, the same condition Moura Budberg was in, and how wonderfully she exploited that. He said that if he, Rod, or I, any of us, were to happen to consort with a Russian spy, we must never forget that he is a Russian spy. I happened to consort with Guy Burgess. Coincidence or opportunism . . . whichever—I never forgot what Guy was for a moment."

"You know, you used the word loyal three or four times just now . . . but not about yourself. Now, why would that be?"

"I don't feel any necessity to state my loyalty. I do my job."

And he kicked himself. He'd almost got ratty with Westcott and that would be a hostage to fortune.

"Johnson," he said, burying the annoyance he felt.

"Johnson?"

"Samuel Johnson, in the dictionary—'Patriotism is the last refuge of a scoundrel.' I would not be able to state mine without the echo of Dr. Johnson, I fear."

"But . . . since you bring up scoundrels. Burgess. Let's go back to Burgess. How long have you known Burgess was a spy?"

"Always, I suppose. He never said he was a spy, at least not directly, but I never really believed in his conversion to democracy. I never had any idea on what or whom he might be spying, and most of the time he seemed to be too indiscreet to be a spy. Many people must have drawn that same conclusion. He was easily dismissed. A bit of a joke. He could have walked around London in a black cape with a parcel marked 'bomb' and got away with it. The queer buffoon was near-perfect cover, I just never believed it."

"Yet you never told anyone?"

"What's to tell?"

Westcott mused awhile. He could not seem to go ten minutes without a cigarette. Troy wasn't certain whether lighting up and fiddling with matches bought him time or merely satisfied a craving.

"Fifty-one. The last time you saw Burgess. And the time before that?"

"Oh, that's unforgettable. He threw a farewell party in 1950 just before he set off for Washington."

"Ah. You were there. Well, that's gone down in the annals of debauchery, hasn't it?"

"Quite rightly so. I don't think I'd ever seen him play the queer buffoon to the hilt before."

"Drugs?"

"I wouldn't know."

"Sex?"

"Of course."

"And quite a . . . how should I put it? A Who's Who of queer London?"

"I wouldn't know about that either. A smattering of men in uniform if that's any kind of indication. Sailors, soldiers. But Guy Liddell from MI5 was there, Anthony Blunt was there . . . and so was the Deputy Foreign Secretary Hector McNeil—Guy had worked directly under him for years, after all. Of those, the only one I can recall speaking to was Blunt, and that was about art. He wanted an opportunity to come out here and look at my father's Turners, Constables, and the van Gogh we have in London . . . I think he came to lunch later that summer. And I've no idea of the sexual preferences of any of those men. Moura Budberg was there. She insisted on talking to me. She usually does. I can't remember about what—I have always found her presence somewhat disturbing. And quite possibly a couple of what Guy used to call 'rough trade'—he was mixing a heady cocktail that night."

"And your part in this?"

"To be appalled, I think."

Troy's memory flashed. A full, immediate picture of the moment he went into the bedroom to look for his notebook. Burgess naked and erect. The naval uniform strewn across the floor. The moment Guy's conquest, whoever he was, sat bolt upright as though stung, only to collapse back on the bed with a thump. Yes, appalled was the right word. He wasn't going to mention this to Westcott. It added nothing and was a memory he'd done without for years and would rather do without now.

"I left when McNeil did. He gave Guy a fairly plain warning to watch his step in Washington—a fraction short of calling the USA a nation of strait-laced prudes who would not take kindly to his antics. Guy laughed it off. But I'd had enough of him by then. He was drunk and clearly going to get drunker as night crept into day. I walked to the next corner with McNeil and bade him goodnight. It was the only word I spoke to him and I never saw him again—although I believe my brother was at his funeral. His embarrassment when the truth about Guy came out must have been unbearable."

"Vienna," said Westcott. "Let's go back to Vienna."

Troy gave him a potted version of meeting Voytek, the anonymous invitation, omitted her performance and cut to her surprise in the dressing room.

"Burgess?"

"Burgess in a crude disguise which only served to get him giggling. He cracked a joke or two, and as soon as Miss Voytek left us alone he dropped his bombshell. Hardly bothered with any preamble. The merest beating around the merest bush. He was homesick, he missed his mother. He wanted to come home. Would I oblige him by asking? I think he might have meant me to ask Rod, but I'd never do that. I wouldn't want to involve Rod, and besides, Rod could never stick Guy.

"Once I'd agreed, he said nothing more of any note, asked a lot of questions about life in London, had I seen so-and-so—half the names meant nothing to me, but he did ask about Guy Liddell, whom I've met a couple of times since Guy's farewell party, about Goronwy Rees, whom I've never met, Tom Driberg, whom I know only too well . . . had I seen anything of his brother, Nigel—and was such and such still a thing there, was his favourite second-hand bookshop still open, and so on.

"In the morning I went to the embassy, asked for a secure line to London, and got through to Jordan Younghusband at Five. That evening we met again in a restaurant. He was even more unhappy, still the Englishman in exile, still on the brink of tears with every sentence. But somehow we got around to what he'd done. To his sins. He got drunker and drunker. Resentful that he was always badgered about what he knew and who he knew. The world expecting him to name names. So I played a game with him . . . took up the question every newspaper's been asking since he defected . . . 'is there a third man' or 'who's the third man?'

"I suppose I meant it as a joke, but once I'd started the game Guy seemed only too willing to play. I said something like, 'You're the first man,' and Guy said, 'You can always trust the alphabet.' I said, 'Maclean second,' and got 'Good bloody grief, is he really?' And when I said, 'Who's on third?' I think the reference to Abbott and Costello was lost on him and he simply said, 'Philby.'"

"No surprises there, then."

"No. We all knew that. Only an idiot or a *Daily Express* reporter would have believed a word Philby said at his press conference. So, I said, 'Fourth?' And Guy said, 'Blunt.' And I was surprised."

"I'm not."

"Really?"

"Oh Blunt's a wrong'un, alright."

"Do we knight our wrong'uns now?"

"Touché, Mr. Troy. Sir Anthony is . . . what's the word . . . contained. Not a problem. And I'll spare you any conflict of loyalty—I would not expect you to betray a friend—when you asked him who came next he named Charles Leigh-Hunt, did he not?"

"So, you knew about Charlie?"

"We do, but we didn't—if you catch my drift. His sudden resignation from Six in 1956 was all that alerted us. Prior to that he was not, to my knowledge, under suspicion, except insofar as we are all under suspicion. Did you get Leigh-Hunt the job in Beirut?"

"No. I had nothing to do with it. My brother, Rod, and my brother-in-law Lawrence Stafford arranged it. They offered him the job, and it's not much of a job from what I hear. Not much more than stringer really. If he's hiding, he's hiding in plain sight. You could pull him at any moment if you so chose."

Westcott paused for thought, drew his scarf up around his neck, then sunk his hands deep in his pockets.

"We have no solid evidence he's a traitor. Less than we have on Blunt, in fact. Your word, Burgess's word. Nothing that would stand up in court. Similarly, Inspector Cobb vanished only a couple of weeks before Leigh-Hunt resigned. I'd put money on Leigh-Hunt having killed Cobb, but neither you, in the Murder Squad, nor I, in Special Branch, could prove that."

"I think I told you a little earlier, my squad wasn't asked to investigate Cobb's disappearance. It is a Scotland Yard unwritten rule—the Branch investigate their own."

"We did, and came up with nothing. Nothing except a whisper of Leigh-Hunt, that is."

Troy said nothing. Westcott picked up his thread.

"Did you ask Burgess about anyone else?"

"I pushed ahead with the game of numbers. I asked who was number six—or six hundred six, or whatever silly number we'd reached by then."

"And?"

"He told me to mind my own business and fell face down onto his plate. I got nothing more out of him. Indeed, there was nothing more I wanted. It was just a game. It's not the business I'm in. I got him back to his hotel, rolled him onto the bed, took off his shoes, and left him to sleep it off. I saw him twice more. Around noon the next day to tell him MI5 were sending someone out, and when I ushered Blaine in and I ushered myself out. I don't think I even shut the door between entering and leaving. Blaine didn't want me there, and I was more than happy to oblige. I never saw Guy again.

"When the Vienna police let me go, I went straight round to Guy's hotel, but needless to say he was long gone. Roderick Spode had checked out."

"Why Roderick Spode?"

"Guy was fond of literary jokes. I believe he told Melinda Maclean he was called Roger Styles—an Agatha Christie character. Roderick Spode is from the Jeeves books, and ironically enough, he's a fascist caricature. The Russians must have offered him a fake passport in whatever name, he could hardly travel as Guy Burgess, and he had to have his little joke with them."

"Did he leave a note?"

Troy took his left hand from his overcoat pocket and handed Burgess's note to Westcott.

"I thought you might ask," he said.

Westcott took it in at a glance.

"Pudding Island?"

"Another of Guy's jokes. A double joke, in fact. It's Lawrence Durrell's contemptuous term for Britain. Stodgy and tasteless. Double in that Guy was always rather fond of pudding."

"Hmm."

Westcott handed the note back.

"Should we be looking into this Durrell chap?"

§98

Just before three, the Fat Man brought the Bentley round to the front, to take Westcott back to the railway station.

He shook Troy's hand, a glimmer of a smile visible above the tartan scarf wound about his chin.

"Thank you, Mr. Troy. May I say it's been a pleasure."

"You will understand if I say it hasn't?"

Westcott dipped his head, looked up again, the smile still intact. He wasn't taking hump. Troy was glad. He had no wish to upset the old man, but temptation tugged at him all the time.

"Will we be meeting again, Mr. Westcott?"

"I don't know. A little too early to say, and I need hardly stress that our conversations are secret, and you shouldn't discuss what we've said with anyone else."

Westcott was still smiling as he said this. As though a routine remark uttered at the wrong point in the routine should be accepted by Troy as a matter of routine.

"You've got to be kidding," said Troy.

"About secrecy, Mr. Troy? I never joke about secrecy."

"Mr. Westcott, surely you can't believe any of this is secret? To single out just one issue, Norman Cobb—when he disappeared the back of the bog door on the third floor at the Yard was covered in graffiti for weeks. 'Comrade Cobb.' 'Nikita Cobb.' There was even one that read 'Burgess, Maclean, Cobb—who the fuck is next?' But you retired early in '56, didn't you? You would have missed all that."

"I rather think I did. It may be ambitious, and possibly naïve, to think that secrets will remain secret, but it's my job to try."

§99

If Troy had one trait in common with Burgess, it was that boredom made him wicked.

By the middle of the following week, a dull, grey, wintery Wednesday, Westcott had not asked for another meeting, but the plods continued to traipse after him.

Troy walked down St. Martin's Lane, down Villiers Street, to Charing Cross Underground, and caught a Circle Line train, on the inner track, towards Liverpool Street. At Liverpool Street, where trains regularly departed for "Harwich and the Continent," a slogan vividly displayed and which he hoped might induce a touch of panic in his pursuers, he dawdled awhile by the ticket office, then exited at the far side, and climbed the steep outside staircase to Broad Street Station, and the North London Railway—suburban trains for Highbury, Hampstead, and Richmond. A grim little place which had once been the busiest station in the world. And if memory served, Mr. Pooter had gone to his office on this railway line in *The Diary of a Nobody*.

He got out at Hampstead Heath and set off uphill in the direction of Kenwood House.

A few hundred yards on, roughly level with the end of Well Walk, was a huge oak, battered by time and wind and rain. As a boy he'd climbed it dozens of times, and he knew that at chest height was a hollow about the size of a football. One summer, he'd found a red squirrel in residence. She had shrieked as loud as any goose. Today the hollow was empty.

He slipped in the envelope, looked quickly around, and walked back to the ponds in the lee of South Hill, where he found an empty bench, took out a paperback book—*Burmese Days* by George Orwell—and read until the light had dimmed. Then he packed up, walked to Belsize Park Station, and caught the next Northern Line train home to Leicester Square.

Somewhere in Scotland Yard or at MI5 HQ in Leconfield House someone would be trying to make sense of the note he had left. An extract from *The Hunting of the Snark* by Lewis Carroll:

They hunted till darkness came on, but they found
Not a button, or feather, or mark,
By which they could tell that they stood on the ground
Where the Baker had met with the Snark.

In the midst of the word he was trying to say,
In the midst of his laughter and glee,
He had softly and suddenly vanished away—
For the Snark was a Boojum, you see.

Troy had always been fond of Boojums. He'd never wanted to meet one—a sensible precaution considering the fate of those who did—but the affection remained.

$100

About Ten Days Later

Someone was following Frederick Troy.

He was pretty certain the Branch had given up tailing him, and in keeping with their habitual, lazy practices they knocked off sharpish at five thirty every day—that was in all probability how they had lost Burgess and Maclean. The new man, caught in reflections from shop windows, was much more persistent. Troy had yet to see his face clearly. All he knew for certain was he was a big bugger in a black macintosh. No hats to disguise him, no change of outfit from one day to the next. Troy had always thought such tactics crude—after all, who could disguise posture or gait, which were giveaways as much as any item of clothing—and so it seemed did his follower. He relied on distance and concealment rather than disguises. A man in a black coat? How obvious was that? London in winter was a sea of black overcoats and gaberdine macintoshes. A flotsam of trilbies punctuated by the odd bowler. All the same, Troy had spotted him two days ago.

Emerging from the Gay Hussar at lunchtime, Troy had gazed idly around and seen no sign of him. But by the time he passed the window of Foyles booksellers, less than two hundred yards away, there he was, a sudden flash in the plate glass.

Early that Friday evening, Troy emerged from the London Library in St. James's Square. It was time to call it a day and go home. Or—time to turn the tables. The logical route home was along Pall Mall, through London "Clubland," to the top of Trafalgar Square, by the National Gallery. It was time to test logic. If he gave his tail the idea that he was trying to lose him, then the man might more readily accept that he had been lost. At the end of Pall Mall, Troy turned up the Haymarket, and into the "mighty roar of London's traffic," as the BBC put it nightly, at Piccadilly Circus. There, quite certain his tail had followed, he vanished into Swan & Edgar.

Emerging into Regent Street he joined the throng around the base of Eros and waited. Eros was about as cosmopolitan as the cosmopolis got, the tawdry hub of empire: tourists wandered, took photographs in the half-light that would look awful when printed up, gazed in awe at the illuminated advertisements that silently mocked the architecture; drug addicts shivered, twitched, and begged—Troy saw one off with a ten-bob note and "You're blocking my view"; prostitutes, tired of pacing Piccadilly in high heels and tight skirts in search of a fare, kicked off their shoes and sat on the pedestal beneath the demigod of their trade.

"You up fo' it?" said one, a beautiful black girl with crimson lips and green eye shadow.

"Do I look as though I'm up for it?"

"Dunno. I can't see what ya little chap's tinking from heayah."

"Well, my big chap is saying off-duty copper to you."

"*Off* duty? So ya might be up fo' it, den?"

He waited a full twenty minutes—so long that the prospect of drugs or sex or both might begin to seem tempting—before his man emerged, a look of frustration on his face. He was younger than Troy, perhaps thirty at most, tall, lean, and quite handsome. He glanced at his watch, stared into the crowd without seeing Troy, turned up his collar and headed off past Eros and into Coventry Street. Troy could almost swear he had silently mouthed the word "bugger."

His destination was obvious. The Northern Line tube station at Leicester Square. If he'd gone down to the Underground at Piccadilly Circus, he would have taken the Bakerloo or Piccadilly lines. A tourist might be a slave to the tube map and its carpet of coloured thread, a Londoner wanting the Northern Line would simply walk the four hundred yards to the next tube station rather than change lines at track level.

The trick now was to get ahead of him. Troy cut across to Lisle Street and ran like hell for the Charing Cross Road, hoping the crowds of shoppers in Leicester Square would slow his man down.

At the tube station he waved his warrant card at the barrier and ran down the escalator to track level. The question now was "north or south?" and logic was no help. It was a simple gamble. To stand where the lobby divided travellers north or south was to be spotted. He had to be on one platform or another, huddled among the tired and the impatient Friday-night Londoners.

He chose northbound. If he was wrong, so what? It was odds on he would be followed tomorrow or the day after that or Monday, and equally odds on he could lose him again.

A train came and went while he waited, and he began to feel exposed, but in minutes the platform filled with passengers again. Among them, his man, eyes glued to a copy of the *News Chronicle*. He'd given up. Accepted that he had lost Troy. He didn't look around, simply glanced at the destination board and went back to his paper.

The next train was for Edgware. When it pulled in, his follower slipped through the sliding doors into the nearest car without a backwards glance. Troy followed one car behind. At every stop he stepped onto the platform. Tottenham Court Road, Goodge Street, and Warren Street he deemed unlikely, far easier, even quicker, to walk; the probabilities opened up at Euston, with the possibility of a change to the main line—Mornington Crescent, Camden Town, Chalk Farm . . . Belsize Park.

At Hampstead, the man got out, stuffed the newspaper into his pocket, and joined the burgeoning, slow-moving queue for the creaking, ancient lifts that hauled you up from the deepest station in London to street level. There were three. Troy had only ever known two to be working at any one time. Surfacing at Hampstead could be an ordeal. Troy took the emergency staircase. Unless his heart gave out, there was a chance that he could get to the surface first.

By the time his man appeared, Troy was standing on the far side of Heath Street in the darkened doorway of a closed shop, his blood roaring in his ears—he felt he must be breathing as loudly as a charging rhino. He watched the man head south, towards Church Row. He could almost believe the man was about to call on his brother, but he walked on, walked on and turned right into Perrin's Walk, and suddenly all this began to make sense to Troy.

There was only one thing to do.

He stood outside the house in Perrin's Walk and rang the bell.

He heard footsteps on the stairs. A voice yelling, "Get that, will you."

Then the door opened, a familiar face appeared, a familiar jaw dropped, a familiar eye popped, and Eddie said, "Oh, bloody Norah."

"I'll take that as an invitation, shall I, Eddie?"

Eddie was speechless.

A voice above them, "Ed?"

Eddie closed the door behind Troy without another word. Troy went upstairs to the first-floor sitting room. His follower had shrugged off his macintosh and stood in shirtsleeves with his back to him, pouring vodka on the rocks for two. He turned.

"Eddie, get us a third glass, would you?"

Then he stuck out his hand.

"Joe Holderness. I've heard a lot about you, Chief Superintendent Troy."

Troy shook the hand.

"And I you, Flight Sergeant Holderness. Or do I call you Mr. Wilderness?"

"Nah. The women call me that. You can call me Joe."

§101

Troy could not work out whether Eddie was angry or embarrassed. He seemed to have only one shade of red to cover both emotions. He sat in silence while Wilderness told Troy a little of their time in Berlin together in the years just after the war. Nothing really surprised Troy. Eddie, after all, had given him a fragmentary narrative over the last two years in which Wilderness had figured almost as a comic book hero. However, Troy had not quite realised the extent of Eddie's criminal pursuits. Nor had he realised that it had all ground to a halt only hours before he and Eddie had met in 1948. The next time they met had been in 1956. Eddie had been a constable in the City of Birmingham Constabulary. Troy had recruited him to the Yard, promoted him to sergeant—or as Eddie put it, "rescued me from copper's drudgery." However . . . Troy did not give a damn that Eddie had been on the wrong side of the law ten years ago. Where he was now was where he was now.

"Eddie," Wilderness said. "Nip and see if Judy needs anything."

"Such as?"

"Anything, Ed. Anything at all."

Eddie seemed begrudgingly slow to recognise what Wilderness was saying, but took his by-now-watery, untouched vodka to the kitchen.

"No point in involving him, is there?"

"No," said Troy. "I need him in the dark for the moment. Besides, he won't handle divided loyalties at all well. You're investigating me, Joe. Tell me Eddie is not part of that."

"He's not. He found out less than two minutes ago."

"You just told him you've been following me? I spotted you two days ago."

"Well done. Five out of ten."

"Meaning?"

"I've been following you for three weeks."

This shocked Troy. For a moment he had nothing to say.

"Good God, I have fucked up. Three weeks? The Branch have been following me almost that long. I spotted them at once. Give me ten out of ten for that."

"They're idiots. We both know that. I followed them, they followed you. They hadn't a clue either of us had spotted them. They were called off on Tuesday."

"Called off? Why?"

"Westcott submitted his report."

Wilderness paused. He was going to make Troy tease this one out.

"And?"

"And perhaps this is when your chickens come home to roost."

The same cliché Stan had used. Apt and inadequate at the same time.

"You may be right," Troy said. "Westcott gave me a checklist of everything Five had against me. A catalogue of my sins."

"People die around you, Mr. Troy. In particular, Special Branch officers seem to die or vanish . . . and MI6 agents resign for no apparent reason. That's a shedful of chickens."

"So, he hasn't cleared me?"

"No. He hasn't. And that note you left in the hollow tree on Hampstead Heath didn't help."

"It was a joke. Burgess vanished just as though he'd come face-to-face with a Boojum."

"Was Bill Blaine the Boojum? If so, it was a very good joke, but the plods, having never read a word of Lewis Carroll, wouldn't have a clue it was a joke, and whilst Jim probably does know what a Boojum is, he could not afford to write it off as a gag. I'd imagine it was pored over for clues for hours. You succeeded in wasting their time, you slowed down Jim making his report by a day or two, I should think.

"Nonetheless—Boojums or not—his report went into Five on Tuesday morning. By Tuesday evening a copy was on Dick White's desk at Six . . . and mine too.

"Jim Westcott works on the principle that most of the time the man he's interrogating, however gently he goes about it, is already compromised and feels compromised. And all Westcott has to do is puff on his Player's Navy Cut, listen carefully, and expose the contradictions in what he's being told. That's how a good spycatcher works, and Jim is the best. That's how he nabbed Klaus Fuchs. He's adamant that you show no sense of feeling compromised. Not a hint of guilt. No self-contradiction. Whatever the circumstances, in a London club . . . strolling by the river like two old pals . . . your story and your tone never varied. You were not intimidated by the formal approach, you didn't unbutton when he went casual on you. He even joked that he wished he'd been able to take your pulse. That way he'd know for certain you were alive. You may be the only man ever to fox Westcott. Put simply, his report says he cannot prove you are a traitor, nor can he prove you are not. It's not damning, but it's the kind of ambiguity that cast Philby into no-man's-land. They can't prosecute, but they could use it to end your career."

"I don't think of it as a career. It's a job."

"But it matters to you, all the same. I've Eddie's word for that. It matters."

"It does."

"So . . ."

"So?"

"So, I'm going to clear you."

Again, Troy was shocked.

"How, Joe? What do you know that the Branch don't?"

"They're idiots . . . 'scuse me, I may be repeating myself here . . . lazy, clock-watching, unimaginative idiots. They followed you. They did exactly what Five told them. No more, no less. Nobody thought to tell them to work shifts, so they didn't, and there was no twenty-four watch on you. Now, every investigation requires a bit more . . . a bit more imagination than the orders allow for. They tailed you, they know who you met, where you took lunch, what newspaper gets shoved through your letter box each morning. I did all that too. But I also searched every house you own or even have a stake in. I've been through every cupboard in Goodwin's Court, every closet in your brother's house in Church Row . . . he should get a new safe, the one he has is Victorian and far too easy to crack . . . and every attic, lumber room, and cellar out at Mimram. I've searched your ex-mistress's clinic in Harley Street, and I've turned over that lunatic accountant she's married to. I've upended every wastepaper basket, read every saved letter. I've cross-examined your bank manager. I've even had one or two of your narks hauled in and threatened with fictitious charges. They're very loyal to you, by the bye. You obviously pay well. I won't say there's nothing I don't know about you . . . I can even tell you Miss Foxx's bra size . . . 34C in case you're wondering about lingerie for Christmas . . . but I know enough."

"Enough to justify the illegal search of an MP's house?"

"Contain your rage, Troy. Enough . . . enough to clear you. Every spy leaves some trace. It's a given. I've never known anyone manage to conceal everything. You have left nothing. But, there's a deciding factor. You are not the spy I found, but there's the spy I did find."

"My wife."

"Yep. Tosca."

"Eddie knew her in Berlin in '48. I may assume you did too?"

"Yep. I knew Major Toskevich. She chatted me up in a bar in the American sector when I was nineteen. I'd've put Tosca at thirty-five or so. At first I thought I was being pulled and what nineteen-year-old wouldn't succumb to the fantasy of the older woman? Particularly one looking like Tosca. Instead she was teaching me how to survive among the rogues. I was a rogue, but Berlin was full of bigger rogues. I made my fair share of mistakes in Berlin. I'd've made a lot more if I'd never met Tosca. I've every reason to be grateful to her. I might even say I owe her my life. If MI6 had to set anyone on your tail, then you can count yourself lucky it was me. I'd no more betray Tosca than I would Eddie.

"What I didn't know was that she'd defected. Eddie can keep some secrets."

Lucky seemed almost an understatement to Troy. He hoped deep down in his heart that Joe Wilderness meant what he said. Or they were both damned.

"Defected?" he said. "Hardly the word. She ran for her life. In what way is Tosca the deciding factor?"

"I'm getting to that. But, a question. Did Jim Westcott ask you about her?"

"Once. Just once. It came up over lunch. He was in his relaxed mode. As tactical as his pro mode, but less obvious. Threw it out over the bangers and mash as a casual query. The kind of thing that didn't require privacy or security clearance. Just brown ale and ketchup. Asked how I'd come to marry an American, which is one of her many legitimate nationalities, and the one she presented when we married in Vienna."

"And?"

"I gave him the short version of the truth. It was a wartime romance. No lie there. Jim has old-fashioned manners and didn't ask why we were separated, merely asked where she was now. By the time we got to plum duff and custard he was telling me who he favoured in the 3:30 at Sandown Park. He never asked about her again."

"She's in America. I found her airmail letters."

"She is. And now you know as much as I do."

"Jim can't know who she is. She isn't mentioned in his report. If he had even an inkling . . . he'd have risked it.

"If . . . big if . . . you were a Soviet agent . . . Moscow would have told you to have absolutely nothing to do with Tosca. It's as simple as that."

Troy mused on this. The winning card tossed down almost as an afterthought. Too casual for words.

Wilderness got up and refilled their glasses with vodka.

"I acquired a taste for vodka in Berlin. Actually, I acquired it in the company of your wife. But, there's every other tipple if you'd prefer something else."

«Нет, товарищ, я за водку.» No, comrade, vodka is good.

Wilderness grinned.

"Cheers, comrade."

Troy said, at last, "Two things baffle me. Why did Six feel they had to duplicate a Five investigation?"

"Dick White was at Five when Burgess defected. He knew they'd cocked it up and didn't want this to go the same way. Plus, however briefly, Burgess was one of ours. He worked for Six. Sometime during the war, I gather."

"It was the summer of 1940. He told me at the time."

"God, was he really that indiscreet?"

"Oh, he was far worse than that."

"Two things, you said?"

"Why have MI5 overlooked Tosca?"

Wilderness knocked back half his vodka. Stared momentarily into the glass. Then looked Troy in the eye.

"I don't know. It's unbelievably stupid. But it's saved your bacon. Tosca was always a liability to you. It's little short of ironic that she's turned out to be your Get-Out-Of-Jail-Free card."

Wilderness's wife appeared at the kitchen door.

"Joe. You didn't tell me we had another guest."

Troy stood, realised he was still wearing his overcoat and looking at odds with Wilderness in shirtsleeves and a woman in a pinafore. He looked like what he was. A man about to leave.

"You must be Freddie," Judy said. "Odd we've never met. I often chat to your sister-in-law in the baker's or the greengrocer's. Now . . . I've got Swift Eddie knocking up toad-in-the-hole. Can I persuade you to join us?"

She turned her gaze to her husband. Troy gently shook his head.

"Freddie already has a Friday night date, Judy. Single man, after all."

"Ah, well. Perhaps some other time. So pleased to meet you at last."

When she'd gone, and they could hear the banging of pans in the kitchen, Troy said, "I don't think we should get to know one another too well, do you?"

Wilderness shrugged, "I'd've gone for it. But . . . you could be right. I can't read Eddie at the moment. So . . ."

The sentence led nowhere.

"I was thinking more of Tosca," Troy said. "I doubt whether I've seen the last of her. And who knows how often I'll have to play that Get-Out-Of-Jail-Free card. You may find yourself investigating me again. Be far easier for both of us the less we know one another."

"Yeah. May be. It's a pity, all the same."

§102

It was eight-ish by the time Troy got home to Goodwin's Court. Foxx had her nose in a book, her blue-jeaned legs tucked beneath her backside, the pink tips of her socks just visible.

Troy tilted the book so as to see its title:

Venetia: A Regency Romance
by Georgette Heyer

A woman on the cover—heart-shaped face, improbably slender, in a pink dress that matched Foxx's socks. Things could be worse. She might ask him to get a television set.

"Troy, you're sneering. Stop it!"

"No, I'm not."

"Yes, you are. I can hear you. Your inner sneer is nagging at you even as you tell me lies."

"Force of habit. My education ruined me."

"Liar. You mean mine ruined me, don't you?"

Troy shrugged off his coat, flopped down next to her.

"Is it interesting?"

Foxx said nothing, gathered herself with a squirm.

"OK. Then give me the gist of the plot."

Foxx flipped open the dust cover, as though refreshing her memory from the publisher's blurb.

"Well, Venetia's an orphan . . ."

"Score one."

"Shut up! Venetia's an orphan . . . well, she thinks she's an orphan . . . lives on an estate in Yorkshire . . . and she falls for Lord Jasper, the wicked baron who lives next door . . ."

Troy aimed for a blank expression—blank even if the muscles in his cheeks turned to agony suppressing a grin.

Foxx suddenly slammed the book shut.

"Oh God. What am I saying? It's utter fucking tosh, isn't it?"

She stood up sharply, threw the book at his groin, and stomped kitchenward.

"I'll cook. Cooking and fucking. The only things I'm good for. You utter fucking bastard!"

Troy let the book fall to the floor. Lay back against the sofa. His inner sneer gave way to something fatter and fluffier and several degrees warmer. A voice that said, "It's over."

§103

At dinner he opened a bottle of the "good stuff," as he and Rod always called the thousands of bottles they had inherited from their father. A Pouilly-Fumé that might well have been a little past its best. All the same, Foxx glugged it as though it were Tizer, and her mood audibly relaxed.

"Bastard," she said, and blew him a kiss across the cod-and-mash pie.

"Guilty as charged."

"If I say tell me about your day, will it be as dull as mine? . . . starting a book I'll never finish . . . or did you achieve something?"

"Yes. I think I did. It's over."

"Over?"

"The Branch are off my back. No one is any the wiser about Tosca, and the Burgess affair is safely contained. As the Prime Minister might well put it . . . a little local difficulty. I can report back to the Yard on Monday and play the honest copper."

"Well," she said. "We all kid ourselves about something."

"Ouch."

"No . . . no, Troy. I wasn't saying you're bent . . . different, not bent . . . I meant, well . . . usually things are only over when you've cracked them wide open. It's over when you say it's over."

"This is different. This is very different. Burgess is not my problem. Blaine is not my problem. As I told Rod, if Blaine had been gunned down in the streets of London it would be another matter entirely. But he wasn't."

"You can walk away from this?"

"Yes."

"I wish I could believe you."

"Just watch me. I'm going to kick off my shoes in about ten minutes and with them the metaphorical dust of Vienna. I shall put up socked feet, stick Schubert on the gramophone. Blow the cobwebs off a Balzac novel I've been halfway through since August. In an hour or so I may even help myself to the old man's Armagnac. Listen to the late news on the Home Service. Then I may undress you, tumble you into bed and ravish you so fiercely you might think I had been rechristened Sir Jasper. Tomorrow I shall sleep in, spread the morning papers across the eiderdown, read snippets of the new nonsense aloud to you . . . a demarcation dispute in Scunthorpe between the Guild of Putters-On and the Amalgamated Union of Knockers-Off, an advert for washing machines at a guinea down and five bob a week for infinity, a life peerage for Fred Fatarse, the supermarket magnate, the life and loves of the newest, tuneless teen pop idol, Randy Racket . . . while I watch you dress, then have all the pleasure watching you undress again at my immediate behest and Sir Jasper you once more. In short, I shall spend a blissfully spook-free weekend with Franz Schubert, Honoré de Balzac, the *Manchester Guardian*, and the girl of my dreams."

"I'm flattered, but . . ."

"Oh fuck . . . but what?"

"You sister phoned."

"Masha?"

"Sasha. That sanatorium where she's been drying out, up in Derbyshire . . . she's leaving on Saturday. Wants you to pick her up and drive her home."

"What sanatorium?"

"The one Rod packed her off to."

"Am I missing something here? When the fuck did this happen?"

"The day after we got back from Amsterdam."

"And why, may I ask? I thought she'd been relatively sober after we left Siena."

"She was, but I think she was storing it all up."

"None the wiser."

"The morning after, at breakfast, she loaded up Hugh's old army revolver and took potshots at him across the tea and toast. Missed every time, thank God. Hugh did not go running to the cops—well, he couldn't really, could he?—God be thanked twice in one paragraph. He came to Rod. Rod called him the C-word and said he'd had it coming. Hugh was in shock, told Rod she kept yelling gibberish at him, something about 'I'd rather fuck a swan.' Made no sense to anybody. Rod told him to bugger off, but he collared Sasha, insisted she check in to this place in Derbyshire . . . not so much to sober up as straighten up. Although I think the two might be connected."

"I shall kick myself."

"Why, oh sweetest?"

"I'm Deadeye Dick with a revolver. I could have taught her."

§104

It was a dreary drive north. England in December. Phrases such as "It's trying to snow" came to mind. A use of English that had always baffled Troy. In French it was snowing or it wasn't. In Russian it was always snowing and worthy of comment only when it wasn't.

The Minister of Transport, a three-ring showman by the name of Ernest Marples, had promised a north-south autobahn to be called a "motorway." Until it was finished, Derbyshire was many crawling hours away up the A5. Troy did not like driving at the best of times. Being at the beck and call of his errant sister might make it the worst of times.

To his surprise Foxx had insisted on coming with him, and at seven in the morning, as he waited by the car at the back of the alley, in Bedfordbury, he realised that she was packing a more-than-overnight bag.

"Tell me," he said.

"Simple really. Winster Priory . . . which is where Sasha is, is about ten miles from Belper. I thought I'd have a few days at home."

"I thought this was your home, and Belper was . . . the day I met you . . . the 'all this' from which you wished me to 'take you away'?"

"Could we just get going, Troy? I'll explain on the way."

They'd passed the North Circular before Foxx spoke again, and then only to comment on the drizzle.

Troy put the radio on. Arthur Rubinstein playing Beethoven's Fourth Piano Concerto.

She slept.

Round about Tamworth she woke with a start.

"Oh hell. I must have nodded off."

"Nodded off for two hours," Troy said.

"Damn. Must be all the Sir Jaspering, Troy. You've worn me out. What was I saying?"

"A few days in a one-horse town in the north of England you now grace with the word 'home.'"

"Oh. Yes. Silly me. Well . . . it's like this . . ."

The pause stretched and stretched. To interrupt seemed to Troy like the snapping of a magic thread. Then she spat it out in one rapid, careful sentence.

"I've realised you can't just walk away from everything that makes you what you are."

This was scarcely one word different from what Burgess had said to him after two bottles of red wine, minutes before he fell face down in his lemon tart. Foxx was at least sober.

"Do places make us what we are?"

"Oh yes. Think of all those Forces kids you can meet, or the children of Empire, the sons and daughters of colonial district officers, bounced from place to place and nanny to nanny, then sundered from their mothers at some insanely early age and bunged into a prep school. They don't have any sense of belonging, do they? It's why the English upper classes are mad. It's why they inflate the notion of country or empire because they cannot relate to any one place in either. All they have is their patriotism. And if patriotism isn't localised it means nothing. It becomes abstract. It becomes Tory bombast. They have a big picture and no little picture."

The last sentence came as a relief to Troy. It sounded like Shirley Foxx. The rest . . . the rest at least assured him she'd been reading something else besides the romantic tosh.

"So . . . you're going, and I use this word cautiously, 'home' to reconnect with your roots?"

"Not really. I think I never disconnected. And that's the matter. I want two things . . . a second look, the certainty that I did the right thing when I left with you two years ago . . . and to put it all in the right place. The right piggy hole in my head, where it can sit safely and not trouble me. I'd much prefer to be supported by my childhood than haunted by it."

"And how long do you think this will take?"

"Dunno. A week. Maybe two?"

For about five miles he let silence rule, if not reign.

Then she said, "Friends. I still have friends up there."

"Aha. Friends you never mention."

"Friends I treated badly. I said no goodbyes. I was angry with a place and angrier still with a time . . . the time being my entire life up to that point. I found a small town oppressive, I hated being singled out as bright . . . all those taunts of 'smart arse' and 'oo er . . . ow's swallowed a dictionary' if I used a word with more than three syllables . . . all that made me so angry . . . and in the end you presented me with an opportunity to blast it all by leaving. I took a shotgun to my childhood. I needed a sniper's rifle."

"So. You're going back to slay the beast. What you mean to put in that piggy hole in your mind is the stuffed and mounted head, horns and all."

"God, what an appalling image!"

"I'm right, though."

"Yes, you are, my very own smart-arse. I shall be kinder to the few friends I have. I shall treasure the memories that are to be treasured, and the rest I shall leave headless corpses upon the field of battle."

Troy roared with laughter. It had taken her an age to articulate all this. Two years with him and almost four hours up an English highway, and he could not but agree. He had watched his grandfather yearn silently, through his years of exile, for the old country. Heard his grandfather give voice to his grief at every far-from-silent opportunity. His father had it down pat, so did his uncle Nikolai . . . their stories, tinged with nostalgia, had never broached heartbreak. They each had found the right piggy hole for childhood, and on that basis had created a secure home, a physical and mental realm Troy had always thought of as Troy

Nation . . . the piggy hole was in the domain of the head, according to Foxx, and the nation in the kingdom of the heart, according to his father. What was the alternative? To go mad? To fall face down in the lemon tart ever after?

§105

It was almost noon when Troy parked his Bentley in front of Foxx's house, on a hill high above the town.

Foxx hefted her one bag. Troy stood with his hands in his overcoat pockets, looking around at the mix of inter-war and post-war houses, with the odd stone cottage breaking the uniformity, unrepentant reminders of a Georgian past, of a pre-industrial peasantry that had raised pigs and hammered out nails in the days before the machines came. And over it all, the red brick chimney "up at t'mill"— except that the mill was not up, but down from where he stood. Nor was it dark or satanic, by all appearances.

"What're you looking at?"

"Oh, just seeing if the curtains twitch."

"Don't worry, they will. They may not twitch for me in my own right, but I am Stella Foxx's sister and if the scandal has died down so soon, I'll be flabbergasted."

"Ask not for whom the curtain twitches. It twitches for thee."

"Oh, yes. Very funny I'm sure."

Stella had left home well ahead of her twin sister. Run off with the man from the carpet emporium, to be set up in a love-nest in Brighton— and to be murdered. Not one scandal but two. Troy had solved the murder, and in keeping with Foxx's new-found philosophy, had found the right hole in which to lodge it. Foxx was here and Foxx was Foxx. He gave little thought to the circumstances of their meeting.

He'd never done this. Returned to an empty house he had once called home. Let cold, and that hollow sound that empty always made, ferret around in his feelings.

Foxx had set down her bag and sighed.

"Bugger, bugger, bugger."

The house was clean. Troy realised someone had to be coming in once in a while and, if nothing else, dusting. It had been remiss of him not to ask, callous not even to have wondered. How much had she packed the day they had, true to cliché, run away together? Bra, knickers, spare T-shirt, spare jeans? He doubted it had been more than that. If he had to run what would he have taken? Books? Well . . . he could have done without the complete Jane Austen. Although he knew a man who couldn't.

"Troy. Why am I doing this?"

"The heart has its reasons."

"Isn't that a book title or something?"

"Duchess of Windsor. Dreadful woman. Never bothered to read it. I just like the title. She pinched it from Pascal. *'Le cœur a ses raisons que la raison ne connaît point.'* Or something like that."

"Oh God. Am I being that irrational?"

"No, no, you're not. Do this. Take your time. Take as long as you need. Salvage what you will, then kill the beast."

She disappeared upstairs.

He put the kettle on. Made tea. Found an ineffectual one-bar electric fire in the broom cupboard and plugged it in. In a year or two it might just take the chill off the kitchen.

Foxx heard the kettle whistle.

"If you're making tea, you'll need to nip out for milk. That'll be a first."

"Eh?"

"I'd bet that you've never been in a corner shop in the north of England, and I'd bet the woman behind the counter has never heard an accent like yours before."

"So much for one nation."

"Just buy the fucking milk! I am, as they say around here, 'parched.'"

§106

He found her in her bedroom. Childhood spread out across a hand-knotted rag rug—one large doll, one small lacking its left arm, half a dozen Ladybird books, a dozen Collins Classics, a shrivelled bouquet of posies in a faded red ribbon, a bar of soap in the shape of Minnie Mouse . . . a couple of Anya Seton's novels . . . *Dragonwyck, The Hearth and Eagle* . . . *The Albatross Book of Living Verse*, Warne's *Wayside and Woodland Trees*—and adolescence . . . a scattering of Johnnie Ray 78s, a Vince Christy long-player: *That Old Black Magic, Vol 2*—and emerging adulthood . . . Orwell's *Animal Farm*, Huxley's *Brave New World, The Catcher in the Rye* . . . the Elgar Violin Concerto, recorded by Yehudi Menuhin circa 1932.

"Not much, is it?"

"But there's more?"

"Not a lot. Mostly clothes I wouldn't be seen dead in any more. And God knows there's nothing like a visit to either of your sisters to make me feel like Fanny Frump."

"Ignore them. Their taste is simply the Russian version of Milly-Molly-Mandy. Doesn't require any idea of fashion or any sense of colour. You wear the same damn thing all the time. All you really need is an open cheque book and a good seamstress to look like my sisters."

"I wouldn't want to look like your sisters. That's my point."

"What do you want?"

"Now? Right now? I just feel like weeping."

"Then in the words of your chosen pop idol, just go ahead and cry."

She smiled, a sad smile that barely suppressed a tear.

She sat on the bed.

"Just hold me, you stupid sod."

He did.

"I'm not going to cry. Really, I'm not."

§107

He'd taken off his overcoat and wrapped it around the two of them, thinking she might sleep and with sleep cease to weep, but it was he who dropped off.

Rain on the skylight woke him.

Foxx was staring at him. Her finger touched the end of his nose.

"I can't hear you think when you're asleep. I find your silence quite relaxing. No buzz of 'what is he thinking? what will he say next?' Almost peaceful."

"Is that a complaint?"

"No."

She paused. Looked up at the darkening sky.

"I always loved rain on the roof. Erotic."

Troy glanced at his watch.

"We have to go. It's almost two. Sasha is expecting us at three."

"You go. I need big sis like I need an extra belly button. I'll stay here. Press on. Get things done. Call me when you get to London."

"Really?"

"I can handle this, Troy. Honestly."

"It's a journey without maps."

"What is?"

"Childhood. And I'm quoting someone yet again. Not sure who. Probably not Graham Greene. But it's childhood revisited for you now. You have your map. It's called hindsight. You just need to know how to read the signs and contours."

"What to keep and what to throw away."

"Exactly. You can start by throwing away all the records. I have the Elgar. I can probably live without Johnnie Ray and I could never stick Vince Christy."

"You're a bastard, you know that, don't you?"

"Is that a complaint?"

§108

Winster Priory stood alone in its Jacobean redbrick grandeur at the end of a long cobbled street, chimneys twisted like barley sugar, roofs steep and red against the Derbyshire downpours, gates rusted open as though they had not closed in a century or more.

Troy's was the only car and as he pulled into the drive he felt he had landed on the set of a western . . . all he needed was rolling balls of tumbleweed and a glimpse of Kirk Douglas or Burt Lancaster. He looked back down the deserted street, straight as an arrow, sloping gently towards the valley, every cottage tight and huddled, belching coal smoke from every chimney, bound by the silence of a winter's Saturday afternoon. Only the glut of television aerials told him it was the twentieth century, and that in every huddled house every huddled family was watching the racing or the football results.

"You're late!"

Sasha was in her black Russian outfit and, quite possibly, her black Russian mood.

"I thought coppers were supposed to be punctual."

"It's five past three, you pedantic hag."

A woman, slightly more colourfully dressed, stepped out from the porch. Sasha stuck her tongue out at him and said:

"You remember my little brother, PC Plod, don't you?"

This was a looker. A stunning blonde. Deep, magnetic blue eyes. The top lip from heaven. A perfect arch. A smile to rip the heart from any man. Troy would put her in her late thirties, perhaps coming up to forty. He was being introduced as though they'd met. He was faintly concerned that if Sasha was right he'd forgotten someone he should not lightly forget.

"Of course, I remember Freddie," the blonde said. "Although the last time we met I fear I didn't. And now, the boot's on the other foot. From the look in his eye Freddie doesn't remember me."

Troy held out an ungloved hand in greeting.

"Frederick Plod. And it's Chief Superintendent not PC Plod."

She shook.

Sasha said, "Bags, Freddie," and installed herself in the back seat of the Bentley. Troy ignored her.

"You're going to have to remind me, you know."

"Oh, no reason you should remember. It was an age ago. In the Blitz."

"That explains it. I couldn't see you clearly in the blackout."

She giggled at this.

"No, no excuse there. It was in La Popôte, you know, underneath the Ritz. You were with Guy Burgess."

Memory burst in him like a dam busted.

"Venetia Maye-Brown?"

"The same, although I've had a few names since then. It's Stainesborough now. Has been for a while."

"And is there a Mr. Stainesborough?"

"I don't know how to take that question. Fishing already, Chief Superintendent? But no . . . there was a Lord Stainesborough but I'm pleased to say he went to the great distillery in the sky some time ago. I am a very merry widow. Or I was until I checked into this place."

The voice from the car.

"Freddie, do get a move on! I'd like to be home before midnight."

Troy hefted both bags into the boot.

As he drove he wondered why he had not recognised Venetia, Lady Stainesborough. A surfeit of expectation, perhaps? Once or twice . . . no dozens of times . . . over the intervening years Sasha had mentioned her, and based on their last brief encounter he had built up a mental picture of someone as degenerate as Sasha herself. She had, after all, been headed that way. But Venetia wasn't. She'd aged remarkably well. Forty or so was wide of the mark. She was nearer fifty, but few would ever guess.

No one had any inclination to talk. Troy put on the BBC Third Programme. A late afternoon concert recorded at the Proms last August: Schubert's "Unfinished."

Past Burton-on-Trent Sasha's snores risked drowning out Sir Malcolm Sargent and the BBC Symphony Orchestra, and, seemingly certain she was asleep, Venetia turned the volume down a little.

"At last we can talk."

"We can?"

"Oh yes. Sasha can sleep for England. Russia as well, I'd imagine. Booze can do that."

"The point," Troy ventured, "of you two being in the priory was not to drink, to dry out in fact. Or have I interpreted this wrongly?"

"Oh, she's dry for now. Until the next time. And I wasn't in for the treatment. She wouldn't do it alone. Masha feels she has done her bit with drink and drugs where her sister is concerned, so I volunteered. I've been clean since the end of the war. I buried the woman you used to know shortly after VE night."

"I see."

"No, you don't. My first husband and I wanted children. More important to me by far than the pleasures I'd indulged in for the best part of fifteen years. But . . . too late . . . my system was . . . well, I don't know what to call it . . . unwilling to conceive."

"So . . . no children?"

"No, and before you point out the possibilities for adoption, Bruce wrapped his car . . . a car very like this one actually, the Mark VI with the soft top, lovely shade of red . . . around a tree in 1947 and that was the end of that. I married Gerontius two years later . . . and he didn't want children. In fact, he was hardly home long enough to make a child."

"Gerontius? You're kidding?"

"No. His mother had a passion for Elgar, so Gerontius he was. Gerontius Stainesborough. Could be worse. He might have been christened Nimrod. And Nimrod does not abbreviate well. He was always known as Gerry."

The penny dropped. Gerry Stainesborough.

"Ah . . . the polar explorer."

"The mountaineer, the Amazon and Orinoco explorer, the trekker of the Northern Territories. You name it he'd been there. If there'd been mountains in Acton or Ealing he'd have climbed them too. A jungle in Highgate, he'd have hacked his way in. As I said, not home long enough to impregnate even if he'd wished to. Then on the '53 Everest expedition he took a fall. Broke his pelvis and was told he'd never climb again. I think he would have preferred to vanish like Mallory. As it was, he vanished into his single malts and was dead by '56. Hence, as I said earlier, I play the merry widow. Which sort of brings me to the point. Why did you ask if there was a Mr. Stainesborough? You used to be such a shy little boy. I can't believe you were just chatting me up."

"I wasn't. But if there had been a Mr. Stainesborough I was curious to know why he wasn't collecting you today instead of me. I've given up expecting anything of Hugh, after all. That marriage is over, it's just a matter of who kills who, of who reaches for the gun first."

"Ah . . . well. I'm disappointed. Just a little. Still, it won't last."

She said nothing. And more nothing. Troy turned the volume back up. Schubert had finished. The orchestra had gained a soloist and moved on to Rachmaninoff's Second Piano Concerto. Troy was not sure he would ever have put these two pieces on the same bill. The Schubert evoked no memories, no pictures. It simply was. The Rachmaninoff was now forever associated in his mind with steam trains and the buffet at Milford Junction, with Celia Johnson and Trevor Howard . . . "I'm a doctor, let me help" . . . a line which lost all romantic power once you substituted the word "policeman" for "doctor."

He dropped Sasha in Highgate and drove Venetia on to Eaton Place in Belgravia.

Her bag was small. He set it down on the steps while she rummaged for her key. It occurred to him she might ask him in. He hoped she wouldn't. All other matters aside, it was nearly nine o'clock, dark and cold, and he was tired.

"Do coppers carry cards, or do you have no room in your pockets once you've got your truncheon?"

Troy handed her one of his private cards. No rank, and the Goodwin's Court address.

"Thank you, Freddie. You've been so kind, I must find a way to thank you properly."

He might bump into her again, if she remained loyal to Sasha, a woman whose command on friends' loyalty slipped lower with each passing day, but he'd never hear from her again. He was quite certain of that.

§109

It was Sunday evening before Foxx called him.

He heard the remote mechanical crash of falling pennies and button A.

"Why are you in a phone box?"

"What? You think we had a telephone at home? And I've been paying the post office for it for the last two years without being here?"

"Sorry. That was stupid."

"It's not like you to make class-based assumptions. Phone? As if we could afford a bloody phone!"

"And it's not as if I'd asked if you rode to hounds. Now, how are you?"

"Better, resolute. I took all my old clothes to the Congregational church for their next jumble sale. I gave Johnnie Ray to the kid next door. I gave Elgar to the vicar's wife, and I decided to keep Vince. And . . ."

"And?"

"I decided to let the house. It's paid for. No mortgage. We might as well have the income."

He warmed to the word "we." The income did not matter, the pronoun did.

"Have I ever mentioned Rosie and Malcolm to you?"

"No. You never talk about any of your friends in the north."

"They're my oldest friends. They have another baby due in April. They could do with the extra rooms. They want most of the furniture, and what they don't want should probably be taken out into the back garden and burnt."

"Do you have a Meccano kit?"

"No. Why do you ask? They were boys' toys."

"You could build a bridge and burn it."

"Ha bloody ha."

"I'm right, though."

"I know. You're a smart arse. Of course I'm burning bridges. What matters is what I bring away, what and to whom I come, and how securely I store the troublesome remnants of childhood."

"I'm impressed by the use of 'whom.' And you have the map of childhood."

"I do. I have the piggy holes of the head to store it all. But it's the what-whom that worries me."

"Eh?"

"You, Troy. I've never been really sure I . . . had you. Oh, bollocks. There's some old trout banging on the door with her brolly. Oh fuck, it's Mrs. Jessup . . . hang on . . . Yes, I know it's a public phone . . . I'm using it . . . Well, you'll just have to . . . oh fuck off!"

"Are you sure that was wise?"

"Absolutely not. She's gone to get her Ernie now. I'll have to go."

"When will you be back?"

"Dunno."

And then he heard the dialling tone.

Almost at once the phone rang again.

Onions.

"Tried calling you yesterday."

Instant reproach in only four words.

"I was rescuing my sister from one of those clinics."

"Again?"

"No comment."

"No matter. Not why I was calling. Westcott's put his report in. So you can get back to work."

"You've read it?"

"No. I agreed to you being put on leave while Jim questioned you. If Jim's submitted his report, then he has no more questions and we play it by the book, to the letter. You're back on duty. If the report raises issues Five can't settle, then they'll have to ask me all over again, won't they?"

There were times when stubbornness and bloody-mindedness were Stan's most appealing characteristics.

§ 110

In his office at Scotland Yard Troy met with Swift Eddie and Jack Wildeve, feeling for the first time in a while that they were not working under a cloud. He explained what had happened briefly to Jack, leaving out that Eddie had been present when he had tracked down Joe Holderness. It seemed like a complication too far. Eddie had known Joe since the end of the war, Jack knew that Eddie knew Joe, Eddie knew that Jack knew and it could be left at that.

"Normal service has been resumed, eh?"

"Something like that, Jack."

Deliberately vague. Troy would not count anything as normal until Onions signed off on it. He wasn't going to call on Onions and invite questions on how he knew he'd been cleared, he would wait for Six to tell Five and for Five to tell the Yard, and then at the bottom of the heap, Onions could tell him, a mere Chief Superintendent of the Murder Squad, and Troy would not even attempt to feign surprise.

"What do we have? Jack?"

"The Roehampton Lane hit-and-run. Turns out the victim was a minor member of the Lambeth gang—a small fry known as Spider Webb. I'm less inclined to regard it as an accident now I know that. Then there's the Wimbledon wife-strangler in the cells. As soon as the rush of adrenalin brought on by meeting his brief and being made to feel important passes he'll confess everything. And lastly, unknown gent in his mid-thirties fished out of the Thames by the River Police at Limehouse Reach with two bullets in his back. Kolankiewicz has the bullets. I'm waiting on him now . . . until then I will admit to being clueless."

None of these cases meant a thing to Troy. They'd all happened while he was in Italy or Austria or sucked into the dark and dirty mindscape that was Burgess-land. He found it hard to care.

"Eddie?"

"I've some very nice medium-roast Kenya coffee on the go, and I nipped into Soho on me way to work and I have a rather succulent panettone."

"Not a lot for me to do, then?"

"Nope."

"Then I'll take my coffee black. One slice of cake. Bring me the bill."

§111

With coffee and cake Eddie brought a pile of manila envelopes almost a foot high. Before Troy could say anything Eddie had nipped out and returned with a second pile even higher.

"You're kidding. You called the pile an 'alp,' as I recall. This is a bloody mountain range."

"That was more than a fortnight ago. Do you really think the work stops piling up just because you're not here?"

"If it's just sign-and-initial stuff, then just forge my signature."

"It isn't," said Eddie as he closed the door behind him.

Troy stood in the window with his cup of coffee. All he had wanted the last God-knows-how-long was to be back in his job—not quite the same thing as being back at his desk, and he felt no more inclination to dig into Eddie's pile of paperwork than he had to dig into Jack's list of murders. Jack would not welcome such intervention. If he needed Troy he'd ask.

Troy did not need Eddie's piles of files. He needed a murder of his own.

Winter sunlight danced its diamonds upon the river, sun slicing in over Southwark. He'd watched this a hundred—no, a thousand—times over the best part of twenty years, ever since Onions had plucked him out of the East End and installed him in this office. Up through the ranks . . . Detective Sergeant Troy, Inspector Troy, Superintendent Troy, and last year, Chief Superintendent Troy. Two and a half years as head of the Murder Squad. He'd never felt this way before. He needed a murder of his own.

Troy needed somebody to die soon.

"Boss?"

Eddie had come in silently.

"Anything wrong?"

"Yes," said Troy. "Nothing I should ever articulate even to myself. The idiotic tangents of thought."

§112

On Wednesday a postcard arrived from Derbyshire, a black-and-white picture of what declared itself to be Chatsworth but was so faded it might be Waterloo Station or the Eddystone Light:

Getting stuck in. Don't worry about me. May take a bit longer than I thought. Will have to find another phone box, so no more calls for a while. Old man Jessup called me a whore and every time I leave the house the curtains twitch. He's itching to catch me on the phone and dot me one with his walking stick. I will be so glad to finally put this place in . . . its place.

SFXX

And on Thursday, just as Troy was lying to Eddie about his progress with the paperwork, Onions appeared in his office.

One nod of the head towards his left shoulder, and one syllable to Eddie, "Out."

Most things in life washed over Eddie. He reacted minimally at the best and worst of times. He had a very English "I'll put the kettle on" response to anything resembling a crisis. Troy did not scare Eddie, he exasperated him, and if his stories of life before he joined the force were to be believed, not half as much as Joe Wilderness did. The one thing that seemed to scare Eddie was Onions.

The door clicked to. Troy could almost hear Eddie's ear flattening against the panel from the other side.

"You're in the clear."

"That must annoy one or two people in this building. Still, do we really care what Special Branch think?"

"Knock it off, Freddie. They bloody near had you this time. Jim Westcott gave a mixed report on you. I've no idea what you told him, but it wasn't enough."

"But it was all he was ever going to get. Now, Stan, could I get you a coffee? Eddie's been shopping again, we have some rather nice roasts on offer, and an Italian delicacy that knocks an Eccles cake into a cocked hat."

"I haven't bloody finished yet! Sit!"

Times there were when Stan would address him much as though he were a badly behaved dog.

Troy took a chair next to the sputtering gas fire. Onions sat opposite him, stuck a cigarette through the grill and lit up.

"I've had to fight for you. Time after bloody time."

"And time after time I have expressed my gratitude."

"This time they nearly had you."

"So you say, and I don't agree. This time they *thought* they had me. Not the same thing at all."

"The Branch wanted your balls. Five wanted your balls. What saved you was some bloke in Six that Dick White set on to you."

"Let me know who, and I'll send him a postcard."

"You're not taking this seriously, are you? I've said this before and I'll say it again, for the last time, do not mess with the spooks. You've got a bloody long lifeline, money, class, family . . . but one day, Freddie, it'll just bloody snap."

Troy leaned a little closer, breathed in the acrid scent of cheap fags, and lowered his voice.

"It was you who told me to stay in Vienna after Burgess approached me. I wanted nothing to do with him. You wanted none of this coming back to us. But that's exactly what staying on led to. A man ended up murdered, then you pulled me out. I could argue that spookery was none of my business, but murder was. But I won't. It wasn't my murder."

"At last, summat we agree on."

"There's more. I want no more to do with spooks than you would have me do. But—there is one distinct advantage to the bastards setting Jim Westcott on to me."

"Which is?"

"The slate has been wiped clean. They'll not dare come back at us with a chronicle of my sins again. I am washed clean. I have bathed in Jordan waters."

Onions didn't know Jordan Younghusband, and would not see a joke. He exhaled a cloud of noxious smoke.

"There's more," he said at last.

"Bad news is never-ending."

"Dunno whether this is good or bad. Sir Clive Potter is announcing his retirement tomorrow."

Potter was the Commissioner of the Metropolitan Police Force, the top copper in London, the top copper in the land—a man who answered only to the Home Secretary. He'd been commissioner since 1951 and the re-election of Winston Churchill—he had been Churchill's own choice. Few men served as long, few men would want to serve as long, and over the last year he had been muttering about his time being up. Troy thought the racial tensions bursting in London, particularly in Notting Hill over the summer, might be the last straw. The Met, Troy thought, was stuffed when it came to race. Whatever they did would be wrong.

"I see," he said. "And you are come to tell me they want me as the next commissioner?"

He got a grin out of Onions with this.

"You cheeky bugger. You know as well as I do . . . you're looking at the next commissioner right now."

"Congratulations, Stan. It's deserved and it's overdue."

"A couple of things bother me."

They would, inevitably, not be the same things that bothered Troy. A knighthood went with the job. He could not help but see Stan as being uncomfortable as Sir Stanley. Few, if any, Met commissioners had been working class, none had ever had a northern accent as strong as Stan's, most had a capacity for flattery and dissembling that seemed beyond Stan, few had his well-honed skill at being the right bull in the right china shop, and Troy doubted that any of them were as straight and decent as he. That was not to say that he was not devious, but that his deviousness was usually in the service of his decency. He was quite capable of telling Troy to break the rules if breaking the rules got the job done. And none of them, to Troy's knowledge, had ever favoured brown boots as footwear. Perhaps he'd have to take Stan to Lobb's in Jermyn Street and treat him to a couple of pairs of hand-made beetle-crushers?

"Such as?" Troy said.

"I'll have to wear a fuckin' uniform. Not all the time but, you know . . . I hate being in uniform."

"And?"

"I'll have less time to keep an eye on you. You'll be running the Murder Squad without yer Uncle Stan at yer shoulder."

"Really? Then bring on the bodies. I could use a good body right now."

VII

Venetia

§113

On the Friday, early in the evening, coat barely shuffled off to the peg, the telephone rang. He was half-expecting it to be Foxx, then a voice he could not place said, "Coming out to play?"

"Do I play with strange women?"

"I'm not strange. I'm Venetia."

He'd not expected this. He had not expected to hear from her. He had thought that all he wanted of a Foxxless Friday night was beans on toast; he had a can of Heinz's finest—a few glasses of claret; he had an Haut-Brion '45; perfect with baked beans in tomato sauce—and a novel. He had the new one everyone seemed to be talking about, *Saturday Night and Sunday Morning*, written at the kitchen sink by some bloke in Nottingham. And now he had doubt as well.

"What did you have in mind, Venetia?"

"Buy me dinner."

"Buy you dinner?"

"Yes. You won't regret it. I know everything."

"Why the sea is boiling hot, and whether pigs have wings?"

"And much much more besides."

§114

Troy called Venetia back fifteen minutes later.

"I've booked us into La Rave. I'll pick you up in about twenty minutes."

"Never heard of it. Where is it?"

"Quite near you, in the King's Road."

"OK."

§115

"King's Road?" she said. "We're practically at World's End."

Troy pulled over, parked his Bentley opposite La Rave.

"Perhaps that's why I was able to get a table at no notice on a Friday night. But it got a cracking review in the *Spectator* a while back."

"What does La Rave mean? I was always useless at French."

"It doesn't mean anything. They just Frenchified an English word."

"So it's rave? As in 'we'll go no more a-raving'?"

"I think you'll find Byron wrote 'roving' not raving."

"He probably meant raving."

"I'm quite certain he did. And I imagine the touch of French makes La Rave sound a bit more like Le Caprice, to which they no doubt aspire."

"Aim high, I suppose."

Once they were seated, Troy looked at the menu. Venetia looked for the wine list. There wasn't one.

"It's a dry restaurant," Troy said.

"A dry restaurant!" Venetia said a little too loudly. Then she leaned closer to him, her eyes darting to either side, and mouthed, "What bloody good is that?"

"I chose it because it was dry. I thought you'd prefer not to watch me drink if you can't drink yourself."

"What a load of bollocks, Freddie."

"If you like, they will send out for wine."

"I do like."

Troy beckoned to the waiter who had shown them to their table. "What would you have, Venetia?"

"Hmm . . . How about a claret?"

"OK. There won't be a lot of choice, but—"

"As long as it's not plonk. Anything Cru Bourgeois or better. After all, you're not going to pinch the pennies on me, are you?"

The waiter told them he'd be back in five minutes.

Troy said, "I thought you were dry?"

"No, Freddie. What I said was 'clean.'"

"What's the difference?"

"Dry means you don't touch alcohol, clean means *you* are in control, not it. I am clean in that I can and do say no to booze. Order a second bottle and you'll have to finish it yourself. Your sister is aiming for dry, because she knows she cannot manage clean. It takes too much will power. There's actually less involved in stopping completely than in keeping control. But, keeping control of anything was never Sasha's strong point. She was a lesson to me. By the time I met Bruce in '42, I was ready to clean up. To say the least, I'd led a raucous war. I'd even admit to being notorious. I'd have settled down happily with Bruce, but of course the minute we were married he was posted abroad to crawl up the spine of Italy, and I scarcely saw him until the winter of '46, and in '47 . . . well, I told you . . . Bentley, tree . . . tree, Bentley . . ."

"Yes," said Troy. "I think notorious might well be the word."

She smiled, unembarrassed by her "raucous" past life.

"I was promiscuous, but not casually promiscuous."

"Again, what's the difference?"

"I can remember all their names."

Troy thought back to that night in La Popôte, and Burgess opining that several men might get lucky in the ladies' loo if Venetia felt so inclined.

"And, I don't need to take my socks off to count them either."

"You mean fewer than twenty?"

"No. Perhaps the sock idea was poorly chosen. Seventy-two to be precise. Seventy-two between the Blitz and VE night."

Troy said nothing.

"You're shocked, aren't you? But you were such an innocent in those days."

"I think I was such an innocent until I was nearly thirty, actually."

"And now?"

"I suppose I've learnt a thing or two about women. Enough not to run a mile in the opposite direction."

"Oh, Freddie. You underestimate yourself. Notorious might well be the word for you too."

"Now I am shocked."

"Shocked, notorious, but in control?"

"I am very much in control. And I would not say I was promiscuous."

"And I would not say it of myself. But . . . I'm a widow. The ties do not bind."

"And I am married."

"So I've heard. No one seems to know much about her."

"There's not much to tell. The marriage lasted weeks at most. It's now . . . a technicality."

"And Sasha tells me you have a live-in."

"I do, and again, I don't count that as promiscuity."

"You're in control?"

"I think so."

"Hmm . . . don't you think it's time to lose control?"

"You mean order that second bottle and finish it myself?"

"No, that's not quite what I had in mind."

The arrival of the soup course broke the thread of the conversation. Troy thought it little short of a miracle.

§116

She pecked him on the cheek, a gesture probably at odds with her nature and her history.

And once she had found her key she looked at him, a teasing glint in her eye, and said:

"So we'll go no more a-raving so late into the night. Though the heart be something something. Oh fuck, I forget."

"Though the heart be still as loving, and the moon be still as bright."

"Yes, that's it. Thank you, Freddie."

He watched her up the steps. Some remnant of gentlemanly code telling him that he had not seen a lady safely home until the door had closed behind her.

The key turned in the lock. She turned to him. Almost gone but not gone.

"I know everything," she said.

And then she was gone.

It was the second time she'd said that. He still didn't know what she meant by it.

§117

Another postcard arrived from darkest Derbyshire. In an envelope. Not to conceal the sepia image—"The Annual Belper Toad Racing Festival" circa 1910, men in clogs and white tabards, each clutching what seemed to be a large, disgruntled toad—so much as for the content:

This is really hard. How do you move on without the sense that you are throwing your life away? Why does every little thing seem to matter? Has anyone ever moved on, moved away without a permanent ache of regret? Why isn't nostalgia a sin? Why isn't it illegal? Why isn't there a motto for psychological good health dunned into every child before they're ten: "Don't Look Back!"

I begin to wish I'd known your parents. How did they ditch a country? All I'm trying to ditch is a one-horse mill town up north, possibly even a one-donkey mill town. Dunno, 'cos I haven't seen a horse or a donkey yet, just the fucking mill chimney. God—if only I could dynamite it.

I've thought about talking to your Uncle Nikolai, but I think the only country he acknowledges is between his ears, and all his "things" are ideas, the ultimate portable property.

I've thought of talking to Kolankiewicz, but who was it said "Poland is not so much a country as a state of mind"?

SFXX

That was a Crispism. Quentin Crisp's faintly damning critique of a friend. Troy must have told Foxx this at some point, probably on one of those days when talking to the Yard's senior pathologist proved too exasperating.

Troy was not at all sure how to help her with this. Telling her to burn her bridges was easy. His own childhood had left him with few loyalties, even though both morality and intellect told him loyalty should be valued as a virtue. He had no handle on nostalgia. He had never felt remotely English, yet not only did he know no other country, he still owned the house he was born in, and his brother owned the house he had spent much of his childhood in. Could one have nostalgia for what is, as well as what was? And logic told him nostalgia was possible even for what never was.

And the telephone rang.

"Are you doing anything this evening?"

Lady Stainesborough. The usual slip-sliding inflections of irony or sarcasm utterly absent from her voice.

"Just drinking alone."

"Been there. Done that. A tableau of misery. Why don't you come over here and drink in company? I might even join you in a glass or two if you bring a decent bottle."

Troy's wine cellar was less a cellar than the space under the sink, between two red brick columns, Chateau Stopcock with vintage old-growth lead pipe, in amongst the cartons of Vim, the bottles of Dettol, and the packets of yellow dusters he bought on the doorstep from the bloke who came around with the knife-sharpening contraption, and home to half a dozen spiders, but it abounded in decency. He'd even been known to keep a thoroughly decent first-growth claret in his desk drawer in case of an unforeseen claret emergency.

A Latour '34. That should do the trick.

And then he paused.

What, if anything, was "the trick"?

§118

He remembered the moment of surprise when he realised that Foxx had hired a cleaner for her hillside semi in Derbyshire—so that, he had assumed, she might never return to layers of dust or piles of mouse shit no matter how infrequent her visits.

Venetia seemed oblivious. Not to give a damn. The huge lobby of her Eaton Place house—he fought shy of calling it a mansion . . . London had grander houses by far—was strung with cobwebs, coated with dust. Something crunched underfoot, the dead leaves of last autumn, blown in from the street and never swept up, scattered across the threshold along with dozens of unopened letters.

Venetia was in working mufti. A pair of loose blue jeans, tennis shoes worn to holes, and a baggy, collarless man's shirt spattered with paint and what looked like woodchip. The mass of blonde hair piled up with kirby grips and rubber bands.

"Sorry. Lost track of the time. I had meant to be dressed to kill by the time you showed up, something sleeveless or something backless, not still in me work clobber."

"Work?"

"Don't sound so bloody surprised, Freddie. It's work that pleases me, occupies me, and on occasion pays. Gerry left me oodles of dosh, but if he hadn't I'd scrub the floors in Selfridges if it kept the wolf from the door."

"Whereas my sisters would simply buy off Mr. Wolf with sexual favours."

"You said that, I didn't. Now, follow me."

She led off into what Troy took to be the drawing room in the house's original configuration, windows facing slightly west and north. Now it seemed to be some kind of studio, the clumpy, big-footed furniture of the last century piled up in one corner, the Persian carpets rolled back—all to make way for easels and work benches.

Two easels were empty. A third had a portrait set in its wooden grip, half-finished, the face unidentifiable, the setting blurring into abstraction.

"Don't look at that," she said, throwing a sheet over it. "I learnt my lesson."

"Which is?"

"Can't paint to order. Can't do anything to order, in fact. Should never have accepted the commission."

"You won't finish it? Even later?"

"Only if my arse is struck by lightning. Now—"

She upended a two-pound jam jar of paintbrushes and picked out the corkscrew.

"Make yourself useful."

She blew the dust off two china mugs. Beneath the dribbles of congealed oil paint, they were still recognisable as coronation mugs. She handed him the Edward VII, and held on to the George V.

"Are you pulling a face, you little bugger? You are, aren't you? You won't taste the paint. Honestly!"

She held out King George. Troy did not pour.

"I wasn't pulling a face at the mugs. I was shocked that you don't think the wine might need ten minutes to breathe."

"Oh . . . you utter fucking snob. OK. Ten minutes it is. I'll show you work in progress, and if that doesn't kill ten minutes, I'll show you the house. You can marvel at all the crap five generations of Stainesboroughs have squirrelled away."

Behind the easels was a woodworking bench, perhaps the only neat thing he'd seen in the house thus far . . . every chisel in its drilled socket, every knife in its predetermined slit.

The sculpture, if such it be, was about eighteen inches across, and looked to be a carefully arranged pile of leaves carved in some dark, biscuit-brown hardwood. There might be a hundred of them, all joined together with thin strips of blackened leather to make . . . what?

Venetia lifted the leaves and suddenly its form was obvious—a cloak. And beneath this cloak of leaves, foetally curled, a small, naked priapic man in the primitivist style. His father had collected a few sculptures rather like this, they had become fashionable once Picasso had adopted them around the turn of the century—their features visible in *Les Demoiselles d'Avignon*. To this day "Minnie" stood in the hearth in his study out at Mimram, a Pygmy astride an even pygmier elephant, its tusks long since snapped off. This man had the same huge eyes and wide mouth as Minnie, a fundamentally black figure carved in a pale wood, almost ginger.

"Well?" she said.

"Well," he replied. "It's got to be, hasn't it? He's Caliban. Hiding under the cloak before Trinculo sneaks in."

"I'm impressed."

"And Trinculo?"

"Oh, I didn't feel like carving a Trinculo. Just another jester, just another bloody Englishman abroad, after all. No, it was Caliban who interested me."

"When did you take it up?"

"Sculpture, about nine months ago. Painting . . . about the time Gerry's drinking started to get fatal. I set up an easel in the attic. I knew Gerry would never bother to climb so many stairs. One by one the staff quit on us. He wouldn't hire more, and if he'd tried I rather think no one would have worked for us. I found myself alone in a huge house . . . with a madman . . . if you'll agree that drinking oneself to death is a form of madness. Had to do something. Gerry had been mumbling incoherently since 1953 and stopped speaking altogether in '55. In '56, he died. The next day I rolled back the drawing room carpets—no doubt a violation of every social code the Stainesboroughs ever stood for. I've worked in this room ever since. I cannot say I am happy, just happier."

"Is there more?"

"More what?"

"Are there more sculptures?"

"Oh yes. I tend to work on two or three at once."

She led him behind a screen. A Chippendale credenza, scuffed and dusty, had been turned into a plinth for three more sculptures.

"Take a guess."

She placed her hands upon a wooden devil, clutching some kind of spear.

"Lucifer?"

"Poseidon."

She pointed at the next. A sightless head with a tangled mass of snaking hair.

"Medusa?"

"Yep. I shall have to steel myself to finish the gorgon gaze and give her eyes. And this . . .?"

The last was more baffling than the first. Two bodies intertwined— more than intertwined, melded. A beast with two backs. Shape rather than feature, everything tending to a curve—the hint of a pendant breast, the suggestion of a sweeping feather. Then it came to him. Siena, Sasha's awed response in the Bargello.

"Leda and the Swan?"

"Of course."

"You're drawn to Greek myths?"

"To myths . . . and to Shakespeare. Bring your bottle down to the kitchen and I'll tell you. I have soup on the hob."

The kitchen was as it would have been had either of the two gentlemen on the coronation mugs dropped in during their respective reigns. A blackleaded range, now rusting—copper pans large enough to boil spuds for a couple of dozen diners. The only hint of modernity was a New World gas cooker, incongruous, untimely in its glaring white enamel and Ideal Home eye-level grill. He began to wonder if the conspicuous neglect was not some form of vengeance. The tale of the drunken, dead husband notwithstanding, he could not help but think of Miss Havisham in Satis House. A cruel world conspicuously rejected in a twenty-year display of cobwebs and mouse shit.

Over dinner, claret and onion soup, seated at the twenty-foot-long, scrubbed deal table in what had been the servants' hall, Venetia answered his unasked questions.

"In my family education was for boys. We 'gels' weren't allowed or expected to get an education. We got a nanny, then a governess, and then we were presented at court. I was a debutante of 1928. Same night as your sisters. I felt about it all much as they did. They smoked reefer in the lavatory and were stuck in front of Queen Mary smashed silly. To this day Sasha still does her impression of the old Queen when she's pissed."

"After . . . afterwards . . . it was marry well and breed, wasn't it?"

"My sisters had choices. My father would not have stopped either of them going to university. They showed no interest. My mother intervened and suggested finishing school in Switzerland—the voice of desperation, I think. I can still hear Sasha's cackle of laughter. My mother never spoke of it again. She just hoped silently that Sasha would marry well—although the English definition of 'well' just means 'wealthy,' while my mother might have meant 'happily.'"

"Then she did not marry well."

"Indeed, she didn't."

"I had two books as a child. No one thought to buy me more. The *Complete Shakespeare*. Four volumes nicely printed and bound in leather. Meant, I rather think, as an ornament than ever to be read.

And a huge, fat collection of *Greek Myths*, flaking gold leaf on the cover, cracked boards and loose pages. They were my education. Yes, to answer your question, I am drawn to them, and they are what I draw on. You won't find me sculpting a London bus or Sir Winston. I know them all, I could recite almost any legend, any Shakespeare plot . . . although I never thought his plots much mattered . . . and for much of my life, and I am forty-eight, they're all I have known . . . my archive, my library, my vocabulary . . . but, and to the point, when we were kids you thought I was a noddlehead, didn't you?"

"Yep."

"And you're not?"

"No, I'm not."

"Masha, and I think she thinks about you more than her sister, told me there was . . . let me get this right . . . 'a thing of darkness in young Fred.'"

Troy said nothing.

"And I am drawn to darkness also."

"Don't be."

"Hence . . . Caliban."

"I'm not Caliban. We're none of us Caliban."

"I was hoping you'd tell me what he is. I'm not a noddlehead, but I can't pretend the play makes a lot of sense to me. I deal in images not ideas."

"It's a very common theme of those times. Nature versus Art, capital N, capital A. Science was beginning to tell us that we might not be the centre of the universe and hence not the apple of God's eye, and the discovery of America, meeting warriors in loincloths who still fought with bows and arrows, who'd not even invented the wheel, set us thinking about what was man in his natural state . . . as Locke put it, 'once upon a time all the world was America.' Montaigne was fascinated by the New World. His most famous essay is about cannibals. Cannibal is Caliban. Caliban is Nature, Prospero Art."

Venetia made lines in the pine top with the tines of her fork, swirls of chaos, crossing and interlocking.

"Don't worry. I'm still with you. You haven't lost me yet. If anything, you've confirmed what I half-thought. If I have this right, and you said we're none of us Caliban, it's because we are all of us both Art and Nature?"

"I think that's what the seventeenth century had to tell us."

"And what do we do? Do we balance the two?"

Troy shook his head.

"Can't be done."

"Does Shakespeare try?"

"I don't know. The play has an ending that baffles me. There's so much at work besides the nature of the savage . . . there's power and tyranny, and vengeance and forgiveness. I'd have to read it again, or hope someone stages it on Shaftesbury Avenue in the near future. I've not seen it performed since I was about fifteen."

"Gielgud?"

"Yes. And Richardson as Caliban."

"Then it was at the Old Vic in 1930. I went too. Several times, in fact. And to most productions over the last thirty years. You seem to have missed Gielgud's latest Prospero in Drury Lane only this year. Now, why do you say balancing Art and Nature can't be done?"

"It'd be more accurate to say it doesn't get done. Art will always smother Nature. If it doesn't, you get a sort of social rebel who is cultured and debased at the same time, and will always be judged not for his Art but for his Nature."

An image sprang to mind, seemingly from nowhere.

"The sort of man," Troy said, "who can listen to a Schubert concert at the Wigmore, and duck out before the encore to get a hand job in the nearest public lavatory."

She was grinning now, that beautiful top lip pouting with delight.

"I think you've just described our absent friend."

"Eh?"

"Guy Burgess."

"Guy Burgess? A well-balanced man?"

Her grin burst to laughter. Laughter so infectious it brought tears to Troy's eyes.

As they calmed down, he said, "Those might just be the stupidest words I've ever uttered."

"All the same," she said, "Guy was hardly ashamed and certainly never repentant about his Nature. You might say he was in touch with his 'thing of darkness.'"

Troy wondered where the conversation was headed. Back to his own "thing of darkness"?

But she changed the subject.

"Sasha tells me you breed pigs?"

§119

He walked home. Across St. James's Park, into Lower Regent Street. Along Orange Street, where he had first spent a night with Tosca.

1944.

A garret under the eaves.

Melting pizza and stolen chocolate.

He wondered about the "thing." He knew exactly where Venetia's line was leading, and he hoped she never got there.

1944.

His other lover, Diana Brack. A friend of his sisters, so almost certainly a friend of Venetia's.

1944.

He had shot Diana dead.

"The Tart-in-the-Tub Case," as an insensitive press had so cruelly put it.

The case that made him famous.

He hoped Venetia never got there.

That was "the trick," after all, to see she never got there.

§120

Another envelope. Another Derbyshire postcard. Four frames: a spartan, stone slate-roofed chapel; a loaf in the shape of wheat-sheaf; a bloke clutching a giant stripy marrow; two boys in Sunday best, matching grey jackets and shorts, hair plastered with Brylcreem, each posing with an untrimmed leek taller than themselves. And the caption:

EBENEZER METHODIST CHAPEL
HARVEST FESTIVAL, 1933

What chance you could lend me £100? The bathroom here is out of the ark and the kitchen is little better than a calabash and an open fire. I can't expect Rosie to live here with a new baby, not in conditions like this. I thought it was all pretty grotty when I was growing up, and Mrs. 1958 expects a lot more than my mum did. Next door still ponches clothes in a dolly tub and puts them through a wooden mangle! All her husband's shirts have to have rubber buttons. Next door, t'other side, they keep coal in the fucking bath! So . . . so . . . I've decided to refit, new bathroom suite, new cooker, and get rid of that horrid Belfast sink. God . . . I hate to think of it . . . but mum used to bathe us girls in that, it's so big.
Anyway, a hundred ought to cover it. I will pay you back. Honestly.
    It'll slow me down a bit. If I can get a plumber sharpish I could be home in a week. Or maybe two.

SFXX

He posted Foxx a cheque for two hundred pounds. How readily the unravelling plot skeined into his hands. How easily his conscience salved.

§121

"If you're free tonight, I can promise you something a bit better than onion soup and me in jeans."

Eddie was hovering on the other side of the desk. A sheaf of papers in his hand. Troy put his hand over the mouthpiece.

"What?"

"Work is what."

"What work?"

"Paperwork. Read and sign."

"Has anyone been murdered?"

"Not today. Not yet, at any rate."

"Then forge my signature and don't come back 'til there's a body."

Eddie paused, tried to give Troy the eye. He was not good at it and found he could not resist blinking.

"What?" Troy said again.

"Do you intend doing any work today?"

"When there's a corpse, you'll find me both eager and efficient."

"Meanwhile, you slope off when it suits you and leave me with all the bum fodder."

Troy dearly wished he could point to stripes on his arm or pips on his shoulders—any silent way to pull rank.

"Do I complain when you nip out to place a bet?"

Eddie blew a raspberry and left.

"Venetia . . . you still there?"

"Of course. About seven. And remember, I know everything."

Troy still had no idea what she meant by this. She hadn't let the phrase pass her lips last night, and he had thought it might be some whimsy she had adopted and then dropped.

§122

Was her promise empty? Venetia was still in jeans and her paint-spattered shirt.

Her glass was not empty.

She held it out to him. Brimful of vintage claret.

"Here is that which will give you language."

Troy sniffed and sipped and swirled and thought.

"Go to be a *Tempest* quotation, hasn't it?"

"Yes. But where?"

"Not a clue."

"Act Two, Scene Two. Clown to Caliban."

"And I'm Caliban?"

"Perhaps. However. Your wooden counterpart is finished."

She led off to her studio. Caliban lay curled up in his cloak of leaves, eyes wide, staring into nothingness the way his cat out at Mimram often did. Unperturbed, but sleepless all the same.

"I'm not sure I see a difference," Troy said.

"I've added more leaves. He seemed a bit exposed to the weather. And I trimmed his nose. See?"

She bent down and pointed.

The nose was a fraction smaller, but then he had to conclude that sculptors dealt in fractions and in slivers.

"He was a bit too brutal," Venetia added.

"Can Caliban be too brutal?"

"Oh yes. Too wild? Not sure. After all, he isn't an animal. He's human feral."

"I thought you said you weren't an intellectual."

"Not quite, Freddie. I said I wasn't a noddlehead. That might imply that I might also not be an egghead . . . but for me two penn'orth, Caliban is a marvellous creation . . . the personification of rage against injustice . . . a living lust for vengeance."

"And Shakespeare wastes him."

"Indeed, he does, throws him away on stock-in-trade drunk scenes with a couple of boring clowns. Playing to the pit. So . . . we do see him the same, don't we?"

She didn't wait for an answer.

"Now, if you'll excuse me, I'll slip out of duck, muck, and mufti and emerge as a swan. Look around. You will see wondrous changes."

She ran upstairs. Soon Troy heard the sound of old pipes groaning and knocking—enough to set the house shaking.

He wandered back to the hall. She was right. Not a dead leaf or a cobweb to be seen.

He drifted up the wide crescent staircase, wondering which bedroom was hers. Everything had been vacuumed and polished. Not a trace of Satis House.

On the first floor a door was ajar. The room faced south. Logically this might be the master bedroom, one she might have chosen for herself. But she had been a widow for some time, he could not remember how long, and had the pick of any room in the house. This wasn't hers. It was piled with cardboard boxes.

He sat on one box with his glass, flipped the lid on another. Books. Lots of books. Gibbon's *Decline and Fall* in several volumes. He flipped another. Books. Lots of books. The works of Dorothy L. Sayers in the wartime economy editions. Plain covers, paper light as tissue. He picked one up—*The Unpleasantness at the Bellona Club*. His dad had bought him that when he was about thirteen. He'd sat up most of a long night to finish it. His dad had also bought him Gibbon's *Decline and Fall*. He'd never finished that. He'd never met anyone who had. It just looked impressive on a bookshelf.

He opened the Sayers and read a page, then two, then three.

At page ten Venetia appeared in the doorway.

"Downstairs!"

"What?"

"Now! You're ruining my entrance."

He dashed past her, brushing through a cloud of scent, and ran to the foot of the staircase.

She stood at the top, just visible beyond the curve, and slinked into view.

He would not have missed this for the world. Her hair piled high on her head, her body sheathed in a scarlet dress that all but swept the floor. On the first half-landing she spun, and he could see that the dress, low-cut in the front, was even lower cut in the back.

She glided towards him, her motion invisible as a Russian folk dancer's.

"You like?"

"Oh yes."

"Been shopping."

"And cleaning."

"Not personally, you understand. I hired a team of ladies who do."

"I might die happily in a cloud of Betterwear wax polish and Miss Dior."

She laughed out loud.

Kissed him passionately.

As she drew back, blue eyes looking down at him, she said, "Y'know, Freddie, most men wouldn't know Miss Dior from Mrs. Beeton."

"Perhaps I am not most men."

"Indeed, you're not. Guard your thing of darkness well, Freddie."

A fingernail stroked the tip of his nose.

"Now, let's eat."

§123

The long deal table looked freshly scrubbed. The iron range newly blackleaded. But Venetia was cooking on the gas stove.

"You should knock back the red stuff, Freddie. We're having fish. Bouillabaisse. So we'll be switching to white. A tangy Vermentino from Sardinia."

"Well . . . I'll bet you won't find a recipe for bouillabaisse in Mrs. Beeton."

"What? You think she was so narrowly English? Au contraire. She has a recipe, although she feels obliged to subtitle it 'a kind of fish stew' just in case her readers didn't get it. And take it from me, it was very fashionable in the day. Thackeray even wrote a hymn to bouillabaisse. Not that I could quote you a word of it."

"Thackeray? I thought you only read Shakespeare."

"Well . . . I was underboasting, wasn't I? He calls it a hotchpotch . . . a noble dish. There, I have quoted it."

She took his glass to the sink and returned with King George and King Edward, freshly stripped of their paint dribbles.

"Take your pick. It'll taste the same out of either."

"Oh, I think I'll stick with Edward and try not to think of the size of his belly."

"A good choice. A noble choice."

She poured white wine into each mug.

He sat quietly as she served "fish stew" on saffron rice.

Parsley, thyme, and hints of cayenne wafted upwards.

She sat as quiet as he. Her George V mug in her left hand.

She took her first sip.

He followed. Neither reaching for fork or spoon.

Then:

"It'll keep," she said. "Even better the day after."

§124

Even in high heels she raced him to the top of the stairs. On the first landing he thought she'd dive into one room or another, but she carried on upwards, up the next flight and the one after that until they were under the eaves.

The door to what might once have been a tweeny's bedroom stood open.

"You sleep up here?"

"I had to get away from Gerry's snoring. And after that, I never wanted to move back down. It's warm. It's a room that wraps itself around you."

There was just enough room to walk down one side of a full-sized double bed.

She turned. Arms outstretched in crucifix, her back to him.

"It's just one button, Freddie."

He flipped it loose without a fumble. She lowered her arms and the scarlet dress slid to the floor.

Naked but for her shoes.

She took him by the tie, slid the knot down his chest.

"C'mon copper, come an' get me."

§125

Afterwards, on the floor, wedged between the wall and the bed, she slept in the crook of his arm, her hair spread across his chest.

Then he realised she was awake again. Her left hand stroking his cock back to life.

And when it rose, she slipped into his lap and deftly took him inside. Her lips at his ear.

"The game you and Guy played that night in Vienna?"

"How do you know about that?"

She rose up and slid down on him.

"If you want your secrets kept, never tell Sasha."

Yes. He had told Sasha and even as he had done so knew it was a mistake.

"Let's play it now."

"Do you really think this is the right time?"

She rose up and slid down on him.

"Oh yes. Go on. Ask me. Remember, I know everything."

The only words that could have made him go along with this.

"Go on."

"Alright, number one?"

She rose up and slid down on him.

"Burgess."

"Number two?"

"Maclean."

She rose up and slid down on him.

"Number three."

"Philby."

She rose up and slid down on him.

"Number four."

"Blunt."

"Venetia . . . this really—"

She rose up and slid down on him.

Troy said nothing.

She rose up and slid down on him again.

"Go on! Five!"

"Five?"

"Your pal and mine, Charlie Leigh-Hunt."

She rose up and slid down on him.

"Now ask me about six."

"There was no six. Venetia, we never got to the sixth man."

"But I know everything."

"Fine. Number six?"

She rose up and slid down on him.

Her lips touched his left ear once more as she whispered:

"Bill Blaine."

Troy slipped his hands under her arms and lifted her gently off. Her bottom slapped softly against his thighs.

"I told you," she said simply.

"How? How do you know this?"

"Freddie? What's my name?"

"What?"

"Just tell me."

"Venetia Stainesborough."

"No. That's my title. My name is Venetia Frances Adelaide Parker-Blaine. Bill was Gerry's little brother. It's his book you were reading not half an hour ago."

"*Parker*-Blaine?"

"Gerry never used his surname. Inherited the title aged three. He was always Lord Stainesborough or Gerry Stainesborough. Bill . . . Bill had a rough time at school, and after his first year at Cambridge dropped the Parker. He'd had quite enough of hyphens and silly nicknames."

Troy heard, clear as a bell, a drunken Burgess replying to his last question in the Café Landtmann—"who was number six?"—and Burgess muttering, "Nosey Parker" as he fell into his lemon tart. He had assumed Burgess was telling him to mind his own business. He hadn't heard the capital N. He'd no idea that Burgess had actually answered his question—until now. And he did not doubt that Venetia was telling him the truth. She knew everything.

"*Nosey* Parker?"

"Yep."

"You've known all along?"

"Yes. I was Bill's confidant. Everyone has to tell someone, and after Gerry died, I think I was the most important person in his life. He told me all about it—getting recruited at Cambridge, all about his handler . . . even the secrets he passed on. I knew and did not tell. Mea culpa. I chose a man over a country.

"I won't be telling anyone else. All I have is a room full of Bill's books. The ones you were sitting on. Arrived yesterday. Probate was granted a few days ago. I am next of kin, if not all kin. He left me about two thousand in cash, a flat near Marble Arch, and a zillion books. There are no diaries, no letters. I doubt he ever wrote anything down, so there's nothing for anyone to find."

"But you choose to tell me?"

"I think Bill owed you that. He nearly got you killed. What he told me was a secret we shared. Now you and I share it, and there it stays. I don't have much patriotism in me, and nor do you, I think, but let's not destroy Bill's reputation. He's dead and that's an end of it."

§126

He dressed and sparked the hob.

By the time Venetia appeared—not dressed, wrapped in a sheet—the bouillabaisse was hot enough to serve.

"Jolly good," she said. "I'm famished."

She reached for a spoon, flashed him a smile of irresistible warmth and beauty.

He resisted.

Faked a smile back across the table.

And they ate.

§127

When conscience makes cowards of us all, what does the thinking coward—the man previously untroubled by that hysterical and unreliable organ—do?

He runs away.

"No, I can't make Friday. I have to be at Mimram. I haven't been there since I got back from Vienna. There's stuff piling up."

"Stuff?"

"Family stuff. I'm the son and heir, after all. Rod got the title, I got the house."

"Freddie, you wouldn't be avoiding me, would you?"

"No," he lied.

"I don't expect flowers and chocolates, but it's a pig of a man who doesn't call a girl the morning after . . . and don't you dare say 'after what?'"

He hadn't called her. She was right. He was being a pig, but telling him so would not stop him.

"I'll be back Sunday evening," he said.

"Back here? At Eaton Place?"

(Pause)

"Freddie?"

"Yes . . . at Eaton Place."

There was nothing piling up at Mimram except dead leaves.

He was a pig.

He got there an hour before dusk.

The first thing he saw was a pig.

A large Gloucester Old Spot, playing football on the edge of the orchard. The Fat Man was booting an old, softly deflating casey. The pig was in goal.

"He's a marvel. Look at him," the Fat Man said. "Never lets one through. I tell yer, old cock, if Manchester City knew about Bertrand here, they'd dump that Bert Trautmann in the wink of a pig's eye."

Trautmann was the most famous goalkeeper in the country, a former Luftwaffe paratrooper, he had famously played on in the cup final a couple of years back despite suffering a broken neck. He was also the only goalkeeper Troy had ever heard of.

"Bertrand? I thought you named all your pigs after Churchills?"

"There's only so many Randolphs and Winstons you can have at one time. And as I have both still up an' gobblin' the new boys will be named after philosophers. Next boar I get will be called Ludwig. Or maybe Aristotle."

He kicked the ball wildly in the rough direction of the goal. The pig snouted it back with startling accuracy. The Fat Man let the ball bounce off his shins and said, "Wot brings you 'ere, then?"

"I live here. Surely you haven't forgotten?"

"Have you forgotten it's yer bruv's weekend to meet the voters?"

Troy had forgotten. Every second Saturday, except in August, Rod held constituency surgery in the village—excising social ills, prescribing political placebos.

"Oh fuck. I really wanted to be alone."

"Righty-ho. We shall pack our piggy bags and leave you to it."

"No. Not you. You stay. It's just . . . Rod."

"You in trouble, cock?"

"Yes, but not the sort you might be imagining. Right now the last thing I want is the company of my family's self-appointed moral philosopher."

"Then don't tell 'im. Whoever she is, don't tell 'im."

The Fat Man could do that to Troy. Catch him off guard every time. He secretly prided himself on his silence, his contrived lacunae, his well-preserved privacy . . . and every so often the Fat Man made him feel utterly transparent. A man whose world seemed to revolve around pigs and vegetables and beer, who probably read a book by the light of a blue moon, could read Troy as though he were a novel. In this case, though the title was undoubtedly *Venetia*, he hoped the author was not Miss Heyer.

"I can't tell you, so don't ask."

"Wasn't going to. So there."

§128

Troy heard Rod come in shortly after midnight and managed to avoid him at breakfast with a pretence of sleeping in. Pretence, as he had not slept a wink all night.

He breakfasted at ten. Peered through the French windows of his study, regretting that it was too late in the year to breakfast outside unless you liked porridge with added drizzle.

Rod would not be back till well after lunch, which he would take in the village pub with his party agent and some of the party faithful.

Troy reckoned he had five hours of uninterrupted thinking ahead of him. But only one thought to think.

"What have I done?"

He was, in summary, a married man seeking a divorce, co-habiting (at least he thought that was the neologism . . . his mother's genera-tion would have called it living in sin), and until two nights ago doing so *faithfully*—a palæogism if ever there was one, and not an adverb that had ever troubled him until now. Casual sex did not bother him because the adjective never occurred to him. Sex bothered him, per se, simply because it was sex, and he had from his first encounters with the *opposite* held that there was no such thing as "just sex." Venetia was not "just sex." She was an open invitation to fuck up every aspect of his life, every shred of stability he had achieved in the two and a bit years since Tosca had walked out on him, and now . . . now . . . mid-coitus . . . she had slid neatly, wetly, nipples dragging along his chest . . . from *her* erotic heaven into the mundanity of *his* work. It was bliss. It was a trap. She knew everything, she had said. How right she was.

On the north wall of the study was a seven-foot-tall armoire. Troy vividly remembered the day it had arrived in 1922 or 1923—hauled up from the station on the carrier's cart by a gigantic Clydesdale, quite the largest living creature the boy Troy had ever seen. Mostly it was still full of his father's junk. Almost fifteen years after the old man's death Troy had still not sorted through it. He had, in fact, added to it. A dozen or more shoe boxes, crammed with scraps of paper he had turned out of his London house and stored here. He'd even attempted method. Each box bore a year that might or might not accurately reflect the nature of its contents.

He took out 1940.

Postcards from his best friend, Charlie, serving in France with a guards regiment.

Eight-page letters in Russian from his father, all in the vein of Montaigne, instructing Troy—twenty-five years old, but still a boy to his father—in "how to live."

And a creased pen-and-ink sketch, once screwed up and lobbed mercilessly into the wastepaper basket, only to be retrieved, smoothed out, and stored the following day.

An obscene cartoon of Troy and Venetia fucking by the statue of Eros at Piccadilly Circus, captioned "Morituri te salutant."

At the bottom was the artist's note and signature.

If I were you, I'd fuck Venetia Maye-Brown under floodlights in the middle of a hundred-bomber raid.

Yrs Ever,
Guy.

They hadn't bothered with the floodlights, but in every other respect it seemed like a prophecy merely delayed in its fulfilment. Burgess, a man Troy thought of as distinctly lacking in self-knowledge, knew him better than he knew himself.

He retreated to the armchair by the fireplace.

"Mind if I join you?"

Troy looked over Rod's head at the grandfather clock standing on the other side of the room, exactly where it had stood for the last forty-seven years. Six o'clock. He had worried away a day. Low autumn light draining into the crepuscular plug'ole and he'd not even noticed.

Rod did not wait for an answer. Plonked himself on the far end of the sofa—his thumb curled around the neck of a bottle of whisky, two glasses held precariously against it by one finger each of one huge hand, and a soda siphon in the other.

The words "not for me" formed on Troy's lips without utterance. Rod would not take no for an answer—he never did—and the sheer bollock-numbing boredom of listening to Rod and "the day I've had" would be a welcome, inane distraction.

"It's a bugger," Rod said after his first gulp of Strathpiddle.

"Yep," said Troy with no idea what Rod was talking about and no inclination to ask. Sooner or later Rod would tell him.

"It's a good thing no one goes into politics for the glamour."

Ah—it was going to be a familiar complaint. Rod whinge No. 12 sub-section B: "The Hon. Member feeling unappreciated."

"I dunno," Troy said. "You get to hobnob."

"Lloyd George knew my father," said Rod, lyrically.

"Father knew Lloyd George," Troy replied—the only two lines in a Great War marching song, properly sung to the tune of "Onward Christian Soldiers."

"And with what nobs do I get to hob? *George* Brown? Doesn't have the same ring to it as Lloyd George, does it?"

"No, but you know Uncle Harold."

Their nickname for the Prime Minister.

"Quite."

(Pause)

"He had me round to Number 10 not that long ago."

"On what matter?"

(Pause)

"You."

Troy shifted from the laconic near-horizontal to a semblance of the vertical attentive.

"Why didn't you tell me?"

"Freddie, I haven't seen hide nor hair of you since Vienna."

"And?"

"And he was checking you out . . . sort of. No real suspicion. Just the usual Mac caution mixed with the usual Mac subtlety to create the usual Mac ambivalence. He didn't want you adopting Burgess as a cause. One thing he wasn't ambivalent about, however, was that he wasn't sending anyone out to Vienna to accommodate Burgess. Told me he didn't want him back at any price."

Troy doubted Rod could know about Blaine. He might have heard a whisper, but all sides had tried to keep it under wraps.

"Rod, try to remember. What exactly did Macmillan say?"

"I'm not addled and I'm not yet pissed. I can remember quite clearly. His exact words were, 'There'll be no de-brief, no attempt to bring him in from the cold.'"

"When was this?"

"My first day back. You were still in Vienna with your strange friend. Obviously."

"You're sure?"

"Absolutely. Unforgettable. It was the same day my PPS, Iain, quit on me because he'd been nabbed with a guardsman in the park. Macmillan brought it up in the same conversation. Switched from asking me about you and Burgess to asking me about Iain. Coincidence? Non sequitur? Just one of those things."

"Just one of those queer things?"

"If you like," Rod said, much as Troy might have done himself.

"The queer thing you didn't get at Oscar Wilde's tomb?"

"The queer thing I still don't get."

And Troy pondered the queer thing and everything Rod had told him. Just one of those things? It did not seem like coincidence to him.

§129

They got through an evening meal and Sunday breakfast in a condition akin to armed neutrality—a buzz-phrase of the times—Troy suspicious of what Rod might not be telling him, and Rod just suspicious.

A neutral condition might have been more fun if Rod had had hobbies they could talk about. Troy thought he had none. His work was his life. Then Troy remembered stamp collecting. His brother's Great Britain and Empire collection in its worn red album. Victoria penny reds, a lone, precious penny black, all the way to King George and Queen Mary, those exemplary middle-class monarchs. Then. He couldn't remember the last time he saw him open it, and vivid images of his teenage brother sprang to mind, in a regular Rod activity—trying to pick a folded stamp hinge off the end of his tongue and cursing Man and God and Glue.

The Fat Man joined them for lunch, well-armed with pig monologues. Troy watched Rod glaze over as Randolph anecdote followed Winston anecdote, all ending with "Ya gotta larf, ain't ya," even though no one did.

By five o'clock Troy was no nearer a conclusion than he had been on Friday.

He'd promised Onions.

He'd let this one go.

He couldn't.

He'd promised Foxx nothing.

Let her go?

He couldn't.

He'd promised Venetia nothing.

Let her go?

He couldn't.

The phone rang. Saved by the bell.

He heard Rod yell, "I'll get it. Probably for me."

It wasn't.

Rod was yelling, "Pick up the extension! It's Jack."

"Freddie. I think you should come back tonight if at all possible."

"Murder?"

"Could be. Looks like an accident to me, but it could be."

"If it's that ambiguous, you handle it. I have other—"

"You'll want to take this one yourself. It appears the deceased is an old friend of your family—Venetia Stainesborough."

Troy said nothing.

"Freddie?"

Troy said nothing.

"Freddie?"

"You're at Eaton Place?"

"Yes."

"Get Kolankiewicz. I'll be there as soon as I can."

He could not let her go.

It had occurred to him that she might let him go, but never in this way.

§130

A crash on the Great North Road cost Troy half an hour and more. By the time he reached Eaton Place it was past seven—a dark autumn evening, rain not falling but hanging in a slick miasma. One lone, bedraggled bobby on the door. The man straightened up and saluted as he saw Troy approach.

Troy did not return the salute.

"Mr. Wildeve's inside, sir."

He thrust the door open.

At the foot of the staircase a body . . . the body . . . her body . . . lay covered by a bedsheet.

Kolankiewicz sat on a hall chair by one of the ornamental half-moon tables—his vacuum flask out, sipping at black Russian tea.

Troy turned on the threshold.

"Go home to the wife and kids, Jim," he said to the bobby. "I think we've all the coppers we need here."

Kolankiewicz looked up, said nothing.

"Where's Jack?" Troy asked.

"Kitchen. Waiting for you."

Troy knelt and lifted a corner of the sheet.

She was as beautiful dead as she had been alive. She was wearing the same scarlet dress she had worn when last he had seen her. The one that had cascaded down her back like a waterfall. Expecting him. She had been expecting him. He must have held up the sheet far too long. He felt a hand take it from him. Heard a voice call his name.

"Freddie. Freddie. Let go now."

He looked up.

Jack.

"Let's all go back to the kitchen."

Troy did not move.

"Freddie. Nothing more can happen. Leave her now."

In the kitchen, Kolankiewicz handed him his plastic cup. Troy muttered thank you and tasted strong, sweet tea.

"Let's all sit down, shall we?"

Jack sat on one side of the table, Troy and Kolankiewicz opposite him. He was being far too gentle. Troy could guess why.

"You've fingerprinted the house?"

"Yep."

"Any prints besides hers or mine?"

"Three sets of prints from small hands, which I take to be the cleaning ladies. It was one of them found her. Let herself in just before five today. Said she'd forgotten her bag. Had enough sense to dial 999, but it soon evaporated. She was near-hysterical when I got here. I sent her home in a squad car. We'll get prints and a statement in the morning. Otherwise the house is uncommonly spotless."

"They scrubbed the place from top to bottom. Tuesday, I think. Possibly Wednesday."

"And when were you last here?"

"Wednesday."

"All night?"

"Yes. My prints will be in Venetia's bedroom, the loo, possibly in here too."

"They are. How long had you been lovers?"

"Just that night."

"But . . ."

"But what?"

"But there's more."

"Of course," Troy said.

"Do you want to tell me or would you prefer to recuse yourself?"

"Neither. I'll tell you everything when I can, but first I want to hear from him. You say it looks like an accident. What does the pathologist say?"

Kolankiewicz sighed, said, "I would prefer to get her to the lab, but I know you will not wait that long. Yes, it seems like an accident. Tripped and fell the length of the staircase from the first floor. Neck broken. No other apparent cause."

"To which I'd add," Jack said, "no signs of forced entry or a struggle. It seems Lady Stainesborough was alone."

"But," Kolankiewicz continued, "I am with Hamlet. I know not *seems*. This is a suspicious death, so I have my suspicions."

"Based on what?" said Troy.

"Based on one simple but complicating fact. And that fact alone will suffice to make me suspicious. The spanner in the works, as you English are so fond of saying—*she* was fucking *you*."

§131

Troy had never walked away from an autopsy.

Until now.

He sat at his desk.

Two in the morning.

Listened to Kolankiewicz.

"Cervical fractures, C4 and C5. I would say death was instantaneous. Two fingers on the right hand broken at the proximal phalanges, third and fourth fingers. After death, I think. There is paint in the skin and I'd assume the hand trailed along the bannisters as she fell. Bruising to the skull beneath the hairline, and visible bruising to the right cheek, where she landed after the fall. I conclude Lady Stainesborough bounced off the stairs several times before she came to rest.

"Stomach indicates she had not eaten in a while. Modest amount of alcohol. Perhaps a single gin and tonic. Not enough to make anyone unsteady. Anyone used to alcohol, that is. And . . . no evidence of recent intercourse."

For a while neither man said anything.

Then Troy said, "Time of death?"

"Around five."

"What time does Jack say the cleaner arrived?"

"Around five. I got a call from Jack before half-past."

"So . . . she just missed him?"

"Him?"

"The killer. You think there's a killer. I know there was one."

"My boy, perhaps what you are not yet telling Jack you should tell me."

Troy said nothing.

"Just tell me."

"The name Bill Blaine means nothing to you?"

Kolankiewicz shrugged.

"He was an MI5 agent. Five sent him to Vienna to de-brief Guy Burgess. I assume you know Burgess approached me while I was there. Blaine was shot only yards from our embassy. I was standing next to him. It's a secret, at least for now, and it's assumed on high that it was a KGB hit. Blaine was Venetia Stainesborough's brother-in-law. But . . . he was a double agent. Venetia knew he was a double agent, and that kind of knowledge is dangerous. It's what got her killed."

Kolankiewicz had sat holding an envelope. He opened it and took out half a dozen large photographs.

To Troy they were all but abstract.

He turned them one way, Kolankiewicz turned them the right way.

"Upper arms, left and right. Triceps and biceps. You might mistake the marks for skin blotches. They're faint, almost invisible . . . but the spacing is the giveaway, thumbs and fingers. Large hands, a big grip, not hard enough to have created obvious bruises, indeed I flatter myself many a quack would have missed it . . . but someone, someone taller than she, held her from above, and in front—"

"And threw her down the stairs."

"Did you ever doubt it?"

"Not for a second."

Not so long ago Troy had needed someone to die.

Now he needed someone to kill.

§132

Shortly after eight. Jack appeared.

He had slept and shaved.

Troy had not.

Troy told him what Kolankiewicz had said.

Then he told him what he had told Kolankiewicz.

"And you still don't think you should step away from this one?"

"No, I don't. I stand the best chance of any of us of solving this case."

At this point Troy did not know which way Jack would jump. He was watching the low wintering sun glinting on the Thames, his back to Troy.

"OK," he said without turning around. "Then you need to know everything I do. And that amounts to bugger all. No other prints. The cleaning lady saw no one. It's not the sort of street where neighbours peer through the curtains, so a house-to-house yielded nothing but dignity firmly stood upon. Definitely no forced entry. If, as you and Kolankiewicz seem certain, there was someone there, then Lady Stainesborough let him in herself. And what does that tell you? Right now . . . if this were a blank case, a tabula rasa, not loaded with spy connections, and if I didn't know you were out at Mimram . . . you'd be the only suspect. I wish I could be more help, but I've nothing to go on. Absolutely nothing."

He turned.

"If you want this case, Freddie, you can have it. It's a stinker."

"I know that."

"You realise we can't tell Onions? If we do, he'll say two words to you and hand the case back to me."

"Which two words, Jack?"

"Diana Brack."

Of course.

"This is different. This was just a one-night stand," he lied.

Troy knew Jack was right and wondered if his own persistence didn't have as much to do with Diana Brack as it had with Venetia. Given his propensity to reoccupy his childhood, how long had his affair with Venetia been going on? More than a night, more than a week . . . had it been latent in his adolescence?

"Well . . ." Jack said. "There's one vital difference, isn't there? We both know who killed Diana Brack."

§133

Troy went home to Goodwin's Court.

He tried to sleep, but dead women tumbled through his dreams, identities shifting and merging. He'd embrace Diana and find he was kissing Venetia. He'd fuck Diana and hear Venetia's voice playing the Burgess game . . . "fourth man . . . fifth man." He'd relive shooting Diana and find he'd shot Venetia.

And a loop of sound in his mind, at first indistinct, loud but distorted and metallic, and then clarifying, close and human and Germanic: "Put the gun down, Herr Troy." Put the gun down, Herr Troy. Put the gun down, Herr Troy. Put the gun down, Herr Troy.

Around three he got up. Sat at the kitchen table with a packet of blank postcards and played a new game, one he'd never tried before. Regard each card as a player in the game . . . name them as they come to you . . . rearrange like a croupier at casino poker.

BURGESS.
VOYTEK.
BLAINE.
VENETIA.

So far, simple and uninformative. Prompting no thought.
Then he added:

ROD.
MACMILLAN.

And took away . . . **VOYTEK**.
He'd just lined up

MACMILLAN—BLAINE—

And pondered the blank.
A knock at the door.

Swift Eddie.

"You never got your morning cake."

A shiny box of panettone dangled from a loop of ribbon on his little finger.

"Make coffee too," said Troy without greeting, almost throwing the line over his shoulder as he headed back to the table to scribble down the name of the player that had occurred to him. And filled in the blank.

JORDAN.

He needed to talk to Jordan Younghusband.

He looked at his watch. Five thirty. If today was an office day, he might just catch Jordan at Leconfield House.

The harridan on the desk knew Troy. Didn't like him—did she like anyone? —but knew him.

"I just saw Mr. 'Usband heading orf downstairs. I'll put you through to the bar."

After much yelling, Jordan picked up the phone in the midst of the hubbub.

"Whoozat?"

"Troy."

"Can't hear you!"

"Jordan. It's me, Troy."

"Freddie. Great timing. It's Bob Chaplin's birthday. Come and join us."

"No. I need you here."

"Here? Where's here?"

"Goodwin's Court."

"Not more bodies?"

"No. Just the one, but you'll want to know."

§134

Eddie made Troy bathe and shave. Even laid out a clean shirt for him.

"You look dreadful."

"Thanks, Ed."

"I'll be off now."

"No, you stay."

Jordan arrived a little the worse for booze. Just when Troy would want him keen and attentive.

"Black coffee, Eddie. And pile on the cake."

Jordan did not so much sit as slump.

"Freddie, is this really quite so urgent? I mean, I was in the middle of a . . . y'know, the top came off the bottle at lunchtime . . ."

"How urgent do you want murder to be?"

"OK. Murder is what you do. It wouldn't be anything else, would it? So, who's dead?"

"Venetia, Lady Stainesborough. You may have known her as Venetia Maye-Brown."

Jordan was nodding.

"I did. Not seen her . . . oooh . . . I dunno . . . since the end of the war. I seem to remember dancing a conga with my hands on her backside on VE night. She was . . . what's the word . . . very *popular* during the war. But . . . I tell a lie. I'm sure I've seen her a couple of times since. Parties and such. Sorry, can't remember where or when. But, as I said, rather popular in the blackout."

"Indeed, she was. And after the war she cleaned up her act. Married into the aristocracy."

"Ah. And how did she die?"

"Someone picked her up and threw her downstairs yesterday afternoon. But this is almost a digression."

"Good. 'Cos if it isn't, I don't see how I can help you. Is Eddie making coffee? Good man."

Troy gave Jordan a moment then said, "Bill Blaine."

"Ah . . . still not laid to rest, eh?"

"Jordan. Who pulled you off the Burgess trip?"

"Section head. Bloody annoying, I was all set, packed . . . and it seemed like an adventure. At the last minute something arose and I got switched."

"What was it?"

"Suspicious activity at Liverpool docks. Some nonsense about IRA explosives. You know, four pounds of fertilizer and an alarm clock. Turned out to be complete bollocks, but it took me away from London for two days . . . and of course, by the time I got back, Blaine was dead. Part of me thought 'could have been me.' But I suppose that's natural without being logical. But any complaint I might have had about my time being wasted got swallowed by the 'but for the grace of God' thingie."

"Section head?"

Jordan hesitated. Eddie nipped in with the cake and coffee. Jordan sipped, munched, and pondered.

"Well," he said. "That's secret. Or if it isn't, it ought to be. But I don't suppose it's a secret that matters much. Denzil Kearney is his name. But as it is nonetheless a bit of a secret . . . I have to ask . . . why are you asking?"

"My brother got called into Number 10 just before you were pulled and Blaine flew out to Vienna. Mac told Rod unequivocally that he didn't want Burgess back and that MI5 would not be sending anyone to de-brief him or bring him in from the cold."

Jordan paused with a chunk of panettone at his lips and stuck it back on the plate.

"Freddie, where's this leading? Macmillan told Rod who told you . . . is this more than gossip? Is anyone sure Mac wasn't just sounding off?"

"Oh, he was definite. 'Not at any price' did he want Burgess back. And I believe him. I think Kearney acted off his own bat. Disobeyed an order from the PM. Pulled you as told, but then substituted Blaine. You were never at risk. No one walked over your grave. You were never the target. Blaine was. He was dead the minute he boarded that plane for Vienna."

"Jesus H. Christ. Why? And what on earth does this have to do with the Venetia woman?"

"Blaine was a Soviet agent. Venetia was Blaine's sister-in-law. She was the one person he'd told about his double life."

Jordan knocked back his coffee, turned to a blank, befuddled Eddie.

"You wouldn't happen to be hiding a drop of Scotch back there, would you, Eddie?"

§135

Eddie poured Laphroaig for the three of them.

"I can't take all this in," Jordan said. "Bill Blaine a double agent. I mean . . . I've known him since God-knows-when. We were contemporaries. We propped up the same bars in London . . . "

"The vital difference is that before that you propped up bars at the LSE and Blaine propped them up in Cambridge."

"That's why we made him our man on Burgess, Maclean, and that slimy bugger, Philby. I seem to recall telling you he was a better man to de-brief Burgess than I was."

"Cambridge is also where they recruited him. Blaine seems to have done a very good job of not attracting attention either at Cambridge or after. As the Cambridge spies go, he seems to have been the sleeping partner. I knew most of Guy's friends. I met a lot of his dubious acquaintances. Blaine wasn't one of them. If he was a homo, he wasn't one of Guy's homos."

"Oh no, Bill wasn't queer. First marriage went belly-up before the war. Divorced. Second wife just walked out. He never bothered with a divorce that time. No intention of ever marrying again. He was happy with prostitutes. Had a regular high-class whore who used to visit him at his flat. None of the 'hello dearie, fancy a good time' on Soho street corners. All very discreet. He had his good times at home. She'd invoice him every month, just like a tailor, and he'd post off a cheque. But . . . Cambridge . . . Burgess . . . I never asked . . . did Bill get to see Burgess in Vienna?"

"Oh yes, they spent quite a long evening alone."

"Ye gods . . . it makes you wonder what they talked about, doesn't it?"

Troy had thought much the same.

"I mean," Jordan went on. "They'd have been laughing like idiots at us, wouldn't they? They had to be. Making twats of us all. And all the while the KGB had a bullet with Bill's name on it."

Troy thought Jordan might have worked it out. He hadn't, but as he was still uncertain himself, he let the remark pass.

"Tell me about Kearney."

"What's to tell? Posh Scottish. You know the type. Shares in a distillery. Wears a kilt on New Year's Eve. Not a trace of an accent. Fettes and Westminster. Greats at Balliol. Then straight into the navy. Joined Naval Intelligence during the war. Transferred to us in '55, I think it was. Ian Fleming recommended him. They'd been pen-pushers in the same back room in '44. There were even rumours Fleming based his Bond character on him. Well, he's certainly tall, dark, and handsome . . . but a man of action he ain't. He wouldn't know a Beretta from a Bazooka. The sort of bloke whose handshake is a bit too limp, and if you sniff your hand afterwards it smells of Nivea. I hope I can say this without false modesty—he got the job he has because I turned it down. It's a desk job. I'm a field agent and I want to stay that way. Kearney is a desk jockey. Happy with his pencil sharpener and all those pens with different coloured inks."

"Can you get me the file on him?"

Jordan straightened noticeably, as though Troy's words had magic. An open sesame to sobriety.

"No . . . No, I can't. Do you have any idea of the scrutiny involved in getting hold of the file on a section head? I'd have to sign it in and sign it out. Given Kearney's seniority, they might not even let me take it out of the room, and as there are two clerks on permanent supervision, somebody is bound to ask me why I want it. I'm sorry, Freddie. I understand your concerns and if you're right, I'm as concerned as you are yourself . . . but we can't go down that route. There is a bag, inside that is a cat, and the minute I ask to see Kearney's file the cat leaps out and craps everywhere. Whatever the nature of your investigation, do you really think it will help to alert, provoke, and antagonise an MI5 section head?"

§136

Troy slept as badly as the night before. His dreams but variations on a theme, ending the same way in the same words— "Put the gun down, Herr Troy."

He couldn't understand why the Austrian detective's words haunted him . . . he'd expect to hear Venetia's habitual "I know everything," as it had turned out to be her swan song. But he didn't, just the prosaic, procedural phrasing of a Viennese flic.

He went into the Yard.

Bypassed all contact with Onions.

Brought Jack up to speed.

He was not in a mood to smile. Tolerant and disapproving.

"An MI5 section head? Good God, Freddie. One of these days you'll get us all killed."

Around noon Jordan called.

"Sorry about last night. Bad timing."

"You remember what you said?"

"Yes, and I stick to it. Meet me in the park in an hour."

Everyone met in the park. Troy doubted that there was a single innocent newspaper reader or duck feeder to be found anywhere in St. James's Park. They were all running dead letter boxes, trading secrets, or looking for guardsmen to suck off.

He had no difficulty finding Jordan. They'd met at the same bench half a dozen times over the last ten years. Meeting here was the shabby side of a relationship that, by and large, remained social and affable. Troy had eaten dinner at Jordan's and Jordan at Troy's. Foxx adored him. They, as Jordan was wont to put it, propped up the same bars—usually the Criterion. If they met in the park, it was work and it was fractious. Troy never felt more distant from Jordan than when talking shop.

"I'm sorry I was pissed," Jordan said. "Sorrier still to sound pissed off. But—I thought it over. I still can't do what you ask. Too damn risky."

"But?"

"But there's another way to skin a duck . . ."

"Cat."

"Eh?"

"The phrase is 'to skin a cat.'"

"If you say so . . . the cat-skinning is this. I can't get you the service file on Denzil Kearney without alarm bells going off in Leconfield House. But you can get hold of the copy at the Yard."

"Not wholly sure I'm with you, Jordan."

"Special Branch have files on everyone. They have one on you."

"Of course."

"I know—I've read it. And they'll have one on Kearney. Might be out of date. I'd doubt they've added to it since 1955, but up to that point it will be as fulsome as your own, which, by the bye, is a mass of innuendo, speculation, and resentment worthy of a cod-Regency novel in which you get to play Sir Jasper."

"Which," said Troy, "is why they wouldn't show me Kearney's file for love or money."

"So. The Branch hate you. They've always hated you. But now you have Eddie. A man for all seasons. You've needed an Eddie for a long time. Jack is far too like you. Another tearaway toff. Quite the wrong class to click with the bowler-hat-and-beetle-crusher brigade. But—if Detective Sergeant Edwin Clark can't wheedle the file out of Special Branch, I'll eat my hat."

Jordan was right, and Troy knew it.

"Of course," Jordan added. "You may find bugger all. Kearney a Soviet agent? I think not. In fact, Freddie, let me ask—do you actually know what you're looking for?"

"No. I don't."

"But . . . you think Kearney had an ulterior in sending Blaine out to Vienna."

"Yes. I told you last night. You weren't at risk. The target was always Blaine."

"Kearney knew Blaine would be shot? That means he was dealing with the KGB. Something I won't believe until you slap irrefutable proof in front of me. Freddie, it would make more sense, if you're right about Blaine being a wrong'un, to have nicked him before he got on a plane to a neutral country. We don't let the opposition wipe out their double agents when they're done with them. We arrest them and we interrogate them and we prosecute them."

"I never said it made sense," Troy said. "But it's what happened."

It wasn't what happened, but now was not the moment to say so. It was a puzzle to which Troy had the solution, but so many pieces of the puzzle were still missing. Without the missing pieces, Jordan would never believe him.

§137

"Oh, bloody Norah."

"Ed, can you do it?"

"In the old days it would have been a doddle."

"The old days?"

"Rationing. Nothing's rationed any more. Upshot . . . people are a damn sight harder to bribe. If this were Berlin in '48, I'd bung someone two hundred fags or a couple of pounds of coffee. Even just three or four years back you could corrupt a man with a soddin' Mars Bar."

Troy hated Eddie's occasional obstinacy. It might be his only weakness, to sound like a plumber confronted with a gas tap you have painted over in violation of common sense and the Guild of Plumbers moral code: Thou shalt not paint over the gas tap.

"But you'll try?"

"I'll try. Might take a day or two. I can't just go upstairs and knock on a door. It means hanging around the canteen in the hope of bumping in to the right chatty bastard."

"OK."

"And it means you keeping out of the way. You can kill any conversation dead as a doornail when you come into the canteen."

"So I'm told."

"What we need is an NCO's mess . . ."

"Ed—just do it."

§138

"This is the last thing I can do for you . . . if you come up with enough evidence to nick Kearney . . ."—a shrug as Jordan indicated his disbelief in such a possibility, then, "That will change everything."

He set a brown envelope on the bench between them. Troy picked it up. Inside were copies of two memos.

One signed, dated the day after Blaine was killed.

> I misunderstood you. I'm sorry, but when you said to pull Jordan off Vienna, I didn't think you meant send no one at all. So I assigned Bill. By far the better man for the job. My cock-up. I take full responsibility. DK.

And one unsigned, dated the day Troy had returned to England.

> Denzil, it's everyone's cock-up. Can't be helped. I made our apologies to the PM in person. Probably burning with rage on the inside, but you know Mac—the smoke never shows. He just wants the whole thing forgotten. He's due in Moscow to meet Khrushchev in less than three months. He's not going to let what happened in Vienna muddy the waters. Sad but true, a good meeting with Khrushchev counts for a damn sight more than a dead agent or a live traitor.

"Who wrote the second memo?"

"Roger Hollis."

"Then I think the director gave Kearney his Get-Out-Of-Jail-Free card."

"As I said, Freddie. Bring me evidence."

"What we're missing is what Hollis actually told Kearney."

"I refer the Hon. Member to my previous answer."

"You didn't find a memo?"

"Most likely it was a phone call. If it was anything like the one I got . . . late at night, rushed, confusing . . . plenty of room for error.

And don't go looking for a Hollis/Kearney conspiracy. You won't find one. Roger's straight."

Jordan stood up to leave.

"You know," Troy said, "one of us really should bring something to feed the ducks or we'll look like a couple of spies."

"Very funny, Freddie."

Jordan snatched back the envelope, turned up his collar, stuck his hands in his pockets, and walked off in the direction of the Mall.

§139

It took Eddie forty-eight hours to appear at Troy's desk. Smug, triumphant.

He slid a buff-coloured file across to Troy.

```
Kearney, James Denzil Carnegie
```

No rank, just his date of birth—5.10.12.

And rubber stamps recording the occasions on which the file had been accessed—twice only. Once in 1940 and again in 1955. A man so above suspicion as never to have earned even curiosity.

"To whom do I owe?"

"Geoff Quigley. Sergeant in the Branch."

"And what do I owe?"

"He'd like a job."

"What?"

"He hates the Branch even more than you do. He'd prefer to work in Murder."

Troy pondered this one. A Trojan horse? An honest, simple, rather difficult request?

"Tell Jack. If he thinks we're short on coppers we might be able to get him transferred."

"OK."

"Do you think he'll make a detective?"

"You're asking the wrong person. Whatever made you think I'd make a detective?"

"Just tell Jack."

When Eddie had gone, Troy opened the file. An unadorned record of a naval career of no particular distinction. Public school, Oxford, the Royal Navy. Kearney had been twenty-six when the war began, a lieutenant commander on a frigate in the Indian Ocean. By 1940, he had risen to commander and was working in Naval Intelligence at the Admiralty in London. He had not seen combat, he had not been to sea again. If he'd remained a regular sailor he might well have been a rear admiral by now—short of cock-ups. But this was Intelligence. Rank did not matter. Power did. As Eddie had reminded him just a few weeks ago, Joe Holderness was a lowly flight sergeant and had the power to call off the dogs—or throw him to the wolves.

Troy learnt nothing he could not have anticipated. A career at once spotless and banal. Not a hint of anything out of the ordinary. If his own file was, as Jordan had put it, "fulsome," this wasn't. It was less a "cod-Regency novel," more like a chit for new regulation-issue boots. No speculation, no innuendo, but then Kearney was one of their own. Troy was not.

He flipped the folder over, venting a little of the exasperation he felt. A photograph slid out. He'd missed that.

It wasn't large, a 620 contact print.

Troy rattled around in a desk drawer for his "Sherlock Holmes Kit." A six-inch magnifying glass.

Kearney was in uniform, and Troy thought the photograph was probably the best part of twenty years old, taken at the point when he moved from ships at sea to a desk in the Admiralty's back room.

He was handsome in a very British sort of way. A passing resemblance to the film star Stewart Granger. He looked straight into the lens. Not a sign of self-consciousness or nerves. A face that you might warm to if it smiled, but in the meantime was giving nothing away.

Troy stared, willing Kearney to speak.

$140

Perhaps hours had passed. The light outside was fading. But it was November—or was it December? Nights that fell too soon. Troy realised he had lost track of time in both the immediate sense of its passing and in the bigger sense of the calendar.

He had stared so long at Kearney's photograph he could see nothing any more.

Voices echoed in the mind's ear.

"I know everything."

But she hadn't told him everything.

"I know everything."

Venetia disappeared at the end of a long tunnel, a slow diminuendo into silence just when he thought he would hear her voice and those same three words forever. And another voice, another past, rang in his ears:

"Captain on the bridge!"

And he could see a young naval officer springing to attention in Burgess's bedroom on Bond Street, pissed as a fart, booze-blind to Troy's presence, only to fall straight back down next to Burgess.

Kearney.

Guy's last night in England, his leaving-for-Washington-fuck-you-England party that day in 1950.

Kearney.

Guy Burgess's farewell to Blighty had been to fuck Denzil Kearney.

He slid the photograph to the middle of his desk. He'd binned his collection of name postcards but in the mind's eye he could see them laid out like a royal flush, ending on the ace—Kearney.

He pressed the intercom.

"Eddie, what day is it?"

"Friday. Are you feeling alright, sir?"

"And the month?"

The line went dead. Eddie appeared in the doorway.

"Are you OK? You don't speak for hours then you can't remember what day it is?"

"You told me. It's Friday."

"A Friday in December, as it happens."

Friday again? Fridays came around so soon.

"And the time?"

Eddie pointed at the clock on the wall.

"Half past five."

Troy pushed up his sleeve to look at his watch, but it was too dark in the room. Eddie flicked on the light and said again, "Are you feeling alright, sir?"

§141

The Fat Man was seated at the kitchen table, filling in a pools coupon.

"Do you reckon Arsenal versus QPR for a draw?" he said.

Troy said nothing.

"Yer bruv's 'ere. Was you expecting him?"

"Yes. I'm not trying to avoid him. In fact, he's the reason I'm here."

The Fat Man looked up.

"Wonders'll never cease."

Licked the end of his pencil and went back to picking draws.

"Have you eaten?"

"O' course. In fact me and him had steak and kidney pie with spuds and peas at this very table not half an hour ago. Yours is in the oven. Rod's in your study 'avin' a snifter I reckon. It'll be rabbit tomorrow night. The cat brought one in, but it could do with 'anging for a day."

Troy sloughed off his coat and jacket and looked in the oven. When he turned around the Fat Man had set out a plate for him and was holding out a pair of oven gloves.

"Fingers," he said simply.

Troy ate.

"I think I missed lunch," he said. "At least, I don't remember lunch."

"You alright, cock?" said the Fat Man, much as Eddie had done, but without any "sir." Eddie forgot his sirs only when he was feeling urgent or irritated, and largely remained purposefully conscious of rank. The

Fat Man, on the other hand, knew no deference and "cock" or "ole cock" was the best Troy or anyone would ever get.

"Things on my mind."

"You can always talk to me, y'know."

"I know, and thank you. But it's Rod I need to talk to. Telling anyone else would be burdening them."

"Well, I 'opes you get a word in edgeways, 'cos I learnt more about the perils of being in Parliament than I ever wanted to know. Just as well I wasn't thinking of standing meself."

"Jack would be the cold voice of reason. Eddie would mutter endless bloody Norahs . . . so it's Rod I need."

"I getcher. You finish yer grub and nip in there while he's still sober. But since you're here . . . Derby County versus Accrington Stanley?"

§142

Rod had usurped Troy's study. Fire lit, feet up. The look of a man happy to have escaped constituents and children.

He was a little the worse for wear, but hardly drunk.

"Were we expecting each other?" he said.

"No. I rang Hampstead first. Cid told me you were here."

"Needed a bit of a break. You haven't come to ruin it for me, have you?"

"I think I have. Pour yourself another drink."

"Can't it, whatever it is, wait?"

"If it could I wouldn't be here."

"Work thing, is it?"

"Yep."

"Yours or mine?"

"Both."

"Then I will have that drink."

When Rod had settled again, poked the logs in the fire into life, Troy said, "Tell me about your meeting with Macmillan."

"I thought I did. I've nothing to add and the old man hasn't summoned me since."

"Yes, but there's emphasis. It's how you say it."

Rod, having made so many speeches in thirteen years in Parliament, had an excellent memory for the right words in the right order, and told Troy of his meeting with the Prime Minister almost exactly as he had before, ending, "Burgess to Iain? A bit of a non sequitur? Just one of those things. I don't know why you're making so much of it."

Troy said, "Has it occurred to you that it wasn't a non sequitur? That Uncle Harold had not changed the subject?"

"What, you mean the subject was the queer thing all along?"

"Guy is queer, Iain Stuart-Bell is queer."

"But Iain isn't a traitor."

"And treason was not Macmillan's subject. Being queer was."

"Let me get this straight here, bro. You're saying Macmillan didn't want Burgess back because he's queer?"

"Yes. And he wasn't the only one."

"So it had nothing to do with him being a traitor?"

"I wouldn't go that far. But ask yourself this. What secrets has Guy been keeping all these years that might not be so secret once he's back in the RAC or the Reform Club with too much Scotch inside him?"

"Such as who fucked who in the blackout?"

"Or who fucks who in cabinet and who in the cabinet is also in the closet."

Rod got up, reached for the decanter of Scotch.

"I don't fucking believe this. Or to be exact, I do."

He necked one neat, then, with a twinge of conscience, squirted a dash of soda into his second.

"He wasn't the only one, you said. So tell me. Who else wants dear old Guy to stay in dear old Russia?"

"Denzil Kearney."

"Do I know him?"

"Section Head, MI5. Jordan's boss. His boss, but not his equal."

"And am I to conclude that this Kearney bloke is, as you so succinctly put it, 'in the closet'?"

"Yep."

"You're certain?"

"Yes."

"And how does this tie in with Bill Blaine and your brush with the Vienna coppers?"

"The KGB didn't shoot Blaine, our people did. Kearney had Blaine killed to make damn sure Guy's attempt to come home failed."

"It wasn't the Russians? It's always the bloody Russians!"

"No, it was our lot. And it worked. Guy will be there for ever now."

"Clutching on to his secrets?"

"Dreaming of England."

"Drowning in vodka?"

"No, I think he's learnt to swim in it."

"Cursing man and God and fate?"

"Pretty much."

Rod leaned his head back, the Scotch and soda warming in his grip, eyes closed.

"What a mess, what a fucking mess."

"Quite."

"It reminds me of where we came in."

"Eh?"

"You know when we used to go to the flicks as kids. You could buy a ticket at any time, walk in half an hour through the Jean Harlows or the Clark Gables and watch until the film came full circle. Made a bollocks of the plot but we did it often enough. This reminds me of our first encounter with Mr. B. Do you remember what Dad said when he told us Guy was a spy?"

"'Fraid not."

"I said, 'who do we tell?' and he replied, 'we tell no one.'"

"Ah . . . yes, of course he did."

"He said it because there was no one to tell. And I say it to you now, Freddie, we can tell no one."

The eyes flicked open, the gaze locked on to his, far from pissed and deadly serious.

Just as seriously Troy looked back and said, "Rod, it isn't going to be that way."

"Yes," said Rod. "I was afraid of that. Why don't you pour a drink for yourself and tell me what you're not telling me. You've already ruined the weekend and I've got all night."

§143

"I saw it in my mind's eye as a series of blank cards. Imagine it as a kind of white jigsaw puzzle. The pieces only make sense if you write on them. And then I set it out for real, on the physical plane.

"I wrote . . .

> Burgess
> Macmillan
> Iain Stuart-Bell
> Blaine
> Venetia, Venetia forever saying 'I know everything'

then . . .

> Jordan
> Kearney

"And then the line I couldn't get out of my head or out of my dreams: 'Put the gun down, Herr Troy.'"

"I'm sorry, I don't get it."

"It's what the flic in Vienna said as I came round after Blaine was shot, two minutes before he arrested me."

"You had a gun?"

"That's not the point. The gun was Blaine's. The point is he knew my name and he spoke to me in English. And it's run around in my head ever since. 'Put the gun down, Herr Troy.'"

"So?"

"So . . . how did he know my name? Logically, he should have had not an inkling who I was. But he did . . . he knew me . . . and I doubt I was out cold more than a matter of minutes . . . how did he and a team of armed rozzers get there so quickly? Only one answer. They were wait-ing for us. The flic had been briefed. The KGB didn't shoot Bill Blaine, the Vienna police shot him on orders from Kearney. Kearney being queer is the key to it all. He was a one-time lover of Guy's. He was the last man in London who'd ever want Guy back again. If Guy blabbed, Kearney's career was over. As surely as Iain Stuart-Bell's. He'd never get a shot at the top job. He'd be shuffled off to the Scunthorpe branch of MI5 and never let near a secret again.

"At some point Kearney realised Blaine had told Venetia Staines-borough he was a double agent, and he killed her. I don't really know how he found out, still less why he had to kill her. Except that the more people she told, the more flimsy his own story might seem. Even then, he might have got away with it. As long as the queer thing didn't come out. But of course, he didn't know her. Venetia wasn't about to broadcast Blaine's treachery."

"But she told you?"

"Yes, she did."

"Can you prove any of this?"

"Not yet."

"And not ever . . . Freddie, I believe you, I believe every word you say, but I say again, tell no one. This can end no other way but badly."

§144

On Monday morning Troy asked Jack, Jordan, and Eddie into his office. He kept it short and far from sweet, and ended as he had begun with Rod.

"The KGB didn't shoot Bill Blaine, our people did."

And more or less as he had predicted, Jack said, "Here we go again, poking around in the fires of hell" and Eddie said half a dozen "Bloody Norahs" in lieu of Hail Marys.

Jordan turned to both of them and said, "Would you chaps mind giving us the room?"

"Willingly," Jack replied.

Eddie left, still mumbling his private mantra.

When they were alone, Jordan said, "Spit it out, Freddie."

"You already know everything I know."

"One more time. Just sum up what you have refrained from speculating on until now. There is no room whatsoever for us to misunderstand one another."

"Kearney would have pulled you off the Vienna trip regardless of any call from Hollis. He was always going to send Blaine. He was going to have Blaine killed the minute he heard about Burgess. It was the perfect cover. If he was caught, then he could play the Blaine-was-a-double-agent card, and bargain his way out of the mess. Sacrificing you would have no get-out clause. Blaine was disposable. Either one of you dead would have put paid to Burgess's attempted return . . . but Blaine came with a guarantee. I told you last week—it was his Get-Out-Of-Jail-Free card."

"Why send anyone at all after Macmillan made it clear he wouldn't have Burgess back?"

"Why take a risk when he could make returning impossible for Burgess for years to come?"

A pause of the kind to which Jordan was not often given.

"You're really convinced of this, aren't you?"

"Yes. And you're not?"

"Oh, yes. I am quite convinced."

Another unfamiliar pause.

"Then there's something *you're* not telling *me*?"

They'd been standing for several minutes, ever since they assembled around Troy's desk. Jordan sat down with a thump, unwrapped his scarf, took off his gloves, loosened his buttons. Shook his head like a wet dog.

"Venetia," he said at last. "I've remembered where I saw her. A party. Bloke I work with turned fifty. Threw a party at his own home. Not sure when, '55, perhaps '56. It should have stuck in my memory. It's rare for agents to gather socially—almost entirely against the grain of the job. What would we talk about, after all? Most of our office gossip is marked 'Top Secret.' Venetia Stainesborough turned up on the arm of Denzil Kearney."

"A beard?"

"So it seems now. If I'd had my suspicions . . . but I didn't. And it's not as if every homosexual in the service hasn't been considered a security risk ever since Burgess defected. Guy queered the pitch—literally. We've wallowed in suspicion, mostly without cause. And Kearney escaped it all. Over the last three years, I've seen half a dozen women escorted by Kearney. All much of a muchness. Tall, English, good-looking, aristocratic. All blondes. All beards. All part of the mask of heterosexuality. It worked. We all thought of him as promiscuous. Single, promiscuous, and lucky. The perfect bachelor. In all probability what half the service think of me. Queer? I didn't get so much as a whiff."

"Except for the Nivea handshake."

"I know. I've been stupid. Rub it in. But it's not as if he hung around Piccadilly Circus. If he has boys, then he's even more discreet than Bill Blaine was with his whores."

"It does, however, explain one thing."

"What?"

"Why Venetia opened the door and let him in."

Jordan sighed.

"There's more. I had hoped not to tell you this. I'm no fucking good as a secret agent if I can't keep a secret, but this one's had its day. We searched Burgess's flat after he skipped the country. Someone had been in ahead of us . . . done a quick clean-up—I rather think it was Blunt . . . there, another damn thing I shouldn't have told you."

"It's OK. I know about Blunt. You're not the only one who can't keep a secret."

"Westcott?"

Troy said nothing.

"But he . . . whoever . . . didn't bother to open Burgess's guitar case. It was crammed with love letters. Enough dirty linen to send our latter-day Oscar Wildes down for another stretch in Reading Gaol. And if I were to tell you the names of those Oscar Wildes . . . well, I won't. Some secrets I can keep. Let me just say that Guy Burgess has enough dirt on the English Establishment to plunge it into eschatological chaos. I understand exactly why Macmillan doesn't want him back. Indeed, I understood the minute you told me. My reservations were all about Kearney."

"Were there letters from Kearney?"

"I doubt it. I'd've remembered, and from what you've told me this morning I rather think Guy and Kearney were ships that passed in the night."

"But . . . close enough to get Bill Blaine and Venetia Stainesborough killed?"

"Oh yes."

"So . . . we agree. Kearney had Blaine killed and killed Venetia himself?"

"We do, but . . . we can tell no one."

Such a familiar phrase. A haunting whisper of impossibility.

"Exactly what my brother said," said Troy.

"Rod's right. There's no one we can tell. Not without evidence. And you have none."

Now Troy paused. Gathering up the thought that had dogged him all weekend.

"There is one person I can tell."

"Really?"

"Yes. I think it's time I paid Commander Kearney a house call."

§145

The address Jordan had given him was a redbrick mansion block on the southern side of Battersea Park. To the north all the tawdry pleasures of the last remnant of the Festival of Britain still rattled on in the form of the fun fair, with its Big Dipper and its House of Horror, which had stood seven years now and was surely due to be torn down any minute. It was quiet now, nine o'clock of a Monday night in winter.

Troy looked up at the lighted windows of the flats. The orange glow of a hundred shaded reading lamps. It seemed to him, the fun fair notwithstanding, to be a building tailor-made for the single man. And for the singular man.

He pressed a button in the brass plate of numbered and lettered apartments.

After a short wait a tetchy voice said, "Whoever you are, what do you want at this time of night?"

"Chief Superintendent Troy, Scotland Yard."

"Y'don't say? Well, can't keep the Yard waiting, can we? Second floor, on the left."

An electric bee buzzed and the lobby door swung open.

The apartment door stood ajar, a faint stream of music curling out. Schubert's *Death and the Maiden*, in Gustav Mahler's orchestral arrangement.

Why was he disturbed by this? A shock, however slight, to think that Kearney might be cultured? Somehow rendered less of a criminal by good taste, taste very much his own? Of course he'd be cultured. The man had read classics at Oxford. For all Troy knew, he was listening to Schubert in a panelled study lined with the works of Homer, Catullus, and Ovid.

The door was yanked wide.

Kearney stood in his stocking feet, tie at half-mast, towering over Troy at more than six foot. It reminded him of dropping in on his brother—so far the only real difference was that Kearney's socks matched and Rod's never did.

"Do come in, Troy."

A false smile, an arm spread to point the way.

Troy stepped into a panelled study lined with the works of Homer, Catullus, and Ovid. There they were on the shelves behind the radiogram in their neat, pocket-handy, pastel-coloured Loeb editions, next to the twelve-volume edition of Gibbon's *Decline and Fall*.

Troy turned back to speak. Kearney banged him solidly on the side of the head with his fist and dropped him into the nearest armchair, as light and limp as a feather pillow.

Kearney flipped the buttons on Troy's overcoat and then tore his shirt open, buttons pinging off the walls, the cloth tearing in his hands.

He stood up, breathed in deeply.

"Sorry about that, old man. But we could hardly talk about what you've surely come to talk about if you were wearing a wire, could we? Now, Scotch OK for you? Ice or soda?"

Troy said, "I might almost think you were expecting me."

"Oh no. Oh no. I most certainly was not expecting you. In fact, I thought I'd left not so much as a loose thread. Yet . . . here you are."

The arm was yanked mercilessly off the vinyl. Troy could feel the scratch on Schubert more painfully than the lump swelling on his head. A Scotch and soda was thrust into his hand. Kearney sat down opposite him. Picked up his drink, pushed a lock of dark hair out of his eyes.

Troy's eyes swam towards focus. Jordan had been right in his description—tall, dark, and handsome. Indeed, Kearney looked remarkably like the depiction of James Bond on the paperback of *Casino Royale*—the strong profile, the ever-errant lock of hair, the unfeeling brown eyes. The same cover on which Vesper Lynd was shown wearing the red dress Venetia had worn the night he had killed her. Troy wondered about the "desk jockey." There was a scar on his right cheek, faintly tracing the bone, that might speak of something outdoors and hearty . . . but the punch had been amateurish. Anyone who knew how to throw a punch would have knocked him cold.

"Cheers, old man. Sorry you have to catch me a little déshabillé, but so are you."

Then.

"Spit it out."

Nobody seemed to have any patience in MI5. Spit every damn thing out.

"I know you killed Venetia Stainesborough."

"Really?"

"You knew she was Bill Blaine's sister-in-law. After you had Blaine shot in Vienna she was the only loose thread. You had her followed, and when you realised she was seeing me she became too much of a risk."

Kearney was shaking his head.

"No, noo, nooo. I'm amazed you ever made it out of uniform, Troy. I have better detectives emptying the wastepaper baskets at Five. Try again."

"There is no 'again.' You killed them both."

Kearney knocked back his drink, reached for the bottle and topped them both up. The hospitality of the captor. Troy thought he was buying a few moments of time. Wondering how much to tell.

He sat back down, glanced away at nothing for a minute, then looked straight at Troy.

"OK. This is it. This is what you get and all you get. Killing Bill made perfect sense. Even with you there. I just didn't think you'd be there at the precise moment the Austrians took him out. Silly really. I should have known they'd fuck it up. All the same, I thought you'd walk away from it. I was pretty certain Stanley Onions would make you. But I didn't allow for Dick White's reaction. He came at it all . . . what do they say these days? . . . out of left field. So, I didn't have a deal of choice. When you'd seen off the inevitable Special Branch posse, seen off Joe Holderness . . . I still had you followed around London. And you didn't spot that, did you? I never followed Venetia. I followed you."

Troy said nothing.

"Imagine my surprise, as the clichés of pornography would have it . . . when you led me straight to Eaton Place. A connection I didn't know existed. I'd no idea the two of you had ever met. But London is a smaller place than one ever imagines. Society more closely knit than one ever likes to think. Of course I knew Venetia was Bill's sister-in-law. It was Bill who introduced us, after all . . . but . . . it was a simple sum . . . two and two made four . . . Troy and Venetia made a rather risky four . . . I wasn't certain she knew all about Bill, but it seemed highly likely . . . we all need someone we can tell, don't we? . . . and she knew about me . . . wooing her for a week or two didn't fool her for a second . . . she knew my . . . my tastes . . . and . . . the prospect of an exchange of information between you and Venetia . . . well . . ."

Troy said nothing.

"No. I didn't kill her, Troy. I had no intention of killing her. It was an accident. All I wanted was to know what she had told you."

"And when she wouldn't tell you, you tried to shake it out of her."

"Alas, yes, but she was a strong woman. She broke my grip, took a step away from me, and went over backwards down the stairs."

"And?"

"And what?"

"And what did you do next?"

"I let myself out and walked away. What would you have done?"

Troy would have checked her pulse, called an ambulance, tried anything that might have stood a cat in hell's chance of saving her life. But he said nothing.

"Believe me. It was an accident. I meant her no harm. My weakness was I had to know. Call it a spy's weakness, if you like, a copper's weakness even, always wanting to know. And I knew your reputation for doggedness. I didn't want you turning up on my doorstep."

"Yet here I am."

"Yes. Here you are. Mea culpa. All the same, you leave with nothing. Your consolation prize is the same as mine—I know, you know. We both know everything and have gained nothing—and now you can just fuck off because there's not a damn thing you can do about any of it."

§146

He called Gus Fforde. It seemed stupid not to check out one last possibility.

"Are we on a secure line?"

"Scotland Yard to a British embassy? I should bloody well hope so."

"Méret Voytek is still in Vienna."

"So I gather."

"She's going back to Moscow on the twenty-third. Can you get a message to her? She rehearses most afternoons at the Konzerthaus."

"Don't see why not."

"Good. The message is for Guy Burgess—"

"Oh bloody hell . . . Freddie . . . no no no!"

"Gus, just do it."

"Freddie, have you a death wish? You've only just climbed out of the last pool of shit over Bill Blaine."

"Gus—I wouldn't ask if there were any other way."

"OK. On mine own head be it, I suppose. Fire away."

"It's simple. Just jot this down . . . Number 7? Number 8? Denzil Kearney?"

"OK. Easy enough. Will Burgess know what you're on about?"

"Yes."

"Denzil Kearney. Sounds familiar."

"Don't ask."

"Wasn't going to. I was going to ask how do you expect to get a reply without our lot and their lot reading it?"

"She's back for the New Year's Eve concert. Catch her then, pick up Guy's answer. Call me."

§147

Troy got home to Goodwin's Court.

Two small suitcases stood just inside the door.

This meant nothing.

Then Foxx rushed up and kissed him, jumping from the chair she sat in.

Then he knew.

"You bugger," she said. "You've forgotten what I look like, haven't you?"

He fought against himself and kissed her back.

"Don't be daft. I just wasn't—"

"Expecting me? Look, I'm sorry. It all took far longer than I thought. But it's done now. The loo works, hot and cold running in a new sink, the house is let and Rosie and Malcolm installed. I am . . . home!"

Of course she was. He didn't think he'd noticed his home in days. He had fallen through a hole in time and space. He had lived with the dead, and could not handle the living woman in front of him.

They ate out, in Giovanni's, the Italian restaurant just across the yard.

After a silent minestra, over the linguine, Foxx said, "Where are you? You seem very distracted."

"Oh, you know. The job," he said truthfully, feeling as he spoke that it was a lie.

He woke around three in the morning. The reading lamp on. Foxx with her knees up. Scribbling on a notepad.

"What are you doing?"

"Christmas list."

"Christmas isn't for . . ."

"It's next week, Troy, less than a fortnight away. And I bet you've done nothing about it."

After the war, Troy and his mother had hosted Christmas out at Mimram for the whole family. When his mother died he would gladly have stopped playing host to quite so many, but his sister-in-law, Cid, had offered to take over his mother's role and they had carried on. Foxx had been at the last two family Christmases and had accepted it as a tradition to be maintained and relished. To Troy it was little more than an exchange of socks and hankies, but he knew he'd never be able to cheat her out of this one.

"Fine," he said, and turned over.

§148

It was Christmas Eve before the inevitable row burst. He was dressing for dinner, which they did for just two nights and had Boxing Day in mufti—kids in new pullovers, Rod in new socks and slippers, and, if he showed up, the Fat Man in a shiny new "weskit" or a bow tie Troy would see him wear once and never again.

From Sasha and Hugh's room came the first low-flying cliché.

"Bitch!"

Well, she was, wasn't she? But she was their bitch, and every time Hugh called her that Troy would happily have thumped him.

He was in his own room, which was unfortunately next to theirs, trying in vain to ignore the swapping of insults, and to tie his own bow tie.

He heard a door slam, then the door to his room opened, and when he turned around Sasha was pressed against it, tears of rage refusing to roll from her eyes.

"I swear, Freddie, one day soon I'll kill the fucker."

"Don't," he said simply. "I am awash in death right now. Save it for the new year when you're bored and having nothing else to do."

She moved off the door, neat and beautiful in her little black dress.

"Sorry," she said, a word that hardly ever passed her lips. "Wasn't thinking."

She stood in front of him, took the two ends of his bow tie in her hands.

"Venetia?"

Troy nodded.

"Was it your case?"

"It was Jack who was called out," Troy said, only half lying.

"But it was an accident, wasn't it? I mean, I'd hate to think . . ."

"Yes," he said, lying. "It was an accident."

Her hands created the knot that always seemed to elude him, saying as she did so what she had said to him since childhood whenever she tied his tie, "The little rabbit runs round and round the tree, and then he goes down the little rabbit hole."

And with that he was looped, and tied, and dressed.

§149

In bed, after Boxing Day, the wee small hours of the twenty-seventh, aligned like spoons between the sheets, Foxx said, "Where are you?"

"Eh?"

"Well, you're not here with me. You're not even in the same room, so where are you?"

"There are things I have to do. Won't take long."

"And when they are done?"

"I'll be back. I promise."

"Then I won't ask who she is."

"*Was*, not is."

"Oh fuck, Troy. What have you done?"

§150

Normal service, as the BBC always termed it, was resumed on January 2. Another Friday.

Troy had been in his office less than an hour when Eddie put through a call from Vienna.

"Freddie?"

"I'm here, Gus."

"I have a few words from our friend. 'Absolutely not. Straight as a die, and queer as a coot.' Does that answer your question?"

It did. It lent a certain purity to what he knew. A singularity to his purpose.

Eddie, clearly, had listened in.

He stood before Troy now.

"You can't do it."

"Do what?"

"You can't just kill an MI5 section head."

§151

Troy had grown used to the Fat Man seeing through him. They had known each other . . . what? . . . fourteen or fifteen years . . . since 1944. He'd known Eddie since '48, but had seen nothing of him for most of that time. For the last two years, they had worked side by side. Coffee and cake. There was bound to come a moment, and clearly it had come, when Eddie would attain Fat Man perception.

But for one thing.

It had not occurred to Troy that he might kill Kearney.

It had not occurred to Troy that he could or should kill Kearney.

Eddie had worked out the fate Troy had meted out to Inspector Cobb. God alone knew how he had done this, but he had. And he had leapt to a plausible, if wrong, conclusion.

It had not occurred to Troy that he might kill Kearney.

Until now.

He'd known, from the second he had worked out the truth, that he would do something.

Kearney had killed the woman he . . . the past participle of the verb "to love" went unuttered in both speech and thought.

He knew he would do something.

He had to do something.

He could inform . . . accuse . . . arrest . . . the list chugged on awhile in his mind only to hit the buffers at Jordan's "Who do we tell? We tell no one." The logic of which rested on there being no one to tell who would believe, and worse, no one who would listen.

It had not occurred to Troy that he might kill Kearney.

Until now.

§152

Kearney was a creature of habit. Most men were. It took Troy only three days to establish his pattern. Not being of sufficient rank to merit a Special Branch watch, he was abroad in the city indistinguishable from any other Londoner, apart from the fact that he was probably better dressed.

His morning routine was to walk to the far end of Prince of Wales Drive and catch the 137 bus across Chelsea Bridge to Park Lane, get off at the Dorchester, and walk the few remaining yards to Leconfield House in Curzon Street. He was a late starter. Hardly in the office much before ten, but also a late leaver. Scarcely out of it before eight, and even then with a briefcase full of documents under his arm. Troy felt certain that if he watched for longer he'd find plenty of nights when Kearney was still in his office at midnight, but time was running out. There is only so much squatting on the rim of the volcano a man can do.

Kearney's indulgence was not to travel home by public transport. A cab met him in Curzon street, every night, and bearing in mind that it was never quite the same time every night, it looked to be an arrangement set up and varied daily. The cab always dropped him on the far side of Chelsea Bridge, at which point Kearney would cut across Battersea Park, south of the fun fair, to the eastern end of the boating lake, which he would then follow on the southern side, parallel to the road, until he reached the exit pretty well opposite his own apartment. Troy ascribed it to the illusion of exercise. It was less than half a mile, but it probably appeased Kearney's conscience and took up less time than yoga or Sunday morning soccer. After that, he'd bet money that Kearney kicked off his shoes and poured himself a large Scotch. It did not seem that he did rough trade, but the advantage of no watchers was that he could do anyone. Again, if time permitted and Troy waited he felt sure he'd see young men at the door. What he wouldn't see was a visit to any Soho bar known for its homos. This was a man with a secret. That he'd ever bedded Burgess struck Troy as a stupid mistake, and one Kearney no doubt had regretted ever since. And, there was no live-in. Kearney spent his private life largely alone. And largely frustrated, Troy thought. Just as well. Frustrated or not, Troy needed Kearney alone. He'd no wish to kill him in company.

§153

Troy took a day off. Caught the train down to Brighton and sought out a man he'd known for twenty years and not seen for twelve—Danny the Deserter.

Troy had nicked him in his last days in Stepney, Danny—real name Herbert Smith—was still a teenager, and Troy himself not much older. Danny had been a fence, passing on everything and anything from jewellery to guns. He'd won in court. The judge had reprimanded Troy from the bench for a poor presentation of evidence and instructed the jury in a verdict of "Not Guilty."

As they left court, Danny had had the cheek to accost Troy and say, "No hard feelings, Mr. Troy."

Troy said nothing.

"You taught me a valuable lesson. This manor's too small for me. I'll be moving off your patch an' up West."

The brass neck of this was startling. This man was still a boy and treating Troy, a serving police officer, like one of his low-life pals.

"I'll be in the caffs in Old Compton Street. If you need me, just try 'em, I'll be in one or the other. A sort of office that ain't an office, if you know what I mean."

Troy said nothing.

He could not think of a single reason why he would ever need the services of Herbert Smith. Soon after, Troy himself moved "up West" with his promotion to the Yard and the Murder Squad. He'd encounter Smith in the streets of Soho, return his cheery "Wotcher, Mr. Troy" politely, note his newly acquired wartime nickname, and think little of him. He dealt in what he dealt, and as long as he didn't kill anyone he was of no interest to Troy.

Until 1944.

When Troy had needed to buy a gun.

§154

A ruined face answered the door in Kemptown. Forty years old and spent.

"Hello, Danny."

"'Allo, Mr. Troy. It's Bert now. I dropped all that malarkey when I left the smoke. Danny the Deserter? Deserter my arse, I never even got called up. 'Cos to call you up they gotta be able to find you first, ain't they?"

Rheumatoid arthritis had rendered Smith pitifully thin, lopsided in his walk, and blind in one eye—he sported an affecting eye patch, attractive but for the perished skin surrounding it.

"You come all this way to see your old pal, eh? Must be summink special."

Smith led off down a narrow corridor, up a short flight of stairs into the front room facing the sea.

"Always wanted a sea view. Ever since I was a nipper. Used to come to Brighton of a Saturday a'ternoon with me old man. Now I can look at it every day."

The room was bare but for a deck chair, plonked in front of the floor-to-ceiling sash.

"An' now look is all I can bleedin' do. Still you din't come 'ere to listen to me whinge, did yer?"

"No," said Troy. "I'm enquiring into the theft of municipal deck chairs."

Smith almost doubled up with croaky-chokey laughter.

"I swear, you are a wag, Mr. Troy. Now, last time you came to me it was for a shooter."

"Yes, it was."

"Well, I got another room for shooters."

He pushed open the double doors that separated this room from what had once been the dining room. In total contrast, the back room was full and filthy. It seemed to Troy that Smith probably slept in the bursting armchair by the fireplace, put his feet up on one of the piles of newspapers, and ate off any one of the dozen dirty plates scattered around the room. All this in a network of cobwebs, offset by fading and faded Georgian wallpaper.

Smith closed the doors. Most of the light vanished.

"Shooters needs darkness. I'm sure you'll agree."

"Herbert . . . it would take a man in France with a telescope to spy on you."

"All the same, I takes no chances."

He flicked on the light bulb. And the room seemed filthier still. He opened up the cupboard built in next to the chimney breast to reveal a rack of half a dozen guns, quite possibly the only things in the room that had been cleaned lately.

"As I recall, it was a .22 Beretta last time, wasn't it? A ladies' gun."

Appropriate. Troy had killed a lady with it.

"I'd like something with a bit more . . ."

"Wallop?"

"Yes, wallop."

"Then I think this might do the trick. An Inglis HP 9mm."

He handed an automatic pistol to Troy.

Troy turned it over and looked at it from every angle. All guns were alike to him. This one was about eight inches long and a bit on the heavy side.

"This," Smith went on, "has wallop. HP for high power. Canadian made during the war. A Browning by any other name, reverse-engineered by our colonial cousins. And it's good in a shoot-out. Magazine holds fourteen. The Belgian model only had thirteen. You'll be popping the bad guys long after they run out of ammo."

As ever, Troy felt blinded if not by science then by detail.

"I was rather hoping one shot would do the trick."

"Best make it two, eh? Just to be on the safe side."

Smith took a cardboard box of 9mm bullets from the cupboard and closed up.

"I won't ask who."

"That's OK, Herbert. I wouldn't tell you."

"But . . . what's your plan for disposing of the gun?"

"I hadn't thought."

"Well, think. And don't be thinking you'll just drop it nonchalant next to the body like. Get rid of it proper. Off a bridge would be best, and not the first bridge you come to neither, 'cos that's too obvious."

"It's . . . it's a bit public."

"So?"

"A silencer?"

"No can do, Mr. Troy. Even if this was threaded for one, which it ain't, the reason criminals like me can get hold of guns is 'cos they're legal, they got a legititimate use. Soldiers use 'em, coppers use 'em. You name me a country wot has silencers as legal?"

"Is it loud?"

"'Fraid so. Crack of doom. You'd best be careful where you pull the trigger. Shoot the bugger and leg it would be my advice."

Well, Troy knew that already.

"Now," said Smith. "About the ackers. I can do you a special copper's rate . . ."

§155

Battersea Park, London SW
Friday, January 9, 1959

Troy stood under the canopy of a vast ornamental fir tree, where two footpaths met at a rough crossroads. There was just a sliver of moon, and the light from the streetlamps in Prince of Wales Drive was too far away and filtered through too many trees to dispel the shadows.

It was almost a quarter to nine. His eyes had long since adjusted. He'd been on the spot since eight o'clock, deeming it better to be ahead of Kearney than to be following him. Not a soul had passed him in that time—it was a bitter January night, after all—but he'd set himself a practical if irrational time limit; he'd wait until nine, and if Kearney hadn't shown by then he'd chalk it up to one of his late nights in the office and come back on Monday.

His left hand was wrapped around the butt of the Inglis. The safety was off. All he had to do was not shoot himself in the foot.

He was worried that he might not be certain. In this light, how close would he need to be to be sure he had the right man? How stupid to shoot the wrong man. How distinctive could Kearney be as an outline? He was over six foot, he never wore a hat . . . but as a man approached from the direction of Chelsea Bridge Road all doubt vanished—there was something about the way he walked, and there was the briefcase he always tucked under his arm rather than gripped by its handle.

Troy slipped the gun from his pocket and held it against his thigh, counting the seconds until he'd step out to face Kearney. Chest shot first—bound to hit one vital organ or another—head shot to finish him off. Don't flinch at the bangs. Leg it.

Seven paces to the centre of the path, Kearney heading towards him, eyes down, seemingly oblivious to his presence.

Then he looked up, Troy levelled the gun, and as he did so a man stepped swiftly from the darkness to the right of Kearney, put a silenced automatic to his head and shot him. Kearney dropped at once. Blood gushing from the exit wound. The assassin shot him through the heart for good measure, glanced once at Troy, and unscrewed the silencer. It slipped into the right-hand pocket of his overcoat, the gun into the left.

Then he walked towards Troy. Troy lowered his gun. The man stopped only inches away. He looked much the same as he did himself, Troy thought, two short, dark men in black winter overcoats and tight leather gloves. He had the same black silk scarf at his throat. The same razor-nicked scar under the left eye. He'd even shot Kearney left-handed. The assassin in the mirror, as if an alter ego had been summoned up like some personal golem—this thing of darkness.

Troy stuck the gun back in his pocket.

The man smiled pleasantly, said:

"Have this one on us, Mr. Troy."

And walked on.

But—he'd said it in Russian.

«Это вам подарок от нас, Господин Трой.»

§

ends

Stuff

Guy Burgess

He really did ask to come home. Not in 1958 and not in Vienna, but in Moscow the following year while Macmillan made his famous fur-hat visit. When I ascribe the line "I don't want Burgess back at any price" to my fictional Harold Macmillan, I doubt it is even a paraphrase of what the real Macmillan said.

I began this book . . . well . . . years ago. Came back to it a few times, and finally got stuck in 2016. I had put it aside in 20-whatever to write *Then We Take Berlin*. Came back to it yet again. Packed all the research books into a backpack of crippling weight and set off for Tuscany and a winter hunched over QWERTY. Before I'd even reached the airport, I found I was writing *The Unfortunate Englishman*, and this book, at that time called *The Worldling's Pleasure*, got stuck on the back burner.

All that time, and for long before, Andrew Lownie (literary agent, biographer, publisher—we go back thirty years and more) was at work on his life of Burgess (published in 2015 to great acclaim as *Stalin's Englishman*) and if I asked a question Andrew would reply to the question, but no further. Who could blame him? Once the book was published, I had many more questions and Andrew replied to them all and was very generous with his material. It's safe to say I probably would not have written this novel without his help, and it would have been a mistake to have written it any sooner than I did. The delays seem, with hindsight, to have been so ordered.

We disagree but slightly on the man himself, but I hasten to add that my Burgess is an interpretation, a fiction based upon a real man rather than a representation of the real man.

While I wrote this I avoided any cinematic portrayal of Burgess. I'd seen Alan Bennett's television play *An Englishman Abroad* when it was new . . . more than thirty years ago . . . and apart from thinking Alan

Bates to be perfect casting, I couldn't remember much about it. It wasn't filmed in Moscow (it was Dundee, in fact) so watching it wasn't going to tell me much about the city, and I'd rather reinvent Burgess than copy Bennett. I watched it four days after I finished this novel—slightly startled at how alike his Burgess and mine were, even to his singing of the same Anglican hymns (at the urinal) I had learnt at school. I was not, I hasten to add, at school with Burgess (I'm not that old!). Oddly, I went to the same school as Bates, but we did not overlap by a small margin (I'm not that old either). But memory refreshed, the Burgess I hear in the lug'ole of the mind is Alan Bates. As I said not a moment ago, perfect casting.

Defection
Anyone who claims to know why Burgess defected is guessing. Neither he nor Maclean left an account, and their movements after they caught the train in Rennes are subject to question. I made my guess—a Burgessian mixture of curiosity and inertia took him to Russia, and after reading the memoirs of his KGB handler, Yuri Modin, I stuck with my guess. That said, every bit of dialogue uttered by either Burgess or Maclean in that chapter is made up. Come to think of it, I think the "Don't fuck Paul Robeson" line in Chapter 18 might be the only line of dialogue I didn't make up.

Peredelkino
Burgess did not have a dacha there. I don't know where his dacha was and the closest I can get ferreting around is the phrase "in the direction of Sheremetyevo." Not helpful, so I opted for the most famous "colony" of all, well-recorded, as Pasternak also lived there.

Mimram Branch Line and Tewin Water Station
Both are made up. England abounds in the remains of railway lines in daft places, testimony to the folly of Victorian investment, but this was not one of them, and I dearly wish that all the lines and stations that closed in my teens were still up and running . . . Midsomer Norton, Lyme Regis, Millers Dale.

Dobell's Jazz Record Shop

It went under the wrecking ball years ago. There was a recording studio in the basement . . . if memory serves, Bob Dylan cut a record there in the early sixties. I never, knowingly, met the real Mr. Dobell. My Mr. Dobell is fictional.

The Wrong Mozart Piano Concerto

I didn't make this up, I just ascribed it to my fictional pianist. It happened to the greatest pianist Earth has, Maria João Pires, in Amsterdam, in 1999, at an attended rehearsal (i.e., a lunchtime performance with audience, preparatory to an evening performance) of the D-Minor Concerto with the Concertgebouw under Riccardo Chailly. It appears MJP was expecting the Twenty-first Piano Concerto in C. Interviewed, it was Chailly who talked of the opening rhythm of Mozart's Twentieth and the feeling of despair. I took my cue from him.

There are Internet "comments" (trolls . . . whatdafukk is a troll? Answers on a postcard, please) to the effect that this was all a PR stunt, although I cannot see who might need such PR—but, two days after I wrote the scene into this novel I found myself, by chance, at dinner with the first viola of the Concertgebouw, who assured me it was real. Thank you, Peter.

Wheresies

Books get written all over the place. This one was kick-started in Tuscany, tweaked in Père Lachaise Cemetery in Paris, tweaked further in Provincetown Public Library, Cape Cod, and finished at home in England. I think there are even bits of it written on the back of a room service menu from a hotel in Texas.

I didn't see much of England in 2016. It seemed to rain whenever I was there, but I got me bike fixed up and managed to repaint the verandah in between the showers. A pleasing shade of green.

Caliban

The sculpture is real, and was carved, pretty well as I wrote this book, by David Mackie in his studio in Tuscany.

Caliban

Acknowledgements

Gordon Chaplin
Sam Brown
Marcia Gamble Hadley
Peter Blackstock
Bruce Kennedy
Clare Alexander
Ion Trewin
Nick Lockett
Allison Malecha
Tim Hailstone
Sarah Burkinshaw
Morgan Entrekin
Cristina Zadi
Christine Hellemans
Amy Hundley
Joaquim Fernandez
Niki Chang
Michael Rimmer

Spiggy Topes
Lesley Thorne
Sarah Teale
Gianluca Monaci
Deb Seager
Angela & Tim Tyack
Antonella Piredda
Sister Beryl
Fran Owen
Karen Duffy
Francesca Riccard
Nikky Ward
Sue Freathy
Nev Fountain
Zoë Sharp
&
Andrew Lownie